I0611513

the tender void

copyright Greta Medlin 2012, all rights reserved
Published by Off-time Press
Charleston, South Carolina

ISBN 978-0-9854361-0-0

This novel is a work of fiction. All of the events, characters, names, and places depicted in this novel are entirely fictitious or are used fictitiously. No representation that any statement made in this novel is true, or that any incident depicted in this novel actually occurred, is intended, or should be inferred by the reader.

All rights reserved. Printed in the United States of America. No part of this book may be used or reproduced in any manner whatsoever without written permission except in the case of brief quotations embodied in critical articles or reviews.

.

Cover artwork by Oceanside Design
Proofreading, interior book design, and production services
by Harvard Girl Word Services

the tender void

greta medlin

Off-time Press

To John

And for all good daddies, and all the people and dogs I love, dead and alive. And especially for my dumb little brother, in a league all by himself—more like our own daddy than anyone else in the world, but even better.

Huge thanks to Peder Zane, great teacher and advisor, as perceptive and supportive as he is kind, and to Linda W. Hobson, a real gem whose phenomenal editing gifts, taste for quirky humor, and uncanny feel for the characters delivered me to the finish line. That was when Heidi of Harvard Girl Word Services took over. Bottom line: If anyone thinks they know of anything Heidi Connolly can't do, then they've got the wrong Heidi Connolly. Also many thanks to Christopher White, and to a handful of test readers for their good catches and insights. No words to say how much you helped. Ann King, aka Annyos—Pinckney beams from on high.

And for the nudges to dig a yellowed old manuscript out of a drawer, especially from that goofy guy on the traveling landscaping crew (sorry I can't remember your name) . . . well, you asked for it. It was lots more fun the second time around.

About the cover, my favorite part of the book: thanks to Sparky Clark for dreaming up such a perfect concept; to Jane Norton for the terrific art that brought his rough sketch to life; and to Heidi Connolly for the cheerful, skillful, and tireless experimenting and coordinating to make it work, and for marrying the print to the art to make it shine.

At long last, bookies can shut their windows on this particular bet. Lots of money lost today. Wow. I actually beat the final deadline! Imagine that.

1

Cooper Barnet should have had no trouble identifying himself as a professional reporter because he carried a Professional Reporter's Notebook in his pocket and employed it in his profession. As of Monday, May 16th, 1988, he had written a total of 4,747 columns for the Columbia *Herald-Journal*. Mainly chronicles of this, that and the other. Accounts of people and animals, plugs for good causes, tear-jerkers, funny stuff... "Odds & Ends," the name of his column.

Cooper's way with words had won him a closetful of big prizes. But it hadn't been an easy run. There was always a deadline to miss. And there was often something new to figure out, another test to fail, another baffling journalistic conundrum that made him wonder if he, a former salesman of ladies' shoes, was worthy of the job.

Like the article in *Editor & Publisher*. Cooper had read it so many times by now that the print was a blur of creases and smudges.

"It's about parity," he explained to his friend Duke Chang. "You know, what newspapers can do to achieve it."

Duke owned the Bangkok Garden, where Cooper was eating lunch. "Hear that, boss?" he asked, speaking to his wife Layla, gathering up some menus behind them. "Parity. Never too late to learn."

"There is no reason to," Layla said. "I have upper hand."

The Changs operated their thirty-seat restaurant in a hollowed-out corner of Columbia that locals called The Bowl, just a block away from the switchyard where Southern Railway boxcars bedded down for the night. The surroundings weren't much—a branch bank, an appliance store, a small Burger King, and consignment shops that changed hands more often than their recycled goods—but when the couple went shopping seven years before, the affordable real estate prices had helped filter out the view.

Duke and Layla spent their savings on a boarded-up pool hall beside a laundromat, remodeled the inside, painted the stucco exterior butter yellow, and began serving what Cooper proclaimed in his column to be the best Thai food in the state. He considered himself qualified to make the judgment, since he ate it practically every day.

"See, the point is, the world has outgrown the press," Cooper told Duke. "We need to be more tuned in."

Duke rolled his eyes. He didn't want a synopsis of the piece. He just wanted Cooper to lift the magazine so he could sweep some crispy fried noodles off the table. Duke moved the book himself and bomped into "Wipe Out" by the Surfaris—*"bompbompbompbompbompbompbompbomp"*—but Cooper kept on going.

"... More sensitive, you know? Inclusive. Respect differences, yet treat everyone the same. With dignity. It's pretty shameful that...."

Duke laid out a fork and spoon. "In the mood for Som Tam Salad today?"

"With shrimp?"

"If you like," Duke said.

"I mean, lip service is one thing, but this guy's really dedicated."

"What guy?"

"The professor who wrote it. He's a real thinker. He's set up a committee. They're designing a new textbook for first-year students, so they'll learn to be conscientious early on."

"Dedicated to wallet," Duke said. "Educators make big money with specialty gig."

Cooper laughed. "He doesn't care about money. He's from Syracuse University. They have a topnotch journalism school."

"Better have something," Duke said. "Weather is very crappy in winter." He started singing "Good Day Sunshine" under his breath, even though it was burning up outside.

Carrying on a productive conversation with Duke when he was working was impossible, but Cooper relocated to the counter to try again. He was eager to get Duke's take on how to handle quotes. The committee was basically suggesting that they be sterilized, so that people who didn't express themselves in standard grammatical sentences would be playing on a level field with those who did.

Altering quotes in any way was supposedly forbidden, although historically there had always been room for an innocent wriggle. Too many "you knows" or mismatched tenses? Edit a few of them out and it wouldn't change the meaning. You could also paraphrase a comment rough on the ear or just skip it altogether. No need to make anyone look bad unless they deserved to, and those people usually didn't need any help.

You had to be careful, though—a little bit of permission can breed a lot of danger. When does a tweak become a transgression? And now there was pressure for the broom to sweep entirely clean.

Take Duke and Layla, who had fled to America during the Vietnam War. They had both been schoolteachers in the Hmong Province of Laos and were very bright, but neither spoke textbook

English, and the way they put words together added to their charm. Duke loved colloquialisms and dished them out with his own novel twist, his wit threaded as tightly into his persona as the laces on the Reeboks he wore to pound the duckboard between the stove and the grill. Yet according to the professor, to quote Duke as Duke the way Cooper had done in the past might be disrespectful to him.

When Cooper explained this, Duke wagged a finger and told him to be patient. "Soon you will no longer have to concern yourself with such weighty matters," he said. "*Herald-Journal* will be going out of business. Same disrespectful dialogue forbidden to newspapers is available in living color every time you turn on TV."

Cooper's head ached trying to figure it out. A human interest story was different from a news story. You had to make the subject come alive. A person's traits and speaking habits were as much a part of his identity as his eyes, nose, and mouth. In the future, how would people who didn't know Duke feel as though they did by the end of the column? Cooper had even begun to have doubts about including details he used to toss in without a thought, such as the tennis shoes. But when he asked Duke if being described as living in a pair of Reeboks would offend him, Duke said, "Only if you mention the way they smell at the end of the day."

Cooper smiled, although he wished Duke would get serious for a minute. The noble goals of the committee made him proud. But to Cooper's mind, taking someone's essence away from them was like saying their essence was flawed.

"Say I wrote a column about you," he said to Duke, "and made it sound like it wasn't you. What would you think?"

"I would think I was somebody else," Duke said.

"Would that make you happy?"

"Sure. I would like to become Abraham Lincoln."

Cooper's quandary was significant because many of his subjects were people society pretty much overlooked. They had patterns of speech that were colorful in an engaging way because they were colorful, which was one of the reasons he wrote about them. Under the new system, the adjustments would take some maneuvering. Cooper would have to do something he'd never done before, doctor quotes to a degree that drained the humanity from a patient who wasn't sick.

He came to a decision as he drove back to the paper. He made little tweaks from time to time, trying to find a balance between color and clarity. He might as well go ahead and run the length of the field. He didn't want to hurt anybody—he couldn't stand to see people hurt—and he didn't want to risk any misunderstandings about his intent. Besides, he'd made a few fairly big tweaks in his own life, emending and adding color, and as far as he knew the results had been harmless enough. So he went in and wrote a piece on Maxine Springs, a woman whose speech was as rural as the five-room lean-to she'd been born in, and after he was done she was talking like a banker's daughter from middle suburbia.

Duke had a point about television, though. Roll the cameras, stick out a mike, and everything was right there, the bad and the ugly included. On today's news, hardly five hours later, a clip on *Six at Six* showed Dan McDonald, the familiar "Face of the City," dodging a rotten plank beside the Christmas tree on Cooper's front porch to peer into his living room window.

Cooper missed it. He was in the Dart, on the way to see his girlfriend Percy. She missed it, too. She'd just finished giving a dancing lesson, and was ushering the girls to their mothers' cars. But a minute after seven, her friends started calling.

It was hard for Cooper to take in. His house had been on the evening news. The very house he lived in, basking in unaltered squalor, challenging the taste and sensibilities of each fascinated and disbelieving viewer.

One viewer in Charlotte decided to take action. Brave, impulsive action. Action intended to alter Cooper's life. But Cooper didn't know that when he got out of bed the next morning. When you're about to be blindsided, the future doesn't issue a bulletin, even to professional newspaper reporters in the business of reporting the news. The main thing he knew was that he dreaded the ragging that would be waiting for him in the newsroom, so he holed up at home with his dogs until it was almost past time for lunch.

Now he was back in The Bowl, hurrying down the sidewalk, his head lowered, working hard to be anonymous, counting the cracks in the cement and studying the passing shoes. He stopped to check his pockets. More bad luck. He'd just spent all his change.

·

As usual, the Bangkok Garden was jumping. The big rush was over, but fifteen customers were waiting to be fed, and requests for take-outs hadn't let up since noon. Duke ran a towel over his short damp hair, dried his glasses, and shoved them toward the top of his head. He'd been squeezing a lime into a wobbly pot of Tom Yum Gai, a delicate chicken soup offered with the Tuesday special, and his face was so sweaty the heavy horn-rimmed frames had slid down his nose and landed in the simmering stock.

"No more shrimp," he yelled, when the phone began to ring again. Layla grabbed an order pad before she answered. She listened a second, but didn't write anything down. "Here," she said, passing the phone to her husband. "Operator for long distance."

Duke secured the receiver between his neck and chin. "*Hello, op-per-a-tor, could I help you with this calll,*" he sang.

"Hello to you," she said. "You can help Cooper. He's calling collect. Will you accept?"

Duke nudged Layla and pointed towards the window with the end of a cracked wooden spoon. "Short distance," he said. Across the narrow street, Cooper was standing in a grimy phone booth, its Plexiglas walls streaked with vapor. He sent them a halfhearted peace sign. Layla laughed, then rushed off to ring up a tab.

"Sorry, Mrs. Stroman. Delayed by call-in," she said, stripping four ones from an old National cash register and sliding them across the counter. "Heat is terrible. Too hot for cooking today."

"Tell me about it," Maggie Stroman said. "I was perspiring so much I didn't bother to add any salt to the peanuts this morning." Maggie and her husband Chum prepared their Stroman's World Famous Boiled Peanuts in a former bakery near the State House and sold them from the mountains to the coast. They made good money, enough to spend the month of January at their time-share near Jackson Hole, Wyoming; the more snow the better. Hard to imagine it now.

It was 101, two degrees higher than the day before. Only the third week in May, but it felt like August without the benefits of a Grand Strand vacation. Columbia, the capital of South Carolina, is located in the center of an oppressive sinus belt, and the humidity added ten more degrees to the torture.

"Hey, Chang," Cooper said. "It's me."

"Mr. Chang is unavailable," Duke said. "Stepped out for Whopper and fries. Left Honest Abe Lincoln in charge."

"Did you intend to make this person to person?" the operator asked.

Duke added stewed chicken to the soup and gave it a little stir. "*Walk right in, sit right down, baby let your hair hang. . . .* Pad Prik today, with Tom Yum Gai. Shrimp went fast. You shouldn't wait. . . ."

"Whoa," the operator interrupted. "You need to accept the charges first."

"What's Barnet doing out there in the phone booth?" Tiny Tuttle wanted to know. Tiny, a ping pong fanatic with a USC

Gamecock tattooed on his neck, was the Bangkok Garden's only waiter and part-time studio musician.

Duke shrugged. "*Op-per-a-tor, let's forget about this call....* Croce's greatest hit."

"One of," Tiny said, as he ladled out two bowls of soup.

"To clarify, sir," said the operator, "you refuse to accept?"

"No reason to when party is already here."

"Which party?"

"The party holding up my line, Miss . . . *Mrs. Jones, Mrs. Jones . . . we got a thinng goin' onnn. . . .*" Duke plucked off a sprig of coriander and began to chop.

"Is Cooper there with you now?" the operator asked, curtly.

"May as well be." Duke tossed a little coriander into the bowls. "I can see him clear as day, right across street, even without eyeglasses on. His shirt is blue. Sleeves are all rolled up."

"Sir, assuming you're ambulatory, why not cancel the call and speak with your party inside?"

"Come on, Duke, say yes."

"'Yes' cost money. I'm broke."

"*Yip yip yip yip yip yip mum mum mum mum mum get a job. . . .*" Tiny chirped.

"Hey, how about unlocking the alley door?" Cooper said, but the operator had already yanked the plug.

Duke cut off the burner, shoved on his glasses, and strode across the street. "What kind of ridiculous fish you trying to fry, man?" he asked, pushing open the folding door of the phone booth to let in some air.

Cooper looked like he'd been boiled with Maggie Stroman's peanuts. His dark hair was a river of ringlets swimming down the back of his collar, his clothes were steamed to his skin, and his eyes were as lifeless as his faded blue oxford-cloth shirt. In a profile for *Sandlapper Magazine*, a female reporter had described them as

"Newman-like stunners that light up his next thought before he thinks it and are always ready to play," but at the moment they were drifting down the road in a fog.

"I'm goin' to Bangkok City, Bangkok City here I come," Duke sang. "Get a move," he told Cooper, "before they drag you out of there in body bag."

"Sorry, Duke," Cooper said. "A broken meter just ate me out of house and home. I was calling to ask you a favor."

"A call-in favor? Give me a break. All you have to do is cross threshold and it becomes a walk-in."

"But look at all those people in there." They glanced over at the long picture window splotched with condensation. Most of the diners were staring out. Some of them waved. Duke waved back.

Cooper wasn't sure what he wanted to do. He wanted to bust out and run down the sidewalk as fast as he could and he wanted to stay in the booth, stay until Duke's warning came true. First he wouldn't be able to breathe and after that he would know how it felt until he didn't know anything at all. He hung up the phone and tried to rub out the glare from his eyes, as well as the scene that was flashing behind them. Being shut up always brought it back.

"Hold up a second, Duke," he said.

"Too busy. Come inside."

"Okay, but if it suits, I'd like to eat by myself today, in the kitchen."

"Eat in kitchen? What show you on now, *Candid Camera*? You want privileged dining, book four o'clock flight to the city. Four Seasons will fix you up in VIP room. 99 East 52nd. Beats boxes and crates all to hell."

"A crate's fine," Cooper said. "Just shove it up against the wall, out of the way."

"Customer has two options," Duke told him. "Eat in space allotted, or take out."

"Where would I take it?" Cooper asked. He checked Duke's wrist for the time. Already twenty past two.

His clothes leeched to his itchy skin like a bathing suit that was wet before you put it on. The advice of Dr. Marlin Fue suddenly came into his head. In a syndicated Q&A that ran every Monday in the *Herald-Journal*, the popular celebrity healer encouraged his readers to be bold, uncork the soul, let it all hang out. Cooper usually did the opposite, but he was getting weak. The Stouffer's lasagna Percy had split with him last night was long gone.

"Listen, buddy, I'm feeling overwhelmed right now," he said. "Shy, you know? Like I want to pull over and park it for a little while, all alone in a private lot . . . far from the maddening crowd, and all that. You can see where I'm coming from, can't you?"

Duke was drying his eyeglasses on the dishtowel he'd jammed into the waist of his cargo shorts. "I can see you acting crazy," he muttered.

"They're waiting for the story in there. How my house got on TV."

"I know," Duke said. "Let's roll."

"You go ahead. I think I'll pass."

"You telling me you for real?" Duke said. "All this elaborate cloak with dagger just to eat in hole like alley rat? You are well aware of situation. My girls play in dollhouse with bigger kitchen. Not even room to cook back there. Heat went to your head, puppy. Turned brain into small fried egg. Learn to face medicine, like normal person."

Cooper's grin curled left in a slow, sly promise that females often found sexy, an Elvis come-on look, but it was unintentionally crooked. His baby brother had jabbed Cooper with a pencil when he was eight, leaving a miniature blue lead scar and some dead nerves. "Honest Abe Lincoln," he said. He used a palm to catch some sweat running down his neck, wiped it on his hip, and sighed. "You're right, Chang, I'm a fool. It's a wonder they let me walk the streets. I didn't mean to put you out like this. Tend to your customers. I need to get to work, anyway, rustle something up for tomorrow."

A woman tapped Duke on the shoulder. She had on white shorts, a black halter top, and an oversized white visor that covered most of her frosted blond hair.

"May I have a word with Mr. Barnet?" she asked.

"Mr. Barnet is feeling bashful. Maybe you can check by another time."

The woman moved a few steps back from the phone booth, then held out a sticky Bic pen wrapped in a piece of soggy notebook paper. "Ask him to make it out to Dot. And tell him not to be intimidated by the brown stuff. It's just Diet Coke."

"Here," Duke said to Cooper, shoving open the door. "Just diet cola. It won't kill you. Hurry and sign."

Cooper gave him a look. This was what he'd been trying to get away from. But he quickly straightened up, ran a hand through his hair, and grabbed the receiver, holding it out towards Dot. "I think it's for you," he said.

She lit up. "Really? I told him not to call me here."

Grinning, Cooper spread the paper out on the glass, using it as a vertical desk. "Anything in particular?" he asked.

"No," she said. "Whatever you want to put."

"Dot." Cooper said it softly, almost with reverence. "I had a teacher named Dot in second grade. My first big teacher crush. Dot Drummer. I was probably as much in love with the name as anything else. She was cute, but not as pretty as you."

Dot blushed. "Pretty? I look so bad, I almost didn't have the nerve to stop and speak."

"Where're you from?" Cooper asked her. He was having trouble. The pen wouldn't write over the soda and the paper was coming apart.

"Originally, Washington State."

"Where'd you get that Southern accent, then?"

"My mother's from Greenville," Dot said. "I ended up at Columbia College and married local, you know how it goes."

"Local catch, huh?" Cooper said. "Lucky catch, for him." The Newman-blue eyes were playful now, like the *Sandlapper* writer had described them. Dot edged closer, the way most people did, responding to the invitation, the only person invited to the party.

"I just wanted to say, I don't think it's fair, them not giving you a chance to tell your side," she said. "I'm sure you have your reasons for the condition of your house and all. You're so busy doing for others, you probably don't have the time to do for yourself."

"Busy goofing off," Duke said.

"Dan went overboard," Dot said to Duke. "He shouldn't have done him that way."

"I wasn't privy to actual broadcast," Duke told her. He turned to Cooper. "Li had indoor tennis match at Kroger Center. Was worth it, though. She scored winning ace.

"Li is oldest daughter," he explained to Dot. "One of top junior players in state."

"Congratulations," she said, taking the folded paper Cooper handed her. He'd managed to find a dry spot big enough to write, "To Dot, from your newest local fan—C. B." She dropped the autograph into her straw tote bag. "Those preservation ladies can get mighty horsey," she said, giving the phone booth a commiserating pat. "Hang tough, Cooper."

"See that freight train pulling out?" Cooper asked her, pointing to the railyard over her shoulder.

Dot turned around, adjusting her visor to block the sun. "Yeah?" she answered slowly, in a puzzled tone.

"I'm about to hop it."

"You won't do," she said, and took off across the street.

Duke hurried off behind her, aiming a hitchhiker's thumb toward the alley. "Better hold dining room in loving memory," he said. "Boss will never allow you to mingle with law-abiding citizens again."

Cooper reached into the back pocket of his khakis. The Professional Reporter's Notebook, always there, even when it wasn't. Flipping to an old grocery list, he stepped outside and started walking, keeping his eyes on the page. A quarter in a vending machine bought a front row seat to his life, access on demand, but there were no customers chasing him at the moment, and after a quick turn behind Jake's Rebuilt Bikes and a stumble over some broken bricks, he entered the hot and spicy sweat of Duke's kitchen. It was the first welcome heat of the day.

Duke came in dragging a ladder-back chair, parallel parked it next to a storage crate, and slung a white dishtowel over the top, but he didn't take Cooper's order. Alley rats like him got the special. Layla delivered it, Chicken Pad Prik, along with a look that let him know he wouldn't be offered seconds.

Cooper ate slowly. The quicker he finished, the sooner he'd be in the newsroom and up against Hitchcock's cigar stench, exorcizing any Asian spices and herbs still clinging to his worthless pores. The managing editor usually weathered most of Cooper's lame excuses with more ambivalence than he had a right to expect, but he doubted he'd get a pass this time. Maybe he'd ask Hitch if he could lay low until things cooled off, do obits for the rest of the week. But who would write his column?

He set his napkin on the plate and rubbed his eyes. It was the reporter's KP, burying the deceased. Although the deceased couldn't be buried. They had to be interred. He would sit lashed to the phone taking dictation from genial morticians who said "Mizrez" for Mrs. and told jokes they stole from preachers. The prospect seemed fine to him right now, especially since the funeral home got the byline. That would be the best part.

Cooper went over the format as he drove to the paper. *Name, age, address . . . died today, last night, this morning at . . . Funeral arrangements are incomplete . . . Funeral will be held at . . . The Rev. So and So will officiate . . . Interment will be . . . The family will receive friends . . . Survivors include. . . .*

His first assignment had been obituaries. He'd never written one before, but they had come easily. They should have. The first time he read one he was ten years old, and for years after that he'd gone to sleep reading it in his head.

A car was pulling out from a spot across from the front entrance to the building. Cooper pulled in. Seven minutes to go upstairs and bum some change before the meter maid rode by in her little red cart. Bonnie. He liked to flirt with her. She knew his license number by heart.

2

The Columbia *Herald-Journal*, the largest newspaper in South Carolina, was produced for 179,000 regular subscribers inside a faded black slab that was more like a prefab in an industrial park than a guardian of the fourth estate. Cooper Barnet wasn't the only reporter who spent more on parking fines than gasoline. The office was ten blocks from the capitol and five blocks from convenience. The designated lot was narrow and often full, dead ending at a paper-strewn loading dock that serviced foul-mouthed circulation drivers and squabbling pigeons, which made backing out tedious, especially for visitors.

The aesthetics inside were no better. The first area to meet the public was the last to be redone. The project had been scheduled for the previous spring, but while the budget was stalling on its promise, the fiscal year had moved on. The original collection was left behind: a lumpy brown imitation-leather sofa, and chairs that matched before the sun baked out most of the color.

The switchboard was a relic. Only two people knew how to make it work, and one was retired. She filled in for Jo Rainey, the lady who drew the weekly check. Jo had powdered wrinkles and stiff silver hair, and performed in a small glass cage. Her affinity to the people inside the plugs and wires didn't extend to visitors waiting for her to notice them in front of the glass. Jo rarely removed her ear-piece when spoken to or mentioned the moody elevator, but wore a key on a spiral bracelet in case it stopped on a phantom floor.

Cooper took the stairs. He stopped at the door of the newsroom and looked in. Everything was gray, like a tent show in heavy fog. Metal desks were mated head to toe in rows of five or six, each with a metal partition halfway to the ceiling and a ledge to the right holding a word processor and the Remington Selectric, tools of the trade. The only accent colors were the muddy green carpet and the dull red utility fabric covering the chairs. Also, the brown cork on the bulletin boards, largely hidden by untended displays.

A gummy Milky Way wrapper was stuck to the floor. Cooper picked it up and tossed it into the trash can, then flipped his toothpick in after it. He could feel the atmosphere changing around him. Everyone was aware of him now, squirming, not sure what to do. He pulled out his notebook and began studying a blank page as he walked past the glass partition dividing the managing editor from the people he managed—the Hitchcock Wall.

"Hey, Odds & Ends, over here. It's yours," called Jazz Liebman, a veteran reporter with busy hazel eyes and frizzed blond hair he swore wasn't permed, though he didn't mind being kidded about it. He was most admired because his grandparents' riding stables in North Brooklin, Maine, adjoined the farm that belonged to E. B. White, author of the newspaper writer's holiest bible, *The Elements of Style*.

"Want me to catch it?" Jazz covered the police beat, and per-ceived a ringing phone to be a siren he couldn't ignore.

"That's okay," Cooper said.

He headed toward a jalousie window missing a handle that was in the bottom drawer of his desk. Jazz sat in front of him. In front of Jazz, desks were breached in a string of three. These were for the city editor, assistant city editor, and Ginna, the world's greatest newsroom secretary, who looked the other way if you didn't want to be in, and issued editor warnings with a bravado fostered by fifteen years on the job. She was shaking her head. Four o'clock, his first appearance of the day.

The copyeditors were already in the first round of crisis mode. They were huddled at a horseshoe table near the back of the room, cleaning up messes, writing headlines, and mining the wire machines for fillers to add to the mother lode. Cooper saw theirs as a thankless job, with reporters complaining that their stories were overcut and undersold and readers thinking the opposite. Editors went with the political winds.

But all succumbed to the Chief. Boom-Boom Bradley was a disheveled sixty-year-old rock star with a built-in mike; a cranky human bullhorn sprouting fringe on the sides above the ears. His vocal chords were made to shout one word: "COPY." The manner and tone of his single-word delivery told reporters more than any of them could define in long inches of polished prose. He made it both a statement and a command. You heard the affected impatience of a seasoned newsman, the confident importance of his role as final arbiter of the finished product, the relief that another baby was ready to be tucked into bed, and the resignation that plenty more were in line to be cleansed from a plague of sins, some arriving too late to be fully scrutinized by his quick and weary brown eyes.

One of the things Cooper had liked best about the salad days was hearing Boom-Boom yell "COPY," and watching a copygirl or copyboy race over to grab the stick of dynamite he was waving in his hand. That was it—the copy. The grail. Typed on porous beige paper. Pasted together sheet by sheet with glue from a rubber pot.

The copy person rolled the pasted pages into a log and stuffed the log into a thick plastic sleeve, then slammed the sleeve into a miniature El to be suctioned into a wild ride on the newsroom wall. Last stop, composing room. Near deadline, the tubes flew up the wall like runaway cars on a roller coaster, then crashed hard at the end of the line, one on top of another. Blam. Blam. Blam. Blam. Blam. "COPY!" Computers made the deliveries these days, but Boom-Boom still sang it out. He took a second to look in Cooper's direction.

"Answer your goldurned phone," he bellowed. "It's the Local Brotherhood of Handymen."

Jazz couldn't stand it any more and picked it up. "He's on the way," he said, muzzling the receiver against his sleeve. "Hey. It's Safer. You made *60 Minutes*."

Cooper loped the last few yards. The blinds were open in Hitch's office and the volume tone was softer than normal, the rings short. An inside call.

◆

"You're just begging to sell shoes again."

It was his good friend Sam on the phone, a former Army medic with a Southern velvet voice and more concern than his large brown eyes could handle. Samuel A. Reaves, Jr., was how his byline put it, even though he wasn't the "Junior" type. As far as ability went, he could call himself anything he wanted, including one of the best investigative reporters in the country. When he received offers to write the news up North, he usually responded that he couldn't live in a place that didn't serve grits. Sam hated grits as much as he hated the cold, but couldn't resist playing out the stereotype.

He grinned at Cooper, whose desk was a convenient whisper away, and pulled a pencil from his sandy curls. "You must have a foot fetish that's off the charts. What's the going rate these days, five bucks an hour plus commission? You'd do better pushing corn pads at a filibuster."

Sam had been running the shoe thing in the ground for years. Cooper's father had been that way, squeezing mileage out of the same old joke long after the trip was over, and Cooper was programmed to go along for the ride.

"The job wasn't all that bad," he said. "I kind of liked it."

"Good," Sam said. "Hope you kept your measuring stick handy." He grabbed a legal pad and glanced at the clock. "You could've found yourself a diamond-studded widow if you'd just given 'em the time of day."

Cooper looked out the window, squinting through the sun for a gray Honda Accord with DELE on the tag. Hitch's vanity plate. He was disappointed to find it parked in the reserved space, and quickly turned on his word processor to check the messages. "You need a haircut," the first one said. Anonymous.

"He's after me," Cooper said.

"He should be," said Sam. "Shoot. Driving in the wrong lane is what they pay you for. But driving in the wrong lane backwards down a one-way street while you're mooning everybody in sight. . . . Come on. That might be the slightest bit of overkill."

"That bad, huh?"

"McDonald was a riot. You woulda thought he'd outed Deep Throat. I can't believe you didn't see it."

"I didn't know it was on until it was over."

"You would have if you ever watched the news."

"I don't need to. Everybody else does."

"All those years I spent sitting in that booby-trapped living room of yours, wondering when the ceiling would cave. The survival odds were better in Nam. No wonder half my check goes to Liggett & Myers."

Cooper smiled and felt behind his neck. The growth surprised him—all the way down to the ragged edge of his damp collar. When did the barbershop close? Tuesday was the half day. Or was it Wednesday? Maybe he'd go to one of those places in the mall. Get a bowl cut, be done with it.

"Journalists generally take an interest in the news," said Sam. "It's a natural craving, like mac and cheese." He trapped the pencil he'd dropped on his chest before it could get a rolling start down a peach polyester rise stocked with rations from the vending machine. The shirt also had forest-green stripes. Sam shopped at K-Mart's Big and Tall on a grab-and-go basis, sticking to the sale racks.

"I see you did another one on Maxine," he said.

Cooper was skimming the rest of his messages and didn't answer.

"You may as well give her your column. She just about writes it anyway." Sam scrawled "writes it anyway" at the top of a lined yellow page. Performing for the editors. "She seemed a little strange today. Had a different air about her or something."

Sam hadn't read the article in *Editor & Publisher*. He told Cooper he'd get around to it when he had time, but Cooper knew he wouldn't. Sam wasn't big on feature stories. Claimed fluff was only good for stuffing pillows.

Cooper frowned at the monitor. All the comments had been funny until this one from the entertainment editor, Janice Dean. She told him she was pulling for him to straighten out his life. If he wanted, she could recommend a good therapist, a woman who had helped her when she had some issues after her divorce. He sent her a thank you. Said he was okay.

"Do you intend to grace me with your presence or not?" Sam asked. "Ernest just brushed the Little Debbie crumbs out of his beard and I still have some calls to make."

Ernie LeCraft, the city editor, was beginning his visual sweep to assess the prospects for tomorrow's paper. Based on the criteria of delinquency, Cooper was the first to be appraised. He nodded back casual confidence, although the only thing in his notebook was a grocery list, and quickly turned to his keyboard, typing air, conducting a telephone interview for Ernie's benefit—his subject, Sam Reaves Jr., sitting at the desk right beside him.

Uh-oh. A second message from Hitch. "ASAP. H. H."

"Hey, Reaves," Cooper said. "He's on here again."

But Sam was still railing about Maxine. "You flip out every time she plants another dad-blame dwarf on her grass," he said. "What do you think this is, *House & Garden*?"

"Calm down." Cooper glanced behind him. H. H. usually wore suede moccasins, with ties to adjust the fit. They sneaked up on you.

"How many mutts did Snow White pal around with, anyhow? I thought there were just seven. Maxine must have seventeen of those tacky little bastards by now, and that's just in her front yard. She could sell wholesale to South of the Border."

"They're gnomes. Dopey was the last one. She had to drive all the way to Kingsport to find him. People relate to stories like that. Everyone's seeking something."

"Great god a'mighty, Cooper. I know you're yanking my chain, but you're still about the dumbest smart man I've ever come across," Sam said. "When are you planning to get out of the clouds, hold a meeting with your brain again?"

Cooper gave him his slanted grin but he was already hanging up, his attention on the next piece of equipment. He cleared space for a memo pad and punched "Play."

Hello, Cooper. Hi, Cooper. Cooper, is that you? Cooper, are you there? Mr. Barnet? I keep getting this recorded message . . . Cooper? . . .

. . . Charlie Cross. Squash bigger than last year's. . . . Julius Cobb playing Owls' Club this Friday. . . . Woman from Dixiana, number, no name, niece gave birth to quadruplets. . . . The entire *Six at Six* viewing audience. . . .

The answering machine. A mechanical secretary, man's best invention. Even a Luddite can figure it out. All you have to do is stick a few wires in the right places and program a little greeting. Cooper's sounded like Lloyd Bridges conducting his final *Sea Hunt* in dysfunctional scuba gear. A muffled fumbling was followed by a tone that imitated the CONELRAD alert. Regular callers knew to hold the receiver at arm's length until it ended.

Pick it up, baby. I'm in a little jam here. . . . then nothing. As a newspaper columnist, Cooper kept many secrets for many strangers. Malachi Patterson was the brilliant alcoholic train wreck who kept his. Cooper moved along.

"Hello, sugar, this is Maxine."

"Hello, sweetheart," Cooper whispered. He turned the volume down as low as it would go and leaned forward to glance at Sam, now on the line grilling an actual source.

"Pier and me were talking a minute ago," Maxine was saying, "waxing philosophical-like about this, that, and the other, you know how we do, and a thought come to me about the peculiar way life is set up."

Something small and fluttery swam from Cooper's chest to his throat. He used his last drop of ink to scratch through a reminder to pick up his cleaning and blew a kiss toward the tiny little town of Irmo.

The first time Maxine Springs had saved him was nineteen years ago, on a rainy November morning back in 1969. He'd been about to premier as a columnist without a column when Jo Rainey rang him up from the lobby.

"Some kook's down here, chomping at the bit to tell the world about her husband's ears. They tick."

Maxine had a copy of *Ripley's Believe It Or Not!* to prove it. She also had the living evidence waiting in the front seat of a brown and white station wagon parked at a twelve-minute meter. Pierre didn't want to come in, so Cooper went out and did the interview while feeding pennies into the slot. His account of life inside a clock that never stops became an instant classic in the South Carolina Midlands. He spelled Pierre's name wrong, though. Maxine pronounced it "Pier," which he'd assumed was a family name.

After the column had come out, Maxine checked in regularly. She told about her exploits but more often commented on current events, such as an unsuccessful attempt by the San Diego Zoo to mate Le Ya the panda with a male that had been imported for the job. Maxine compared the disaster to a documentary on arranged marriages in rural Chinese villages. When material was scarce, Cooper treated readers to one of her original observations. But lately, Maxine's life had taken over the column, like her quest to find the seven gnomes. He was in trouble about it. He couldn't make himself stop writing about her, though, and couldn't say why.

"The way I see it," Maxine always entered the answering machine like a confessional, "you've got two kinds of people." She stopped to clear her throat. Although she wasn't a smoker, Maxine cleared her throat a lot. "You've got your caught, and you've got your uncaught." Cooper heard some rustling noises. "Says here in today's paper—and I'll just go on and read it verbatim—it starts off:

"'A Piggly Wiggly cashier, a deserted mother of a physically disabled child, was sentenced Tuesday afternoon to twenty days in Richland County Jail for reporting to work instead of jury duty' . . . and so forth and so on. . . .

"Now compare this to Pier's first cousin. She's a preacher's widow, and she's just plain sorry. As lazy as the day is long. Pier's right here beside me on the couch, and he'll tell you the same thing hisself."

Cooper pressed "Pause." Lately, he had begun to edit Maxine when she spoke. Consciously, like a censor. He reminded himself to focus on the content.

"Wellsir, every time her name comes up to serve, she marches straight down to that courthouse and claims she's tending her invalid husband, and him nothing but dust for fifteen years. Can you believe she gets away with it? Goes around braggin' about it, too. I says to Pier, I said, 'Everything's all upside down and backwards. Wonder what Cooper thinks about that?'"

Your caught and your uncaught. Maxine was a genius, the reincarnated Voltaire. Most people, even the most righteous intenders, lived in a state of caught or uncaught in one way or another, didn't they? What else could existence be? Cooper turned back to the word processor and typed the set-up for his next column.

Brooke Cameron, the new summer intern, rolled a chair beside Sam's desk and plopped down, adjusting the fall of her long blond ponytail and flipping off her pink Pappagallo flats. She had on a pink blouse with a peter pan collar and a matching grosgrain ribbon in her hair, and she didn't look a day over twelve.

"That guy's cute," she whispered. "Hey, isn't he the Odds & Ends man?"

"Sure is," said Sam. "At least for a few more days. He's leaving. Plans to take his old job back."

"What old job?"

"Selling shoes."

"Selling shoes? Why?"

"He likes to wait on people."

"Really? Weird. Well, he was on the news last night. *Six at Six.* Did you see it?"

Sam innocently shook his head.

"Dan McDonald had a thing on about his house. It's a wreck."

"Do tell."

"He must be kind of out there." Brooke kept her voice low. "He's done some pretty wacky things."

"Yeah? Like what?"

"Like auctioning off a bunch of stray dogs down in The Bowl, for one."

"Come on," Sam said, although he knew the story well. He'd been there.

"No, honest. I went with my mom back when I was in tenth grade. It was at that Chinese restaurant. It was wild. Dogs running around all over the place."

"They weren't leashed?"

"Some were, but the people in charge were kind of slack. They lined up the dogs and tried to strut 'em up and down like they were in some fancy pedigree parade or something. They were playing 'Walkin' the Dog' and everything. You know, by Rufus Thomas? I love that song. Well anyway, the dogs wouldn't behave. They kept breaking free and running for the kitchen."

"Must've been the chow mein," said Sam. "Which one did you get?"

"Huh?"

"Which dog?"

"Oh. We didn't bid. We didn't see anything worth having."

Chuckling, Sam dialed Cooper.

"Mr. Barnet. Take a second to meet our intern, Brooke Cameron, from Columbia College. She likes your looks."

Brooke kicked Sam under the desk.

"Sorry, couldn't hear you with the machine on," Cooper lied. "Did Sam say Columbia College? I just bumped into another lady who went there, out in The Bowl."

"Really?" Brooke said, shyly peering over Sam's green-striped shoulder. "Who?"

"Dot. You probably don't know her. She's a good bit older than you are. Closer to your mother's age, I'd guess."

"Oh."

"Well, anyway, welcome aboard," Cooper said. He was still holding the phone, with Sam on the other end.

"It's an honor to be here," Brooke answered.

"It's an honor to have you." Cooper told her, the blue eyes waking up to her smile. "Has Sam been treating you right?"

"Yessir," Brooke said.

"Let me know if he doesn't." His eyes were dancing now. "These old men can get a little out of hand."

Brooke giggled. "I will."

"You want to be a newspaper reporter, huh?"

"Either that, or TV."

"Probably be wiser to go for the glitz. They pay you over there, and you don't have to do any work for it."

"Really? Like Dan McDonald?"

Sam beat his hands against the desk. "Take a bow, young lady," he said, after he stopped laughing.

Cooper grinned, feeling the flush rise from his chest to his cheeks. "You're all right, Brooke Cameron," he said. "If I can help you with anything, just let me know."

"She's been talking about that harebrained dog auction," Sam said. Holding the phone with his chin, he stretched and rolled his head toward Brooke. "That nut over there ended up with the rejects," he told her. "Hid 'em in the photo lab while he wrote the column. Two of the saddest-looking canines you ever saw."

"What kind were they?" Brooke asked.

"A screwy dachshund named after some mountain nobody ever heard of and a Boykin spaniel," Sam said. "He was decked out in a smelly old cowboy bandana. One of his ears was gone."

"Yuck."

"Not the whole ear," Cooper said, winking. "Just a piece."

"But, still . . . what's his name?"

"Reba."

"Reba's a girl's name."

"I know. He was already named when I got him. They all were."

"That makes sense," Brooke said. "Where is she now? He, I mean."

"Probably scouting out a nice spot for a territorial marker," Sam said.

"He's a political artist," said Cooper. "Does indoor abstracts, kind of protest portraits."

"She's quite prolific," said Sam, then bent over in a writing frenzy. Brooke leaned in to read. "Now is the time for all good people to come to the aid of their country . . . country . . . country . . . country. . . ."

"Got a minute?"

The eyes were black, the voice muted. The Tampa Nugget was a blur of cold ash, hanging off a downward slope of lip. Benjamin J. Hitchcock, managing editor of the Columbia *Herald-Journal*, was wearing the jacket to a blue serge suit and his brown suede moccasins. He was called "Hitch" not for the obvious but for his habit of pulling up the waist of his Sansabelt slacks during awkward moments like Arnold Palmer did after hitting a drive in the Masters.

After a long career of hurdling annoying—and to his mind often superfluous—roadblocks, Hitch's moods ran from discomfort to disbelief, generally in the sarcastic range. As far as he was concerned, newspaper reporters and kindergarten children belonged to the same genus, class, and species, with one exception. Reporters didn't evolve.

He motioned for the receiver on Cooper's ear and put it to his own. "He'll talk to you later," he told Sam.

Brooke wriggled into her flats and headed for the ladies' bathroom. Sam flipped to a new page and continued scribbling, speaking into the phone without making a sound: frowning, smiling, nodding, gesturing, pondering the perforated asbestos ceiling tiles.

Cooper followed Hitch to a metal chair with a thin hard bottom and thinner metal arms that was shoved close to the belly of a Mack bulldog ashtray. Hitch was his own designated smoking area, self-exempt from a recent newsroom ban. Cooper took a seat as Hitch lit up and phoned his secretary Ruth Ann, at her desk on the other side of the partition.

"Hold 'em," he said.

"All right," she said, and got up to close the door.

Cooper watched the receiver bang into its cradle. He watched the blinds close. He watched the cigar join the pile in the ashtray and wondered if Hitch could tell it from the others. They all looked alike, corpses turning to dust. *I'm Goin' to Obit City. . . .*

"Some woman was on the machine just now," Cooper said. "Her niece had quadruplets."

"That doesn't help you one damn bit."

"Didn't think it would. I called you from Duke's. Nobody answered."

"How many rings? One?"

Cooper shrugged. "About a half."

Duke had placed a portable phone on the storage crate, telling Tiny Tuttle that Mr. Barnet was a big TV star now—"Requires telephone on silver tray, like Cary Grant."

"Myrtle's writing something for tomorrow," Hitch was saying. "Bottom of B-1, around ten, twelve inches. With a shot of your so-called house." Myrtle Bailey, who covered local government, was one of a dozen minority reporters hired by the *Herald-Journal* since the mid-sixties, and one of the few who had stuck around long enough to gain seniority. Although she was Cooper's friend, she was too conscientious to give him a ride, which he knew put her in a painful spot.

"Do you have to use a picture?"

"She'll need a few quotes." After a tug at his trousers, Hitch sat in the chair behind his desk.

"I'll be out of reach. Having my hair trimmed."

"The hell you say."

Cooper knew the protocol. Hang his head and offer a reasonable explanation, though he had no clue what it might be. Straighten in earnest and agree to talk to Myrtle. Then stand and excuse himself quickly, apologizing his way out the door. The trouble was, he didn't see himself as the subject of the story. He saw himself as a person he may have written about in a throw-away column long ago, some minor character involved in a silly predicament, someone with a name and face you wouldn't recall. So he sat there and watched Hitch go bottom fishing in a pondful of ashy cigars. He hooked the same slimy monster he'd just thrown back and jabbed it into his mouth.

"Do a column," he said.

"I can't."

"How come?"

"I already have one."

"Won't it hold?"

"Not really. It's a reaction story."

"What on?"

"On the caught and the uncaught."

"On what?"

The cigar headed back to the ashtray. Cooper leaned away from the smoke. "It's a theory about. . . . It concerns the human condition."

"The human condition pertaining to what?"

"Pertaining to . . . well, I guess you could say pertaining to a philosophical revelation."

"Pertaining to a philosophical revelation," said Hitch. "I'll be a son-of-a-bitch."

"It's about how man fluctuates between two states of being."

Maxine was a genius all right, Cooper thought. He'd spent his adult life fluctuating between being the caught and the uncaught, overshooting deadlines, then writing his way out of trouble. He'd been caught by the historical police yesterday and by morning he would again be among the caught, as soon as Maxine's mug shot was discovered smiling above the fold. Unless Hitch found out that she was the guest philosopher before he left for the night.

The bad thing about obits, you had to come in early.

Hitch was holding up a palm. A cigar-fingered palm. Cooper watched the smoke waft across his knuckles and evaporate. But that fog was easier to follow than the premise he was trying to explain. Why was he feeling so confused?

"For Chrissakes, Barnet." Hitch grabbed the bulldog by the ass and yanked it across the desk. "Is there anything I can do?"

Cooper didn't know whether to be frightened or touched. He'd never known Hitch to be much on personal extensions, at least in the newsroom. He tried to think of an answer to the question, but Hitch's bout with the bulldog had reminded him of the dogs at home. He couldn't remember whether he'd left the electric fan going on the dining room floor. Sophie, the only dog he'd owned before the auction, was fourteen. She could barely hear or see.

"I understand slack," the editor said. He was still talking to the bulldog, which was more responsive than Cooper. "But we've crucified slum lords with dumps better off than yours." Hitch finally looked at him. "What happened to you, man?"

"I don't know. Things just kind of built up."

"Don't you have any pride?"

"It doesn't seem that way, Hitch. I'm not sure."

The state of his house had driven Cooper to eat in Duke's kitchen, but he knew the motivation went beyond the limits of simple shame. It had more to do with being the center of something. Talking was part of the job. He'd never been all that comfortable with it, and as the years moved along his reticence had become worse.

Now he bored himself, and somewhere along the line he'd lost the spirit of the story. This made him feel guilty. Because it was a natural gift he had, entertaining people, and he'd always had a crazy notion that it was up to him to make the world a happier place. Him, of all people.

"Sig's steamed," Hitch said. "They're all holed up in their hideaway at Roaring Gap, watching the eleven o'clock news, and there you were."

"You're kidding. It aired in North Carolina, too?"

"Afraid so," Hitch said. "We got a publisher whose wife is treasurer of the state preservation society, and he's got a prize-winning columnist wearing a 72-point condemned sign around his neck."

"Sorry," said Cooper. He was, in a disengaged way.

"He called me in the middle of the night. Sloane wants him to print some sort of public reprimand. Here. He even dictated it to me: 'The *Herald-Journal* fully supports the regulations mandated by the city building code for the upkeep of residential properties and congratulates the Richland County Historical Society in its efforts to seek compliance. We strongly encourage the fulfillment of these obligations by all our employees.' What the hell are you grinning at?"

"Nothing much." In the kitchen, while scrubbing big pots in a small sink, Tiny Tuttle had suggested that the hysterical czarinas set fire to their girdles, get in sync with the modern world.

"Know how he got our home number?" Hitch asked. "Called Sandra Sawyer at midnight, rooted her out of bed."

Finally, after a round that had yielded little concern beyond the health of his dog, this simple statement moved Cooper to painful contrition. Sandra, the company's personnel director, was a divorced mother of an autistic son, a teenager. Cooper didn't see how parents could take the everyday setbacks experienced by normal children, but someone like Jimmy....

Routine was important, Sandra had told him. She always put Jimmy to bed at eight thirty. She read him a chapter in a book about animals. Numbers and facts were his ice cream and cake. He craved them, so she doled them out, one chapter a night, never more, never less. She sat on a chair near his bed until the medication did its job and he fell asleep. It was just a small dose, much less than the doctor had prescribed.

That's why she asked her friends not to call after nine. Cooper imagined the poor kid startled by the phone. Frightened, then agitated. Sandra, waking up, scared half to death, finding the publisher on the other end, asking for a telephone number.

"Wonder why he didn't call information?"

Hitch deposited his cigar on top of the bulldog's head and stood. "You got brown shit all over your pants," he said.

Tom Yum Gai. Cooper had gulped down what was left in the pot before Tiny could toss it down the drain. He'd been just as careless with his life.

·

In forty-two years he'd made few calculated decisions. He hadn't meant to be married and he hadn't meant to be divorced. He didn't plan to apply at the *Herald-Journal*. It just happened one afternoon on a whim. He'd never thought about being a columnist, either. Didn't have the credentials, unless you counted a job as manager of a low-budget shoe store and travels to Florida, Rock City, New Orleans, and the New York World's Fair. Nor did he have a chip on his shoulder he wanted to blame on anyone else or a crippling despondency over anything he wanted to share.

He was fiercely pro-underdog and anti-bigot, but beyond that, he had no desire to comment on the daily ins and outs of the political scene. In short, he had nothing he wanted to say. That's why it had surprised him when just a month after his twenty-third birthday, editors offered him a fifteen-inch hole to fill five days a week and wouldn't let up until he'd accepted. He couldn't say why he did, other than somehow it had seemed ungrateful to refuse.

He'd come along at a time when each day was like a bailout from a puddle jumper, the engine blown, the rip chord caught in the zipper, and a story overdue before you crashed. He loved hurrying down the greasy third-floor corridor, past the windowless cubbyhole where the publisher hardly ever shut his door, past a morgue bloated with the yellowed print of overtime work and illegal pay. Heading toward the metallic alto of manual Underwoods jumping across the metal tops of battered desks, he'd slog through the never-ending smoke of Camels and Winstons and Lucky Strikes and ashes too busy for ashtrays, then stride past the rowdy parade of copy tubes slamming the bottom of the chute, listening to reporters and editors shouting at impatient telephones and vagrant copy boys and early deadlines and missed deadlines and an uncooperative composing room and everything caught in between, aching to reach his own desk and join in.

Gradually, as technology advanced new vistas of opportunity and profit, the free-flying stunts were reigned in by sanity and order. Editors were sent off to tanks to develop their thinking. Psychologists were brought in to reorganize the newsroom with an ingenious personality test. The Myers-Briggs Type Indicator was designed by a mother-daughter team to help place women in industrial jobs during World War II. It determined your "natural energy orientation"—whether it was "outer or inner." Decided whether you had "sensing characteristics" or "intuitive characteristics," "thinking characteristics" or "feeling characteristics." Evaluated responses to statements like: "I work first, plan later," or "Enjoy now, finish the job later," or "I'm really in between." Cooper had to guess at the answers.

He couldn't say when the lassitude began, because it had sneaked up on him, like Hitch's moccasins. He continued to fake it the best he could, which seemed to satisfy his readers, if not the editors. He wanted to do the right thing, even if he wasn't sure what it was anymore. He felt an obligation to the integrity of his craft. Besides, he was good at his job. He could write. He liked people, and he had a soft spot for originals who couldn't find a niche. He could lose himself in other lives without making a dangerous investment, anonymous lives that would provide a temporary port in his own storm. Better yet, he could reward them with a little prize in return, the celebrity they'd never expected, while giving the readers a minute or two to forget about their own troubles. Fulfilling his verdict with community service. No question it was a lifetime sentence, but after so many years a person starts wearing out, especially if they've buried a tombstone in their gut. The deeper it sinks, the heavier it is to carry.

Sometimes, though, a shadow of a sensation would take him by surprise, a nudge from the past, when it was fresh and fun. Like Duke back in stride beside the grill, ringing up receipts and inquiring after customers and taking call-in orders, all in the ebullient ease of his general operating mode, while at the same time shielding a columnist on the lam in the kitchen, a refugee from Tiny Tuttle's girdle-bound historical czarinas and his own hapless life.

Something about the mood, the moment, had made Cooper want to hurry to a keyboard and describe his predicament with irony and desperation and humor, the way he would have done it before.

But that creative desire seeped out with the steam rising from his third cup of tea, so quickly he wasn't sure it had been there in the first place.

After a brief pit stop down the hall, Cooper headed for his desk, his shirttail pulled down to cover the soup stains on his khakis. Maxine was wound up and waiting to roll. In another hour the editors would be at their posts chopping the soul from incoming copy, but now they were on reconnaissance, wandering in and out, stopping by one desk and then another, glancing at the clock—a nice little round of window shopping with a baleful undercurrent of life and death. Soon Ernie would be leaning over his shoulder, barking "Gottahaveit," though he knew there was nothing to have.

The caught and the uncaught. Cooper wasn't sure anymore if it made sense. But the readers would figure everything out, one way or another. They always did.

3

By the time he got to Percy's it was after ten. She came to the door the way he liked her, in ballet slippers and shortie Pjs, the sleeveless pair with valentines on the collar. The hearts were red and the shoes were pink, scuffed at the toes. She wasn't the type to apply lipstick or mascara every day, only when she went to parties or to church, or when she gave recitals. Cooper liked Percy's organic lips. They were nice to kiss. He wanted to kiss them now, just a friendly hello, but they were trapped behind the screen.

"Good evening," he said. "Are you the lady of the house?"

"Want me to be?"

"I'm pretty sure I do. Can I get a closer look?"

Percy shook her head. "It's not evening anymore." Her thick black braid ran to her waist. She rarely wore her hair loose, except occasionally when she slept. She claimed she kept it corralled because it was one less thing to account for.

"Come on," Cooper said. "Open up."

"Nope."

"Why not?"

"The small cost of fresh notoriety. You look pooped. You need a mattress with some sleep on top."

"I want to sleep on top of you."

"With or without the dogs?"

Percy sprung the latch, but she was coming out. "Better behave," she threatened. "I can turn a pretty mean cartwheel myself."

Cooper faked a wince. Percy was referring to a knee injury inflicted on him by one of her students. Last night had been bad all around. Two attacks. The first by an over-the-hill talking peacock, and the second by a ten-year-old in a pair of leopard tights.

"Mean is the operative word," he said. "Hey, lady. Got any salve inside?"

Percy was right. He was too tired for sex. He just wanted to stretch out next to her on the bed for a while, rest his swollen knee. Actually, it didn't hurt that much right now. It was just something else teasing him for attention, another link in the chain of his confusion, one more reminder of his increasing loss of control.

It had been wild. Pretty funny, all but the pain, and as far as Cooper could tell, completely unprovoked. After Percy's six o'clock class, he'd come over to help her work on the scenery for her annual spring recital. The kid had been sitting on a kitchen stool. She'd announced that her name was Little Linda Lister and asked him for a bowl of ice cream. She said she needed something to hold her over until her mother picked her up. "It might spoil your supper," Cooper said, and went off to the den to ask Percy. "Go ahead," Percy told her. "Help yourself."

Then she'd filled him in. The child's mother was Belinda Lister, a redheaded exercise guru famous for leading aerobics demonstrations in a series of popular workout videos produced by The Firm. She had begun calling her daughter "Little" Linda a few months after she was born and the name stuck, even though Linda now weighed more than her mother and was four-feet-eight-inches tall.

"It's just baby fat," Percy had whispered. "She has a great set of genes. In three or four years everything she doesn't shed will shift to the right spots and she'll look like a million dollars."

Fifteen minutes later the baby fat had landed full force in the center of Cooper's left kneecap. He'd been on the couch waiting on Percy to come back with some duct tape when Little Linda approached him to show off her new pair of silver tap shoes—from his angle, a pair of ladies' nine-and-a-half wides.

"Want to see me do a cartwheel?" she'd asked him.

"Sure," he said, touched by her hopeful smile. The next thing he knew he was moaning and holding his knee and she was back in the kitchen, giggling, while Percy defended the attack.

"Little girls can be possessive about their dancing teachers," she'd said. "A man doesn't belong in a dancing school affiliating with the teacher unless he's a daddy coming after his daughter. It spoils the magic, and that's all there is to it."

Percy was just as stingy with her compassion tonight. Cooper was tired of standing out in the heat, and she was still planted in front of the screen, blocking the way. She'd seemed preoccupied since he got there. A mosquito bit him on the hand.

"I think that's the phone," she said, yanking on the door. "Daggum humidity. This thing is really stuck." The ringing stopped. "Too late to be calling anyhow," she said.

She leaned up and kissed Cooper on the chin. He grinned. "I have a cautious observation to make regarding your favorite political cause."

"Well?"

"There appears to be a double standard."

"Oh yeah?"

"Physical abuse seems to be acceptable if the person on the receiving end happens to have a penis attached."

"You got that straight," Percy said.

He grabbed her braid and followed it to the end, just above her tiny waist, then gave it a little tug.

"Are we even?" she said.

"Never. Unless you dig up some of that salve."

He ran his hands over her body. She was taut and erect, a perfect form, and her breasts fit precisely with the design. Three deep lines spread from each outer corner of her eyes, spaced so uniformly apart they could have been drawn by a graphic engineer. Sometimes Cooper wondered if her physical properties, balanced to precision, formed the plumb line to her emotions and anchored them with such easy control.

"Let's go in," he said.

"Uh-uh."

"I need somebody to cut my hair. I'm about to get fired."

"Then you don't need a haircut. I kind of like it that way. Makes you look a little reckless."

"Like I am?"

"Like you're not. Well, except when it comes to keeping up houses. And keeping deadlines."

She nudged his foot.

"Listen," she whispered.

This time the caller had stayed on the line. Ernie LeCraft, looking for Cooper. It was important, he said. City editors were shameless. They'd been known to track reporters to a honeymoon bed on the wedding night. If nobody picked up on the first ring, they'd dispatch a copyboy posing as a bellhop.

Ernie could be having trouble understanding the nuances of Maxine's caught-uncaught thesis. He was a straight news man. But by now the column should be set in type. He was probably making one last try to pressure him for some quotes before the composing room shut down for the night.

"Myrtle did a story about my house," Cooper said. "They want me to talk. Think I'll pass."

"Looks like you already did," Percy said, and took his hand to lead him down the steps and over to the driveway, where she packed him into the Dart. Her preoccupation hardened beneath the sickly yellow gloom of the yard lamp.

"What's bugging you, baby girl?" Cooper asked her.

"The recital. I only have five more days."

Her students were to perform Sunday in the Fellowship Hall auditorium of Ebenezer United Methodist Church. Percy's older brother, Stuart Ray, was the associate pastor. Without a curtain or even a stage, she told Cooper, she had to improvise to come up with a place to prompt.

"Why don't you just lay low in a bathroom stall," he suggested. She paid him for the stupid joke with a grin, which to him was better than gold. Often her narrow mouth bore the strain of resolve, primarily engendered by her résumé of bad history. She smiled only when she meant it.

Hooking the back of his ankle with her foot, she swung it toward the floorboard. He yelped. "What do you teach in there, anyway, combat karate?"

"I guess I'll just have to stand flat against the cardboard sets," she mused, "and hope that does the trick."

"Don't count on it," he said, reaching through the window to rest a hand on her butt. "Something might pooch out right . . . about . . . here." He took his time with the last three words so he could get a good feel. One person's albatross is another's delight, he thought. He started to say it but instead prodded the engine and pumped the gas, since Percy's mouth was set in a line again.

Periodically the *Herald-Journal* auctioned clunkers that cost more than they saved the stockholders. When the rusty brown Dart didn't sell, Hitch decided his columnist should have a bonus. That was around 70,000 miles ago, although the car couldn't claim the prize for unserviced automobiles valued at $350 or less since the odometer hadn't been able to make the turn past 99,999. Cooper had stopped buying Freon after the A/C died its last death and his mechanic had refused to install a new unit in a vehicle that old.

He hadn't missed the air conditioning, though. Unless someone was riding with him, he'd rarely used it. When people told him he was crazy, he claimed he liked a jolt of real life blowing through the open windows. But tonight not even speed could stir the heat. It would be just as bad at home. Six years ago, in his only attempt to fall in line with the movement to revitalize the neighborhood, he'd broken down and replaced the window units with central air, and was already having problems with the compressor.

"Better go on in," he said to Percy. "Engine's running hot."

"In a second. Don't you have something for me first?"

He leaned out and puckered up.

"No. Next to you. On the seat."

"Oh."

On the way over, Cooper had finally gotten around to shopping for his groceries: oat bran, milk, yogurt, and raisins in place of bananas, which the drug store didn't carry. Percy had asked him to pick up some shampoo for normal hair. He handed her the bag. She dug out three Hershey bars with almonds and a bottle of crème rinse.

"There's always Ivory soap," she said, mouthing a kiss before backing away from the car to let him go. "Give it some thought."

What was she talking about? "I will," he said, "if you come over here and send me off with something to remember you by. Ummm, that's more like it. You dream sweet tonight, okay?"

He slowed in front to wait for the signal, two blinks of the living room light. She was locked in, at least until he was out of sight down the street. Percy often opened the door after he left so she could listen to night noises through the screen. He found this out once on a whim, when he'd turned around to check and caught her. "I'm a grown girl," she'd announced. "If you want kids you should've had some."

Although her house was a palace compared to his dump, it also needed a serious tune up. Cooper had first come upon it when he was aimlessly cruising the streets on the way to the paper, trying to make himself care that he had nothing to write. That had been more than ten years ago.

He'd circled the block three times to take it in. The white paint was shedding its coat by degrees and had stripped down to the lining on the south side. One of the black shutters was missing and the other three sagged dejectedly, as if they were mourning the loss. But a playful pink had been brushed on the steps, promise of a brighter day. The sign propped against a concrete column was what told the story and won his heart. The letters, printed in black by a hurried hand, advertised "The Columbia Academy of Dance." Beneath, written so small he had to pull to the curb to read it, was a list that offered tap, ballet, toe, and acrobatics, and in a different slant, an afterthought, baton. The border was done in pink to match the steps.

A column lives inside that old place, he thought. Yet even on days when he'd been buried neck-deep in a deadline hole, he couldn't make himself ring the bell to ask for an interview. Something told him that if there was one wilting bloom worth saving in this deflowered world, it was the proprietor of the Columbia Academy of Dance. Funny, the only thing he'd been protecting was his fantasy. When a spilled beer at the Owl's Club had finally introduced him to Percy Sims, she'd *asked* him to write about her.

Cooper suddenly swerved left, sliding halfway off the seat as he reached out to anchor the groceries. Drifting in his reverie, he'd almost missed the bad curve on Saluda Avenue. He wiped his clammy hands on his pants and moved on, trying to keep himself awake by visiting a scene he hadn't thought about for a long time. Percy's short black skirt sopping wet with beer, the mountain of napkins he'd dumped in her lap, his lame offer to make it right.

"Fine," she told him. "I could use a little shot of pub."

He'd let it go, not sure if she meant publicity or another beer. "I believe I already know you, at least in passing," he said.

She raised her thinly plucked brows and threw him another curve. He'd imagined a woman behind the Academy door with the black eyes and dark secrets of a gypsy, an exotic daughter of tragedy. Unless the bar lights were deceiving him, Percy's huge eyes were the gold of varnished oak. They met him straight on and bored in like a pair of electric drills.

"What I mean is, I pass your house every day on the way to work. Sometimes I see you standing near the porch with four or five girls holding batons." He usually drove slowly to watch, although nothing much was ever happening, even when he double-checked in the rearview mirror.

"They're my smallest class."

"You look different up close. That silver streak. It's nice."

"You like it? It's real."

The gray extended from the peak at her forehead to the crown of her head, which came just above his chest. From a distance she'd seemed taller.

"I've wondered what you'd be like in person," she told him. "You should make them use a better picture in the paper. I'm looking at dreamboat material here."

Dreamboat material? What a crock. He had a straight nose, a crooked smile, the infamous eyes, and a healthy stand of finely textured hair that liked to roam. His six-foot frame wasn't exactly a stick but his few muscles were lean, making him appear thinner than his weight.

"They don't make magic cameras," he said, glad it was too dark for her to see him blushing. "I don't even look in a mirror unless it's dirty."

"It's not just the externals," she said. "There's this other thing, this vibe going on. Sort of like you're surprised at what you're seeing even though you expected it to be there. There's something seductive about it."

He admired her dancer's calves as she lifted herself on tiptoe to reach over the counter and pluck a towel from the bartender's belt. Percy Sims was as tentative as a hammer on the way to a nail. Her straightforward manner made him a little ill at ease, yet he was attracted to it. He accepted when she asked him for a date.

"What took you so long?" he said, relieved when she poked him on the arm and grinned.

"It only has one 'm,'" she said.

"What does?"

"My last name. Make sure you spell it right in the paper."

•

A bump of tires against the curb told him he was home. This late at night, travel between their two houses didn't take much more time than it did for his man Otis Redding to finish putting the moves on Carla Thomas, one of the pickiest women he'd ever encountered: calling the King of Soul a tramp from the Georgia woods just because he happened to be born in a rural part of Georgia, accusing him of having no money, not even twenty-five cents; claiming he couldn't buy her all the minks and sables and who knows what other ridiculous stuff she wanted, and him with more gold records than she had sense.

Tonight Otis would have to fend for himself. Cooper was too miserable to sing along, too worn out to care. He reached down and felt along the dirty floorboard. During his bout with the curve, the aspirin bottle he kept uncapped next to him for emergencies had taken a dive and was now trapped against the passenger door. The tablets were down among candy wrappers already losing color after a week of afternoon sun. He'd eaten two bags of Tootsie Rolls getting up his nerve to break another promise to take Percy to Cherry Grove Beach.

Why did he keep promising her in the first place? He didn't do beaches, not since his little brother had died, but Percy didn't know he'd ever had one. When she'd asked him if he had any brothers or sisters, Cooper had said no. Because he didn't. Hadn't now for going on thirty-three years. It was the same when anyone asked if he'd had a happy childhood. Yes, he would tell them, and it was true, though his childhood had ended the summer he was ten.

He grabbed the bottle, giving it a shake. A single pill rolled out and disappeared. **"Gutter Ball Ends Match for Former Champ."** I should moonlight as a copyeditor, he thought. He had no idea why his mind kept generating headlines, but since they were there, driving him crazy, he might as well get a check for it. He envied copyeditors like Boom-Boom Bradley. Easily categorizing, constantly simplifying, voyeurs of the world in brief. Reporters didn't like to admit there was a skill involved, but for Cooper summing up a story with a few catchy phrases was harder than writing the article that ran beneath it. It required a pragmatic personality type, which he appreciated now that he was old enough to understand that foresight and decisiveness had perks. As far as his own story went, **"Landlocked Man Treads Water"** pretty much summed it up.

His life was a broken record. Lunch at Duke's, supper either at Percy's or the Toddle House, the same short-order diner he'd been going to since before he'd quit college. The only thing that ever changed on the menu was the plastic cover when the stains got too bad to read it.

Next time he'd come back as Liebman, always on the prowl for something new. Or maybe he wouldn't. Jazz was embedded with enough wires to start a fire in the deep end of the YMCA pool where he swam every morning to build stamina for running down all the crime in Richland County. Cooper had bumped into him outside the drug store an hour ago when he was buying Percy's crème rinse. The little man had been wild, threatening to kill the vending machine for eating his quarters without coughing up *The Times*. Beating on it like he was Butchie Trucks at Fillmore East. Humidity had coifed his frizzy hair into a blond beehive, sparkling in the floodlights with droplets of tupelo honey. The machine prevailed. They generally did, just like the parking meter Cooper had battled that morning, leaving him no opportunity to spot his friend a second round of change.

"You got a weird call a while ago," Jazz had told him. "Female. Hysterical. Asked me to track you down. She find you?"

"No."

"She wanted you bigtime, man. She was begging. A real basket case. Wouldn't say what it was, only said it was extremely personal. Said she needed to get hold of you before you talked to the police."

"Extremely personal? Did she leave a message?"

"Not with me. I was up to my ears and shipped her to Ernie, but we had some late stuff coming in and he got rid of her quick. Think he told her he'd call her back."

Maybe that was why Ernie had been looking for him at Percy's, Cooper thought. A little bit of fresh notoriety and they came flying out of the woodwork. She could be his ticket for tomorrow's column, though. No. He'd pass. He had more kooks around than bogus headlines.

The dogs were barking. Reba was butting heads with the screen, about to win. It wouldn't take much.

"Damn it," Cooper said. "Do something."

It surprised him to find the engine still running. He turned the key and leaned over to fish two aspirin from the floor as the motor knocked itself dead. He swallowed them fast, then grabbed the groceries and remembered not to lock the door.

4

Cooper tried to block out the noise by concentrating on the lullaby from the electric fans, but he couldn't stop counting. Twenty-seven rings. Nobody should have anything to say at five fifty in the morning unless they were talking in their sleep.

The only working telephone was in the living room, volume turned sky high so he could be forewarned from any place in the house, yet he didn't want to get out of bed to find out who it was. If they were waiting for the recording, it couldn't be anyone he knew. Once the tape was full, the mechanical voice no longer picked up, more or less its chronic state, since he seldom retrieved his messages. This was either a wrong number or the preservationists, trying to take him by surprise while a deviant with a ten-inch tail was inspecting his body parts. Hard to believe the dogs hadn't reacted to the bells. Ordinarily, the first amped-up chords out of the ringer and the two that weren't deaf turned into ACDC Live, using him as the stage. He held his breath. The instant he stirred they would demand breakfast—if he survived the show.

Yo, Liebman, come and get it. It's the phone.

Three and a half hours sleep. Ten and a half hours until deadline. Tuesdays, Wednesdays, Thursdays, Fridays, Saturdays, news holes snapping open under Cooper like the mouths of giant piranhas with editor heads.

> *Dear Dr. Fue:*
>
> *I'm writing to you paralyzed nude on a decomposing red-plaid futon seven inches off the floor, surrounded by three hungry dogs—dachshund fixated on privates . . . help! desperate for advice.*
>
> *For many years I've been a faithful follower of your column. Every week, I felt the twitches, pangs, pains, and aches exactly as your readers were describing them, and I was sure I'd been inflicted with the same maladies. God, I hurt, and I could hardly wait for your advice. It made me feel better on the spot.*
>
> *But that was before my own illness. My condition is hard to pin down in the space allotted, but the upshot is that I can no longer feel the symptoms. My question is this: If it's possible to have symptoms without a disease, then is it possible to have a disease without symptoms?*
>
> *Dear Dr. Fue:*
>
> *My nose itches. Is there any way I can get relief without activating the dogs?*
>
> *Dear Dr. Fue:*
>
> *Can a person who's in the doghouse for living in a doghouse be a suitable caretaker for dogs?*

Dear Dr. Fue:

Worst of all was coming in last night and finding Malachi Patterson passed out on a dog bed underneath the baby grand.

.

The paper wasn't in the yard or on the porch. The light hurt his eyes. His knee ached. He was wearing dirty khakis but had drawn the line at yesterday's boxer shorts. His chest was bare. His only clean shirts had words written across the front and he wasn't in a conversational mood. *Dear Dr. Fue. . . .*

There it was, stuck in a rotted-out piece of step. He'd been looking up instead of down, looking at the Christmas tree, amazed at the number of needles still attached in May. Amputated trees, even evergreens, weren't expected to hang on practically five months after field surgery, were they? Especially without a nurse.

This spoke well for the health of Maxine's woods, where he and Percy had found the tree December 21st. Pierre had sawed it down, a medium-sized blue spruce, shapely, with a fine set of sturdy arms that were wearing old-fashioned trinkets, many of them homemade, in Cooper's living room later that night. Sam, his wife Laura, Duke, Layla, and all four of the children had come over to help. Turned out to be a good party.

In early January, Percy had stripped the tree and dragged it out on the porch. He'd almost gotten it to the curb. Okay, it had been February by then. Mount Maxwell had escaped and hopped aboard the trunk as Cooper was dragging the tree down the steps. The dachshund hadn't been fixed and saw sexual promise in the impossible, such as a spruce with a nice little swish. Cooper had to heave the tree back up the steps while Max was still engrossed in the challenge. Either that or watch him fly off down the street to get creamed by the garbage truck.

In her secondhand holiday finery, the tree looked as frowsy as he felt this morning, the shapeless silver icicles frazzled in the heat. Some carousing reporters had done the redecorating. In the wee hours, after a newspaper party in March. Sam had been involved.

Cooper's reaction disappointed them. He'd been pleased. A tree covered with ornaments from other people's lives was comforting. The decorations were funky and intriguing. A pipe-smoking Santa sitting in a Model T Ford pulling a trailer filled with brightly colored balls, a glittery green alligator with a sly grin and a red wreath around his neck, a red felt stocking with "Merry Christmas Joey" crudely stitched in black across the cuff. Who had they belonged to, these personal memories? Why had they let them get away?

When someone kidded him about the tree, Cooper would say it distracted from the woes of the house, gave the porch a little lift. He would say he was curious to see how long it would last in the elements without water. It was a no-maintenance botanical study, a column in the bank. That's the kind of thing he would say when anyone forced him to come up with a reason for keeping it. But really, he just couldn't let it go.

Where was his pride? Hitch had been right to ask. This house deserved to be pampered and he was running it into the gutter, along with the degraded tree. Maybe he'd sponsor a contest. Who would go first, Cooper Barnet or his crib? The prize would be a fill-it-yourself news hole in Odds & Ends. He'd make sure there were multiple winners.

No question about it, he was a blight on the neighborhood, and every other cliché the Face of the City could manage to roll out on his eager silver tongue. If he'd written the newscast as a column, Cooper would have lightened it up, substituted Dan's righteous edification with a touch of irreverent humor. Said he believed in preservation

Beatles' style—"Let It Be." But at Channel 6, about the only levity during the newscast was a daily riddle from the weatherman.

One of the unique assets of the Palmetto State is her beguiling mischief, a capacity to let down her hair without detracting from an elegant style. Propriety was taught with a child's ABCs. Proper homes were appropriately dressed, even when their underwear was dirty. This wasn't the case at 57 Park. The exterior was as grubby as its owner's rejected boxer shorts.

The previous summer, Cooper had hired a down-on-his-luck painter named Frisco, given him fifty dollars, and sent him to the local Sherwin Williams to buy five gallons of Colonial Gray. Frisco had come back with a pint of Metallic Watermelon that he'd found in the closeout bin. Before going on his way, he'd splashed a farewell above the living room window, a rocket-shaped red glare that trailed up toward the roofline—a defiant bird flicked in the faces of aristocrat cousins, preservation, and civility, any perceived symbolism unintended.

McDonald had made Cooper's perversion of property clear on *Six at Six*. The Face wasn't the heartless type, but head-to-head combat was what they got paid for. It would be a kick, his print buddies scrambling for a follow-up to his story, Dan razzing them about having to do it. It was usually the other way around. Sure, everyone liked Barnet, but even good guys have to pay the consequences sooner or later, and he'd had plenty of time to clean up . . . like, years.

"I'm here today in Shandon Oaks, one of South Carolina's charming historic neighborhoods," was the way Dan had started, pointing to the new carved wooden sign for proof: "Established: 1891," as a woman in a station wagon tooted and waved.

"A community bursting with the kind of satisfaction that diligence and dedication can provide. A community emerging from a thorough going-over, a lengthy spring cleaning, if you will, a joint restoration effort by homeowners and volunteers from the Richland County Historical Society. And the payoff is readily visible, as you'll see when we enter this canvas of freshly doctored lawns and houses, a whitewashed wonderland of yore."

The camera went along. Pointed out a bed of red and white impatiens and a scalloped white verandah. Gazed at a golden cedar rooftop and a shiny copper drainpipe. Closed in as McDonald admired a lacy gazebo newly shored up to support thick vines of yellow jasmine, the state flower, "whose late winter blossoms are the glorious belles of the South Carolina ball," then opened up again as he extended an arm to enfold the panorama.

"These good citizens of Shandon Oaks have joined hands to toil long and hard for a common purpose," he said, and yoo-hooed to a burly man on a ladder placing a state flag in a polished brass bracket.

"Residents, supported by the historical society, have applied to have this lovely little pocket of long-buried treasure, one of the oldest residential districts in Columbia, added to the National Register of Historic Places. They believe they meet the qualifications, and are awaiting approval."

McDonald stopped and frowned as he assumed an oracular stance.

"But as we are about to see . . ." he paused to make a vocal adjustment, solemn now, and stern ". . . not everyone has cooperated with the refurbishing effort."

A slatternly house came into focus behind McDonald. The dissenter. The feckless miscreant on the bad side of a good war. The newsman didn't want to shoot but did he have a choice?

"This domicile"—backward gesture—"was once the proud, enchanting home of Ann Rucker Rutledge, whose cousin was the first poet laureate of South Carolina, Archibald Rutledge, a nationally known scribe who brought joy to countless readers with his vivid and exquisite portrayals of the out-of-doors, publishing his first book of poetry in 1908, and continuing to write well into his eighties.

"Today, the single sore thumb in this historically significant district belongs to another Columbian also known throughout the city and beyond. Someone who has promoted many causes, both for individuals and the collective good. Like Rutledge, the present owner also is a writer—Cooper Barnet."

While McDonald read biographical data, the camera crawled along a wall inside the *Herald-Journal*, scanning all the columnist's plaques and awards before ducking into the newsroom for a pan of reporters creating stories with ferocious concentration. Then viewers were back at the house: first, to a close-up of red paint splotched on the decayed German siding, then to a group of broken-down steps, finally to a seedy-looking Christmas tree that listed to the right after a bad night in the wind. The camera flattered the icicles.

Now the reporter ascended the porch steps, avoiding a caved-in plank to take his stand beside the tree.

"The historical society is faced with a delicate matter," he said. "President Virginia Humphries declined to be on camera for this story. However, she explained that for a neighborhood to be approved, an inspection is required by officials from the National Registry of Historic Places. She believes that Shandon Oaks will make the grade despite the neglected condition of Barnet's house.

"Yet she is concerned that the eyesore not only is humiliating to and disrespectful of other residents, but a drawback to fundraising tours. The Rutledge/Barnet structure is three doors down from one of the most historic dwellings in the neighborhood, the office of the city's first mixed-race law firm, which included Robert Masala Perry, renowned judge and courageous leader in the early struggle for civil rights."

While the stately Dutch Colonial was on screen, McDonald re-stocked his lungs, and continued. "What path does the society take?

Do they make an official complaint to the city inspections department? According to Mrs. Humphries, this action would not be in keeping with the spirit of the organization or its mission, although they haven't ruled out the possibility. Meanwhile, members have repeatedly attempted to contact Barnet, who has not responded."

A dog with some belly weight rushed the screen and started barking. McDonald flinched and hastened off the porch, managing to clear the bad places in the steps without tripping. The cameraman crept in for a close-up, though, shooting between the limbs of the tree. The camera was good to Reba. The light cast a copper sheen on his dull brown coat and turned his cowboy bandana into a cheery red garland.

•

Cooper sat on a chunk of step. Time to be a man. He took off the rubber band and unrolled the inevitable. There it was, **"The Caught and the Uncaught, A Life of Temporary Reprieves."** It began at the top left of B-1 and ran vertically, ending one column length from the bottom of the page. **"Shandon Sore Thumb"** started where **"Reprieves"** left off and ran horizontally, ending at the right side. In newspaper vernacular, **"Sore"** was a sidebar to **"Reprieves."** The end of one disaster flowing into the beginning of another. Barnet had been unavailable for comment.

What would he have said? That he felt embarrassed, humiliated, regretful? Mortified was too strong. Acute discomfort, maybe. The same thing any trouserless man would feel lying spread eagle on a glass slide the size of the two Carolinas, enduring a public scope. Feelings were hard to figure out, like taking the Myers-Briggs personality test. Cooper wandered aimlessly among the variables, always having to answer "I'm really in between."

For years he'd entertained readers by castigating himself, giving hilarious versions of his "this-could-only-happen-to-me" screw-ups. Trivial. Fun. Good for lunch counter small talk. Nothing that mattered, and he was at the controls. Yet overnight he'd become a serious screw-up, even a villain, powerless to accounts broadcast by other people, those operating on a different frequency. They played it straight, accepted conventional lives. He should've answered their calls. He could have claimed a discipleship to Andy Warhol. The installation was authentic, even historically correct, because 57 Park Street imitated his life. It represented his entire existence.

Funny how a dream can backfire. Shandon Oaks had simply been an older neighborhood downtown when Hannah and he moved in three years after they were married. The homes were quirky, heterogeneous, and affordable. The one they picked was in declining health, but they didn't want an antiseptic suburban shell. They wanted to sleep inside used walls and add on as they lived there. When the realtor mentioned the Rutledge connection, Cooper couldn't believe his luck.

Final Jeopardy question: "What ex-shoe salesman and smalltime newspaper hack inhabits quarters once owned by the cousin of the Dean Emeritus of South Carolina letters?" He wandered from room to room calling Rutledge's name. Hannah disguised her voice and jumped him from behind.

They'd made lists: Paint knotty pine cabinets in kitchen; check. Strip hummingbird wallpaper in bedroom; check. Remove living room carpet; check. Caulk leak around bathtub faucet; done. Later they could afford to refinish the floors, replace the rotten wood, upgrade to central air. It didn't matter so much if their progress didn't measure up to their intentions. The neighborhood was filled with postponed projects.

That changed six years ago, when the city council decided Shandon Oaks was too good to waste. Urban renewal had come to Columbia. The council handed out incentive packages with low interest rates. Yuppies moved in. The historical society salivated. But Hannah was long gone, and Cooper wasn't up for the awakening.

The friendly young couple from the Victorian next door recommended carpenters and landscape engineers. Frank, an amateur carpenter himself, said he'd fix the swing and replace the bad boards in the steps for nothing beyond the cost of materials.

"I'll let you know," Cooper told him. Sometimes he admitted that his days might end as they were now, coasting along in ambivalent disrepair. He could move into a room at the Carolina Hotel, home of transients and anyone else able to fork out seventy-two dollars a week plus a little change for use of the washing machines, but they didn't take dogs.

Besides, Shandon supported his old habits. When the Dodge went on strike, he could count on sidewalks to take him where he needed to go, as long as he didn't get careless and trip over a root from a giant water oak. He lived one mile from the university library, a half mile from the biggest coliseum in South Carolina, and about three-quarters of a mile from the Toddle House, the Bangkok Garden, and Ben Cogburn's Grill, where on Sundays when Duke was closed he could buy a thin cut of tough steak with skinny fries sopping up the juice and an iceberg lettuce salad topped with thousand island dressing made by mixing mayonnaise and ketchup, plus two slices of toast soaked in liquid butter, all for five dollars and ninety-five cents, plus tax.

The presses rolled three-quarters of a mile west on Lady. The state pen was five blocks north. The state mental asylum was four blocks directly to the east, on Bull Street. Cooper's mug shot was posted in all of these locations. In one way or another, his livelihood paid the admission.

On the way inside, he stopped by the tree. Maybe if he removed one ornament each day. He didn't have to throw any out. He could save them, use them again next year. A plastic Santa winked at him. Something about the eye wasn't right. Cooper leaned in to check. The wink was a hole. He tugged at the beard but Santa was affixed to the branch with a paperclip, and didn't want to be disturbed. What about the snowman? Nothing intimidating about him, all cheery in his red and green scarf and matching beret. But that was the problem. He seemed happy where he was. Rudolph looked a little sad, though. No wonder. One of his horns was broken off. Might as well put him out of his misery. Cooper reached through the limbs, then thought of Reba's missing chunk of ear. It was getting late. He'd better go in and see about the dogs.

Dear Dr. Fue:

By the way, don't know if I'm allergic to any medications. Only take aspirin and an occasional Tum—(would that be singular or plural, if you only take one per dose? 'Here, have a Tum,' the doctor offered. 'You're in need of a Tums,' the doctor said. 'Would you swallow a Tum if I gave you one?' the doctor wanted to know. 'If you don't chew a Tums first, it will take longer to dissolve in your tummy,' the doctor warned).

Dear Dr. Fue:

Just considered switching to a Rolaid(s). No good. Same problem.

5

Scary, the number of people primed since dawn to tell him what they thought about "**Shandon Sore Thumb**." So far he'd avoided them, but the dogs were wearing him down. Each time the phone rang, Mount Maxwell howled while Reba backed it up with one of his trademark head butts.

"Okay, that's it." Reba had just come at him from behind, causing his knees to buckle, oat bran raining all over the floor. Cooper put the cereal box down on the counter and headed for the desk, picturing a very wide white girdle unable to restrain the duty-laden maven laying for him on the other end of the line, lingerie image courtesy of Tiny Tuttle, lover of womankind, chauvinist supreme. No wonder feminists became feminists.

Cooper didn't know why he was playing hard to get. Yes, he did. It was too much trouble to listen to the spiel, too much trouble to sound personable, too much trouble to make excuses for not making excuses. "I'll get right on it," he would say, and he would mean it, too, at the moment. He felt like a heel. The historical society, such an easy target, but they were doing something important. Preserving history.

He lifted the receiver and listened, waiting. No reason to initiate anything.

"Didn't anyone teach you how to answer a telephone?"

"Nope."

"The greeter goes first."

"Am I the greeter?"

"In a civil world, yes."

Cooper smiled. "If I'd known it was you, I would've picked up before it rang."

"Which time, dear?"

"How many times have you tried?"

"Are you referring to the number of attempts made or the number or rings per attempt?"

"Neither, really. Just apologizing for not answering."

"But you did, with exceptional style."

Cooper supposed Margaret Motte Burns qualified as a maven. She lived on the harbor in Charleston, which her ancestors had helped establish, and often gave her age as somewhere between that of the Dock Street Theatre, the nation's first, and the Egyptian mummy at the historical museum. But she didn't wear a girdle, and preferred making history to preserving it.

In her mid-thirties she'd swapped her first marriage for a second to a Yankee twelve years her junior and delighted in the shock, which registered as high on the Richter scale as the earthquake of 1886. After her husband died young, she came home bringing more money to add to the inheritance she already had. She liked giving it away. She also liked her own ideas, which were more creative and sensible than those of the solicitors camped at her door. Margaret referred to what she did as sprinkling a little Holy Water, but she considered it an obligation rather than an achievement, so it wasn't advisable to patronize her by telling her how wonderful she was.

Cooper had made that mistake years ago, trying to butter her up about the ongoing generosity of her philanthropy when he'd called to ask her for an interview.

"What would you suggest I should do with the rest of my life," she'd demanded, "put on a bikini and go to Myrtle Beach?"

With that remark he'd become infatuated. That's all it usually took, one little thing. She turned down the column but invited him to dine over an eighteenth-century mahogany table with too many leaves and forks, and enough polish to require sunglasses to tell the carrots from the haricots verts. Didn't matter that much since a lady in uniform put them on the plate for you, anyway. When he'd declined the fingerbowl, Margaret tossed the water from hers into the centerpiece of cut flowers, and he was double-hooked.

The first time she'd come to see him he'd panicked. Thrown every sheet he could find over the ratty furniture and dragged everything to the center of the room. Told her he was remodeling and steered her to side-by-side chairs facing nothing but a bare wall. "What time does the movie start?" she'd wanted to know, and he felt undying love.

He doubted if Margaret realized she was talking to a notorious celebrity this morning. She hated television and rarely turned it on. He wondered how she would have reacted if she'd known about the *Six at Six* story. Probably with delight. The unrequited rebel in her got a kick out of his lifestyle. She'd once asked him the name of the authority who recommended sleeping on the floor with a pack of mange-infested dogs. "It's apparent who gives the orders," she said. "I suspect the only reason they keep you is because you're tall enough to reach the counter."

Three weeks ago, she'd left a wrapped present under the porched Christmas tree. He hadn't opened it yet. They enjoyed standoffs.

Still, he imagined it would've rattled her cage a little, seeing the tree and her present beneath it on TV, the camera eye invading her civil world. Cooper considered confessing, but a brawl in the pantry distracted him. "Hold on a second," he said, and went off to rescue Sophie, trapped in a corner trying to talk an old feather duster out of retirement.

While he was gone, Mount Maxwell picked up his ball and strutted over to the piano. He had a prospect, the brown dude who'd staggered in the night before. He'd seen him around plenty, but not horizontal on the floor. Wouldn't matter, as long as he could throw.

Despite being a dachshund, Max knew how to play it cool. He started smooth and slow. Sniffed an ear, tasted an eye, then a corner of the mouth. Nosed an armpit and checked out the crotch. Nothing doing. He stepped it up. Circled, snouted the left knee, lifted it. Easy to do since it was missing a lower leg. He dropped the ball beside the stub. Not much meat on these bones. One more nudge. Bad news. The cat was dead. Then Max saw the crutch. Nobody looking. Just one quick squirt to break even.

"Back again," Cooper said, holding Sophie under his arm.

"Redundant," Margaret said.

Cooper grinned, depositing the dog into a spot between the telephone base and the answering machine. The mismatched appliances were sitting on some newspapers haphazardly stacked on a handsome walnut desk built by his grandfather, which was situated catty-corner in the entrance hall with a stairwell up the back side.

A small living room, to the right if you were facing the front porch, caught the best light. The sofa sat on a red oak floor in front of a trio of tall windows. The baby grand was on the wall to the right of the sofa, with a single window on either side. An archway opened to a dining room that Cooper referred to as "the den," but it was basically storage for more unread newspapers. Beyond that was the kitchen, two semi-furnished bedrooms down the hall, another two unfurnished upstairs. At least they'd been there when Cooper had last checked, maybe five years ago. The backyard was a small dry patch off a screened-in porch, set off by a shed at the property line.

"I just got your note a few minutes ago," he told Margaret. He'd stuck the envelope in his back pocket and forgotten it was there.

"Evidently, the Pony Express delivered it."

"I was a little late checking last week's mail. Here, it's open now."

Three lines were written on thick white paper engraved at the top, the blue ink strong and steady, like the hand that penned it. Cooper read aloud, hamming it up with a dry Charleston brogue. He didn't know why he always raised his voice. Margaret was deaf in her left ear, the same one she used for phone calls, but an amplifier in the earpiece was broadcasting their conversation to the eastern seaboard.

"To whom it may concern: Never mistake endurance for hospitality. My love as always. Margaret."

"Well?" said Margaret.

"Well, what?"

"Did you get the message?"

"Yes. I got the message."

"In that case, dear, try putting it to the good."

Cooper accepted the dare.

"Nice talking to you," he said, and hung up. Soon after they'd become friends, Margaret had told him he had no terminal facilities, and that people took advantage of him because of it. When he didn't understand, she spelled it out. "Time is a resource one can never recover," she said. "You have no capacity for ending a conversation and moving along." She'd been trying to teach him how to terminate ever since.

He collected Sophie from the desk and carried her into the kitchen. He liked playing Margaret's games. She had a way of zeroing in on him that went beyond uncanny. She was brilliant in every category except two: operating her Continental, a '61 convertible, black with silver trim and whitewalls, which she drove like a maniac; and ordering from a fastfood restaurant. At Wendy's drive-thru the other day she'd asked for a small can of prune juice and a slice of apple pie with cheese on top.

The phone rang again. Cooper smiled. Margaret, conducting a test. Grabbing a pot, he added oat bran and a jar of pureed organic carrots, blended in some tepid water, and set it in front of Sophie. She ate on the counter. Reba and Max ate on the floor, in opposite corners, backs hunched over their bowls to prevent poaching: oat bran mixed with vitamin-enriched kibble, no additives or preservatives. Cooper ate standing next to Sophie. Oat bran doctored with yogurt and raisins. Good for cholesterol.

"Your old man's quite a cook," he said.

The phone finally stopped, then started again. Max complained about it but Reba was occupied in washing dishes. Cooper was tempted to fold, but it was getting close to eight o'clock. After facing up to his contribution to the morning paper a while ago, he wanted to slip in early while there was a vacancy behind the Berlin Wall. "**The Caught and the Uncaught, a Life of Temporary Reprieves**" the same day, same page as "**Shandon Sore Thumb**." What had he been thinking?

He picked up Sophie, nuzzling her against his neck as he carried her to the back porch, where she couldn't get lost. After latching the screen, he went in to say goodbye to Mount Maxwell, digesting his breakfast underneath the sofa pillows. Reba had finished cleaning up and was curled against Malachi's chest, eating the raisin box. Cooper worked the mushy cardboard out of his mouth, careful not to wake up Malachi. No time for the call of nature now, he thought. He'd come by on his way to lunch and let them out.

Burning up on the drive downtown, he pictured Margaret sitting by the old red telephone in her library, writing him a note of congratulations. He'd even surprised himself, the way he'd dispatched her, with defiance and flair, a tough guy. Could've been Bogart in *The Maltese Falcon*, Marvin in *The Big Heat*. Hello, Goodbye. Ring me up again all you want, doll, no second chances. Cooper smiled. Margaret knew the training would never take for good but she persisted. It provided a little levity for her in a world of needs she couldn't satisfy or meet.

She accused him of being a cedarbird. "The poor creature occupies the lowest rung on the perch," she'd explained one night as they were finishing up a bottle of Pouilly-Fuissé in her den. "The other birds keep pecking at it until nothing is left but feathers."

Margaret had him tagged, all right. He collected rocky souls in Odds & Ends the way a swimming pool gathers dead leaves. He treated their missteps and idiosyncrasies with acceptance and affection, crafted their legitimacy in black and white so convincingly they began to believe it might be true. Yet the hungry have to be fed. So weeks after the ink had faded in the bottom of the cage, and months and years after that, they continued to peck away at him. What bothered Margaret the most, Cooper knew, was that it made him happy to oblige them.

·

Another telephone, inside ring, this one jangling underneath the sports page. Braves 9, Cards 8, extra innings. Cooper jumped.

"Yeah?"

"Transfer," said Ruth Ann. "Relax. It's not him."

But the call had come in on Hitch's line, so it was probably the historical society. Caught, 2, Uncaught, 0. Cooper plowed through his hair, raking in a little respect. No haircut. He'd forgotten again. He put an elbow on the desk and held his forehead. The pressure felt good.

"This is Cooper Barnet," he said.

"Indeed it is."

Malachi Patterson, slumbering degenerate of the keyboard, had arisen from under the piano.

"Where are you?" Cooper asked.

"What difference does it make? At the desk. Where else am I likely to uncover a telephone in this godforsaken house?"

Brooke the preppie intern walked up with a cardboard tray filled with canteen coffee. Cooper smiled and shook his head no. Brooke was a lemon popsicle today. Yellow hair, yellow ribbon, yellow blouse, yellow sandals. Cooper watched her hand one of the Styrofoam cups to Sam, who suddenly let out his first whoop of morning sneezes. Coffee sloshed out, drenching the keys of his word processor.

"The dogs need to go outside," Cooper said. "Sophie's on the porch. And, Malachi. . . ." He grabbed up some copy paper to hand to Brooke, but Sam was mopping up the mess with his sleeve. ". . . don't let her get tangled up in the blackberry vines. They're bad behind the shed. Remember, she's practically blind."

"Then enroll her in doggie day care. Saw the van the other day. Camp Bow Wow. Claimed they have a pick-up service."

"I meant to change her water. Make sure it's against the wall where she can't trip over the bowl."

"Buck up. I don't have the patience to humor your neurotic Jones this morning. Man obsessing about the heat doesn't leave his dog on the porch in a heat wave. Look here, you had a visitor."

"Visitor? When?"

"Early enough to disturb me. Not long after you left."

"Who was it?" Malachi was right. Here he was trying to keep the dog from being sliced into minute steak by the fan and he was frying her whole on the porch. Serial killers established an M.O. early on. He had his—frying, complicated by lack of foresight.

"A member of Columbia's finest," Malachi said. "Banged on the door hard enough to break it down. Wouldn't take much."

"You mean a policeman?"

"Those fools up there pay you to be that dense? I assume he was a cop. The milkman don't deliver anymore."

"Doesn't."

"What?"

"You just said 'the milkman don't deliver.' You do that all the time."

"Do what?"

"Use improper grammar when you're a genius."

"I've been speaking the same way since you were eleven years old and you just now asking about it? It's a form of cultural license, in this case employed to indicate frustration for the time you waste with senseless questions. How about passing it along to the Oracle of Syracuse so he can put it in his next paper."

"But if I was quoting you, would I say 'don't' or change it to 'doesn't'?"

"I could give a rat's ass. Please yourself."

"Up until now, I would've used 'don't' and never thought a thing of it."

"In other words, you would have reported precisely what I said."

"Yeah. That's the way I was taught. But I don't think it's right."

"Because I'm a black man."

"Partially, I guess."

"I get special privileges."

"Not really. It's not like that."

"What is it like, then? What if I were white?"

"I'm not sure. It would depend."

"Depend on what?"

"On . . . I don't know. It's complicated."

"For God's sakes, baby. People out there starving to death, and you worrying yourself over the racial ethics of quoting sources."

"I'm not, really. I just think about it every now and then."

"You should be worrying about the policeman."

"What did he want?"

"Didn't say. Just left a note with his name and number. A Lieutenant Lewis. Said to call or stop by the station ASAP. You in some kind of trouble?"

"Probably. Hey, Malachi?"

"What?"

"You think I might be a closet racist?"

"I think you need to do something about these animals. It smells like the inside of a toilet bowl in here."

"Reba won't go as long as you're there with him. He just does it when he's abandoned."

"Is that so? What about this little short-legged character wrestling with my leg?"

"Mount Maxwell's house-trained."

"Not even in the halls of Glory. Damn dog whizzed all over my crutch this morning. Listen, how about bringing a quart of decent bourbon when you come home, and something edible. Looks like the last time you shopped for groceries was with the Pilgrims."

Cooper held the dial tone a few seconds. ASAP? Sounded like Hitch in uniform. Surely the historical society wouldn't have called the cops. But maybe they had. Or it could be his outstanding parking tickets. It wouldn't be the first time they'd issued a warrant.

Now he saw the message from Ginna—"Lt. Lewis up here looking for you. Call immediately!!!!!"—underlined three times.

"This is his direct number!!!!!!" He glanced at her desk but she wasn't in it.

.

"What you got for tomorrow?" asked Sam.

Cooper handed him a napkin. They were sitting at a table in the canteen, where Sam had just splashed coffee overdosed with Cremora on his Banlon shirt. Lucky for him, the stripes were in the taupe family today.

"You probably should switch to water," Cooper said. "That shirt's toast and it still hasn't eaten lunch. Doesn't K-Mart have anything in solids?"

"Change the subject, why don't you," Sam said.

"There is no subject. Not yet, anyway."

"Well, that's it. You're as good as fired. You'll be begging in the streets. The shoe shop won't even want you now. Those worthless dogs'll starve to death." Sam reached for another napkin. "What was all that uncaught crap?" he asked, focusing on the stain again. "Jesus God. You'd have been better off with another dwarf."

Cooper checked behind him for editors in the caffeine line. "I told you they're gnomes," he said. "Pretty big ones, actually."

"If you were that determined to put forth such an idiotic notion, you could have at least let Maxine dig her own hole," Sam griped. "She didn't utter a single word in the entire fifteen inches. Damned thing was so dull they could've run it on the editorial page. It read like somebody else wrote it."

"I'm trying to cut down on quotes. All they do is cause confusion. I wanted to make things clear for the reader."

Sam wadded up the napkin and chunked it in his empty cup. "Clear? It didn't make one bit of sense to me. What was the point?"

"The way life works is the point. It's like any universal truth, simple and complex at the same time."

"It's a bunch of mindless junk, just like those stupid figurines."

"No it's not. Nowhere near. I'll play you the tape so Maxine can tell you about it. She explains it perfectly."

"Why the hell didn't you let her do it, then?"

Cooper looked over his shoulder again. "I might be able to redeem myself in the morning," he said.

Sam perked up like Reba at mealtime. "Good stuff?"

"It depends."

"Depends on what, one of those dinky old dwarfs coming to life and dancing a disco boogie on top of your head?"

"Might happen. You never know."

◆

Liebman could drive Mother Theresa to battery. There he was, holding the phone like a sputtering land mine, begging Cooper to hurry. Why couldn't he learn to respect his system, leave him be.

Cooper pictured himself writing the action for a series of cartoon panels. Ram Jazz with back of chair, jam him against desk, squeeze "HURRRRRY" and all related synonyms from memory compartment in brain, force nuclear reaction that zaps overwrought blond frizz and every telephone line in building. HAHAHA, the evil red-horned robot would go. HOHOHO.

"Tell 'em I'll sell my entire sorry soul for a column," Cooper said as he sat down, fumbling around for a pen. "Anything they've got."

Then he took the receiver from Jazz and listened. And what he ended up scribbling across the front of a photograph had nothing to do with incidental odds and ends. It had to do with the caught, and the no longer uncaught, and the very soon-to-be discovered. It had to do with a child on a Greyhound bus, a missing child—a stranger, and with a man by the name of Barnet who had just busted the bank on reprieves.

6

Malachi found a clean t-shirt on the floor of the bedroom closet. Barnet called it his "payola pile." As in, "Thank you very much for the write-up, and by the way, here's a ridiculous advertisement to remember us by if you have the bad taste to wear it."

The background was white, had a bloated red frankfurter running down the front, two mini-sausage links in black studded boots for legs, and another semicircular link for a pocket. Malachi smiled. A poor sartorial choice for a cat who'd just read in the morning paper that he'd been breathing the same sanctified air as Archibald Rutledge, but the closet was dark and small and his only accomplices were a crutch and a decrepit old mutt lunging herself at his heel, doing her damnedest to influence the selection.

It would be hard not to notice a shirt like that, but the more observant would explore the man who had it on. They would take in the leg that wasn't there and move directly to the face. His was a captivating face, intelligent and commanding, daring you in and warning you off at the same time. A face with the kind of classic features they taught you to sketch in a class of introductory art; the expressive, haunting, seductive face of a seasoned actor who has played all the parts; a Denzel Washington or a Morgan Freeman or a Poitier, except this face didn't act except when the man behind it was playing a mockery of himself.

If you were especially perceptive when you encountered Malachi Patterson, the man and his face, you might sense the potential for an exquisite kindness. It was hard to see, though, because it was carried deep. Mostly what you saw was despair. His despair was bitter. Forty-four going on nowhere and he knew it. Also knew what was waiting for the ones who had the luck to hit on fame before they thought the whole thing through.

Stay, go. Go, stay. Most people found it easier to look at Malachi from a distance.

Sophie wasn't intimidated. Just as soon as her ill-kempt guest topped the zipper on his Bermudas, she cajoled him into the kitchen, wagging her nubby tail in front of the oven until he looked inside and saw the box. Malachi pulled off a piece of petrified pepperoni stuck in a cheesy corner and lobbed it to her quick, before the competition realized what they were sleeping through, then led her into the front room, where he picked her up and put her on the desk.

He had to shove off half of Barnet's life to make a space. He stuffed things in the drawers that weren't mildewed shut, dumped things on the floor. He knew where they landed wouldn't make a difference. Not here—and surprisingly not in a number of other houses. Malachi had been brought up to believe the world was orderly and everything had a place. Then he got out in it.

He sat down, laid his head beside the dog. *"Remember, she's practically blind."* It was crazy, Barnet knowing he was jiving him about his pets and getting in a lather about it anyway. Malachi winced. The chair had a stiff caned bottom. The devil's throne, reserved for sinners on liquid diets. The less you weigh the more you pay.

According to Barnet, the chair was a family heirloom. Went with the desk. Crayon marks on the blotter explained why he'd hung on to it all these years. Faded scratches and scribbles, mostly circles. Kid had been too young to know how to write.

Malachi ran a finger over one of the marks, the finger of a pianist playing the music of an abstract artist. "Herein lies a sad, sad story," he said to Sophie.

She licked his nose. He was on her level now. He reached over and unbuckled her collar, let it out a notch. At her age she'd earned a little space. Poor girl, about to surrender assisted living for skilled care. Swap humiliation for futility. Her thick tangle of hair was a mix of charcoal black and ashy gray, the luster dulled from no longer being able to chase and catch what she wanted. I can identify with that, Malachi thought. He picked a dried clump of oat bran from the white whiskers around her mouth, then grazed a hand over his own chin. "We could both stand a shave," he told her. "You know, I believe we have a lot in common, little dog. Stubs and grooming deficiencies included. And what's with that purple collar? It's about as garish as this shirt."

The fans were making him drowsy again, blowing all over the house. Giant Whirlpool sucking wind up into the attic and out the eaves. A large boxy Walmart Mama dancing the cha-cha at the end of the hall. In the kitchen, an Old Havana table model, pale green, teasing some take-out napkins lying on the counter until they gave in and dashed to the floor.

The dining room where no one dined had been turned into a den where no one sat, since there weren't any chairs. Only some unpacked boxes of books and a large pine table holding up a mountain of newspapers, most never released from the rubber bands, and another fan, a rotator model teetering on a slender pedestal, aimed to travel through the archway toward the desk—more noise than air. The house was shaded by three lusty oaks and a sweet gum. It wasn't as hot without the A/C as you'd expect it would be. Or maybe it was. Malachi hadn't been spoiled to think that way.

He'd always felt lonesome in this house. Lonesome and at home, too. Like most things of interest, it was hard to explain. He wasn't the justifying type and didn't try when he was asked. Round peg in a square hole was what made life life. He pitied folks who had to make everything fit.

Across the room, the dachshund was using his head to butt an overstuffed sofa cushion to the floor. The dog kind of grew on you. He was a noble specimen, looked like a holdover from some prehistoric bodybuilding competition. Ten inches high and two feet long, with fifteen pounds of sable muscle, each one toned to perfection. Bad taste in partners, though. The cushion was an ugly tan, wearing its age in stains. Matched the overall ambiance.

"Give it hell, Yum-Yum," Malachi said. It was the name on the frankfurter shirt. *"Yum-Yum"* painted in stringy loops of yellow mustard across the hotdog on front, and in red letters on back, *"28 Ways to Go,"* with the ways listed in black, the most preposterous being with green chutney relish and deviled egg.

The Yum-Yum was a downtown institution, a duck-in dive selling hotdogs for fifty cents a pop. Blue collar hotdogs, boiled to an anemic pink in a monster pot. It also was the title of a hit song written by Malachi's friend Bogie King, number one in the U.K. *Yum-Yum, gimme some.* It wasn't written with wienie dogs in mind but it sure fit this one. Bogie was in a hot disco group called Fatback. Sang and played guitar.

Malachi loved him when he didn't hate him. He even jammed with him from time to time, as long as Bogie didn't try to mind his business. He only lived an hour down the road in Rock Hill, where Malachi had been last evening when he was supposed to be here teaching piano lessons at the private academy run by his aunt. He'd found a ditch speeding back. He would've been dead if he hadn't just slowed to get his bearings. The whiskey helped, an effective shock absorber. Nice little town, Rock Hill, friendly folk. Gardens are pretty. Any hills or rocks you met were incidental.

Malachi picked up the phone. He had to cover the base, the only one he cared about covering. His aunt Angeline, two months shy of seventy-five, still a tiger. Barnet told him that even to this day Angeline Patterson was the first one he prayed to for the forgiveness of his sins. When Malachi had mentioned it to her once, she'd laughed. "You tell that impudent sinner the only mercy he can expect from me is a strap on his smart behind."

The secretary didn't answer. Any gift horse, baby, even a machine. He left a message. "Tell her I'm safe, as in acceptable company. Tell her I'm sorry, as in apologetic and contemptible. Tell her I'll be in touch."

More than likely his aunt would guess where he was, although he hadn't been here in a while, and another while before that. Hard for him to accept that this was the best place he could find to crash. Didn't matter. Here he was. The least he could do was clear the way for Angeline to get through so she could give him a piece of her mind.

It was a joke, Barnet even bothering with a machine—its belly stuffed full of calls he ignored and that constant infernal ringing following him around the house. Like this morning. Phone had been doing the Freak since the crack of dawn.

"Here, old girl, we'll just do something about that," Malachi said. He reached over the dog, pressed "Delete," then recorded a notice in the spirit of full disclosure. "Try your luck. No guarantees." He wasn't about to go through every message and take it down. Hell, Barnet wouldn't know they were gone.

Yum-Yum had called it off with the cushion. He was bulldozing, front paws flying through a pile of old record albums stacked around a stereo on the far side of the sofa, making himself a cave. A fusion of nurture and nature, some issues from his past mixed in with the badger-catching traits he was born with that required him to do time in holes.

The dog was buried now, everything covered but the snout, poking out from under Horowitz. Malachi smiled a sweet sad smile. Already asleep. The fool had worn himself out.

◆

The music had been selected with care. Bach, Beethoven, and the lot. Hendrix, Clapton. Lennon and the Beatles. The blues and ragtime Joplins. Hubert Sumlin, Robert Johnson, John Lee Hooker. Parker . . . Krupa . . . Blakey . . . Trane. Clyburn, Frampton. Quincy Jones. Miss Billie Holiday. Ella. Aretha. Longhair and all the New Orleans greats. Would take a week naming them all, but if Malachi was going to teach him, he was going to teach him right. He was leading up to his man, the one and only, the wizard of the New Orleans piano.

After putting Sophie on the floor, he helped himself over with the crutch, stooped beside Yum-Yum, and fished around. Little Booker was face up beneath the dog's hind leg, looking just as wild and fierce on the cracked, moldy jacket as he did when they'd seen him in the Paris of the South twenty-three years ago. Same scared look too. Everything was after him that hadn't already caught him, including the CIA.

Cooper's stereo was on concrete blocks, three feet high. Malachi had to go low and sit on the arm of the sofa. He lifted the lid and turned the knob. First a squeak and a groan, the turntable making a decision. It gave in, a spinning Dust Bowl. He aimed for "Junco Partner," landed on "All by Myself." That's fine. He straightened, got his balance, shut his eyes and said hello to his glorious, notorious role model.

Warps, scratches, shoddy machine, nothing could mutilate the mad giddyfying genius of James Carroll Booker, the Third. He still had it, everything but life. 1939 to 1983. Forty-four years old when he checked out, same as Malachi now. Died in the emergency room of New Orleans' Big Charity, liver shot all to hell. Booze, heroin, insanity, the wars of misfitted sex. He claimed they took it from him but he had to know he'd stolen it from himself. Chose all for nothing. Did that make him smart or sorry? Guess that didn't make him either. Guess it made him nothing but dead.

Malachi named the next piece before the needle finished filling in the blank. "Until the Real Thing Comes Along." Thought it had the Friday afternoon he'd yanked Barnet's sheltered young ass out of a Milton lecture and hauled it off toward something he could feel. They'd made it to the Big Easy on five Big Macs and a couple of tanks of thirty-three-cents-a-gallon low-test. Drove straight through. They had to. He was South going South, with a white boy to boot, a white boy who wasn't the one driving, in 1967 definitely a cause for significant caution and in many cases still a mandate for abject fear.

They found Booker in the Maple Leaf Bar on Oak Street, wearing a major 'fro and a polyester suit. His eye patch had a big white star on it. He played three songs and booked in the middle of the fourth. "Tico Tico." The girl in front of them blamed a waiter who'd dropped a glass, but the drummer told her it had been broken since before she was born.

Malachi had seen that the brother was right. Saw it when the man had thrown his head at the ceiling, cackled wild and hoarse, at nothing but cobwebs boogieing across a square of particle board. Saw it in the "Black Minute Waltz" when the base hand outran the lead in the treble. Saw it again in "How Does It Feel?" when what had started as a slow-to-medium stride leapt into a frenzied race to a place the notes weren't meant to go.

But he'd also seen what he'd been hearing about since he was twelve. Booker accompanying Booker, a classically trained magician pulling ecstasy and pain from every empty hat. Could have been two pianos, sometimes three, even to the schooled ear. But it was the Bayou Maharajah, one piano, all by himself.

He'd been a fool, Malachi Patterson, with his dreams of taking over where Booker had left off, of doing it better, sober, clean, and sane. And his young white friend? He didn't have much of a plan.

Cooper had been two years behind him in numbers, two hundred more in the ways of life. A naïve grown boy in his junior year of college, working the same job he'd had since freshman year in high school. He'd started at fifteen, the summer before ninth grade, knocking himself out every Saturday in Butler's Shoe Store, making fifteen cents an hour plus commission for shoving the latest style pump or mule or satin heel past the bunions on a worn-out foot attached to the lucky lady who could manage to scrape up $4.99—$5.17 with tax—for a shoe that might hold up six months, as long as she saved them for special occasions—or $2.99 plus tax ($3.08), if she wanted a sassy little backless sandal that gave her breathing room.

You could see he was a natural. Something about the way he turned it on, nice and easy; walking her to the mirror, those soulful baby blues admiring her lovely foot as he snowed her with mindless clichés. *You make that shoe look good. Not everyone can wear that style. Does it slide up and down on your heel? Remember, it will always stretch. A real pretty shade, goes with everything. Come on, you can afford 'em. A sweet lady like you deserves to treat herself.*

"Nothing wrong with the job," Barnet would tell him. "I might stick around. Work up to manager one day."

He didn't admit how much he liked it, watching a limp become a strut as he appraised the model posing this way and that, nodding his pleasure at what he saw—*would you like to wear them home?*—as if he were sending a dainty glass slipper down a trail of silver moonbeams to the ball. But Malachi knew. He'd sold shoes with Cooper in the same store, to brown feet only. Quit before the third week was over, but he'd seen enough.

They'd spent hours downtown back then, listening to albums at Mo's Music House. The first time they showed up they simplified their connection, explaining that they worked together down the street at Butler's, and that Malachi was helping Cooper build a record collection.

Maurice Stein was a Jew who had empathy for any persecuted race. He knew that since 1954 Angeline Patterson had operated the Calhoun Street Academy, a small, accredited private school for grades one through eight in what used to be a dentist's office in a separate wing off the back of her house, and that her students were reading Latin and solving calculus equations before they moved on to high school. He also knew that her nephew Malachi was a brilliant pianist who discreetly took lessons from Dr. Richard Matthews, one of Mo's customers and a retired professor from Converse College, a highly regarded liberal arts school upstate.

So Mo left them alone as long as they listened to the demos in the last booth in the back and drew the blinds. He took less heat that way, though he'd been willing to take whatever heat he got. If anybody raised hell, he shot some bull about Malachi being a jazz pianist visiting from New York and sent the young men out the same way they'd come in, through the rear door.

Yes, Malachi thought, they'd had some fine times in Mo's, in the days when they heard the music. But fine memories couldn't solve his current problems—like thirst, and the policeman who'd cruised by the house at least four times in the last hour. Could still be after Cooper, but when you drive on a suspended license, disable a "Proceed with Caution" sign and leave the evidence tagged in a ditch, paranoia has a way of setting in.

With his history and connections, he was a trophy deviant, good for a laugh while they poured a cuppa joe at the precinct coffee pot. *Hey. Looks like that education in the classics taught him how to be a classic drunk. Yeah. Guess there ain't as much ivory in ol' Angeline Patterson's tower as she thought.* The times they hadn't been a changin' all that much. Shit. He would've been a joke if he was white.

After they'd come home from New Orleans, Malachi altered his plans. Wanted to spend the money he'd been squirreling for a new piano on a funky little spinet tuned to the blues according to Booker. Of course his aunt wouldn't hear of it, so he bought a Steinway baby grand instead. Third-hand ebony, with some scratches on the roof, but it played. The same piano on the other side of the sofa, getting damp against an outside wall. Barnet told the movers to put it there. Hadn't known better, since there were no instructions on the note taped to the stool.

"To the happy couple," it said. "Please accept this token of friendship, no questions asked. Don't worry. It only speaks when spoken to, and from the looks of things, it's talked out. God help us all. Malachi."

Barnet probably still had the note. He never threw anything away that was attached to somebody he was afraid of losing. Malachi made his way over to the piano. He started to run his fingers underneath the stool, then decided to let that particular sleeping dog lie with the other three, and took a seat.

He touched middle C, then G; came back to F, and crossed over to B flat on the base side. Came back to middle C again. His hand shook. The piano needed tuning. Sophie was at his feet now, throwing her body against his leg, jumping for his lap. He picked her up. Steered her matted black paws to the keyboard. They were about the only parts she had left that weren't splayed with gray. With the treble paw, he pressed F and G and banged six times. He used his own hand for the base. Nothing much to it. The dog was deaf, and Chopsticks spoke for itself.

The phone rang again.

"Pick up, Malachi."

Hold on, I'm comin'. Sam and Dave, 1966, Stax Records. Should be in the pile.

"Are you listening?"

Trying not to. We were in the middle of a concert.

"It's urgent."

Dog needs food. Dog needs water. Dog needs burping. Hell, the dog was getting a piano lesson. What did he want, an egg in his beer?

"I have to talk to you, man. Please."

This wasn't good. The boy sounded desperate, disturbed. As soon as he could get close enough, Malachi flipped the receiver off the cradle with the toe of his crutch. "Go on," he said.

When they'd finished, he went to the kitchen to recheck all the hiding places he'd checked two hours before, and although he knew he shouldn't be asking, prayed to God that this time he would have better luck.

7

For a rare moment the lack of a column wasn't on Cooper's mind. He was too busy drowning in the heavy rain. After Hannah's phone call, a series of instinctual actions had taken him from the newsroom to the police department, where he'd consulted with Lieutenant Lewis and alerted Malachi, and then to the bus station, and after that to places he wasn't sure he could say he'd even been, before eventually delivering him to Percy's sofa five hours later.

A brain wave had directed him to leave his wet loafers and socks on the sunny edge of the porch to dry, and now another one was telling him he should sit, so he did. A shabby red slipcover sopped up the water, leaving an outline like the body at a murder scene, proof that he was actually there. Like a patient in one of the common areas on Bull Street, he appealed to the television for any kind of verification he could get. He was conscious. He was alive. A rerun of *The $10,000 Pyramid* was on.

Percy hadn't seen him come in. The big room was half studio, half den, divided by a long decorative screen, and she was in the studio half, in her opinion the best spot in the house. She'd fixed it up the winter before, after her classes had surprised her with a pink canvas beach chair for her thirty-eighth birthday. The chair had stayed exactly where it was when they'd presented it to her, largely due to her boyfriend's mysterious distaste for coastal travels.

But Percy had a talent for sweetening lemons. She'd gone to an outlet mall and bought two more chairs similar to the first one, as well as a slightly damaged white wicker table at cost, a clear glass lamp filled with shells, and a striped umbrella. In the bargain bin from five dollars up, she'd found a bonanza, a faded pastel print of four little girls holding hands while they jumped the waves; then she'd created what she christened "Happy Isle," a cheery spectator's beach near the floor-length mirror for parents who arrived before the lesson was finished.

To tie everything together, she'd painted a Jamaican blue sky over the Oriental design on the decorative screen and splashed on some silver stars. It had taken her three coats to cover the red. "Stars only come out at night," Cooper told her when she'd shown it off.

"Wrong. The stars are always out when you're dancing," she replied.

She was dancing now in pink tights, swinging her arms from side to side, fingers fanned, wrists cocked, demonstrating hand positions for the shuffle-ball-change as she had done infinitesimal times the entire year, and wondering what about it could be so hard that a group of healthy young girls with no obvious mental deficiencies couldn't get it right.

A teacher workday in the city schools had given her an opening to set up extra practice sessions to fine tune before the recital. Only four girls in the nine-through-twelves had shown up. Three, actually, and Marie Chang, Duke and Layla's daughter, who belonged in a different class.

True, Percy had given them short notice, or maybe it was the flood. One minute the sun had been blazing, the next you needed Noah's help to float out of The Bowl and cross Gervais Street. Now it was sunny again, and hot. Percy was about to run the air back up to total blast, but saw something in the corner of her eye, and glided over to a bobbing blur of mismatched movements in short black bangs and a gypsy halter top, about to collide with the piano behind her.

"Don't make a fist, Lacey Jo. Open your hand like this, see? Pretend you're a princess waving to the crowd. Keep your fingers straight. No, you're freezing up. Be cocky. Be happy."

"Like this?" Lacey Jo waved at a passing hearse from somewhere beneath her chest.

"Not exactly, hon. More like this. That's the ticket. All right, chicks, take five."

"I'm too hot for a snack," Little Linda Lister said. She had on the leopard skin leotard. The smoky blond coils of her new permanent wave were kinky and damp, more from the rain than from exertion.

"Don't worry," said Percy. "This is way better than Kool Aid and cookies. Now pay attention and copy me."

She held up a Dixie Cup and tore out the bottom, careful not to rip the waxy paper along the sides. "Got it? Then let's do the other one. Perfect." She raised the cups up to her eyes and peered out. "Glasses, see?" The girls giggled. "But that's not the surprise. Just watch and do exactly like I do. Firsssst . . . we squeeze our fingers into the hole, and thennn . . . we work them all the way through, like so. The whole hand, that's it, until we come all the way to the wrist. Now the second one. And, voila, what do we have? A shiny new pair of fingerless gloves."

"Look at hers," Little Linda said, pointing to Lacey Jo's sister Katherine, a shy, sandy-haired blonde wearing pink polka-dotted shorts. "They're on backwards."

"That trick is called originality," Percy said. "All set? Here we go. Close your eyes and when you open them again, bingo, you're in the recital, tapping up a storm. Wow. Are you the stuff or what? Now extend your arms. And curtsey. And lower. Beautiful."

The lesson was taking too long for Cooper. All that motion, alien and cockeyed, those funny little girls. . . . Did the little girl on the bus wear polka dots? Did she tap dance? How funny was *she*?

On some level, he understood it was okay to be numb. Out of the blue, he'd been told that he was living the wrong life. He should've been in a different life, in a story with other characters. Or at least with one other character, who'd been robbed of her leading role. He couldn't be expected to absorb it this fast. He was still running. It had to catch up. He had to catch up. Eventually they would both have to stop.

"Ouch," said Marie. "You did that on purpose."

"Did not," Little Linda said.

"Little Linda, you're on very thin ice," Percy said.

"I didn't mean to. She got in the way."

"And kick-kick-catch-up-kick, DANCE. No matter what happens, never stop dancing. Professionals never lose their cool on stage."

"But we aren't on a real stage," said Lacey Jo.

"You will be Sunday night. A good dancer never lets her guard down. Rehearsals are serious business."

Can't lose my cool, Cooper thought. Can't let my guard down. Rehearsals are. . . . Can't imagine. Don't imagine. She was on the bus and then she wasn't on the bus and he would never see her unless it was in an open casket. He didn't think he could look. Which meant everything would be like before. Because he never would've seen her. But he would know that he'd never seen her, and he would have to spend the rest of his days wondering if he was glad or sorry.

Percy finally saw him. He waved a hand toward the mirror, signaling her to keep going. She tossed him a towel from a stack beside the barre. What in the world was he doing here, drenched, in the middle of the day? She wanted to dismiss the class, but a trail of bad experiences had convinced her that if a man makes a call in a crisis, even a small one, it's better to go along until he settles down.

•

She rarely pressed him. Deferring to the territorial rights of private baggage and middle age, they'd knitted their needs into a satisfying union of uncomplicated commitment, threadbare when it came to long intimate stares and the profession of worship everlasting. Few issues were worth getting steamed up about except the sex. Beyond that, it was more the Carole King thing, "Winter spring summer or fall, all you have to do is call," with the benefits of monogamy you could count on. In that department, Cooper hadn't deceived her.

During the week, their connections were loose and easy. In his job, the fewer plans he made, the fewer he had to break, and Percy held classes at odd hours to accommodate her odd mix of students. He once teased her that they had the ultimate relationship: the comfort of knowing he'd be there every Sunday for lunch, divvying up newspaper sections over floppy aluminum trays of turkey and gravy and mashed potatoes, or whatever Swanson's delight the Piggly Wiggly had marked on special.

Did he love her? Yes. Was he in love with her? He didn't know what the "in" meant. Wasn't sure what it felt like anymore. Wasn't sure he had the capacity to feel "in" love. He'd thought he felt it with Hannah. He was positive he had. But that kind of fire didn't burn forever. You were supposed to replace it with more substantial stuff as a foundation for the long run, and for Cooper that was where the trouble started.

Percy accepted what she got and gave back what she wanted to. She had some personal history of her own. She'd married the first two and lived with the third until an emergency room nurse enticed him to start over in Albuquerque.

"But you kept going back for more," Cooper had pointed out to her the night they'd first met in the Owl's Club, after moving to a corner booth. She'd agreed it didn't make sense, and yet, she'd told him, somehow it got easier.

"It's like the first time you lose a favorite puppy," she'd explained. "You can see his big brown eyes looking up to ask if everything's all right, and you can feel his warm, furry body snuggling up against your chest, and you ache so hard you can barely take a breath. After a few months, you don't think of those big brown eyes quite as much, and that makes you feel guilty. So you make yourself conjure them up, and you try to feel the ache along with it, but somehow the caring has dulled more than you want to admit.

"Then you've recovered, and you tell yourself you'll never get attached to another dog. But you do, and the second one's a little bit easier to lose, and. . . . You learn how to streamline your emotions, shorten the stages of suffering. And also"—she'd timed the ending nicely by swallowing a sip of beer—"you unconsciously choose less desirable pets."

Her latest pet was Bob the ferret. How did this relate to his desirability? Cooper decided it didn't matter. As the weeks passed, he'd begun to long for the moment when he could enter Percy's yard sale sanctuary and close the door behind him. It was like stepping inside the booth in Woolworth's Dime Store when he was a kid and pulling the curtain shut. He would twist around on the adjustable stool until his head was in the center of the mirror and wait for the invisible magician to bring him to life. All it took was a quarter in the slot.

In seconds, a whirring noise announced the arrival of four black and white images through a narrow chute. He'd sit behind the curtain, holding the slimy paper and drinking in the sickening chemical smell, until the photos dried enough to find a safe haven in his wallet. If no one was outside waiting, he sat there a long time. It felt good, sitting in the darkened booth.

But now he didn't want to sit. Couldn't sit. Couldn't move, either. Couldn't watch Percy. She made him feel strange. The girls made him feel strange. But he didn't want to remember the other time he'd felt like this. The same feeling, almost. Didn't want to be aware of the recognition that he'd tied the two experiences together. That he'd wanted to run then, too. That he had run. Run and run and run until he tripped over a curb. He was a good runner. Later on he'd lettered in track.

Dick Clark was grinning at a contestant who looked like Doris Day. She was partnered with Betty White. They were smiling, too. The word they couldn't get was "swipe." No wonder. No Hannah. . . . No Hannah no Hannah no.

"Saw you on the news," she'd told him. *"Heard them say your name. Saw them show your house and the desk where you work. . . . Wanted to be the one to tell you . . . didn't want a policeman pounding on your door in the night but I kept calling and calling and I couldn't find you and they didn't want to wait even before they knew what happened and. . . . But I was the one who told you, wasn't I? . . . I got to you first, before. . . . You didn't have to hear it from a stranger. . . ."*

He tried to focus on the Doris Day woman. She was hugging Betty White. They'd made it to the final round, despite missing "swipe." Hannah had exiled Betty White from their honeymoon. They'd spent late afternoons watching *Password*, a mindless interlude during lovemaking. Millions of Americans saw the program every day, switched it off and went on.

But Cooper didn't have a mental eraser. Hours later, when they were hiking to town or riding the T-Bar up the mountain, he would turn to Hannah and say, "If only that sweet kindergarten teacher from Trenton had thought of 'Parliament' when she was. . . ." Percy had brought him back to game shows. By the time he'd met her, it no longer mattered that much who won or lost.

•

Percy held him a while before he could tell her. He was cold. Shivering in the heat. He spit it out like bile. "You can kill yourself later," she said. "Right now you've got to find that child."

She drove him to the newsroom in her tights. His mind was flying faster than the sputtering red MG, which under the command of a pink ballet slipper was breaking the speed limit at the cost of a license and maybe some community service.

Ironic that the job—his enabler and to some extent the reason he'd lost Hannah—might be the only way to find the girl. If he'd been a mechanic or a chef or a surgeon, he would be falling apart, minus power, with few options other than to wait and wonder if he were going insane. Instead he was now on autopilot. He was the reporter in charge.

He'd been in this hot seat too many times for too many years, racing toward another deadline. He'd done it in different cars with different information under all weights of pressure, swearing at the end of each crazy streak-to-the-finish that this was the last, that trying to come from twenty points down with two minutes left on the clock was a game for the young or for the birds. But he hadn't meant it.

Back then he believed he was born to chase life with a pen, and he rode the rush like a Derby stallion, harnessing it to carry him over the finish line, driving it until he was spent of time and words.

He would use the race back to the newsroom to rewind the snatch of history he'd just witnessed, fast-forwarding past the insignificant, freezing the highlights. The lede might come to him in a passing blur of black asphalt, the end in a blank billboard waiting for its next sell, the defining quote in the red eye of a traffic light tempting him not to stop.

At the foot of the Broad River Bridge, he might decide to do a straight write-through. On the other side, he might reconsider and go for a teaser instead—make the reader dig through paragraph after paragraph of exposition to find the prize. He might decide, then he might panic and begin the process again, all on the ride back to the paper. Just as he was doing now. Doing and caring for the first time in months.

Back in high school, he'd thought about becoming a newspaper reporter. Through a lucky connection with an English teacher who dated a *Herald-Journal* photographer, he'd been chosen to cover the local teen scene during his junior year. But after learning that the university didn't offer a degree in blowing time and the old man's money, he'd dropped out to manage the shoe store. Just temporarily. That's what he kept telling Malachi, who'd been giving him relentless hell for still kissing feet when he should've been kissing ass. "I'll figure it out," he'd say.

Temporary became two years. It was going on three when he bought a fifty-cent paperback one morning at a used book store. He started reading in the stockroom during lulls and forgot to go out for lunch. The author was war correspondent Ernie Pyle. His columns were vivid, poignant, and shattering. Cooper was floored that such humble, simple prose could call up the horror and beauty in life. Also death.

At five that afternoon he locked the glass doors of Butler's Shoes and headed east. He remembered the location of the newsroom from his Teen Scene days. Second floor, third door, right. Editors didn't use fancy daytimers back then. The new city editor, Benjamin Hitchcock, received him without pretense.

"What do you wanna do?" he'd asked.

"I want to write like Ernie Pyle."

"Can you?"

"No."

"Well, let's see how bad you are."

Humiliation is a ruthless editor. His first story was a pretty good read if you didn't care about facts, like that the subject's name was Rice instead of Reece. Cooper began jotting things down. Everything. In his Professional Reporter's Notebook, on the tops, bottoms, sides, and backs. Between the lines of printed programs and meeting agendas. On fast food wrappers and napkins; paper, cloth, clean, dirty. On the soles of his shoes, his pen scratching through the grit. On his skin when he couldn't find anything else.

The notebook was an insurance policy. He could flip the cover and find a recorded guarantee, a scrawled piece of memory: a slice of country ham that tasted like fried ocean bottom; a print dress that smelled like the insides of a cigarette lighter. Bad was okay, too, as long as he could call up the feeling, then adjust and refine. You had to feel to make it right. The gut had to work in tandem with the brain. A passionate detachment.

Especially on a column like he was about to write today. In a column like this one, detail was everything. Except this afternoon, for the most important column he would ever write, he was coming to the keyboard empty-handed.

◆

Sam passed him in the hall. "What is it? Something big? Hey. Wait."

"Can't. Gotta go."

He bumped into the intern at the door—what was her name?—and grabbed her by the arm.

"Yes?" she said, tentatively. Was this the same man she'd cut up with in the newsroom yesterday? His eyes were red and wild, and ringed with dark circles, and a dark shadow of whiskers made him scary.

"I need you to do something for me," he said.

"What?"

"Go to the police department. It's in the municipal building, the place they call City Hall. Back side, lower level."

"My uncle used to be on the force."

"Good. Ask for Lieutenant Lewis. Tell him we need a snapshot of the missing child. Bring it back and deliver it to Photo. Quick."

He strode toward the city desk and found Ernie LeCraft checking the AP wire. Ernie kept his eyes on the terminal. A minute or two of squirm time was required. Cooper broke protocol.

"Listen, man," he said, "I need you to back me up."

The city editor slowly turned his way but it was clear he was on another page. The stub of a pencil was jammed in his thick gray beard. He pulled it out and jotted a reminder to check the head on the council story. Touchy situation. The mayor had come to the meeting wasted and wouldn't surrender the floor during the segment open for public comment. When the pro tem intervened, the mayor had gone belligerent and an officer had to escort him out of the chambers. It was a sad story about a good man who'd developed a bad drinking problem after a drunk driver killed his oldest son.

Myrtle and Sam had teamed up to work it. The copy had run way over, and for the second time this week, Boom-Boom had to bump a feature on the owner of a real estate firm who'd just won a national public service award. That would piss off Branch Brown, the executive editor, who'd already promised the realtor's wife that the piece was definitely coming out tomorrow, no ifs, ands, or buts.

Ernie glanced up at Cooper again and saw him. Three hours to deadline and his slumping columnist was standing before him looking like Sonny's new accomplice in *Dog Day Afternoon Part II*, the dope who'd heisted the armored car and lost it a block from the bank. He reached for the Rolaids in his jeans.

"Shoot," he said.

"I've got something coming, a personal column, and I don't feel like talking about it, other than to say it'll shock the hell out of you. When I finish, I'm gonna ship it over and walk. I'll be tied up, so if you have any questions you'll have to wing it or call the cops. I trust your judgment, Ernie. I hope you can still trust mine."

"The cops?" demanded Ernie. "The historical society thing?"

"It's historical all right, but no."

Cooper went to his desk and sat. He checked the clock and the city desk. Ernie was mumbling into the phone. Cooper swiveled toward Hitch's office but it was empty. He dialed Ruth Ann.

"Where is he?"

"Gone to a United Way hoo-do. Shouldn't be back 'til late."

Cooper picked up the photograph that Charlie Cross had brought in, a picture of his magnificent mega-squash, now defaced with vital statistics of a missing little girl scrawled on every glossy inch of space, front and back. After studying the child's height and weight and the quotes he'd jotted beside it, he snatched the receiver again and called the Greyhound station one more time, and made a final call to the police. Then he turned on the word processor.

He stared at the screen, but only for a minute. Only long enough to plow through his hair and try to rub the sandpaper out of his eyes. Only long enough to recall Hannah's voice:

"You have a daughter."

He typed his byline, squared his shoulders, and began to write.

8

"Get you something else?" T-Bone Davis, manager of what he called the "three 'til forever" shift, was talking from the bottom of his chin, mining vanilla for a hot fudge sundae.

"Just another glass of tea and some snow," Cooper said.

He was heading back from the bathroom after a lukewarm splash in a dirty sink. Downgrade that to filthy. Full disclosure was posted in a smudged frame by the door, but customers in this den of fried repute weren't shopping for an A, just instant gratification.

The Toddle House was a comfort stop for university students, beat cops, and other downtown regulars in the mood to elbow the table and drip mustard on a knock-around shirt. Booths along the window wall were usually jammed. The overflow and loners sat across the aisle at the counter. Stoolies got a show in short-order magic in return for a shot of cracked orange vinyl and some cheesy jokes scrambled in with the eggs.

Cooper grabbed his tea off the counter.

"We could top that off with a Spanish omelet," T-Bone said.

"No place to put it. I ate at Percy's a while ago." Three-quarters of an apple. Bob the ferret ate the rest.

Cooper chose a booth near the door, one of three two-seaters against the short wall. Not for privacy because there wasn't any—for a chance to see her first. The tea was too sweet. He made a face, gulped it down, and started on the ice. So far no one had bugged him. The diner was heavy on students tonight, but they faced a newspaper only when it was between them and the parent with the money.

Still, he felt conspicuous in all the cheer. At Duke's they could have rendezvoused in the kitchen, sat on crates, and commiserated with Tiny while he washed dishes from the dinner rush. But the Bangkok Garden closed at nine. Park Street wasn't an option either. The house was haunted by old ghosts and Malachi. That left the best of lousy choices. Highway 21 merged into Main. Three miles later, it practically curved into the parking lot. She knew the way.

Hannah was nineteen when they met. She had Ava Gardner eyes, the cheekbones of a runway model, and a blaze of auburn hair pulled from her face, showing a childhood scar at the edge of her right temple. Twelve stitches worth of rock fight, and she was proud of it.

They'd come here on their first date, after a Peter Sellers movie. She'd told him he reminded her of a kid who had his hand in the cookie jar and knew he'd eventually get caught, and then couldn't explain what she meant. What was the stolen prize, he wondered now. Twelve years of ignorant bliss?

The clock cranked out another stroke, griping all the way. It claimed twenty-seven minutes past the hour of ten, but the hands had to slug through grill grease to jerk forward, and couldn't keep up with the time. Cooper didn't wear a watch. He had enough editors riding him without letting one parallel park on his arm.

The ice chips were water begging to be drained from his bladder. He went off to relieve what he could control, and risked typhoid for another round of sink water. The A/C squealed along with the pipes, more bark than bite.

T-Bone raced the melting sundae to a cute blonde in a blue middy top. "Here you go," he said, winking. "A nice cool bowl of chocolate soup."

Cooper and Hannah had eaten hot fudge sundaes the night he fell into marriage but his inspiration had come from three tall brown bottles perspiring on his side of the table.

"We good here?" a waitress named Happy had asked.

"Not quite," he'd said.

"Alrighty. What else can I get you?"

"Her."

"Nice choice, but I'm afraid she's not on the menu."

"Sure I am," Hannah chimed in. "Today's special. Every day's special, if he swears to treat me right."

Cooper jumped up, hooked an arm through Happy's and danced her down the aisle, singing . . . "Here comes the bride, here comes the bride, here comes the bride, and here comes the bride. . . ." the only words of the lyric he could think of. A rowdy chorus stood and joined in. It was Saturday midnight and the diner was full. A crew of Fort Jackson soldiers hauled him over for a toast. He landed on a drill sergeant's knee.

"She loves me," he said.

"She loves him," they said. "Hear, hear."

Hannah informed him later that she'd been a fool not to see it coming. "What kind of man gets engaged," she'd asked him, "then runs away to celebrate with strangers?"

But it had happened so fast, he didn't know he'd proposed.

◆

The table wobbled as Cooper lifted his head. She was leaning over him, a long-limbed, rumpled apparition, swathed in an odd blur of colors and doused in Chanel-scented sweat. She was standing too close. He couldn't take her in.

"I'm here," she said.

Had he been asleep? A flimsy tin ashtray clung to the side of his face. When he stood it fell off, a fluted edge snagging on the pocket of his shirt. He trapped it against his chest.

"Welcome home." The words came out hoarse and flat. He'd spent some time thinking about his greeting before deciding not to prepare one. Now he wished he had.

"Sorry," he said.

He felt grumpy and perplexed, a sleep-deprived customer abruptly awakened from a ten-minute nap and forced to participate in a Myers-Briggs pop quiz, ordered to make the right choice when they all seemed wrong. What was he supposed to do? Pull her to him and hold her? Pat her consolingly on the back? Shake her hand?

He saw some watery tea in his glass and gulped it down. T-Bone must have stopped by while he dozed. The warm, saccharine liquid made him nauseous. He didn't want to touch her at all, at least in a tender way. He wanted to take her by the shoulders, hurl charges, demand answers. He wanted to tell her it served her right, tell her he despised her, despised her deceit. You stole my half of our child and then you killed her, he wanted to say. But he didn't say anything. She was talking instead.

"I don't think we should stay here. What if she manages to make it to your house and no one's home?"

"Don't worry. That's been covered." He heard the coolness in his voice and didn't care. She slid into the booth. He put the ashtray back on the table. Some ashes were planted in the fluff on his cheek.

"Here," she said, shoving the metal napkin holder toward him. He blinked at it, trying to clear his thoughts. What did she intend for him to do? He pulled out a napkin and tried to hand it to her.

"Never mind," she said, and when he looked at her again his anger went away.

Her hair was stylish, chin length and choppy, but most of the auburn fire had been extinguished by pewter gray. She was thin, too thin, eight or ten pounds lighter than when they were married. She couldn't have lost that much weight in less than a day.

She had on a white silk blouse with a silver bar pinned to the left pocket. "Scheduling Supervisor," it said below her name. The Piedmont wings were there, tiny and bright gold, just above the bar. But Scheduling Supervisor Hannah Smith, notorious clothes horse, was wearing a pair of baggy red shorts. The legs were appliquéd with bouquets of asparagus and tied at the hem with navy ribbon. She looked disoriented. Spent.

"You shouldn't be driving," he said.

"I'm not. Frances dropped me off. She went to find a motel."

Frances was her sister. The sister who'd called him after Hannah had taken off. Hannah wasn't ready to talk yet, Frances had explained late that night, but was safe and would be in touch. As time went on Frances had become a confidante of sorts, telling him things she thought he should know. He wasn't a bad person. He'd been faithful. He loved his wife. But Frances had remained true to her sister where it counted. He wondered how she felt about that now.

"Have you eaten?"

Hannah shook her head.

"What about a sandwich? Or some pie?"

"I can't. Why don't you sit down. Cooper?"

"Oh." He was staring at her eyes. They were alarming— enormous precursors of despair.

"She takes amiodarone. For an arrhythmia. Her heart pumps to the beat of a different drummer. That's the way the doctor explained it. Scotty thinks it's just fine."

"You told me. The first part, anyway."

"She's . . . did I tell you that she's not, as far as her age group goes, that Scotty isn't. . . ."

"Yes, Hannah. You told me that, too. We don't need to talk about it now, okay?"

T-Bone hesitated beside the table. He was refilling salt and pepper shakers for the breakfast run. He picked up Cooper's empty glass and asked if they needed a menu. Cooper knew he meant "the lady" since he hadn't used one in years.

"Give us two coffees," he said.

"Two? You don't drink coffee."

"I know." If he ordered some, Hannah might have a cup. "And a slice of banana cream pie."

"I guess that's the best way to describe her," she went on. "That different drummer thing. Of course, it's trite, but. . . ."

"No. That's a nice way to put it," he said. Why couldn't he think of something more comforting, more profound? The bleakness of Hannah's life assaulted him from across the three-foot space. This slab of cracked Formica, once a conspirator of fantasies, now held the casualties of broken promise. T-Bone had just studied her up and down and hadn't recognized her, and she was wearing a badge with her name on it. Even after thirteen years anyone would've remembered Hannah if she'd lived another kind of life. Cooper reached towards her, not sure what he was going for. He ended up clutching the strip of metal trim wrapped around the edge of the table, rocking the table back and forth.

"This thing really wobbles," he said. He ducked underneath and wiggled it some more.

"The medicine builds up in her system. Her doctor thinks she should be all right for another few days."

Cooper dug out a clump of napkins but Hannah wasn't crying. He didn't have anything to mop up. Did he mean to put some under the table leg?

"We'll find her," he said.

He didn't say what shape they would find her in. She was probably dead by now. Dead or better off dead. He checked the clock like it meant something but all it told him was the wrong time.

Hannah was fumbling in a canvas satchel that had been "Soaring through the Skies with Piedmont." Emptying things on the table, into her lap. When they were together she had a bag like that. She was a flight attendant then, called a stewardess. A toothbrush . . . deodorant . . . the sleeve of a nightgown . . . a piece of notebook paper. It was rumpled and dirty. She spread it out.

"This is what they found this morning. It was in a trash can. In the terminal. They let me keep it. No, that's not exactly the way it was. I wouldn't give it back."

She was edgy, watching.

"She wrote it at school."

Cooper sat still.

"Here," Hannah said.

Slowly, he lowered his eyes. A labored, eager hand trespassed across the lines. He read upside down. MY DADDY SAYS I AM NOT PLUMFF LIKE. . . .

He looked up at Hannah and nodded but she expected him to go on. He pulled the paper towards him and turned it around.

MY DADDY SAYS I AM NOT PLUMFF LIKE THAT GRIL MARY IN THAT NICE LITTLE STORY. HE SAID LISSEN SCOTTY THE CHILDREN WILL NOT MAKE FUN OF YOU.

HEAR IS MY DADDY. I WILL SHOW YOU HIS PICTURE RIGHT KNOW.

A pint-sized man with a squat head was wearing what looked like a red bowtie and carrying a briefcase. One of the eyes was colored cornflower blue, the other a sickly green.

BUT MY DADDY IS NOT ACOUNTINT LIKE THAT MAN WITH THE SHORT BRONW HAIR ON PAGE NUMBER 5. MY

DADDY RIDES TO A JO ON THE BUS AND ON MY MOMMY'S AREPLANE AND ON THE BUS. TODY DAY HE TELL ME THAT HE LOVES ME VRAY MUSH AND THAT HE WILL BE THER IN THE BIG BLUE CAR TO TAKE ME TO HIS HOUSE TO PLAY.

HE SAID NOODLE CAN COME TO. HE SAID SCOTTY YOU BE A VARY GOOD GRIL AND DO NOT WASH TIME AND DO YOUR HOME WORK. AND I SAD YES DADDY I SURE WILL DO THIS DADDY. AND DADDY I LOVE YOU VARY MUSH TO. SINGED BY SCOTTY SMITH.

·

Cooper had heard tales about marriages that ended with an errand to pick up Pampers or a jog around the block. Before Hannah's escape, he hadn't believed anything like that could happen. She'd set off for a weekend at Sullivan's Island, a small quaint beach with a Revolutionary War fort overlooking Charleston harbor. She was going to visit her best friend, Julia. She left with her Piedmont satchel and a kiss goodbye.

Frances had filled in the blanks. Four miles from the ocean, in the little town of Mount Pleasant, Hannah had pulled over at a sidewalk sale and bought two adjustable lounge chairs. Then she'd loaded them in the trunk and taken off. Not south down Coleman Boulevard toward the beach, but north. North until she climbed the rickety curving hills of Grace Memorial Bridge and veered right on the other side. North until she hit I-26. North until three hours later, when she reached the driveway of her sister's condominium in Charlotte. She'd been driving fast.

He got the letter three days after Frances had called. It was written with a felt tip pen. The ink was black and heavy. Smudges made it hard to read.

Dear Cooper:

Thank you for making me feel, at times, anyway, like most women only dream of feeling. You've always called it chemistry. I think you're right.

I remember once in senior chemistry lab, our teacher spent a whole week talking up an experiment she was going to perform. She would add one very powerful substance to another (the technical details escape me) and the union would result in one of the biggest explosions we'd ever heard.

I remember many of us, mostly the girls, had our hands near our ears, ready to cover them the second the chemicals united. But if we had, we never would have known there was a noise.

Funny. After all that planning and talk and anticipation, after all the promise in the air, all that came of the whole experiment was one tiny little poof, like a baby trying to blow on a dandelion. Of course, we laughed our heads off. Looking back now, I guess that was the best lesson I learned about chemistry.

Love, Hannah

P.S. Until it happened, I had no idea.

◆

Cooper wondered if she'd seen the irony in walking out without notice because of his unwillingness to confront things. It wasn't his lack of passion, she'd often said. She didn't care a plug nickel for the paramours in romance novels who wore fervor over their shoulders like a favorite jacket. She'd been brought up to appreciate the mystery of reserve. She loved his easy humor, his ability to identify with everyone he met. He'd once reminded her of this during a fight.

"Did I say *identify*? You're the biggest sucker for someone else's suffering I've ever known."

She called him Reverend Barnet. "The Rev. Mr. Barnet," newspaper-style. Pastor of the Covenant of Holy Redemption for Odds & Ends. Healer of all he surveyed. He would come home late, reporting on the latest tribulation.

Carlos, a party rent-a-clown who stilt-walked while bouncing a volleyball on his head, was caught smuggling doses of blackberry wine to rest home patients. Louie, the paraplegic Korean War vet who sculpted red, white, and blue pipe cleaners, lost what feeling he had left in his right hand just before the Christmas craft show. Short Stroke Driggers, the emphysematic Putt-Putt champion with a photo gallery of strippers from around the world, had uncovered another injustice at the Leticia Florence high rise for the elderly.

In the Covenant of Holy Redemption, solutions didn't matter. The Odds were a world unto themselves, a world revolving around Cooper, a needy, greedy world without Ends. They called him before breakfast, during work, after dinner, in the middle of the night. They told him stories he'd heard before. They wanted advice he'd already given. They had something to show him he didn't want to see. They needed favors he already had provided. They brought him presents he couldn't use. And he loved them all.

"Who initiates these personal affiliations?" she would ask him.

"They do, of course," he would say.

"Cooper is like a member of the family," they would tell her.

"The feeling is mutual," she would reply.

It was true. He was sorry he couldn't make it home for supper. Maxine's goat escaped. Hubert's basement was flooded.

"I didn't mean to be late, but you remember Mrs. Dean?"

"That smelly old woman who carries crocheted potholders around in a wheelbarrow?"

"I hadn't heard from her in quite a while . . . you may recall she had a delinquent son . . . stopped by her house to check . . . her grandson was playing in a checkers tournament . . . needed a ride . . . there weren't many spectators so I. . . ."

"What's wrong with your wife?" she asked. "Am I too well balanced to lure your interest?"

"You're supposed to be a columnist, not a social worker," she reminded him after another phone call at dawn.

"These are strangers," she told him. "You have problems of your own."

"I don't have any problems," he said.

"You have more than they do."

"Name one."

"I'll name two. You can't make a decision about anything that matters. And if you keep running away from your marriage, you're going to end up without a wife."

She sprayed herself with whipping cream. She grew as frozen as the Arctic tundra. She tried adapting a kooky persona. She locked him in the basement. She cold-cocked him with a plate of spaghetti. She cried until she threw up. He held her head.

"But you're perfect," he would say. "As far as I'm concerned, nothing's wrong."

"Then when can we start having children?"

After her letter arrived, he called Frances. Hannah came to the phone.

"I love you," he said. "I'm sorry I haven't made you happy."

"If you'd loved me enough, you would've figured out how to start."

They gave it two months. He called again before the first was up.

"I miss you. Come on home."

"Let's wait a while longer," she said, and that was it.

.

Hannah stirred fake cream in her coffee but didn't drink. She raked a banana from the pie, then stuck it back into the custard. She had no effort to waste. She suddenly sat forward and took the notebook paper from Cooper's hand, as though she just remembered he was there. She gazed hard at the large, sloppy print, and slowly shook her head.

"Quite a little author, isn't she," she said. "Must take after you."

Cooper took a sip of coffee, coughed, and tried not to spit it out.

"Funny, you just kind of appeared in her world one day. She was getting older, paying more attention to the characters in her story books, the children who lived with their mothers and fathers, you know, taking it more to heart than we ever dreamed, I suppose." Hannah ran a hand through her hair, breathed a deep sigh. "I'd always told her you were far away. That our jobs required us to live in separate places. I said I misplaced your address and didn't know how to find you. She seemed satisfied, for eleven and a half years."

Then came Christmas morning. They'd celebrated with Hannah's family. Scotty had wanted a salon hair dryer, the kind Ethel was sitting under in an *I Love Lucy* rerun. Hannah found one.

"Where on earth did you get that professional beauty parlor dryer?" Frances asked her niece.

"My daddy gave me this very nice professional hair dryer," Scotty answered. "And he said I could come over to his house as soon as he's finished with his work and he would play with me and Noodle as long as we want. And this will make you very happy, Aunt Frances—he said you could come over to see him, too."

Next came the call from Mrs. Wiley at school. Scotty was acting out. Making up tall tales. Interrupting the reading period, her favorite part of the day.

"But she's always been the same," Hannah had said. "Ever since first grade. She tries so hard to please."

"She's still an angel by comparison," said Mrs. Wiley. "She's just not Scotty. Is everything okay at home?"

"Yes."

"The reason I asked, she can't stop talking about her father. He's become very important in her life. Which if you don't mind my saying is surprising, since until recently she didn't speak of him at all. There may be a connection, you know. Sometimes a change like this, especially at Scotty's age, can be unsettling. I think it would be helpful if Mr. Smith came in for a conference."

Scotty was playing at home, trying to put Noodle on one of the teeter-totter seats. Hannah called her in. She brought art supplies to the kitchen table. With a Magic Marker, she wrote a first and last name, and the name of a city. Then she drew a picture of a man, using crayons to color black hair and blue eyes. She described his job and wrote down "Odds & Ends." She said he liked people and animals and told very funny stories, and that he was nice to everyone he saw.

"Scotty," she said. "Meet your father."

Two weeks later Hannah and Scotty were watching a rerun of *The Brady Bunch*. Miss Mac, the housekeeper who had been with them since Scotty was a baby, was frying chicken. A promotion came on for the evening news. Scotty ran to the screen to touch Priscilla Roberts, her favorite anchor, as she announced the murder of a Rock Hill man in the Park Circle Mall.

"An asbestos scare has closed the county's largest school," Roberts continued. "Also, from our sister station in Columbia, we find award-winning Odds & Ends columnist Cooper Barnet at odds with neighborhood renewal, and the historical society at the end of its rope. Details at six."

The segment ran at the end of the newscast. There on the television screen was a panoramic scene of the street Hannah had fled, the newspaper she had hated, the desk that had held him captive while she ate dinner alone. And now a gray-haired reporter was easing up the steps in front of their house, Cooper's house—God, it looked horrendous—picking his way across a decaying porch, tapping on the door. A burly brown dog in a red bandana appeared at the window, barking and pawing at the screen. The reporter hurried down the steps.

"Apparently Rascal is the only occupant at home," he said. "This is Dan McDonald signing off from Shandon Oaks, where spring cleaning is a *fait accompli* except in the Rutledge-Rucker house . . ." gesturing back toward the tree . . . "and where Christmas has no specific season in the world of Cooper Barnet."

Hannah turned to Scotty, who hadn't budged from the front of the screen. "That disaster area there," she whispered, "is where your father lives."

Scotty ran to her room to get her paper and crayons. She drew a crooked red house as narrow as a chimney, a brown dog that looked like a bear, and a bright green tree. Then she added a lavender mailbox with a red flag and a wavy black pole. "DEER DADD. . . ." The printing started in the middle of the mailbox, but the letters were too big to fit. They crawled on down the pole until they trickled off the bottom of the page.

•

Frances came to the door of the Toddle House and stood. It was late. Cooper saw her and shook his head. She went back to the car.

He shoved the coffee closer to Hannah. She lifted the cup with two hands and took a sip.

"I can't do any more," she said. "I'm a mess. I better go."

"Try to stay a few more minutes," Cooper said. He no longer wanted answers. Not tonight. All he wanted was damage control. "Come over here and sit by me."

It was tight. Two tall bodies in a seat for one. All legs and arms and bones. Cooper was jammed against the wall. He felt between them on the seat. The printer paper he'd brought in had fallen on the floor. He leaned down and scooped it up.

Printout number . . . what difference did it make? He'd produced enough copy to pave the highway from here to Camden fifty miles away, a paper trail of trivia. At least until tonight. Until this jumble of words and sentences and paragraphs. The most important words he'd written had been created not in the thrill of conviction but in bewilderment and anger and shame. He'd done the reporting and writing in two hours, miraculous considering his state of mind. Driven by desperation, he'd managed to function in a daze. Now he was depleted, too drained for regrets or second thoughts, too empty to care about consequences. Even if changing his mind had been an option, deadline had passed. The column would be in the composing room, ready to go. Probably already gone.

He gave the printout to Hannah; put an arm around her shoulders, holding her too tight.

"What's this?"

"Tomorrow's column. I want you to read it."

Hannah stretched across the table and dug into her Piedmont satchel. "I don't see my glasses. I'm not sure I could read anyway. Please. You do it."

Cooper took the printout. Hannah's hand was shaking. Her nails, always polished and rounded in perfect peaks, were ragged. The pink polish was chipped. Until tonight, Cooper hadn't had any coffee since he tried it thirty years ago. Now, he downed his second swallow in less than thirty minutes. It didn't taste any better. The words on the paper were blurred. He straightened his arm until the letters took form, and then he began.

ODDS & ENDS
By Cooper Barnet

It seems I have a daughter.

Police believe she's wandering lost somewhere in Columbia. She's 11, almost 12. I can't tell you when her birthday is because I forgot to ask. If you see her, you might think she's much younger. She's small for her age.

She lives in North Carolina, in Charlotte. She hasn't been away from home without her mother before except to horse riding camp in the mountains near Brevard. She goes for a week in summer and talks about it the rest of the year.

She's trusting—too innocent to get along by herself in the world—and there are people who might prey on her and do her harm. If someone tried to hurt her, she'd have trouble defending herself, since she weighs only 63 pounds.

Her light brown hair is cut short and topped with soft bangs. She has

pale blue eyes and a fair complex-
ion. She's four feet four inches
tall.

I must rely on others for this
description. I have never seen my
daughter. If I knew her, I could
contribute some definitive detail,
perhaps in the curve of her brow
or in the skip of her step, perhaps in the tilt of her head as she
speaks or in the splendor of her
smile, which I've been told is the
most magnificent ray of sunshine
God ever created.

She left home Tuesday morning with
a mission. She wanted to visit her
father. As best we can piece it
out, the story goes like this:

She went to school on Monday. Mrs.
Wiley, her regular teacher, was
out sick. The substitute teacher
read a story about a little boy
from the city who rode a Greyhound
bus to visit his country grandmother. She told the class they'd
see the real bus station when they
went on a field trip the next day.

On Tuesday, after they'd eaten
lunch at school, a minibus took
them to the downtown mall. They saw
the art and science exhibits, and
ate snacks. They went to a cooking
demonstration and watched a pup-

pet show. The substitute teacher and two room mothers had the responsibility of overseeing 33 students who require special attention in school and especially away from it. As planned, they left at 4 o'clock to return to the school parking lot, where their parents were waiting for them. One student was missing.

No one in the group had seen her cross the street, and once she entered the terminal she was just another stranger. You know how it is in a bus station. People too busy watching or ignoring their own children, or listening to the stories on radios that play TV, or feeding the vending machines with some extra change. Buying themselves a little diversion from whatever troubles put the slump in their shoulders, waiting on the voice from the microphone to tell them when to catch the ride that might deliver them to a better place. She was just a sweet little child, wandering around for an hour or maybe two. The bus left at 5:05 p.m. It was on time.

It seems an elderly lady helped her buy the ticket. A stout, pleasant woman with white hair and glasses that may have been blue or gray. No one knew her and police are

trying to find her. A few people
remembered them talking. They remembered a little girl sitting on
the dirty floor, emptying a yellow
book bag, scattering papers all
around. Chasing after an eraser;
a ballerina, pink. They remembered
her pulling out a stack of new
dollar bills and the lady helping
her count them.

The lady took her up to the ticket
window and told the man behind it,
a Mr. Joseph Murray, that the child
was going to Columbia to visit her
father. Mr. Murray assumed the
woman was a relative. He suggested
that she let the driver know where
she was supposed to get off, and
the driver says the woman did.

Her mother believes she paid the
fare with birthday money from the
housekeeper, whose name is Miss
Mac. Miss Mac always gives her a
new dollar bill for each year of
her age. She kept the money in a
huge piggy bank on a table beside
her bed. She bought it with the
allowance she'd earned picking up
pine cones, and named it "Noodle"
after her pet poodle. The bank is
smashed and Noodle is waiting by
the door.

Police have learned other things.
They know that on the bus she was

sitting next to a man with perox-
ided hair, wearing a lime green
shirt. They know that he behaved
improperly and a woman intervened.
Caucasian, possibly a member of
a religious sect. She was wearing a white turban and a flowing
dress. The driver watched them get
off the bus together at the proper
stop. No one has seen either of
them since.

Now I must relate some personal
information.

For nearly 20 years, I've made a
living exposing facts about your
lives. Many of them you sacrificed
from your souls. Sometimes I'd
write about a silly adventure in
my own life—the night I tried to
stiff a pay toilet and got locked
inside; the time my dog Reba ate
my underwear for supper—and by doing so, I convinced myself that I
asked no more of you than I was
willing to do myself.

But this was a deception, for the
information I revealed cost no more
than the effort to pound it out on
a keyboard. Today I'm forced to
go deep, to pay a price, trusting
that you will follow this column
to its end and want to help.

Close to 13 years ago my wife left
me. I expect she had every right

to do so. Shortly afterward, she found out she was pregnant with my child. She assumed I wouldn't take it well; a supposition based on almost eight years of observation, and chose to keep the news to herself. I don't know how I would've reacted. I wish she'd given me the chance.

Maybe some day I'll know the whole story. Today I know only that this child wanted to meet her father. If she hadn't, I probably would have never known about her, and if she isn't found, the trip she made will be in vain.

The last time anyone saw her, she was wearing a white sundress sprinkled with flowers. Daisies and tulips in yellow, blue, and red. She had on red sandals fastened with Velcro on the side. She was carrying a yellow book bag.

She takes pills for her heart. The medicine is overdue.

I forgot to tell you the most important thing. Her name. It's Scott Norris Smith. Everyone calls her Scotty.

Scotty may be hungry and need to eat. She may be sick and need a doctor. If you see her, please take good care of her and call the police.

And please give her a message for me. Tell her that her daddy is looking for her, and tell her that belatedly, he sends his love.

#

9

Cooper worked his finger through a hole in the mesh to unlatch the screen. He could see Percy asleep on the couch, wearing her pink shortie pajamas with red hearts on the collar, using a plastic grocery bag filled with scraps of fabric for a pillow. When he kicked at the warped door, she stretched and rubbed her eyes. "What time is it?"

"Almost three o'clock."

She yawned, still recovering from a distorted dream about Cooper riding a white giraffe through the lobby of the Wade Hampton Hotel, tossing out boxes of Thin Mint Girl Scout cookies.

"Oh. Wow. You won't believe what I was just. . . ." She sprang up, suddenly awakened to the current crisis. "Have you eaten? How about a glass of ginger ale, or some tea?"

He shook his head and flopped down beside her. "What's that?" he asked, nodding toward the coffee table. A piece of cardboard, about three inches wide, had been painted red and joined together to form a circle, like a crown.

"My pattern. My nine through twelves are wearing headbands.

You know, like the Roarin' Twenties."

"You mean Bloody Mary and her Bali Hai Flappers?"

Percy reached over his knee for a tube of Elmer's glue, and squirted loops over the surface of the cardboard. "If I can get the rest of these finished in time." She plastered on a handful of red sequins before setting the crown back on the table. "See?" she said. "But this is just the first coat. It takes at least three to show up from a distance."

She looked up at Cooper, put a hand on his arm. "Small potatoes, huh?" she said.

It had been after midnight when he had called from the hospital, speaking softly; telling her things had taken a bad turn; that they were stabilizing Hannah; that she'd have to be admitted to the cardiac ward.

"How is she?" Percy asked him.

Cooper deflated like a ruptured tire. "I don't know. She was a zombie when I left."

"I'm sorry. What about you? How are you feeling?"

The classic question in the reporter's guide to a helluva story. How are you feeling? About the murder of your husband by the milkman. About the twenty-four-hour deadline for your baby to find a kidney. About the head-snapping tackle that turned you into a quadriplegic when the coach brought you in off the bench in the last thirty seconds of your senior-high football game so you could tell everyone you played. Do you mind describing it in more detail? I'm talking about exactly, precisely. Okay, that's awful. But how do you really feel?

Columnist's Reaction Unclear

COLUMBIA—When asked today how he felt upon learning he was a deadbeat dad for a runaway kid he didn't know

he had, local columnist Cooper Bar-
net said he couldn't precisely say.
When pressed, he added that the
whole thing was too bad and it would
probably make him sad if he hadn't
been going mad.

•

Life can turn fluky in a heartbeat, Cooper knew. The Theater of the Absurd paid his bills. Stories about people like Harry and Barry Bradley, twins abandoned at eight months old in a truck stop in Rapid City, South Dakota, with nametags stuck to the front of their matching blue diaper shirts. They were taken in by a local Sioux chief, renamed Enapay (brave) and Matoskah (white fighter), and in their late teens began looking for their parents by traveling the country, earning money by jumping teepees at state fairs in identical motorcycles studded with feathers.

But stories this wild didn't exist beyond the chronicles of his most outrageous subjects. Bizarre things like this didn't happen to semi-respectable, dues-paying citizens, not even those on the historical society's Most Wanted list. He'd rethreaded the reel and run it through the projector again and again. Each time, the cellophane shredded as it spun out. Wife leaves. House suffers. News airs. Child watches. Child escapes. Child disappears. Wife, make that ex-wife, returns and collapses in downtown greasy spoon. All in a thirteen-year timeline. Maybe that was the culprit. The thirteen.

"Cooper?"

"All right, I'll tell you. I feel like I'm about to vomit. There's this piece of me I didn't know I made, lost in a world of reprobates. She's not exactly right in ways I can't conceive of, and she's helpless, and she's been through no telling how much, and I'm afraid now she's being tortured or worse, and I'm as powerless as she is to do anything about it.

"The news that I'm a father is dropped on me like the A-Bomb on Nagasaki, and I'm expected to believe I haven't lost my mind and that you're not supposed to be packing me in the car right now and driving me down to the admitting office on Bull Street, where I'll spend the rest of my days stoned on Haldol, trying to count the hairs underneath my armpits. I don't have any feeling. For Scotty, I mean, apart from the fear and dread. For any of it. I have a child and I can't summon up any feelings beyond the urge to puke."

"Hold your horses, bud. You can't expect to start feeling fatherly overnight when you've never laid eyes on your child. You're not the guilty party here."

"There was a photograph. I couldn't make myself look at it. I couldn't even look at her picture."

"That has nothing to do with the issue. You need a shrink, except I doubt even a shrink could help. Your brain's a sieve for every particle of misplaced guilt floating around the universe. I know it's hard, sweetie, of course it's hard, but you have to stay within the realms of reason."

Cooper laid his head against the back of the sofa. The faded slipcover had dried out, but proof of his afternoon flight to Percy's den was still there, a life-sized water stain.

"Hannah's a sane, responsible woman," he said. "How could she do what she did? How did she live with it?"

"Maybe responsible isn't the best word," Percy suggested. "Maybe sane isn't, either."

"You think she saw something I wasn't aware of? Some kind of latent abusive tendencies in me, or. . . ."

"Quit spinning wheels, Cooper. You're the one who paid the vet to euthanize a dying bat, remember?"

"He wouldn't take any money. Let's change the subject, okay? I can't talk about it anymore."

"You're right. It's going on four o'clock, and the woman with the answers is in no shape for true confessions. Come here."

Percy tried to pull Cooper to her, but he got up and walked into the studio, where the blue princess phone had been shoved underneath one of the pink beach chairs. Malachi answered on the second ring.

"Any news?" Cooper asked him.

"None we're hoping for. Officers came by on two occasions, that's about it. Where are you?"

"At Percy's."

"What about Hannah?"

"In Baptist. Not doing so hot. We had to take her to the emergency room."

"We?"

"Her sister's here."

Cooper blamed himself. He shouldn't have shown her the column. She'd listened with fingers dug into her temples as he read, crying softly, barely taking a breath. When he'd finished she sobbed, then wailed and started gagging. She couldn't stop. He'd sent T-Bone out to get Frances, who'd been sitting in the car with the air conditioner running. It was her husband's new Buick. He was home with the kids.

"Her blood pressure was off the charts," Cooper said.

"No wonder," said Percy, who'd come over to sit cross-legged on the carpet where he stood, craning her neck to see his eyes. "The poor woman's been going extra innings every day for almost twelve years."

Cooper was swaying back and forth like a spindly pine wobbling in a breeze. Percy motioned him to sit but he shook his head, so she made herself into an anchor, positioning her weight against the back of his legs. She'd read long ago that the smallest life forms were the hardiest. Look at her. Look at Mount Maxwell and Sophie. Look at Bob, the world's toughest ferret. She prayed the same would be true of Scotty. She liked the name Scotty. It had spunk.

"What did the doctor say?" Percy asked.

"Not much. But Frances let on that Hannah hasn't been a Blue Cross calendar girl these last few years. They'll monitor her vitals; keep her sedated to help her rest. Everything's really on hold until they can reach her doctor in Charlotte. The side effects of tranquilizers can be dangerous. One of Short Stroke's putt-putt buddies took some Xanax to calm his nerves before a playoff in Toledo and ended up in cardiac arrest on the final hole."

Percy groaned. "Probably took the whole bottle," she said, sending a glance toward the phone.

"Oh, hey," Cooper said. "You still there? Where are the dogs?"

"I turned them out," Malachi said.

"Outside?"

"Chill, sweetheart."

His words were tender, calming. Cooper missed the old Malachi. The Malachi who'd led him into manhood. The Malachi with the strong hand.

"They're lying at my feet. All except the one in charge. She's in my lap. Man—that girl's got some breath. You need to start putting Listerine in her water bowl."

"They need to eat."

"You need to eat."

"Oat bran's in the pantry. You can mix it with kibble and cottage cheese but first make sure it's not molded. Make Sophie's soft, with water. Lukewarm. Not too hot. You can substitute cabbage for Reba's Purina if you run out. There's half a head in the vegetable bin. He likes it sliced thin."

"This ain't the Toddle House, daddy. They ate pizza for dinner."

"They can't eat pizza," Cooper said. "Sophie gets diarrhea. That pizza's a week old."

"We upgraded. Look, we going nowhere here. You get some news, let me know. I'll do the same. We're camped by the front door in case God's kinder than I think. Had to drag out that nasty futon. Jesus help. Put it by the side of the road, garbage man's bound to charge you double."

"You'll have to carry Sophie to the bathroom. She can't see anything at night. Watch Reba, too. He'll raid the counters as soon as you turn your back."

Malachi put his finger on the button, then put the receiver in the cradle. Gently. He wanted it to sleep through the night. Cabbage? He had to get out of here.

"I had no business telling her about that column," Cooper said.

Percy didn't say anything. Just stood, took the phone, and led him off to bed.

•

On the back porch, Malachi opened the screen with the toe of his crutch. Reba bumped his round brown belly down the steps and wandered off into the dark toward the shed. Sophie scrambled out the door, came right back in, and walked over to sprinkle a stack of yellowed newspapers piled beside a green plastic chair.

Malachi couldn't do anything about it. He was still trying to coax Yum-Yum out. When he attempted to nudge him with the crutch, the dachshund ducked, circled wide, strutted over to the newspapers, and peed on Sophie's spot. Sophie came back and added a few more drops.

"Let it alone," Malachi said to Yum-Yum. He splashed the puddle with water from the dog bowl, then leaned out the door and emptied his own bladder on a holly bush next to the steps. Reba waited for him to finish, trumped it, and came inside.

Pecking order established, they called it a night.

10

The newsroom was eerie and still, like the Edisto River in a cloudy dawn. After flipping on some lights, Cooper headed to his desk. For once he had a plan. Check both machines. Send a note to Hitch. Be gone before everybody staggered in for coffee.

He switched on the word processor, rolling away from the monitor so he could see. Why couldn't he remember to buy reading glasses? His father had worn them long before this, in his mid-thirties. They were brown, and dangled from his neck on a shoestring necklace. Cooper's brother would beg to try them on. Then he'd hop around and make his Bugs Bunny face. That's what he called it. He didn't look anything like Bugs Bunny, just like a little kid acting stupid, good for a laugh.

They used to go fishing on the Edisto; Cooper and his brother jammed together on the front seat of the old cedar boat, sitting backwards to watch their father gnawing the guts of his Muriel, cutting the sputtering Mercury to an idle, and casting beneath the mossy limbs toward the base of stumps.

Cooper liked watching the lure get hung up in a cypress tree, the boat drifting towards it as his father worked the rod, gently, deftly, until the barbs released, zinging from the branches and plopping back in the water again. He liked the reassuring flow of the place and the easy wonder on his father's face as he took it in and nodded it towards his sons. He hated the conquest, though. When his father set the hook, Cooper would shut his eyes tight and clench the hard wooden bench, sending out brain waves to help the fish break free.

"C.B.: Something or other Hightower called about pet pig. Making her debut next week, coming out at Sterling's Barbecue. Sounds more up your sty than mine. God. Did I really say that? 799–4017. Myrtle."

"Hey, big boy, howz it hangin? composing room party, my pad tomorrow nite. Do not advertise. Editors and scribes uninvited. except for you and Sam. bring your own. Bottle too. ha-ha. Burgers and dogs. Rex."

Cooper scrolled from his past to his present, eager to finish and move on to the phone calls, the likely source of clues from readers who got up to meet the paper when he was just going to bed.

". . .trying to run you down. Sam."

"What can I do? Ruth Ann."

Myrtle again: "We're signing up folks to help search. Organizing right after deadline. Jazz coordinating with PD. P.S. I can just feel you blaming yourself. Don't. All my love. M."

"Bummer, man, but helluva column. Ernie."

Helluva column? Cooper blinked and rubbed his palms on his khakis, the same pair from yesterday, except now they were trimmed in white from the powdered sugar donuts he'd eaten during the drive to the paper. Percy's idea of breakfast. Krispy Kreme could use the residue on the roof of his mouth to coat the next batch riding the conveyer belt and have enough left to paint the holes.

"See me. H. H."

He could picture Hitch huddled with Ernie on the composing room floor, reading the column one last time, then hurrying back to the newsroom. First to call Jo at the switchboard, then to call a meeting. Ernie presiding, Hitch standing in the back, cigar snuffed out and stuffed in his shirt pocket, assessing damage. They'd still have to put out a paper.

How would Ernie begin? He would play it in a low key, pulling on his beard, measuring words like he did the ingredients for his famous granita margaritas. They would be stunned, perplexed, alarmed, and for a second, giddy—the rush of a Geraldo moment. After all, they worked for a newspaper, ruined their health putting one out, and suddenly the biggest story many of them had ever seen, with all the elements they could wish for, had been dropped directly onto their collective keyboards.

Cooper cut on the answering machine and checked the clock. Jazz would be in soon. The tape was sluggish, overloaded with undeleted calls.

"Yo, Barnet? Driggers back at you. More trouble in the lobby this evening. That dirty scalawag I told you about has been feeling up Miss Helen again. Hell, the help wouldn't get off their fat you-know-whats if he stripped her down and glued on pasties and hooked her up to a whirlygig. She could croak and they'd wait for the next shift to cover her with a sheet. Thought you could stop by on your way home and straighten things out. If you could just talk to him, tell him not to take advantage of a woman when she's in that kind of a state. I'd take him on myself but the emphysema's really been kicking my butt. Did I tell you I found the putter I won off Bad Boy Ken in that double elimination down at Macon, Georgia? We ran dead even for seventeen. Then on eighteen, that pesky little uphill slanter. . . ."

Two hours sleep. No. Two hours watching Percy sleep while he pretended. Now the last exam was over, the black beauties were wearing off, he'd flunked every course, and it was time to confess to his parents.

"Lamb? This is Betty from the cleaners. What about your clothes?"

"Hello, dear. Just tried you at home. Is dinner still on? I'll bring everything but the salt. Don't buy any, even if it's on sale. We won't need it."

Margaret hadn't heard. When she did she'd send out for the National Guard. He'd forgotten she was coming to town. She had an appointment at Benedict College to review plans for her proposal to fund a housing unit for married students.

"Hey, man." It was Sam. "Remember that outfit of kooks around Holly Hill near Hellhole Swamp? Thing I looked into about two or three years ago? Some cockamamie Baha'i offshoots decked out in togas and turbans? They talked about setting up more branches around the state but I kind of doubt they ever did. You know how those nuts tend to run out of gas before they get half way around the block."

Cooper glanced at Ernie's desk, specifically the middle drawer where he kept the antacids. Fear and undigested donuts were giving him heartburn. He did remember something about an unusual religious flock wandering around the South Carolina Lowcountry. Sam had heard about them from an Army buddy named Phil, owner of a one-stop shop forty miles north of Charleston, in an area where local kids were born wearing camouflage and baseball caps.

"These dudes are dressed for the second coming," Phil said. "You need to ride on down and check it out."

But Sam decided to punt to the *News and Courier* in Charleston and never heard anything else about it.

What did Baha'is *do*? Cooper believed they were all right, decent and peace loving, but he was too anxious to recall the specifics of the faith. Besides, this was a fringe group. It could even be some type of cult. Cults were bad news. For all he knew, these people offered children as sacrifices, married them at twelve, and turned them into sex slaves. The little girl had one thing going for her, though. She looked younger than her age.

He'd done columns on so many different religious groups. Weren't Baha'is the ones who roamed airports, pulling pamphlets from their robes and waving tambourines, which they used as collection plates? No, he was thinking about the Hare Krishnas. They didn't wear turbans. Their heads were shaved.

And this lady Baha'i, riding the Greyhound by herself. Why wasn't she traveling with the others? Maybe she was a renegade. Or a member of some other splinter group. An Indian sect?

Once, Cooper had written about a Sikh. Surrender Singh, a visiting professor from Punjabi, ticketed for riding a motorcycle without a helmet. Singh wanted to obey the law but the helmet wouldn't fit over his turban. A female judge let him off. Judge Miles. She wore a big white wig but not a turban. Singh's wife hadn't worn a turban to court. Females from India didn't wear turbans. Some of them wore burqas, not the same.

Sam might be onto something. If women weren't required to wear turbans for religious purposes, yet turbans were part of the dress code for the group in Hellhole Swamp, the kidnapper could have been headed there. But why had she gotten off the bus in Columbia? Didn't they have a Greyhound to Holly Hill?

Cooper had a flash of Percy in a turban, then remembered it had been a towel. She'd just finished showering and he hadn't been looking at her head. He'd seen another woman in a turban similar to Percy's. Someone he knew. Was it his mother, after she'd come in from a swim at Folly Beach?

He should rein himself in. Preposterous leads rarely led to reliable stories. But his heart was pumping possibility and calling it fact. The deadline had passed when a shiny red sandal had reached for the first dirty step of a Greyhound bus and climbed aboard. The sandal was held together on the side by Velcro straps fastened by her mother before she'd taken her to school. Fastened tightly, so they wouldn't come undone and trip her. She was accident prone, Hannah said. The step was high for short legs. The driver asked her if she wanted help. She said she could do it on her own.

Cooper shut his eyes. It was coming back to him now. The Baha'is were definitely peaceable. They had this thing about smiling. They did it a lot. Something about being mellowed out down the road to Nirvana. But this was a band of disconnected extremes that had come from out of nowhere, probably hiding behind the name of a good religion to do whatever they pleased. They probably liquefied weed and substituted it for water in the Kool Aid. His imagination was raging, picturing a child stoned and yoked to a mule, ordered to plow the marijuana fields while the tribunals decided who would break her in. Turn it off, he told himself. He hurried to the bathroom, stuck his head under the cold water faucet, and jogged back to his desk.

It was almost seven. He messaged Sam, asking him to check the clips for area Baha'i activity and pass anything worthwhile to the police. Then he returned to the answering machine.

After clearing her throat, Maxine called his name, and began a diatribe on historical societies. "The founding fathers would be rolling in their graves," she said. "You need to come on out our way. Put you up a little double-wide behind the house here until you figure out what to do. You could build something simple on a slab, something brick with a hip roof, so's it won't leak."

Maxine hadn't seen this morning's column. But there were plenty of early birds in the world. People going to work on the seven-to-three shifts. People coming home after working nine to five or ten to six. Retired people who didn't have to get up, so they did. Close friends like Duke, offering to send food to the house. Friends of friends. Friends of friends of strangers. Characters from this or that episode in Cooper's life—or event or accomplishment or tragedy or triumph or screw-up. People he remembered he'd forgotten and people he'd forgotten and couldn't remember.

Some were stingy. They gave first names without the last or no names at all. One Midwestern voice brought up the face that went with it. The mother of Izzy, the four-year-old Perle Mesta who hosted a private tea party with turtle bowl water. After spending two months dying, she decided she didn't like it. "She's eleven now and the picture of health," Izzy's mother said. "You told me not to give up on my daughter. I'm giving you the same advice."

His daughter. They all referred to her that way. Some of the callers had seen her. Cleaning the windshield of a yellow Beetle at the Amoco on Two Notch Road. Playing bongos in a skit at the Lutheran Church of the Redeemer. Riding a bicycle near the railroad trestle in Maxcy Gregg Park, pulling along a fuzzy brown dog on a leash that looked like the poodle named Noodle. Wolfing down a strawberry waffle at the Original House of Pancakes. She was a brunette, about ninety pounds.

A man identified himself as Edward Swinson, a communications specialist at the police department. He wanted to put a tap on the phones. "Taps can work if they demand a ransom."

Cooper sent a message to Hitch, asking him to tell Edward Swinson about Malachi, to assure him that he would handle things responsibly, that he was okay. Cooper needed him there, with the dogs. He needed him there when the news came in.

Another stranger on the machine. This one identified herself as Mrs. Eula Mae Evans, a retired third-grade teacher. When she picked up her granddaughter from the bus station, she saw a little girl in a flowered sundress following a woman from the terminal. They went out the Sumter Street door, both talking away, neither listening. The woman was wearing a white turban and a flowing white dress.

"We always called them muumuus," Mrs. Evans said.

The dress was sleeveless. The woman's arms were large. "Of an ample size" was the way Mrs. Evans put it. She dictated her number and slowly repeated it, then promised she would call downtown. She was referring to the police department.

Cooper's hand shook. He transposed the last two digits. Come on, now, slow down. An eye on the piece of paper, an eye on the dial, a muzzle over his heart because the phone was ringing and the racket was blocking his ear. She answered.

"Of course I'm home," Eula Mae Evans said. "Where else would I be this time of morning? A nice young policeman is here, a sergeant, drinking a cup of coffee with me in the kitchen, and I was about to tell him something about the car.

"Just a minute. Yes? All right. He said to go ahead and tell both of you together since you're the father. Well, what I was about to say was that I saw them get into a black vehicle parked beside the old Sears building, you know, in the side lot they reserved for customers before they moved out to the mall? My granddaughter and I were standing on the sidewalk across the street, waiting for a cab."

Eula Mae Evans said the car looked like the Cadillac her husband had owned before he passed. "I can't be certain, because we had to wait for the suitcases and make a necessary stop, and by then it had grown fairly dark.

"The model? Gracious me. I have no idea. I've never been a car person, and it's been twenty years since George was alive.

"He sure was proud of that car. Washed it on Saturdays after breakfast, and took the kids and me for a spin practically every Sunday after church. It surely did shine."

11

Cooper stopped by the sink to wash his hands. The patient's sink. The long-deposed ex, assuming the liberties of someone who belonged. But he'd climbed five flights after ducking in a side door to the radiology department, and was worried about stairwell germs. The patient was resting; her eyes closed, her arms folded across her chest, a tube taped under her wrist to keep the butterfly needle in place.

He tiptoed over to stand beside the bed. She continued to take quiet, even breaths—this long, thin woman in a hospital issue night-shirt; this solemn, drawn person; her knees angled skyward and joined together, as if they were raised in prayer. Her gown exposed parts she wouldn't want him to remember. He looked away.

He'd seen her for the first time at the State Fair. She was riding the silver Bullet, glowing in the gaudy reflection of the colored lights. A daredevil, spinning high, spinning fast, her auburn hair flying, her green eyes thrilled with life. He'd known then, waiting at the exit to stammer an introduction. They'd dated three months and married, shared the same bed for almost eight years. How had she become a stranger? Why did he feel like he shouldn't be here, that he'd wandered into the wrong room?

"Hannah?"

He leaned over to adjust the railing, lifting it slowly; careful, quiet. It wouldn't go any higher. He touched her shoulder, pulled back. He was as bad as the scalawag in Short Stroke Driggers' nursing home, preying on the comatose.

She reached an arm between the bars.

"Hannah? It's me. Cooper. Can you hear me?"

Slowly, she moved her head. Could she understand him or was it just a reflex, an involuntary response to her name?

"I came by to . . . I have a little bit of news."

Take it easy. Don't scare her.

"I went to the paper this morning . . . to check the messages. A lot of people called, but they didn't . . . I mean, they felt bad and wanted to help, but there was nothing to . . . until . . . there was one . . . don't get your hopes up too much, but there was one that sounded like it could be promising."

She was grasping for something. He took a chance and grabbed her hand. "I called her, the woman who left the message. An officer was there. A sergeant, she said he was."

Her mouth was open. Someone had coated her lips with Vaseline, but the grease had moved inward, leaving a shelf of crust in its place. A used Q-Tip was stuck in foil on the bedside table. He picked it up and swabbed her lips. The Q-Tip was big and greasy. Now Hannah's lips were greasy. She licked at the grease.

Hannah had nice full lips. He watched them struggle to perform. They were beautiful, even cracked and caked with gunk. It was hard, watching her fight to produce a sound. He put an ear close to her chin. He might be making a mistake, talking to her without consulting a doctor.

"A Mrs. Evans," he said. He backed off and belched the taste of donuts. "Eula Mae Evans, a retired schoolteacher. She was there picking up her granddaughter, I think from a different bus. She saw a little girl with a woman in a turban, a woman with ample arms. They left together. The little girl was wearing a flowered dress. She seemed to be all right. They went off in an old Cadillac. The lady, Mrs. Evans, said it was black."

He tried to reconstruct the message, but all he could get was the morning before. He'd been in the canteen jousting with Sam, and then Jazz had crammed the phone into his ear, and then there had been Hannah. Hannah, adrift for five or six lifetimes, telling him he had a daughter, a daughter who wasn't an ordinary child.

"It isn't her physical appearance. Well, except for being small for her age. She's darling, actually. But she's like . . . do you remember the child in your class who didn't fit in, the one all the others teased? She's. . . ."

"Don't tell me," he'd pleaded. "Don't tell me anything else. I can't process it. I don't want to. I need time."

He still didn't want to process it. He still needed time. Maybe the police would get lucky. Eula Mae Evans had seen them leave. Maybe she would be all right and Hannah could take her home. He would write her letters, send toys and money, maybe phone her on Sunday afternoons.

But he wouldn't see her. That's the way Hannah had planned it, so he wouldn't be involved. Hannah had determined the child would be better off. Suddenly, he was angry again. She didn't know what he would want. She hadn't asked. So why had she kept her from him, then? She had no reason to.

With his free hand he reached for the pitcher, shook some ice into a tiny white cup. The ice overflowed and slid across the bedside table. He grabbed a handful and shoved it into his mouth. The ice cooled his anger. Now he was scared. What if Hannah died? Her hand was cold. Where were the blankets? He removed his fingers and fastened hers on the railing. The IV tube was twisted. He tried to uncoil it but it curled again as soon as he let go.

"She has to be close by," he said. "The woman in the turban had a ticket to Columbia. Columbia was her destination. She got off the bus here. Her car was parked right across the street. How many women in Columbia go downtown wearing turbans? There can't be that many, with ample arms."

And a white, flowing robe. He left that out.

"Go get her." The words were faint, trapped inside the drugs, but he heard them. Go get her, she'd said. But how did she expect him to do that when he had no idea where she was?

He dragged the recliner beside the bed and sat in it. What did she look like, this child who wasn't like the others, this child who didn't fit? All he knew were normal children:

Sam's hardy ten-year-old daughter, Sarah, already competing in freestyle and backstroke in the junior-high league. Duke's six-year-old charmer Marie, a paradox of mischief and brains, playing tricks on Tiny Tuttle and reading the Book-of-the-Month Club biography of Lincoln while her parents closed up at night. Myrtle Bailey's Stacey, eleven years old and still her baby. A real head-turner, all arms and legs. Saturday before last, Stacey had stopped by the paper with her mother. She told Cooper she intended to find a cure for cancer and be a supermodel on the side.

But Sandra Sawyer didn't have a normal child. She had an autistic son. He'd asked her out to dinner after Hannah left him. He was passing the personnel department and the door was open. She looked good and he was lonely. Jimmy went along. He was five years old. They went to the aquarium. Jimmy recited statistics on the fish, matter-of-factly, as if he were checking them off a list. Cooper had promised him they'd go again.

He got up and walked to the closet. How had Hannah gotten so thin? He found a pink blanket and tucked it over her white legs. Then he leaned down and put his head next to hers on the pillow.

"I'm so sorry," he whispered.

She couldn't hear him. She was asleep.

12

Brakes yelped, tires thudded, and metal grated the curb. The dogs charged the window. "Got to go," Malachi said to Liebman. "Something's happening out here." He slammed down the phone and did his best to hurry to the door, praying it was the youngster and finding an old lady instead.

She was dressed for tea in a blue paisley shirtwaist, long sleeves open at the cuffs. She climbed out of a gleaming black Lincoln Continental. Its convertible top and the hair piled on her head were both a sparkling white.

Malachi waited with the dogs as she crossed the treacherous terrain without a cane. What did they say she was? Eighty-five? A hundred and ten? Probably infused with Krypton. Doesn't matter who cuts the cards, rich people run the table on genes.

And now here she was, erect beside the slumping branches of the Christmas tree, reacting as if she'd expected to see him, the Baron of Skid Row, reprobate-in-residence, a one-legged bleary-eyed rat wearing a frankfurter for a shirt, halitosis worse than a trestle bum's after a rotgut-guzzling marathon in The Bowl.

Margaret Motte Burns offered the introduction he didn't need. He didn't tell her that, or anything about himself. She was too busy making time.

"Is there any news?" Nothing about her large green eyes told her age except the creases in the skin around them.

"Not any to speak of. Cooper just called. He's heading for the Santee swamps."

"Forgive me," she said. "I'm hard of hearing on occasion."

"He got it in his head the child was kidnapped by some religious fanatics shacked up in a 4-H camp."

"Oh, dear."

"Odds are it's a wild goose chase."

"But there must be a reason he went down there."

"You mean besides shock and desperation? There is. He heard they wear turbans."

"Turbans? Oh, yes. The woman who left with the child. You don't believe there's a chance?"

Malachi shook his head. "Nothing about it seems logical. Where was she coming from? Why would she catch the bus to Columbia and then take off to Holly Hill? Why would she kidnap a little girl?" The dogs were about to knock him down, helping him open the door.

"Please forgive me, Mr. Patterson. I've barged in without even asking if it's an inconvenience."

"Mercy. Here I am racking my brain for a way to explain myself and you already know who I am."

"Doesn't everyone?"

"That's a comforting thought."

"Old women entertain themselves by reading the newspaper, especially when there happens to be a connection to the featured subject," she said, "as you have been in one form or another for quite a number of years."

He didn't answer.

"You may be aware, Mr. Patterson, that I'm quite fond of your aunt, and of course we share a kinship with Mr. Barnet. But waste disturbs me, especially when it involves a remarkable gift. I'm afraid I was disinclined to seek an audience."

"A lady with a head on her shoulders."

She held up a finger. "Although I was about to say, now that our meeting has occurred, I seem to be changing my mind. Mr. Barnet and I were scheduled to dine this evening. Perhaps we'd better go out and salvage the meal."

Malachi followed her down the steps. The car was immaculate, as old as his grandmother's first set of teeth. He glanced toward the front bumper, but the chrome was so shiny with polish he couldn't tell in the sunlight if there were any dents from the curb. Burns was opening a door the size of Solomon's vault, pointing to a blue Igloo cooler. He slid it from the seat to the sidewalk. Damn thing was as heavy as a supermarket.

"Why don't we unload it here?" she said. "I'll manage the wine if you can carry the containers."

"Praise God for the genius who invented Tupperware," Malachi told Margaret on the third and final trip to the kitchen. "Has to be a 'she.' No man is that smart."

They sat at the red oak table. The fan blew around stray oat bran flakes and the air of stale dog as they made small talk while anxiously listening for the phone. Burns explained that she had been waiting to meet with the president of Benedict College when she heard, and rudely cancelled the appointment.

"I suspect I may have misread some traffic signals on the way over," she said.

"Freedom of interpretation," Malachi said. "A human right."

Sophie was clawing at Margaret's skirt, trying to jump in her lap. She reached down and helped her up, then awarded Reba a consolation prize by rubbing the back of his neck with her foot. Yum-Yum was going for the brown utility sandal.

"Our friend has a unique method of training animals," was all she said.

Margaret served the breakfast—pheasant pie and caviar mouse—and called it lunch. The telephone disrupted any conversational rhythm or focus on their forks. The fifty-foot cord was tangled too much to set the phone on the table, but by stretching, Malachi could reach it on the floor. Each time he answered, Margaret watched him intently until he looked at her and shook his head.

The police had come early. Different officers today, two from missing persons. They'd told him what he already knew, that Mr. Barnet wanted him to be there and monitor the calls. "We've been assured you will handle this in a sober and trustworthy fashion." He had to. No more liquor until Sam brought some by later on.

They installed a tracer on the phone, Yum-Yum shining the black patent leather shoe of the one who gave his name as Detective Moore. After explaining the setup, they informed Malachi he was to report any suspicious calls or potential leads to a direct line in the watch commander's office immediately, then sat around and killed an hour, giving him a chance to prove he wasn't up to the job.

"Imagine," he said to Margaret. "Sitting at a rickety kitchen table with the belle of the Broad Street ball, chasing a lemon tart with thousand-dollar wine. Best hallucination I ever had."

"I'm pleased you approve." She smiled. "The declaration on your shirt gave me reason for pause." They were both being polite. Neither of them had taken more than a few bites. "Although it's South of Broad, to be accurate," she said. "You performed there once for the Symphony Guild. The home of Louisa Gadsen, a dear friend. I was out of town."

"Didn't mean to slight the location. Just don't get around much anymore."

"Duke Ellington," Margaret said.

"With Sidney Russell." Malachi played it on occasion back then, his own version, with some extra steps. "It was the summer of 1972, I believe." Alien prodigy, recent graduate of Julliard School of Music, was making obligatory rounds before heading off to fine tune his talent at Yale. Hide the silver, Jenkins. Be gracious, but whatever you do, hide the silver. Didn't matter how civil they were, the pressure was unbearable.

Sometimes he used to think it would be better if he'd gotten his hands sliced off by a machete-wielding adolescent guerilla in a Mekong Delta cave.

"I had it once before, Château d'Yquem. Up North. Vintage 1951, believe it was. Didn't think I'd meet up with it again."

"You should treat yourself more often," Margaret said.

He nodded, toasting her with solemn eyes as he slowly brought a glass to his lips that was meant to hold juice for a child. He set the glass down without drinking from it.

"Donald Duck never had it so good," he said. His thumb stroked the outline of the cartoon stencil; the duck's yellow, slewed feet, his large orange bill, his tiny black gloves. "Especially in this house."

Margaret studied him, her head tilted slightly. The silk collar of her dress played with the side of her throat, in sync with the fan's warm breeze. Her faint smile wandered, distracted by the canned music from an ice cream truck, then suddenly tightened with resolve. "You're aware, Mr. Patterson, that you've disappointed a number of people."

Malachi stiffened. The silence lasted a few seconds. "I know of one or two," he finally said. Resentment burned through the quiet in his voice.

Margaret accepted the consequences, her own demeanor unchanged, determined to finish what she had started. "Every once in a while, Angeline would ask me to intervene," she said. "She has always been of the mistaken opinion that a bullheaded old bag is a formidable force, as long as she happens to be Caucasian, with a commanding bankroll in tow. The last time I declined her request was at least a decade ago. She hasn't asked since."

Malachi narrowed his eyes and set his jaw. "I believe I could have held my own."

"No doubt," Margaret said. "For what it's worth."

"For what it's worth," Malachi repeated. He sucked in a breath, calmed himself. At least Burns had resisted the trespass, realized the futility of it, the disrespect involved. "Thank you for understanding," he said, then wondered why he said it, and took a drink.

"I don't understand one damn thing," Margaret said. She glanced at the floor. The fan had snatched the napkin from her lap. She trapped it under the furrowed heel of her clunky sandal.

The music jangled louder as the ice cream truck came closer to the house. Reba and Max rushed to the front door to chase it away, but the driver stopped across the street to serve some customers, a toddler, and his young mother. Reba barked as Max howled, neither in tune to "Pop Goes the Weasel."

Margaret waited out the racket. "But now that we've been united by crisis, I reserve the right to be enlightened at a future date." She leaned down to pick up the napkin. "At present, though, I can't seem to concentrate on anything beyond the circumstance of our wayward friend, a concern we obviously share."

Margaret told Malachi she had overheard a secretary at Benedict College reading the column over the phone. "The young woman was kind enough to give me her copy. I was so distraught, I had to review it several times."

Malachi sipped some more wine, picturing this ancient Caucasian aristocrat with her fine head of white hair, huddled in a corner, oblivious to the stares, reading and rereading the revelations of a man she'd assumed she knew inside and out. And them, the sisters and brothers who belonged on the campus, assuming she had made a wrong turn and was waiting to be rescued, to be delivered to the university across town.

But he had always heard that race wasn't a factor in the philanthropy of Burns, and based on his aunt's experience, it might be true. One Saturday morning before breakfast, the woman had shown up at Angeline's house, uninvited and unannounced. She introduced herself, saying, "Miss Patterson, I would be honored if you would accept a gift from an interloper who deeply admires the Calhoun Street Academy." Wrote the check standing right there in the foyer. Fifty thousand dollars, no questions asked. That was way back in 1969, ten years before *60 Minutes* had done the story on Marva Collins in Chicago. Angeline's success was as inconceivable as the parting of the Red Sea, but the cats back then claimed it opened up, so why not believe it? As a rule, miracles like that didn't happen in Chicago, either. Not in the day. Rarely in this day, either.

Margaret stood and began to clear the table.

"Her poor mother," she said. "She must be distraught. Have you ever met her?"

"Yes, I have."

Malachi scraped the leftovers into a plate and leaned down to retrieve his crutch.

"That's my territory," Margaret said. "Your post is beside the phone."

She slid the Yquem towards him. Barely a third was gone. No matter the cost per swallow, sweet wine and anxious stomachs don't mix.

"She was taken to the hospital last night," Malachi said. He was speaking to the liquid, admiring the golden color. "I tried to check on her a while ago. Couldn't get beyond 'No visitors, no calls, butt out.'"

Margaret took the bottle from his hand and started to pour, but he covered the top of the glass.

"What about red?" she asked.

"Not now. My keepers might decide to pull a raid."

"Mr. Patterson?"

"Please. Call me Malachi."

"I thought you'd never ask." Margaret corked the Yquem and put it in the refrigerator. She was moving around the kitchen, feeding the dogs pheasant pie from her hand, rinsing their water bowl, filling it up, perspiring the way old people do, a wilted flower misted by dew. She was what Angeline would've been, Malachi thought, excepting the dry wit and the wine. "Perhaps you think me intrusive," she said, "but it's remarkable, the friendship you share. Quite an intriguing gift to come out of that tragic period of history."

"We suffered for it in our own ways, he and I. So did my aunt. His family did, too, although we kept it mostly to ourselves until we were down the road a piece. Makes us seem extraordinarily shallow, but you have to remember we were just kids then, in a time when whites and blacks hardly spoke that much, let alone had dialogs on racial injustice. We each had other issues we were dealing with. Musicians are a selfish lot. Have to be. I had a world view, and I was passionate about it, but life was between me and my piano."

"Be that as it may," Margaret said, pulling out her chair, "it's surprising there wasn't trouble."

"I suppose so. But other than some words and looks, people in the neighborhood pretty much left us alone. They considered the Academy sort of a safe house, like being on base. And remember, a white person coming to a black person's house was somewhat less incendiary than a black person going to a white's house, at least a black person who wasn't wearing a uniform and entering through the rear door. If the white man did the initiating, he wasn't number one on the hit parade but at least he was the one in charge. Angeline wasn't the only black woman in the South taking care of a white child."

Margaret sat again, absorbing the information. "Indeed. But the animosity and suspicion," she said. "A conflict could erupt with the slightest provocation, or even without, particularly when it came to those with superior educations. And the vile cowards who hid beneath the bed sheets. They couldn't abide the thought of an Angeline Patterson." She reached for the bottle of Lafite Rothschild, clasped it hard.

"Yes, but if you recall, compared to some of the other Southern states, we weren't headline-makers when it came to the most violent atrocities, for whatever reason. Hell, in 1963, Harvey Gantt managed to check into Clemson without an entourage of federal troops, and a year later, a handful of black students were living in the freshman dorms at USC. One of my friends from Charleston and her roommate were among them. They were terrified, but some of the white girls invited them to their rooms the first week."

Margaret looked skeptical, but Malachi went on.

"We lived in a unique pocket of town," he said. "The 'colored section,' as you mannered people called it back then, began at our end of the block. As far as the houses on Calhoun went, they looked about the same as the ones white people lived in less than a quarter mile or so away, down on the other side of the intersection. Weren't many of them like that, the nicer houses on our side. I'd say no more than ten or twelve, before they began decreasing in value and size.

"We were isolated, in a sense. White folks in the vicinity stayed on their side of the intersection and pretty much left us alone. We quietly went about our business and it certainly didn't involve them. By the time things got cranked up, Cooper wasn't coming around to be tutored anymore, but folks were fairly accustomed to seeing him when he stopped by. We talked a lot on the telephone. We knew better than to venture beyond the boundaries unless we took the necessary precautions. I guess you could equate it to having a love affair, the lengths we had to go to back then to downplay attention to ourselves."

Malachi used to wonder why he went to the trouble. He started to say so, but the phone rang. A neighbor, calling to offer help. He thanked her, said they were fine.

"We seem to enjoy a unique rapport ourselves, Mr. Barnet and I," Margaret offered. "He related to me once—if I recall, a bottle of wine also was involved—that you know more about him than anyone else, and that he intended to keep it that way, which makes me reluctant to intrude. But despite my best efforts, Malachi, I can't make out how my young friend has managed to find his life in such a sad state of affairs."

Malachi considered the precision of the words she'd just used. "Managed to find. . . ." Barnet in a nutshell.

Why shouldn't he tell her? Share the weight. He'd taken no formal oath, only made an agreement in passing, a young teenager mortified over his outburst, eager to move on to other things.

It wasn't the information. It was the right to release it. It belonged to a man who'd chosen all those years ago to hold it to himself, and without another word since, he'd trusted his friend to guard the gate. Depended on him to do it. Works all right, as long as the watchman's not a drunk. Even then, he'd let the chickens out of the barn only once, but look what happened. Couldn't be any worse, how things were now.

♦

It had been hot then, too, a morning in the first week of June, when Angeline had knocked on the bedroom door. Too hot for patience or understanding, but his aunt expected both, and she usually got what she wanted.

"There's a white boy downstairs with his mother," she said. "They've recently relocated from Charleston. I'd like you to come down and meet them."

"White boy? Here?"

"That's right."

"Sure, and I tore the wrong page off my calendar today. It's actually April first." But he knew his aunt wasn't joking. Not about something like this. "What's a white boy doing coming around where he has no business being?"

Every reason to be shocked—and angry. This was 1957, after all.

"His family moved to Columbia right after Christmas. They live over on Fifth. He's making failing grades and shouldn't be. His mother wants him to be tutored. The association would benefit you both."

"Benefit me? I don't want it to. I don't want to lay eyes on his ugly face. What planet these people drop down from, anyway? How come they want us to teach them when they say we so stupid? Why they want to be associated with our people when it's against the law? Everybody knows they hate us, and we hate them just as bad."

"Hatred is a product of the devil's workshop, Malachi. I've told you that time and again."

"But that boy has no place being here. Either this is some kind of setup or these folks are pure crazy. They need to be locked up on Bull Street. They better put that fool in solitary. Keep him there for life. Nobody else is gonna be around him."

"Shush. Voices carry."

"I don't care. He better get on down the road, find another sucker. Barge in on somebody of his own kind. And I mean right now, before I have to. . . ."

"Mind yourself, Malachi. You know anyone is welcome in this home."

"Yeah, but 'anyone' never came before. Tell him he crossed one street too many. Tell his mama she knows what's good for her, she better learn her way around town. Tell her I don't want to spend my good time tutoring some strange white boy. Nobody's gonna make me, either. Not even you."

Angeline frowned. "And some strange white boy doesn't want to spend his good time learning from you." She leaned close enough for him to smell the Zest soap on her neck and the lavender oil she daubed on her silver hair. It was pulled tight in a severe bun, the same way she'd worn it every day since he was a baby. The large vein above her eyebrow was throbbing. "They came here for a reason, Malachi. God delivered them to us because they need help."

"But I hardly ever talked to a white person before."

"Oh? Are you forgetting about your father? You forgetting about me? About what's in your own blood?"

"You never even saw that man. Ya'll can't even prove he's your daddy."

"Our mother said he was, and that's all the proof we need. How do you think she got the money to raise us the way she did, scrubbing floors for a dollar a day? Now get on downstairs and be the man the Lord intended you to be. You're going to share that beautiful brain He gave you and find it much more stimulating than earning your money cutting grass."

"I won't, either."

"You want me to worry your father over this? Call him up in New York and tell him about your sass?"

His aunt expected him to follow her down the stairs and he did, muttering behind her back. "Go ahead and call him. He'll come get me, sure enough. He'll think you lost your mind, and you have, too."

The boy was worse than he imagined. Awkward in brown penny loafers and long cotton pants, overdressed for the heat. His black hair was skinned in a crew cut, and his blue eyes sparked like the rays from Flash Gordon's gun. Sparking the same disgust I feel, Malachi thought, but he wasn't experienced enough to see the rest, the discomfort and the humiliation, the fear of what was to come next, although he felt it all, too. Especially the fear.

The mother was tall and slim and even whiter than her son. Malachi had never seen anyone as white or as still. She had the same blue eyes without the sparks.

"Malachi, I'd like for you to meet Mister Cooper Barnet," said Angeline. She seemed at ease, almost as tall as the mother and slender herself then in the blue sleeveless housedress she slipped into when she wasn't in school. But he knew better. He could read the pulse in her vein. "Go ahead," she said. "Shake the young man's hand."

Malachi barely touched the boy's fingers; eying his brown penny loafers and watching him stare back at his black Converse All-Stars. High-tops, beyond cool.

"How old are you?" he demanded.

"Twelve," the boy replied. He glanced at his mother. "Well, almost."

They stood looking into their own separate distances, already depleted.

His aunt sent them to the kitchen. He pointed to a chair shoved beneath the yellow Formica table. The boy slid in. His chest was squeezed against the table ledge.

"You named after the Cooper River?"

"No. After my granddaddy."

"He from Charleston?"

"I don't know. He died."

"How come your mama brought you here?"

"Somebody told her about it."

"Who?"

"A lady who works in our house."

"She tell her we were colored?"

"I don't know."

"Somebody's liable to kill us, they find out about you coming over here. Kill you, too. Kill you and your mama and your daddy and everybody else in your family."

Malachi couldn't have known that the boy wasn't brought up to hate black people, that he hadn't been afraid of them until one of them hit his mother in the back of the head with a tomato. It had splattered seeds and pulp in her hair. They'd been in Charleston then, on the colored end of King Street, in Edwards Five & Dime. His mother shopped there because the prices were cheaper. They weren't poor but she hated to spend money. Dragged him with her to buy his clothes. They would usually be the only white people in the store.

Malachi shoved a cookie at him. It was filled with lemon crème. The boy took a bite and dropped the rest on the floor.

"I didn't mean to," he said.

Malachi bent down to pick it up.

"Whose idea was those pennies?"

First the boy took the cookie and put it on the table. Then he leaned down and took off a loafer and dug a finger into the slot. He struggled with the penny until it rolled onto the beige linoleum. The other one was easier. It came out on the first try.

His mother drove him over in a yellow Buick. She stood next to the mimosa tree until someone responded to his timid ring. The furry pink blossoms were startling against her pale white skin. Malachi often waited before he answered the bell, watching her from behind the sheers that covered the door, watching up and down the street to make sure no one was around when he let a white boy in. She didn't look tired or scared or anything else in particular. Just still.

They usually began with math and moved to geography or history or science. Literature they saved for last. Sometimes Malachi read aloud. He had a good reading voice, quiet but edgy, as if he expected a surprise to spring out from the next sentence like a clown from a jack in the box. *Forever Amber* and *Lady Chatterley's Lover* weren't among the selections Angeline had assigned, but Malachi had slipped them from her room and hidden them under his mattress. He removed the gray jacket from *David Copperfield* and used it to cover Lady Chatterley's forbidden treasures. His pupil's interest in the classics soared.

His friends wanted to know why the white boy came over so much, sometimes even stayed late at night. Their parents never heard of such a thing. Didn't think it was right. How come his people didn't believe in segregation? Malachi told them he didn't know and asked his aunt.

"That family's segregated all right," she said, "but it has nothing to do with race. That family's segregated by sadness. With us, they don't have to fit in, to explain. That's why she brought the boy here."

Then she told him about Cooper's younger brother. That he'd been trapped in a car on a hot day with the windows shut. That they'd moved to Columbia to start a new life.

"A person doesn't heal from a tragedy like that without facing up to it first," she said. "And often, not even then."

Malachi had plenty of questions. His aunt answered them the best she could, then gave him his marching orders.

"You aren't to treat this knowledge as gossip," she warned him. "You are to keep it to yourself and try to help the boy any way you can."

He liked to sit on the porch at night. It was hard to get him to budge. Malachi was bored but he was also racking up fees for hanging around. In six months he would be legal to drive, fourteen in South Carolina, and he was hoarding for a car.

So they would sit there in the pitch-black dark, Malachi and the white boy he now easily called by name, hiding from mosquitoes who found them anyway and from people passing down the sidewalk who didn't know there was a reason to look. Just an adolescent boy with a teenager. Nothing to attract curiosity except the different colors of their skin, which wasn't an attraction in the dark. Just two young boys moving back and forth on a wooden swing in an old neighborhood where the races were divided by a few street signs and some root-cracked sidewalks and separate expectations for their lives; two stick shadows framed against the drawn window shade protecting a nightgowned lady's reading by a dim bedroom lamp. Two boys lazy with summer and the squeaky serenade of rusty chains against rusting ceiling hooks; trying to take it easy.

They had fallen into a comradeship of necessity, guarding their private thoughts, letting the night noises do the talking since they didn't have much to say.

"Tell me who they are," said Cooper during one of these nights. He whispered, as if afraid that the action beyond the porch would be interrupted by a strange white boy's words.

"Just plain folk." Malachi spoke in his regular voice. "Some like you and me. Some different."

"Where have they been?"

"Just up and down the street."

"No, tell me. Really tell me."

Malachi stopped to listen to the sounds he'd slept by since his mother died and his father had left him at his oldest sister's home and gone to find work in New York. He heard the clicking of spiked heels and the scraping of metal taps on the grainy cement.

"That's Charlotte Evans and her boyfriend Kenny, probably going for a bite down the street at Jake's." On the way home their gaits would be looser, with less style, soft strokes against the face of familiar concrete.

"And that old lady there, she's old Miss Reethie." They listened for a minute to the slow, scuffing rhythm of bedroom slippers. It was too dark to see her calloused heels hanging off the backs. "She goes to the drug store every night to get her husband a quart of chocolate ice cream. He can't get up from the bed."

"How about him?" Cooper pointed toward a man putting one foot crisply in front of the other. His inquisitive young voice was softer now, as if by making it lower he could apologize for the intrusion.

"Oh. Pastor. Pastor Quinn. Probably just finished up Wednesday evening Bible study. I don't care when you see that man, morning, noon, or night, he's always wearing a suit."

"Quick, listen. Who's coming now? What are they gonna do?"

Malachi had fallen asleep. He rubbed his eyes, and then leaned toward the voices. A man's whining boast. A woman's crooning taunts.

"Hey, girl."

"What you want?"

"I got sum'in for you."

"Nutin' I can use."

"Com'ere, baby. When you gone let me do sum'in for you?"

"Get on home. I ain't got time for your fool tonight."

Loud words. Garbled words. Nonsense words, soused with J. W. Dant and aimless time.

"Nothing but sorry old drunks," said Malachi.

"No," said Cooper. "It's more. Something we need to know."

"Nothing anybody needs to know," said Malachi. His strong mouth was curled in contempt. "Nothing but some worthless liquor trash."

He jammed the soles of his bare feet against the warped wood planks. The hinges creaked as the swing suddenly stopped. Their bodies were suspended against the back railing, straining forward.

"My aunt said you had a little brother." Malachi said it just like that. Blurted it out.

"Did she tell you I killed him?"

"She didn't put it like that."

"Well, I did. I killed him, and that's all I want to say about it. To you or anyone else, from here on out. I never want to talk about it again. Not in my whole entire life. So keep your damn trap shut, you hear? You promise?"

"I promise," Malachi said.

"Okay," the boy said, and jabbed him hard in the side, and jumped from the swing and took off.

Then there was nothing left to hear but the hinges creaking one last song as Malachi walked one foot in front of the other until the swing was level again.

13

They rarely panned out, Cooper's impulsively drawn plans of escape. Here he was chasing a wild hare in Clarendon County when he should have been minding the store in Columbia, working the phones, monitoring drips beside a hospital bed. But Hannah had said "Go get her" and he'd gladly taken off, spinning wheels in a traveling furnace leaking Valvoline, a man of action, missing in action, and smelling worse by the mile. He'd pulled up at Palmetto Cleaning and Laundry ten minutes before it opened at ten, too long to wait. The Dart had needed new tires, water, and oil—even megadoses weren't enough to keep it lubricated during a road trip in the heat—and his mechanic was way out on the Lexington Highway, the opposite direction of where he would be heading. The cost was $165.29 and two more hours off the road.

Cooper wasn't used to being early. It wasn't just wristwatches he avoided. He also didn't get along with clocks. The way they fixed their rifles on you like Dragline in *Cool Hand Luke*, glaring out orders with an infinitesimal jerk of a hand. Move it or pay. He rarely moved it fast enough, leaving his editors and friends stuck with the tab. They loaded him down with daytimers, bought him watches for birthdays and Christmas, and bored him with time management tricks. They pointed out the incongruity—a man hell bent on pleasing, but inflicting so much displeasure by making people wait. Cooper didn't understand it himself, why he put things off. What was he afraid of?

He'd gotten a pretty good column once out of being late to the wrong funeral. He assumed he was attending the service for a tournament Bingo player named Irene Miller. "The Hairnet Woman," Hannah called her, because she always had one on. He arrived at the church sanctuary thirty minutes after the minister had taken the dais. But he was mourning a stranger. The Hairnet Woman's funeral was being held next door in the chapel. If he'd attended the visitation the night before he would've known, but he didn't look at dead people.

Sam gave him hell about that. "A reporter who's never laid an eye on the tiniest little platelet of blood. Damnedest thing I ever saw. You couldn't hunt up another one if you dug the whole way back to Gutenberg."

Car wrecks, plane crashes, shootings—Cooper had covered them all while looking the other way. "Takes skill to do that," Sam liked to say.

Cooper would use his skills on the Baha'is. Be humble. Polite. Make small talk before easing in with questions. Any of you happen to be riding a Greyhound lately? Those buses sure can fly. See many little children on board? How about a little girl? Dress with flowers on it? Small for her age, heart pumps to the beat of a different drummer? She ran away from home, searching for someone. No, not for *something*, for *someone*. She was looking for her old man. Her deadbeat dad. Hey, anybody around happen to have an old Cadillac they might be looking to sell?

They would stare at him, patient, smiling. Them cool and fresh in their brown leather sandals and gauzy white robes, and him, filthy and smelling to high heaven, flushed up from the bowels of hell.

Cooper turned on the radio to find the time. Already quarter past two. His trip to the South Carolina Lowcountry had taken just an hour and twenty minutes, but he'd spent the next thirty-five getting lost. Directions stopped making sense as soon as you drove away from the person who was giving them. In this case, she was a waitress named Pearl, and at the moment he was so distraught he couldn't even figure out how to get back to the Summerton Diner to ask her where he had gone wrong.

He'd driven past the Amoco like she had instructed, and taken a quick right and then a left toward Davis Station. He'd kept it up until he'd passed the maroon double-wide owned by the preacher who once sold sections of his anointed sport coat sleeve on Channel 12, and then he'd started watching for the next left. Pearl had said it was "right around there," which had given him three choices. He selected the one that was paved.

"You'll pass a goodly stand of Rickenbaker woods before you get to a juke joint," she had told him. "Actually there's two, but the one I'm talking about's painted camouflage. There's a little cut-off forks left, and a mile on down I reckon it is you'll see an old boarded up bait shack. Belonged to that blond boy . . . can't think of his name to save my life . . . you remember him, Betty, heavy-set, drove the rig for BI-LO, used to come in for lasagna night . . . well, that's neither here nor there. Where you'll want to turn is beside the hatchery over to Potato Creek. Just be sure you don't. . . ."

Don't what? Cooper couldn't figure out if the woods he was passing belonged to the Rickenbakers, or how much woods make up a "goodly stand." He'd driven to the end of the road and hadn't seen a juke joint yet.

Now he was in a driveway, surrounded by green-armed monsters with pus-filled golden heads. He was burning up and so was the car. He raked the floorboard for some aspirin, and found two of them lodged in a crumpled Tootsie Roll wrapper. A dry ride, but the pills hit bottom without a snag. He hung out the window and backed up.

Broadly speaking, he was in Santee Cooper Country, an underpopulated union of lowlands that took up five sprawling counties midway between Columbia and Charleston. The region was big on fishing and produced quality cotton, and, judging from the jungle he had just escaped, a bumper crop of silver queen corn.

Locals preferred to let Mother Nature put on the airs and she did, with rivers, swamps, and wildlife mimicking the Everglades. But the headliners were two big lakes named for Revolutionary War generals, William Moultrie and Frances Marion.

Interstate 95 and a six-and-a-half-mile diversion canal divided 60,000-acre Moultrie from its twice-larger companion Marion, a major mid-state power source that could pass for the Atlantic Ocean in twenty-mile-an-hour winds.

Cooper was no stranger here. He'd judged turkey-calling contests at the Santee Fun Festival, spitting contests at Hellhole Swamp, and corndodger fry-offs at the state park. He'd also interviewed eighty-three-year-old Inky George, the area's oldest working fishing guide.

Inky caught the world-record channel catfish in Lake Marion with a concoction of spoiled chicken entrails, dead frogs and rotten herring, all chopped and bound together with six slices of Sunbeam bread and scented with eight ounces of cod liver oil.

"When her stomat's growling," Inky said, "a cat'll hit anything from a pecker off a putrified skunk to a bar of Dove soap."

In his spare time Inky wrote poetry at the Summerton Diner—a sparkling white vinyl shoebox a mile off 95, named by *Esquire* magazine as one of America's finest—the same place Cooper had stopped to use the pay phone. His call to Sam had saved him a twenty-mile trip farther down the road to Holly Hill, even though he had lost the time by mixing up Pearl's directions.

"The Big Cheese of the outfit bolted for Orlando," Sam had reported. "Took some kind of trapeze gig with the Cirque du Soleil."

"A high-wire performance in a turban and robe? Sounds like bullshit to me."

"Probably is. But that's what Phil just told me. At least, that was the word going around. Look, you might've gotten lucky for a change. My understanding is that when the others scattered, six or seven stuck around. Ended up together in an abandoned cabin at Four Hole swamp. Poor suckers were as clueless as they were broke. They were supposed to be living off the land but they couldn't tell a turnip from a squash.

"Seems they gave up before they got started. Headed off to some Girl Scout camp in Clarendon County. Anyway, Phil left two years ago. Not much commerce going on in Holly Hill. Says he hasn't heard anything since."

Camp Bob Wilcox. It wasn't too far from the diner. A long row of concrete cabins painted a jazzy shade of lime green, just off the edge of the water. Cooper remembered Inky George pointing it out five or six years ago, when they were riding around Lizzie's Creek in his pontoon boat, Inky helping him find a column.

"What in the world are they doing over there?" he asked Sam.

"Apparently, one of them knew somebody connected to the operation. A cousin, somebody like that. Offered to teach them to grow something edible and make biscuits to go with it if they manned the kitchen and kept up the grounds and promised not to stump for their big boss man, whoever the hell he is, while they were on the job."

◆

Cooper was finally headed toward Potato Creek, his body odor flavored with malted barley and hops. He'd found the camouflage-painted juke joint and cooled off with a beer and an air conditioner that put out something besides a bluff. This time he knew where he was going. Unlike Pearl, the man behind the counter had a Sergeant Friday approach to directions. After turning left onto Rickenbaker Road, he'd take an immediate right and continue down a dirt road until he reached Scarborough's Landing.

And there, he would find a woman with a flowing white gown and matching turban cleaning the privies with her ample arms. Beside the boat ramp, an old black Caddie would be parked in hubcap-deep water, its fins raised toward land with the pride of a world record channel cat.

What was he doing here? Baha'is hung out in melting pots. They didn't form free-roaming bands of offshoots and hole up in rural South Carolina, surrounded by Methodists and Baptists and Presbyterians and Pentecostals, with no funds to buy land that they didn't know how to farm, and their leader flying through the air with the greatest of ease down in Florida.

But this was all Cooper had. Nothing had come in from stories on the evening news or the two wire services, AP and UPI, or from the public service reminders during station breaks. And besides the call from Eula Mae Evans, nothing of substance had come out of the local story offered on the Associated Press's regional menu for papers that wanted to use it—a column written by a man who happened to be the father of the lost child, a father on the run himself.

The radio told Cooper it was three thirty. Someone named Flo was signing off from GNO On-the-Go radio to get her some . . . it sounded like bread and meat. He couldn't find a station closer than eighty miles away in Charleston, and nothing on a Charleston station about a little girl on a Greyhound bus. Something had happened on the bus. A sleazy male passenger had put his hands on her. A woman in a turban had intervened.

Charleston, the lovely Holy City, the start of Cooper's race—Sunday, August 12, 1955. They told him it wasn't his fault, that he was a kid himself and had no reason to assume blame for something God had planned. They told him his brother was in a happier place. But you can't picture a place any happier for your little brother than right here with your family where he belongs.

He'd lost his mother in Charleston, too. She'd gone home that day and put on a funeral and pretended to live in the same house with her husband and surviving son, until they moved to Columbia and she'd dumped him out with a black family on foreign soil so she could finish dying on the vine. It had taken her nine more years.

They called his brother "Scooter." Scooter, Scooter, the big bad pooter. Not his parents, the last part. Just him. Scooter wasn't big or bad. He would've gone by "Peter" when he started kindergarten, and the kids would've made it a bathroom joke. Cooper had planned to always call him Scooter. Scooter, Scooter, the big bad pooter. It fit.

14

The home lap to Scarborough's Landing & Marina was a driveway. Dusty and a quarter mile long, it curled around row after row of squatty campers parked to stay put. The speed limit requested fifteen but Cooper was going under ten, looking for turbans and stolen children in a primitive enclave of functional contraption art set among tall pines and painted signs. . . .

EXPERT MOTOR REPAIR and BAIT AND LURES and LIVE AND ARTIFICIAL BAIT AND LURES and HOME-COOKED FOOD and GAS. ICE COLD BEVERAGES. GRILL FOOD AND SANDWICHES. BURGERS WITH . . . popping up like square shooting gallery targets at the South Carolina State Fair.

He passed a miniature Airstream. The striped awning over its tiny stoop looked to be made from the seat of an old beach chair, and next to the door stood a clay pot filled with Black-eyed Susans. The camper's aluminum was as dented as a tin pitcher Hannah had once bought at a yard sale for thirty-five cents, so lopsided it toppled over when she came home and filled it with lemonade. Up ahead, parked in the crook of a bend was an outfit made from a hearse, painted bright yellow, trimmed in white, and topped in yellow-and-white-checked vinyl that looked like a tablecloth.

The Dart was pumping hard. Cooper's blue shirt, the same one he'd broken in three days ago in a phone booth, clung to his back. Here he was, a rancid family-size teabag brewing in tepid water, ready to meet the locals. He stretched behind him, digging for a comb in the back seat. His left front tire descended into a pothole. The slick steering wheel jumped from his hand. Whomp. He was in somebody's yard.

What had he just walloped? He got out to check. A hit and run might further count against a child already paying for the sins of her father. Her father who was not an accountant. Wasn't that in the story she'd written for school? NOT AN ACOUNTINT who rode the bus to work, but a responsible father who bathed every day and dressed in a bowtie like a grownup. A red bowtie that looked like a dog collar or a hangman's noose.

It was a rubber doormat. His skid marks had sawed through a message stamped in big white lettering. Something without fins wasn't allowed. The doormat led to terra cotta flagstones shaped like fish, swimming down a sandy path to "The Shack That Jack Built." The lean-to was plastered in Bass Pro Shop bumper stickers. The roof had been jigsawed into a huge fish with a big green eye and clusters of curly gray splotches to designate scales. It looked like a kid had done it. In fact, it looked similar to the artwork Hannah had shown him in the Toddle House.

Cooper searched up and down the curves and ruts of the long driveway. He hadn't seen any children. Not in the Summerton Diner, not fishing on the bank beside Potato Creek, not even playing in a yard along the many roads he'd traveled during the hour he was lost.

He scrubbed his face with some floorboard napkins, leaving one more paper trail. Fifteen hours had passed since he'd dropped the wood-pulp bomb that sent Hannah to Baptist Hospital. He didn't think he could force himself to write another one, even if that meant fulfilling Sam's prophesy and exiling himself to the land of the wailing arches. He grabbed the rest of the napkins and got out of the car. This last quarter mile was taking longer than the trip from Columbia.

The word was "Females." "Females Without Fins Not Allowed." What about finless males? Was it okay to trespass intentionally to make amends for a trespass that was accidental? Stalling. How long would this trick work?

He spit on a napkin and worked on the largest mark. The rubber was hot. His back hurt but the pain had eased from his knee. He squatted to get closer. He'd been in this position hundreds of times, surrounded by blue cardboard boxes, sizing a naked foot. Sam didn't get it. If you don't mind eating grilled cheese sandwiches on last week's bread, treating soles is an ideal job. All it takes is a little dose of polite attention to turn a woman into a queen, and a corn is the only risk. Besides, the only hole to worry about is the gap between the toe and the tip of the shoe.

A woman in a black bikini was working by the hearse, kneeling close to a two-foot picket fence, shoring up dirt around a small windmill with a colored propeller. She waved. She was wearing a kerchief, not a turban, wrapped around the orange juice cans she was using for rollers. Her hair was a brassy blond. Something about her was familiar. Cooper stopped.

"Hi," he said.

She smiled. There was no recognition in it.

"Hope I didn't stir up too much dust." What was it? Something about the rollers. The rollers in connection with the hearse. A pickup bed was hitched to the rear bumper, covered by a camper shell. More yellow edged in white.

Cooper leaned out the window. "Where's the front half?" he asked. He heard a man laughing and saw him behind the hearse, cutting weeds with an old-fashioned push mower.

"Had too much to drink one night," the woman said. "Got good and smashed."

She had black roots, Cooper noticed. Why was he so fixated on her hair? He peered through the windows of the hearse. Two youth beds were made up with yellow chenille spreads and white throw pillows.

What if this woman and her husband roamed the country kidnapping children, stowing them under the beds until they could sell them on the black market? Who would suspect such malfeasance in a happy yellow hearse with a plaid oilcloth top, especially if they used the bikini as a diversion.

Don't give yourself away, Cooper told himself. Keep it fast and simple. He knew how to do it. Make the words come out offhandedly, even though they were now slogging through a deep black pit.

"You haven't seen a little girl around here, have you?"

The couple glanced at each other and shook their heads. They weren't smiling any more. "How old?" the woman asked.

"Almost twelve, but she looks young for her age."

"How long's she been missing?"

"Not too long."

Use what's left of your brain, for God's sake. These people aren't up to anything more nefarious than setting out a few petunias. "I think I know where she is," he said. He gave a thumbs-up and moved along.

The signs were everywhere along the road, nailed on posts, too close together to absorb one before another took over. GRILL FOOD AND SANDWICHES. 5 a.m. UNT'L. . . . GROCERY. PICNIC AREA. GROCERY and GASOLINE and BEER. DINING INSIDE

AND OUT. CAMPSITES AVAILABLE. RESTROOMS. Everything but BAHA'IS WITH AMPLE ARMS WEARING TURBANS.

•

Tad and Yolanda Potts ran the marina. The couple leased it from a propane dealer three hundred miles up the road in North Carolina, who'd chased his boyhood dream too far away from his life to survive the logistics. The Pottses worked extra jobs in the winter to stay reasonably in arrears.

But from spring through the first big freeze, they had more than they could handle, and needed help at the GRILL and GROCERY. Cooper walked in, holding the door for a lady in a bathing suit carrying a mesh container filled with crickets.

Had she just called the waitress "Reba"? Small world. Reba had to be fifteen if she was a day. Beautiful mocha skin and straight shoulder-length hair with thick bangs to her eyebrows. Cooper tugged off his shirt, put it over a stool and sat on it.

"I have a dog named Reba," he said. "He's a guy, though. A bad boy. Always up to something. Anyway, you don't hear the name too much. I like it."

Reba just looked around the room, a rectangle twice the size of the retooled school bus Cooper had passed a minute ago, as if she were trying to find out who had spoken. Her smoky brown eyes traveled left, to a topless Coca-Cola cooler stocked with the live bait.

Cooper got up to examine the items assembled on glass shelves behind the counter. There it was, Ban Roll-On, next to Goody's Headache Powder and Murine Eye Drops. He waited in front of the deodorant. Reba waited behind it. He moved on.

A plywood plank led to DINING INSIDE—an open, sunny area twice the size of the grocery and grill. Cooper went in and looked around. The tables were topped in vinyl like the hearse, but these checks were red and white, and worn bare in spots. Plastic-coated windows exposed a scratchy view of the lake. Off to the right Cooper spied Camp Bob Wilcox. The lime green façade had mildewed.

He walked back to the grill, sat on the stool, and ordered a Tru-Ade. "Excuse me, Reba," he said, after she set down the bottle. "I wonder if you could help me out."

Reba didn't answer. Her busy eyes located the second cooler of bait, the crickets.

Maybe it was the hole in his undershirt. It exposed part of his nipple. But that couldn't be it. She worked at a marina in the summertime. He gulped some Tru-Ade. The cold felt good, even though orange didn't go with the donuts or beer. He wiped his mouth with the upper part of his sleeve and gagged.

"I've just come down from Columbia," he said. "The air conditioning went out on my car."

Reba backed up toward the grill.

"Any idea what time it is?"

She pointed to the Muse Propane wall clock behind the cooler of crickets. Already past three. Cooper's stomach cramped. He nodded toward a phone beside the cash register. "Can I use that?"

"Out there's a pay phone," she said, indicating the door.

But he couldn't seem to move. One second he was a zombie, the next he was having a panic attack. What was he doing at Scarborough's Marina?

"Actually, Reba, I'm looking for somebody. A group of people. They wear turbans. I heard they're in the area. I was wondering if you've seen them around."

Reba was slipping a white apron over a tan Scarborough's t-shirt. She wrapped the strings around her waist twice, then knotted them in front. "They fishers?"

"I'm not sure. They're religious. They. . . ."

She turned to remove a hamburger patty from the rounded freezer of a short Frigidaire behind her. After peeling off a layer of Saran Wrap, she threw the meat on the grill.

"Tad's around to the back," she told him, but her eyes were on the sizzling meat.

Cooper waited.

"That's all I got," she said.

•

The manager of the marina was at the end of a dirt drive leading to the picnic area. He was lying on an orange bedspread under a bass boat, unscrewing the cover on a 75-horsepower Evinrude. His brown hair was oily from sweat and grease, and his Scarborough's t-shirt would've been white if he hadn't been in charge of EXPERT MOTOR REPAIR.

The camp wasn't in session, Tad Potts told Cooper. "Summer camps don't open 'til summer vacation, no matter how damn hot it is." Tad grunted this part as he shimmied his big stomach advertising the perks of the grill into a spot an earthworm couldn't reach.

"You see all kind of getups around here," he said, twirling a wrench socket to fit an inside bolt. "People come off without a cap and start to burning; they'll cover up with anything they can get a hold of. You get so you hardly pay attention. Still, a lady in a turban . . ." he strained for a better angle and yanked ". . . the answer would have to be no."

Cooper found the children. They were across the lake, paddling belly down in a chaotic armada of rubber floats, kicking up enough wake to sink an ocean liner, in a free-for-all against anyone with a shrill set of lungs and a bathing suit.

A circle of adults in green plastic chairs supervised them from a small beach at the lawn's edge. The kids shrieked even when the spray missed.

If he hadn't been screaming, I would have taken the time to put on my sneakers before I carried him across the street. If my feet hadn't been on fire, I wouldn't have....

The second bolt was off but Tad had made no progress on the first.

"Damn fools," he said. "They get this idea that pistons are put in for life."

Cooper blushed. He sure thought so. Tad was a column he would've jumped on back when he was a columnist—*a guileless riverbank philosopher at home in his well-rewarded body and in the pines beside Lizzie's Creek, where reality was basic: itching from the sun and the heat, smelling gasoline from the pump at the end of the pier, eavesdropping on chattering engines lined up for a hit of fuel. Here a person could climb inside an evanescent time warp and become a limb waiting for a breeze, or a wave playing slapjack with the dock.*

But now, Cooper's eyes were turning the brown grass a lurid green, and he thought he might keel over on it. He sat at a picnic table and tried to hang on to the bench. He couldn't. The wood was melting, unable to hold him up.

Tad was scraping off rotted pieces of suction ring and stuffing them into a Styrofoam cup. "Ought to be a law against a dawg neglecting his boat this bad."

Christ. I'm about to croak on a man I've just laid eyes on.

Tad was saying something else, but Cooper was listening to another voice: *"Stay with me, baby. Come on. Stay with me now."*

"I said, 'Here to catch your limit?'"

"No, I'm not," Cooper wanted to tell him, but his tongue was wily, heavy one second, light the next. Likewise his arms and hands. His torso was on a foam rubber raft shooting down putrid green rapids, headed for the rocks.

"Stay with me, baby."

He couldn't. He was going under.

"Hold on."

Malachi, reaching to him from a memory he couldn't connect to. It was the weekend after Hannah went away. He'd been poisoning himself on a half gallon of cheap Scotch that Sam had left behind after a party. Malachi happened by to bum some cash so he could get on with his own personal destruction. He'd called Sam. They teamed up, Sam doing the heavy lifting—dragging Cooper into the shower, walking him around and around, room to room—Malachi doing the talking.

"Never learned to drink worth a damn, did you, partner? Hang on now. You're doing fine."

"Crappies bitin' over by the cypress knobs not far from the cut. Not much action on bass, though. Too hot. Best place to try is the big rocks down along the dam. Follow 'em out about a quarter mile, then try your grapes and your yellows with . . . I'd say you don't need no more than eight-, maybe ten-ought line. I like the braided, but that's just me. Near about dusk, switch over to your cranks. But you may as well stay cool while you can. Won't do any good to put in as long as the sun's still out."

Did he just hear "stay cool?" He had to get a grip, figure how to pluck words he could speak from his brain. But all he saw was Malachi, out cold, his head bleeding against the corner of the walnut desk, the disconnected receiver on his chest. Saw Hannah in the Toddle House, thin and pale and scared. *"What if she manages to make it to your house and no one's there?"*

"I have that covered . . . have that covered . . . have that. . . ."

"She's dead, damn it. Your secret child. Your child's already dead."

Tad plopped the last of the rotten O-ring into the cup. He'd been humming a catchy little scat of "Love Is a Many Splendored Thing"—*baa-ba-du-da-du-daa-du*—unaware of Cooper on a runaway raft behind his left shoulder. He rolled his head backwards toward the lake.

"As far as that other thing goes, over yonder's the one you ought to talk to," he said. "You know how these women are."

Cooper was hanging onto the bench, dripping sweat. He took in a breath. It surprised him by coming back out. He wasn't tingling cold anymore.

"Mind if I have a little bit of your water there?"

"Huh? Sure. Help yourself."

Cooper got up and walked to a plastic jug beside the trailer tire. The grass was brown again. He didn't stop drinking until the water was gone.

"Tell me where to get it and I'll buy you some more."

"These women" Tad had referred to must've been the woman grabbing a tow rope from a teenager who'd just cut the engine on his ski boat. Cooper wondered how Tad could see her, lying on the ground, buried underneath a 75-horsepower motor. She was in the company uniform, her t-shirt a bright red. Securing the boat with her foot, she handed the nozzle to a muscular kid in cutoffs. Across the creek, the child armada had stormed the beach, where the junior Seabees were demolishing bologna sandwiches.

"You'll do no such thing," Tad said. "We got more water around here than we know what to do with."

He rolled his head towards the pier and whistled three short tweets. After jamming some bills into her pocket, the woman began sauntering their way, tugging her shirttail from the waist of a tight pair of denim culottes and using it as a fan. Her thighs were thick with muscle. Her hair was thick, too, full of brown curls that she'd pulled back and tied with a frayed piece of nylon rope. She was moon-faced and tanned, and had a big dimple in her left cheek.

Cooper stood and shook her hand. He liked Yolanda Potts, the dimple, the curls, the way she greeted him: "What can I do you for, blue eyes?"

As they sat around the picnic table, she told him about Reverend Jack Riles, the "Pentecostal Holiness" who'd inherited the lakefront property from his grandparents back in the fifties. He'd come up from Kissimmee, Florida, to build a church, saw the setting, and established a camp named "Bob Wilcox" after his grandfather. Church members who couldn't afford trips to the mountains or beach could spend a week on Lizzie's Creek to refresh their souls. To help with expenses, Riles rented the facilities to 4-H clubs and scouts, and did a lot of the maintenance himself. When his stepsister called to report her wandering son and his friends, he told her to send them on.

"He has a heart as big as the U.N.," said Yolanda. "Truth be known, if the devil beat down the door huntin' something to eat, Jack Riles would give him his last slice of bread."

"How many were there?" asked Cooper. He was sitting backwards on the picnic bench, leaning against the table. Yolanda was next to him, watching the dock for customers.

"I'm not sure," she said. "Summer before last—that was when they first came—I believe it was only around six or seven, but I haven't seen them in a good while. They rarely did business with us, I think because they don't. . . ."

She interrupted herself to holler at some people in a red pickup circling the front of the grill.

"Hey, Bubba, red light."

A kid hung out of the driver's window. The tips of his flattop were so much lighter than the brown hair hugging his skull that they looked bleached.

"Hey, Miss Yo. I know what red means. Red means stop."

"That's them," she said.

"Them who?" Cooper asked.

Yolanda stared up at him and cocked her curly head. "Now who have we been talking about the last five minutes?

"That Chris, he's a doll. Jack brings him over for a cheeseburger every afternoon during the week, as long as he behaves in school, lets him drive the circle a couple of times when there's no other cars. Well, he don't actually do anything short of turning the wheel. He's only six. His mother was in the church until she got off track and lost her way. Has a dope habit so bad they say she'll prostitute herself out to get it. They couldn't find his daddy, so Jack and Miss Claire took him in."

◆

"Offshoots? That's a new one on me but I guess you could call them that. In fact, it might be the best word for it," Jack Riles said. "They were off shooting for something, all right, like young people since Moses was a babe in the reeds—wrestling with those old cockleburs that get stuck between your toes when you strike off to choose your own path. These were decent kids, wanted to explore the fringes without straying too far out of bounds, so they meet up with this group of nonconformists with originality. Nice, respectful folks offering a way to get through the thistles with a modicum of courage and hope, and bingo, they were Baha'is."

Cooper nodded calmly, an appreciative student, but his hands were shaking so much he had to jam them into his pockets. Couldn't let the preacher know he was scared. He dug out some coins and put them on the table, like he was leaving a tip. Riles took this in with a quizzical look—Chris hadn't even started to eat—and went on talking.

"Idealists have the best of intentions, yet you generally find they don't think things all the way through, even those that have most of the facts. You need them around to keep you honest, but you sure don't want them running the show."

He paused to cut the cheeseburger in half with a plastic knife. "Hope I haven't stepped on any toes," he said.

Cooper shook his head. The only thing offending him at the moment was an anemic iceberg lettuce leaf dripping from a soggy bun. He turned to the window, watching Yolanda grab the bow of a Boston Whaler before it bumped into the dock.

Miss Yo, his latest infatuation. Just like that, she'd arranged for him to join Riles and Chris in the dining area. Reba had brightened like Haley's Comet the second they'd stepped in the door, calling the boy "Boo" and showing him the cheeseburger on the warming tray. While she was stuffing the meat into a bun, Cooper had grabbed his shirt off the stool and taken it to the car.

"They liked the appeal of communing with nature, you know," Riles was saying. "As an idea, it sounded good. But they were just going on what odds and ends they'd picked up extemporaneously."

Cooper angled his chair away from the burger. The mention of odds and ends reminded him of the calls he should've made. He needed to check in with Sam, Malachi, and the police. Tell Hitch the column for tomorrow would be fifteen inches of blank space. They could run a black border around it. He had the urge to bolt, race outside. But where would he go? The first obit he wrote would be his daughter's.

"I've been a little half-cocked at times myself," he told Riles. Like ten minutes ago, when he'd identified himself as a reporter from Columbia working on a story about Baha'is. Like now, sitting in a theology seminar while a child was possibly being tortured.

"Haven't we all," the preacher said, then went on. "They hadn't really researched the history of the operation. They weren't much on scholarship, which is why they left the university in the first place. They were just a little band of wayward gypsies eager to shake their tambourines, and they jumped on the wrong wagon and got lost. To tell you the truth, they didn't even know who it was that founded the Baha'i faith."

"Neither do I," Cooper said. If he kept stalling, he'd be out of range when they called. It was customary for the father to show up and make the identification. "Is this your little girl?" they would ask. And he would have to shut his eyes and peer beneath the sheet and tell them he didn't know.

"It was Baha'u'llah. He was a prophet born in Persia back in the mid-eighteen hundreds."

"Huh." Go on, speed him up. Ask him and get out.

"He was a forward-thinking man. Had a vision of better social conditions for the poor, mutual love and harmony for all, equality between the sexes, even one universal language. He thought this idea we have about austerity being a prerequisite for salvation was bunk, a roadblock to spiritual growth. Believed people should be happy, you know, that the way to achieve happiness was to be pure in body as well as spirit. Drink pure water. Don't eat meat found in traps and nets. In fact, he believed killing animals of any type was unkind, which is the reason orthodox Baha'i's were vegetarians."

Jack Riles stood up and walked over to the grocery to pull a bag of chips off the rack. He had a graceful, leonine quality, intense green eyes, and flowing silver hair reminiscent of Billy Graham's. His short-sleeved blue polyester shirt was spotless all the way to the pointed tips of the open collar. Cooper twisted his t-shirt sideways until his nipple was covered.

The minister opened the chips, ate a few, then, after making sure Cooper didn't want any, shook out the rest on Chris's paper plate.

"I could of brought 'em over," called Reba from behind the counter.

"I need all the exercise I can get," Riles answered. "Tell Miss Viva thank you anyway," he said to the boy.

"Thank you anyway, Miss Viva," Chris said.

"*What's* her name?" whispered Cooper.

"Viva," Riles mumbled from underneath the table. A bite of chewed tomato had fallen out of Chris's mouth and he was picking it up. "Hand me a napkin, will you, Cooper," he asked. "Like the Latin, for long live."

"It was kind of comical," the minister said, settled again and back on topic. "They pictured themselves as the ultimate form of Baha'i. Believed in love and harmony and laughter, and knew they weren't supposed to be caught up in the temptations of the material world, but beyond that they didn't seem to know much else. Got hung up on some outmoded idea of turbans yet hadn't gotten the message that the hard-liners don't eat meat, and off they traipse to Hellhole Swamp. Started off there were a gang of twelve; no money, no prospects for a job, and they pick a place where everybody learns to hunt and fish before they learn to use the potty. Now you tell me, where's the sense in that?"

Stall him. Keep on stalling. "Nowhere," Cooper said. There was something about the turban. A particle the size of an atom was wedged underneath a rock in his skull, begging to come up for air. "What about the clothing," he asked. "The turbans and robes?"

Riles swiped a chip from Chris and popped it in his mouth.

"That was mine, PopPaw," Chris said.

"I never saw a single robe, not even a bathrobe," Riles said. "Wish I had." He chuckled. "Kids that age have this notion you want to see whatever it is they have to offer."

Cooper's heart raced as he watched the minister walk his fingers down the table toward another chip. What was he doing sitting here? Why didn't he leave?

"Some did have the towers, though, when they first got here. That's what Chris calls 'em, 'towers,' don't you, buddy? Weird looking things, almost like they were wearing fire hydrants, some white, some black. I gave the ultimatum right off: heads covered in the kitchen, whether it be with turbans or hairnets or Betsy Ross bonnets, I didn't care; or get yourself a haircut. I meant skint, too. Couldn't have hair co-mingling with the grits and eggs. Wasn't more than a week or two they'd opted for the clippers, all except my nephew John. He wore that tower . . . was a couple of months, wouldn't you say, Chris, before he gave in and got a flattop like yours? Ended up going to the same barber, didn't he, son?"

Chris grinned and brushed his hand across his head, frosting the blond tips with crumbs. Jack reached over with a napkin, but Chris ducked.

"Uncle Johnny plays in a heavy metal band," he said. "His mom's buying him a new guitar so he'll go to college."

"Good for him," Cooper managed to say. The pain in his side was so sharp he had to fight to keep from bending over. His hands were underneath his arms now, holding on to his chest, which was trying to jump out of his shirt.

"What about the rest of the offshoots," he asked, "the ones who came with John?"

•

"He said they were scattered to the winds," Cooper told Sam. He was calling from the open-air pay phone beside the restrooms. "But it doesn't matter, because nobody in the pack was older than twenty-one or twenty-two, and none of them were women."

Things had been going the same way in the newsroom. Jazz had crafted a system for investigating all leads. Reports were coordinated with the police and Malachi at the house. Everyone on the staff had volunteered, including Ginna and Ruth Ann and members of the copy desk. All they'd come up with were bum steers that led to more bum steers. Hitch decided they would run one of his classic columns each day until he returned, take the pressure off.

After Jack Riles helped Chris into the truck, he walked over to the pay phone and took Cooper's arm. "I've been praying for you and your little girl," he said.

The woman and man were still out by the hearse, sitting on lounge chairs, drinking tall glasses of iced tea, watching a sprinkler water their new petunias. The woman motioned him over. Cooper waved but didn't slow down, and wondered if *Sports Illustrated Swimsuit Edition* gave finders' fees.

The kerchief tied around the rollers. The turban. The hearse. It had gone beyond eating at him to driving him insane. He was in front of "The Shack That Jack Built." A man in a straw hat was kneeling near the mat to open a tackle box. The skid marks bared their teeth. Cooper looked the other way and sped all the way up to fifteen.

15

The traffic was going nowhere, and Malachi was stuck in the middle of it. He'd put off leaving the house until after five thirty, figuring by the time he reached downtown the congestion would be ebbing out to the suburbs, but even the slackers had procrastinated today, keeping cool on the company dime, belting a last shot of carbonated sugar from the vending machine before they slogged through the atmospheric sauna to the steam bath fogging up their cars.

Instead of cruising down Assembly, he was sandwiched between a dump truck and a minivan, waiting for the vehicles stalled two blocks ahead of him, which were waiting for the cars ahead of them to turn left at a light that had no left turn arrow and no opportunities for cutting through due to a stalemate in the opposite lane.

The man in the minivan blasted his horn. Malachi shrugged in the rearview. What was he supposed to do, sprout feathers? He noticed the USC baseball sticker on the windshield and gave him a thumbs-up. In two more hours, the ice cream line at Zesto would be longer than the one they were in now, if the Gamecocks could keep the 10 and 0 run going tonight.

Malachi had played baseball, outfield, initially lured to the sport by the courage of Jackie Robinson and his mighty bat. He started in fourth grade and didn't miss a year until he went off to school. He was good. The coach had a connection on one of the Dodgers' lower-level farm clubs and told him he might have a shot. He would've taken it, if he'd had a different woman for an aunt and known what he was about to find out.

Hell, it might not have changed the score at all. Isn't that what they always say—it was meant to be? It could have been meant-to-be sliced off the first afternoon of practice during a collision with the mowing machine. But losing one for the glory of the game—that was a contribution he might have been able to live with.

He draped an arm behind him, feeling around in the cool cracked leather of the seat pocket, just in case Burns kept a little flask on the side, a little antidote to help her suffer the sycophants. He knew better but he was jittery, looking for a project for his hands. All he found were the white linen towels the wine had been wrapped in for the drive from Charleston. Not much protection with a demolition derby queen behind the wheel.

He couldn't blame her, though. The torque on the steering column was a joke. Aim toward Miami and you're liable to end up in Mississippi, something he'd experienced a few minutes ago when he tried to avoid a busted pavement grate, straightening the wheel after he passed a city bus. Almost hit a Stroman's peanut vendor heading to the plant to park his cart. The cat was lipping the curb, probably punch drunk after a day in the sun.

The boiled peanut. Most peculiar morsel of organic matter Malichi had ever put in his mouth. Shriveled-up mush, cooked to death with enough Morton's Iodized Salt to dry out the Great Lakes. Work one open with your teeth and suck the juice through the grime and the strings. The good old taste of Dixie.

"Way down South in the land of cotton, old times there are best forgotten. . . ."

Malachi had tried it up North. The scenery was different—no rebel flag flying over the Capitol Building—but the bottom line was the same, just better disguised. He felt more comfortable here at home, where he knew the ropes, knew what to avoid, knew when something wasn't right and when something was real. Like Burns. She was real, all right. A real anomaly, in any part of the world.

"Don't get frisky," she had said when she'd handed him the key. "I'm short on cash." Nothing like impeccable timing, and there was a woman who had it.

There was a woman, period. She could send you to the North Pole to plant hibiscus and you would turn yourself into a glacier waiting for something to grow. She hadn't sent him that far, just off to the other room to change his shirt, saying, "I've always been fond of a good frankfurter, but perhaps you'd rather save that one for the Fourth of July."

It didn't offend him, this interference from some audacious old woman he'd barely met. Just brought back memories of being respected as a matter of course. Malachi had been on his way out the door. He didn't say anything, just gave her a look, got one back, and turned around.

The closet didn't offer more than it had earlier in the day, but he was a different shopper. It came down to a knock-off Izod knit or the shirt he chose, a white Brooks Brothers, a can of double-strength Niagara in the collar and sleeves. French cuffs? Not Barnet, not even at a yard sale. Probably didn't notice until he'd gotten home, ripped open the bag, and flown off to collect another prize to keep the t-shirts company on the closet floor.

Malachi rolled up the sleeves, then put on a pair of khakis, using the belt looped around the doorknob to hold them up. A lot of trouble, pinning up the leg. The only shoe that fit was the one he'd come in with, a cream leather loafer with matching patent trim, polished with a little Johnny Walker Red, unintentional courtesy of the long, exquisite neck on a bass guitar he'd encountered in Rock Hill. Curtis Wilmore. Hell of a musician.

"There you are," Margaret said when he'd come out again, and at least in that moment there he might have been.

They'd added a new entrance to the hospital, a bland brick sign lost in a cluster of Bradford pears. Malachi overshot the turn, lunged for the brake again. If the brain is as adaptable as neurologists claim, then why, twenty years later, was it still ordering him to use a leg he didn't have?

Driving this car was a trip. It would be easier piloting a U-Boat in the Battle of the Atlantic. He'd have to ask Burns if her contract called for a functional steering wheel. If it had, she'd been taken through the cleaners and out the back door. The first and only time, he expected. Maybe he'd go with her when she was ready to make a trade.

Trade, nothing. She'd be plowing the sidewalks with this antediluvian submarine after the rest of humanity was floating around in bubbles overhead. Because you better believe some Orwellian genius would be inventing the flying saucer soon, just to keep out of her way. But you couldn't open a window in a flying saucer. And there she'd be, owning the streets and roads down below, splaying concrete all over town in her '61 Continental convertible, fine white hair blowing in the breeze, free as a celestial bird.

◆

"NPO" was stamped across a white sheet of paper in large orange letters, along with "Vital signs q6h," and a warning about trespassing. It worked. It made this visitor apprehensive as hell. Burns had procured the room number, and assumed that he could waltz right in. He couldn't even hop that far. He'd borrowed a wheelchair at the front entrance.

The door across the hall was open. A patient in a negligee, full figure peach, was lying on her side, facing the window, the air conditioning tossing helium balloons around her like ping-pong balls in a bingo cage.

"Forgive me, Burns, but clothes don't always make the man," Malachi mumbled, and rolled himself in. The chair steered as poorly as her car.

The lady was snoring, wheezing in duet with the A/C as it made passes at her nightie. Up close her face was sweet. He hated to disturb her, but after he explained the situation, she hacked a laugh, and told him to be her guest.

When he opened Hannah's door, it banged into an immovable object, setting off a sparring match between his head and the balloons. The woman on the other side was freckled, with lean muscles and a miniskirt. She was wearing a stethoscope and seemed flustered, but only for a second.

"You'll have to wait here. We're not done," she said, and stepped back inside the room.

"Anything else bothering you? Headaches? Dizziness? Nausea?"

"No. Yes. Everything you mentioned. I feel like Ingrid Bergman in that Hitchcock movie, you know, the one where they hold her captive in a bedroom and shoot her full of everything under the sun . . . do you know the one I mean? They're in a mansion and the people are all evil, particularly the old woman, the one in charge of all the men, they're spies or subversives of some type, and just at the last second Cary Grant comes in and grabs her from the bed, not the old woman but Ingrid Bergman, and carries her down the stairs. Or maybe they catch him before they make it down. I'm not sure. I can't think any more."

"*Notorious.* They lived to tell about it."

"Is that it? Doesn't ring a bell. Something's very wrong with my brain, doctor. Please don't give me more medicine. I have to be clear. I'm ready to be discharged. I'd like to check out right away."

"I'm afraid this isn't a hotel, Miss Smith. You're exactly where you need to be. We're giving you medication to lower your blood pressure and medication to keep you as calm as possible, and to be frank, they can have side effects from A to Z. Tomorrow we'll get busy with the fine tuning, try and figure out what's what. Then, once you're more stable, we'll be making some adjustments and substitutions. I agree that you are getting a fairly high dosage, but under the circumstances, when considering the alternatives, it's the best we can do. Well. That was an earful. Any questions?"

"I haven't given my consent. You can't hold me against my will. It's against the law."

"I've left instructions for them to start taking your pressure every hour, both lying down and sitting up. If you can put up with the annoyance a few days, we should be able to get your medication squared away by the end of the week."

"No. That's unacceptable. I want out now."

"When I spoke with Dr. James this morning, he warned me not to let you boss me around. He said you've been bossing him around for years. I'm not being fair, am I? Cary didn't lecture Ingrid when she was under the influence in *Notorious*, did he?"

"No. He just carried her out of the bedroom."

"Clever, aren't you? Good for you. Okay, we'll start again. I understand that Dr. James has been trying to get you into the hospital back in Charlotte for some tests. He says your diastolic numbers have been running borderline and above and you've also been experiencing some dizziness and occasional fainting spells. It doesn't help that you're anemic. Sterling's a fine doctor and a fine man. You need to listen to what he says."

"Yes, but I'm trying to make you understand. I'm dealing with an extreme emergency, a life-and-death emergency, and I need to be. . . ."

"You need to be right here where we can keep an eye on you. I want you on the monitor. Your heartbeat is nothing near what they got in the ER but it's still elevated. The meds you're on are responsible for that to some degree, but we don't know how much. We won't know until later on, when we start bringing you down. Meanwhile there's nothing we can't handle, so don't worry about it. Okay?"

"Not okay. Not at all. Please direct me to your supervisor, or someone who. . . ."

"You're out of luck, Miss Smith. I am my supervisor, and your sister has signed on with the treatment program. You have to get yourself strong, for what's ahead. I don't mean to imply . . . we all continue to be hopeful. You have a lot of folks praying for you out there. Now, then. We'll keep the block on your calls and when we decide to okay visitors, they'll be limited to family and a few very close friends. One person at a time and short visits only. Your sister is making a list."

"But you have me so doped up I can't function at all. Listen to me, talking like Goofy the . . . is Goofy a dog or a mouse? And I can't seem to stay awake. I feel like I'm trapped in . . . in some kind of vacant capsule or something. My head is unattached from my body. It's floating around somewhere up there on the ceiling and I keep trying to catch it and I can't. I have to find my daughter. She's my little girl. She's lost and I'm her mother and I . . . and she's all I want. She's my life."

"Miss Smith. Hannah. I'm a mother, too. Three, and trying for a fourth, and my heart is breaking for you. If I were in your place I'd feel the same way. But you have to trust someone besides yourself to take care of things. You're not capable of doing anything right now, and, in fact, anything you do besides staying right where you are puts your health at grave risk. And that does nothing to help your daughter."

"Scotty."

"Yes, Scotty. We'll evaluate your condition tomorrow and go from there. That's all I can give you for now. It's all I can do."

"But I'm so disoriented. I feel like this is happening to someone else, and I keep fighting to make it seem real because I know it is very real and yet I don't want to believe it, and . . . and, don't you understand? My daughter's life is on the line and I'm up here in this stupid bed, like all I can find to do is lie around and behave like some kind of drunken corpse. You've got to help me."

"You're quite active for a drunken corpse. You're wound up like a top. Your next IV isn't due for another hour, but I'm going to have the nurse bring you an oral sedative and I don't want you to send it back. It's going to make you drowsy again so you can get some rest. Rest is very important, Miss Smith. We're going to help calm you down so you can get some sleep, and then we'll talk about it later on. Will you try for me?"

"Yes. Yes, if you promise to let me go, I'll try."

"And now." A face-off through the balloons. "You are . . .?"

"Malachi Patterson."

"And your reason for being here?"

"My reason?"

"My God. Malachi. Is that you?"

"She knows who you are?" the doctor asked.

He nodded. "You assumed I was the delivery man?" He got a kick watching her blush.

"He's my cousin," said Hannah. "My very first one. We're really close. Please, doctor, I don't want to be alone. Please let him in."

"Her first cousin?" said the doctor.

Malachi smiled but didn't reply.

"All right," she said. "That's fine. Um ... I'm Bunny Carpenter. I don't know. Technically, you shouldn't be here, but . . ." a quick look at the wheelchair ... "since you are and you *are* related ... she's become highly agitated. Maybe you can help her settle down. I want you to understand, though, that I'm talking in the neighborhood of minutes."

◆

Storming in on a bucking bronco, ramming everything in sight, taming a herd of wild balloons. Not what the doctor had prescribed.

"Malachi?"

He should've taken this machine for a test drive first. A wheel was trapped between the side of the door and an open cabinet beneath the sink. The balloons couldn't decide whether they wanted to be in or out, and were squawking like a fiddle with broken strings.

"What's wrong? Are you okay?"

Her heart had to be raising almighty Cain. His was. The whole medical staff was probably racing down the hall, ready to perform Code Blue. Malachi left the balloons with the door. Surgery takes manual dexterity.

"Oh, dear." Hannah said.

He dreaded going in, seeing what he heard. Weak voice. Slurred words. Same as when she was talking to the doctor, except at times back then her escalator had zoomed from high to giddy. He took a breath, came inside. Pulled the door to until it shut, then changed his mind and left it cracked, the balloons bouncing all to be damned.

"Hello, Hannah." His smile wouldn't work. His lips were glued to his teeth, and his tongue was drier than the strips of gauze lying on the table by the bed.

"Hi."

The eyes weren't hers. The green had gone underground, crowded out by pupils black with urgency and dope, staring at him like they weren't sure what they were seeing.

A strip of surgical tape was holding the IV to the underside of her wrist. The tube had been disconnected from the plastic bag over her left shoulder. The bag was empty, another beside it, ready to go. She pulled up on the railing and fell back. A monitor peered from her hospital gown.

"Something's happened to Scotty."

"Be still now. Nothing's happened."

She was lying flat. Not a break in the plain of her body.

"Then what made you leave the house?" she asked.

Malachi pushed the chair closer and pressed a button on the side of the bed to raise her head and shoulders.

"Someone else is there," he told her. "A lady from Charleston. She knows how to handle things."

Her knees were climbing toward the ceiling.

"Hold on," he said. "Wrong one."

"Over here."

Hannah lowered her hand. A motor whirred. Her eyes were crazy. A string of mucous dripping from her nostril was moving toward her lip.

"Fairly high dose" nothing, Malachi thought. They're turning her into a junkie.

"I understood your sister was here," he said.

Not even a lousy box of tissues. He offered her a handful of paper towels. She shook her head. He used one to daub at the mucous and laid the others on her shoulder. Her face was flushed.

"I sent her to the room. She didn't want to go. I made her. She hasn't had a minute's rest since we found out."

A can of generic ginger ale was on the nightstand. Malachi picked up a paper cup.

"No thank you," Hannah said. "Did they tell you about her heart? She needs her medicine."

He put down the cup to stroke her shoulder. This had been a mistake.

"Where's Cooper?" she asked.

He grabbed the ginger ale, popped the top, and drank until the can was empty.

"Out looking. Whoa, here, Hannah, lie down. There aren't any feasible leads. He just needs to be looking."

"Oh, God," she said. "I can't focus. I wanted to ask you something about what you just said and I can't think of what it was. Do you see some colored balls or something? They keep moving. They're right over there."

"Those are just balloons, baby." His ticket for admission.

"I'm in bad shape, Malachi. I want you to take me out of here. I want to go with you to the house in case she . . . in case somebody nice finds her and brings her over. They might, you know. It's possible."

He took her shoulder again, easing her back until her head was on the pillow. Her hair was oily and matted, and turning gray. Thin wrinkles crossed her forehead. She was still pretty, but some hard miles had been traveled since the first time he'd seen her, a vision— the last vision he'd wanted to see at the time.

"Do you remember," he told her, "that the first time we met was in a hospital room?"

"I remember," she said. "You almost died." She closed her eyes. "Malachi?"

"I thought you were asleep."

"I tried to be a good mother. I took her to school. She never ran away before."

"Ssssh. Hush. Hush, now, and try to rest."

His throat was dry. He needed a drink. Craved one. He eyed the box of gauze. "Contains Medicinal Alcohol," it said. He wanted to suck it out.

He picked up the pitcher of water, his hands trembling like he suffered from palsy, and spilled water and ice all over the khaki trousers. The cups around here couldn't hold Thumbelina's thimble. He reached for the paper towels on Hannah's shoulder. His hand was jerking, about to conk her in the nose. Her eyes were swollen, the lashes heavy with grease.

"Why did it have to happen?"

"I don't know, Hannah."

"Why did it happen to her?"

"I don't know."

"She wouldn't hurt a soul."

The khakis were soaking wet. Cheap paper towels don't dry anything. They just leave wet pills of paper.

"She doesn't plan things. She doesn't understand about working things through. Well, maybe she does to some degree, but to figure out how to catch a bus. . . ."

"It's all right. Just go on to sleep."

"She's been on a plane but she's never even been on a bus outside of something related to school. We go to Disney World. She loves it there. We've been a bunch of times. I get free transportation. She loves to fly. She loves to talk to Mickey and Minnie and Goofy, and there's a ride she's crazy about. 'It's a Small Small World.' I hate it. Can't get the song out of my head for days. Over and over, Da-Da-Da-Da-Da-Da-Da-Da-Da-Da, Da-Da-Da-Da-Da . . . you know the one I'm talking about, right? They take you around in teacups."

"Never been."

"They said an elderly lady helped her buy the ticket. What kind of grown woman would send a little girl like that off by herself?"

"Hannah, Hannah. There are all kinds of people." Hadn't she ever been inside a bus station?

"Malachi?"

"Yes."

"Why did *she* have to be the one?"

"The one what, baby?"

"The one punished. You know, for what I did. Did and didn't do."

It's always more than one, he thought. That's what makes it punishment.

"You sound like your ex," he said. "He used to ask those kinds of questions. Questions without answers."

"About me?"

"No, baby. Long before you."

"Oh. You're talking about his brother."

"Not hardly. He asked questions about everything but his brother. He didn't talk about him. Only once, when he was a kid."

"Only once? But I thought. . . ."

"And even then, I was the one who brought it up. He went berserk. Told me he killed his brother and he never wanted to talk about it again."

Hannah pulled herself up by the bedrail. The scar at her temple was throbbing. Ugly red blotches covered her neck, swollen and angry, like hives.

Malachi manipulated the wheelchair, parallel parking beside the bed. Now it was easier to reach her. Putting a hand behind her, he guided her back down on the mattress and slid the pillow underneath her head. Where the hell was her sister? Why didn't the nurse come in?

"I thought, that night you told me . . . I just assumed, you know, that you'd talked about it lots of times."

"No. Only the one."

"I was beside myself, trying to figure out what I'd done. What I was doing wrong."

That was why he'd told her. Because she'd convinced herself that she was the one with the disorder. The type of disorder that could drive a husband away. Cooper's problems were destroying her beauty. Not the physical back then. The beauty of her self-assurance. Her strength.

"I shouldn't have violated the confidence."

"Can you believe it made me jealous? If you were the person he told things to, I wondered, then what was he doing with me?"

Malachi's jaw tensed, but when he spoke his voice was tender. "I was drunk that night. You were distraught. I didn't think it through. I came here to apologize for my poor judgment. I have a feeling it may have influenced your decision to keep your daughter to yourself. It's been tearing me up."

"No." Hannah reached over the rail and grabbed his wrist, squeezing tight. "No," she said again. "You should have. Told me, I mean. It explained so much I didn't understand. The big things, of course, the obvious, like about having children, but beyond that, all the other infuriating stuff that caused the ridiculous fights."

She let go, turning on her side to face him. Her eyes reflected her fight to focus. "Like how he refused to lock the car or leave it without cracking the windows, even in the winter. Heck, even in the pouring-down rain. And the times he would promise to take me to the beach. He knew how I adored the beach, and we'd end up at the mountains or the lake.

"We'd be packed. I'd be excited, and then, at the last minute he'd come up with one of his convoluted stories. With his job and all those helpless people who depended on him . . . I don't know. He had this way about him. You know how he is. You've never seen anybody like him before. It was easy to think you believed him even when you really didn't. I knew he wasn't being mean, though. He wasn't made that way, to be mean like that."

"Hannah?"

"Yes?"

"I want to ask you a personal question, okay?"

"Okay."

"Did you realize you were pregnant when you left him?"

"Yes. Yes, I did. At least I suspected I was."

"Then I am responsible."

"No," she whispered, shutting her eyes. "Just me. No one else."

"I told you right before you left, Hannah. A few weeks later you were gone."

She moved her head back and forth over the pillow, like a stubborn child refusing sleep. "You did me a favor. You did all of us a favor. It just underscored how hopeless it all was, you know, when you told me, when I found out. But I didn't leave on purpose. It just happened."

She was quiet now. He could slip away. He began easing the chair away from the bed.

"Malachi?"

He didn't speak.

"I want to tell you about how it happened."

She waited.

"You know," she said. "The whole story."

"Another time, baby. Not tonight."

"I dreamed he was here today."

"I believe he was, this morning."

"No. It's just this crap they have me on. It makes me hallucinate. Can you believe they're doing this to me? What should I do, call the police? Or I don't know, I probably need some kind of lawyer. Do you know a lawyer I can call? How can you stand it, being in here with me behaving like some silly teenager who just got high for the first time?"

He patted her shoulder again. "You're doing fine," he said. "Remarkably well."

"You see," she said, "I thought he loved me. I thought he would come to his senses and make a beehive, hell, you know what I mean, a beeline to get me, and I would tell him and he would be happy and all the bad . . . the guilt and the fear and all that uncertainty and the . . . oh, shoot, it's so dumb when you can't think of what you want to say . . . his inability to let himself go, it would just. . . ." She raised her arms up and down as if she were dropping a load of air.

"I pictured it over and over, like a scene from the movies, you know? I was here when he found me, I was there. He said this, I said that. God, I screwed it up. About Scotty, I mean. About the movies, too. I should have told her. I should have told him. . . ."

She was crying. No sound. Just tears.

"She's not . . . she's a funny little girl, Malachi. I mean, funny in an awfully sad way. Sometimes when I look at her, I hurt so much I can't tell if it's from love or pain. Maybe it's from both. I don't know. I never know."

A woman wearing baggy white trousers and carrying a tray opened the door with her backside. After parting the balloons, she stopped smiling.

"Hey, what's happening in here?"

"Hey," said Hannah.

"She's not supposed to have visitors," the woman said to Malachi. She looked to be in her late twenties or early thirties, and had moussed blond hair. "They told me she CANNOT be disturbed."

"Please don't fuss . . . I'm sorry, I can't read your name. This is her surrogate father. The godfather. The godfather of my child. He has a right to be here. You can't make him go."

"I'm Megan. They said your sister was with you."

"She went off to get some sleep. She sent him to take her place."

"Merciful father," Malachi whispered. Either Hannah Smith or the dope was a world-class liar. Could be they were teaming up. "Pleased to meet you," he said.

"Me, too," Megan said. "I'm truly sorry about your godchild but they told us she's not to have any company."

"The doctor was here," said Hannah. "She said it would be good for me."

Back when I was the first cousin, Malachi thought.

"All right. She's the boss. We've been busy, so I haven't had a chance to check your chart. But to tell you the truth, I thought they'd lost their mind, sending me in here with a tray. One of the girls told me you were in awful shape. About comatose, she said. I'm sure glad you came to. Sometimes they don't for a long time."

"No need to sugarcoat it," Malachi said.

Megan grimaced at her mistake. "Well, maybe he can help you eat," she quickly said. "You've got a little chicken bouillon here and some Jell-O, but they left off the whipped cream."

"That's all right," said Hannah. "I'm not hungry. What time is it?"

"Exactly quarter past six."

"The sign on the door says no food by mouth," said Malachi.

"It also says 'No Visitors.'"

Point well made. "Just leave it," he told Megan. "We'll have a party."

"You better not," she frowned, but made it obvious she was teasing.

"Megan?"

"Sir?"

"The nurse was supposed to bring her a pill awhile ago. Could you check on that?"

"Yessir."

"And could you do me one more favor?"

"What?"

"On the way out, grab those balloons and take them to the lady across the hall. Tell her the man who sent them says that she's a peach in peach."

"A peach in peach?"

"Those exact words."

Megan looked at Malachi like he had wandered down from the psychiatric wing on the floor above.

"Never mind," he said. "I'm right behind you. I'll deliver them myself."

"You're taking her *her* balloons?" Megan asked, gesturing with her head as she set down the tray. "Whups, there's my pager. Don't you sneak off anywhere," she said to Hannah. "I'll be watching."

"Uh-oh," Hannah said. "That smell. I'm about to be sick."

"No wonder," Malachi said, about to vomit himself.

The bedside caddy stuck out its wheel, but he maneuvered around it and lifted the tray. Bouillon sloshed out of a plastic bowl the color of what was about to come flying out of his mouth. The dietitian had to be a sadist. Holding the tray in his lap, Malachi used his free hand to drive. In the bathroom, he flushed the sewerage still under containment. He decided to save the Jell-O, though, just in case.

"Be there in a second," he said.

Hannah had just asked another question. Her voice was low and hoarse, and it was hard to hear with the tap on. Malachi splashed water on his face, and then drank some from his hand. This made him better and worse. Hannah waited until he wheeled back to the bed before she asked the question again.

"What made me stay too long?"

"Stay here?"

"No, not here. Stay there. Stay married. With him."

"You saw the bars, baby. You thought you could help him break out. That's what a woman always thinks."

"He was so tuned in. He could get under your skin before he finished shaking your hand. I mean, in a good way. He just had this . . . this . . . I don't know. Everybody could feel it was there, even when he wasn't able to say it all that hot. Why did he want to give it away to strangers?"

It wasn't a conscious choice, Malachi started to say. But she was on to something else.

"What were you like when you were little, I kept asking him. You're dying to know this man you just married, what he was like all those years you missed. Did he hate girls? What did he like to play? Where he got the idea for those icky peanut butter and date sandwiches. You know how he does. He tells you something in a way that makes you think you're getting all this information . . ." she rubbed the sleeve of her gown across her nose ". . . then later on, you realize he's hardly given up anything at all. He wouldn't even show me a photograph. He said he didn't have one. But everyone has pictures of themselves when they were growing up."

Her hand flopped through the railing, looking for a part of Malachi to touch. He was putting the Jell-O back on the caddy, close enough for her to reach after he left. Just the Jell-O, red, in a little white saucer meant for coffee. He'd parked the tray in the shower.

"I couldn't let her suffer like I had. A poor innocent child living her life that way, trying to figure out why she had a father but couldn't have him. Insecurity making her a basket case. And then, when they told me she might . . . might be. . . ."

"You weren't just trying to protect the child."

"What did you say?" Her eyes were wide. Confused.

"You were aware of his past. You loved him. You were trying to protect him as well."

Malachi couldn't look at her any more. Her child was dead, and he had a role in killing her. He'd had no business telling her. It had never been his thing, going someplace he didn't belong.

He had to get out of here. The doctor had prescribed minutes and he'd been here for days, nothing to drink but water and a shot of ginger ale. He'd outlasted his tolerance level, but a dried-up cripple with the DTs wasn't the man for the job, godfather or not.

He planned to stop by the nurse's station, though, tell them she didn't eat, that her sister hadn't returned, that she shouldn't be left alone. He would ask about the missing tranquilizer. She probably *should* call a lawyer. There seemed to be malpractice everywhere you turned.

He told her he needed to go.

"You're something," she said. "I never would've considered that."

"Considered what, that I'm over-parked in a stolen vehicle?" But he knew. She'd been wrong about her train of thought. It was definitely on the track.

"You've done it, too," she said. "I mean in different ways. When he was a boy, putting up with him when it couldn't have been comfortable for you. Opening his eyes. He used to tell me you were the person who taught him how to look at things. He might not have made it if you hadn't given him what you did. Something to replace what he didn't have."

There was no way to replace that. No way in this wide, miserable world. "It was a job," Malachi said. "I got paid."

"But it happened so long ago. He was just a little kid. This sounds awful to say but why didn't he get over it? Or at least get better. He had me and he had his friends and all those people who loved him so much. Have you ever known anybody else who had more people so absolutely crazy about them? Why couldn't I . . . why couldn't all of us sustain him? What's wrong with a person who can't let go of something he couldn't help in the first place? And what about his parents? They went off and left them, two kids that young on the beach. What kind of parents would do that?"

"It was a different time, baby. They grew up with the ocean. But I can't answer your questions. Doubt he could either. People are either one way or they're another. The way the boy died, it was bad. The way they found him. Something about a kid dying like that. He put him in the car and shut the door. Be hard to get it out of your mind."

"But his parents should have ... I don't know ... not put it out of their minds. I know they couldn't do that. Never, ever. But it was their job to help him. You told me his mother. . . ."

A woman knocked and came in. A nurse. There was no water in the pitcher. When she went to the bathroom to fill it, Malachi leaned over the bed, picked up Hannah's wrist, and kissed the adhesive tape.

"Take care of my first cousin," he whispered. Then he rescued the balloons.

"You see, you had to," Hannah said. "You had to tell me because I had a right to know."

But he was across the hall returning a favor, adjusting the A/C for a peach in peach. There was no reason for them to blow her out of the bed like that. Malachi stayed a little while. When he left, she thanked him for warming up her night.

16

In a crisis, when insight is hiding just beyond awareness, the conscious self must surrender control. But surrender is tricky. If the conscious is ordered to unlock the gates, it freezes up—a responsible pilot is trained to keep the plane in the air. That's why it must be taken by surprise. Cooper wasn't sure how it happened.

He'd seen a bald-headed child in a gray housecoat collecting tickets on a Greyhound bus, and a pink foam curler rolling back and forth over the sharp red peak of a large stone mountain, and a little girl chained to a bed of yellow daisies inside a miniature hearse. He'd seen a jolly old woman with fat rolling from her stomach and arms and neck, the woman driving a long dark car along the bank beside a lime-green building that was really a snake, the woman getting out in the roiling gray water, the water seeping over the floorboard and flooding the hem of her robe.

And he'd seen a perspiring young man ladling soup from a large black turban into bowls of cracked earthen pottery held out by multiples of the frail little girl locked in the yellow hearse, the girls becoming paper dolls joined one to another by yellow cardboard hands, waiting in an endless line that led from the big dark car at the edge of the bank to the yellow cardboard kitchen of a lime cinderblock camp; then they were girls again, desperate for servings of turkey soup and white-powdered donuts.

Next they were starving old women with heads draped in black like the wizened cripples in third-world countries who crawl up marble steps into gilded cathedrals to ask God for His holy blessing; and then he saw a little girl with stick arms knocking at a giant redwood in the Sequoia National Park, her tiny stick fist pounding and pounding on the massive trunk, the trunk slowly swinging open and pulling her into the shadows of a hollow cave, the cave becoming the trunk of the long black car, and then he fell asleep.

When he hit the shoulder and swerved back onto the highway, Cooper saw the gas gauge fluttering near empty and the sun skipping rope on the dash and the propeller of a 250-horsepower Mercury motor he came inches from clipping before he straightened the wheel. He turned on a country music station and forced Waylon Jennings to strain his lungs, then screamed gibberish along with him, because he didn't know the words to any of the songs. He shook his head like Mount Maxwell killing a cushion. Dug his nails into his wrists and thighs. Banged his fist on the steering wheel and then the dash. He had to stay awake.

He didn't know which of the fragments had triggered the release. He only knew where he was now, on Thursday, May 16, some time after six in the evening, but in the heat of Daylight Savings still afternoon.

He was twenty miles from the fringes of Columbia, ten miles west of Bowman, a small community in an insignificant crevice of the state he'd never explored. He didn't want to waste time on unfamiliar roads, take chances on variables—like her phone being out because she was boycotting Bell South or she'd misplaced the bill.

So he kept going, driving as fast as he dared, not sure whether the fumes he smelled were from the engine overheating or an embedded spill in the upholstery or his own adrenalin fueled with body odor.

"Here I am. Pull me over. Pull me, dammit, please."

If he hadn't chased turbans to the Lowcountry, his brain might have gone through another process to bring him to the same conclusion, or some other development may have resolved the mystery in a different way. But it was this trip that had led to this process of discovery, this trip that had nourished the seed that had burst to the surface like Inky Davis' world record cat.

He knew who had his daughter. And for the first time, he believed she might be all right.

Strange, he thought, how everything came back to Odds & Ends. If it hadn't been for the column, his house wouldn't have been on TV in Charlotte, and Hannah wouldn't have pointed him out to her daughter, and she wouldn't have run away to find him, and he wouldn't have had the forum to circulate her plight. If not for the column, he wouldn't have been contacted by Mrs. Garland Cayce on a stifling August day eleven years ago, or agreed to meet her and view her village made of turkey bones.

He'd known it was a stretch when he heard the message on his machine. A miniature turkey village. Walt Disney. An animated movie. But the story is incidental. What you're doing is listening to a voice, acquainting yourself with a personality, feeling your way inside. Tuning in for an inflection which appeals to your ear, a hint of something in the tone or manner of presentation, anything promising potential. Your gut is what it boils down to. You either have something or you don't, and the closer you are to deadline, the stronger the feeling is that you do. He did, all right, when he heard the voice of Mrs. Cayce.

Perhaps if he hadn't written about the Tribe of the Lost Turkeys, his daughter would have done as instructed and consulted the driver as she got off the bus, and the driver would have realized she was lost. But there had been trouble and a woman had intervened, a woman had rescued her from a predator.

If someone else's byline had been at the top of the column, would he have lost his wife and child in the first place? He didn't ask himself that question. If he had, the answer he chose would have been wrong.

·

The interview had been set for one o'clock. Cooper had arrived ten minutes late, reaching for the Professional Reporter's Notebook in his back pocket as he bounded up the widely spaced steps. It was then that he saw the sign. "PLEASE RING GONG," it said. A green arrow pointed to a corroded brass plate; the bull's-eye. A brass duck was attached to a piece of denim.

He aimed and shot. Hit the spot. Listened. Nothing. Did it again. Another time. One more. Finally he held on to the duck and banged hard. Struck a casual pose and looked around in case anyone was at the window. Still nothing.

Was this the wrong house? It seemed to be the white frame colonial she had described on the phone, a mansion in need of paint, with massive Doric columns and gargantuan English boxwood covering four enormous windows shuttered tight; definitely the centerpiece on the main street of the four-block historic district; definitely located right next to the South Carolina National Bank. She had mentioned the bank but not the clothesline strung up beside it, dressed with ridiculously racy lingerie from the Ziegfield days. This had thrown him and he had driven past the driveway. He might have missed it anyway, lost in a circle of cedar trees.

But now he spotted the Cadillac. On the opposite side from the bank, in a big weedy lot with untended azaleas, shielded by the thick dark bodies of two cedars. The car was ancient, early Garbo and Gable, her husband's contemporaries, his peers. Simon Cayce had been a famous actor. She claimed she would have been, too. Gave it up to rear his children in the old homeplace his grandfather built in 1831. Eleven anonymous miles into Lexington County, thirty miles from the capital of South Carolina. Then Simon died and left his widow to be reared by the 8,205 citizens who lived there, his admirers and acquaintances. Their children had moved away.

"No way that car could run," Cooper told her when she came to the door.

"It doesn't run," she said. "The transmission is busted."

"I must've misunderstood," he said. "I thought you drove an old black Cadillac that was parked in the yard."

"I do drive an old black Cadillac, and it is parked in the yard, but the old black Cadillac I drive is a later model. A competent reporter would have seen it."

Her deep-set wrought-iron eyes smoldered derision as she motioned towards the other side of the house. A second black Cadillac sat in front of a garage.

Hard to be observant when you're facing a woman in her bra and panties, carrying a tray containing a brown plastic pitcher and a black-handled butcher knife. She stood against the large mahogany door and motioned him through. The cavern beyond him was black. He went in.

"Have a seat in the drawing room," she told him. "I shall return."

He could barely see her. She had gone on down the hall, and was standing at an open door to one of the rooms, still holding the tray supporting the pitcher and the butcher knife.

"Don't be frightened," she said.

"Ma'am?"

"They're only bones."

He fumbled his way into a pit of ogres, hoping it was furniture. There was no logical path to take, no way to keep from bumping into something without bumping into something else.

He could see a little better now. He was in a vast bleak room of plaster with gaping wounds and forbidding Victorian wallpaper, packed with chairs and tables, two chifferobes, three sofas, a cobbler's bench, and a stagecoach wagon, confronted by an avalanche of costumes, crocheted bedspreads, table linens and playbills, the whole permeated with odors of soured laundry, bad plumbing, and a death chemical like formaldehyde. And something cooking in the back of the house; a comfort food: turkey.

Was this his designated hell, to be buried alive in a house of horrors operated by a murderess in a Maidenform bra, a madwoman who would soon return and stab him to death while he was trapped in the clutches of a mildewed, sway-backed loveseat next to a tray of petrified donuts and a pile of wilted celery? He prayed to God to let it happen fast. The smells were making him sick.

He found the bones. A hint of white against the dark, arranged on three tables joined together in front of draperies made from plush maroon brocade. Some were dressed as cowboys and Indians, others as soldiers. Two of the larger bones were riding on horseback, wearing tiny sombreros, carrying a banner between them with tiny printing. He stepped over a bolt of frayed silk fabric and read it. "Welcome to the Tribe of the Lost Turkeys," it said.

His hostess came back without the tray. Her red silk blouse billowed with ruffles. But no matching skirt. A painted turkey bone hung from her neck, joined to a crucifix. She began to wave her arms and kick her legs high over her bouncing belly. Cooper sank farther down into the mildew.

Garland Cayce told the story of her life. Meeting Simon, nursing him through his illnesses, grieving over his death. Competing against Babe Didrikson Zaharias in the high jump. Modeling and then dancing with Zeigfeld and the Rockettes.

She acted with the Marx Brothers and Bela Lugosi. She rejected the advances of producers and other Lotharios. She was the girl with a thousand faces.

She pranced, knelt, tiptoed, squatted, struck a Lucky Strike model's pose.

"The only legs in Hollywood insured for a million dollars," she said.

"What about Betty Grable's?"

"A mere publicity stunt."

Suddenly, with a dramatic flop, Garland collapsed on a stack of cardboard boxes. She couldn't go on. She suffered from leg cramps, she said, caused by the large mats in her hair, which developed when she was ill with pneumonia. She patted her lopsided French twist and twirled around so Cooper could see.

Then she went away again. When she came back, she was wearing a skirt over her panties and a white silk turban on her head.

"You make that hat look good," Cooper told her.

Garland curtseyed and beamed.

"An elementary trick of the trade. To survive in this dog-eat-dog business, you learn to cover up your sins at an early age."

•

Cooper pressed hard on the gas. Shifted forward, stood on the pedal. Couldn't get a number past 85.

He knew who had his daughter. At any second a gust of air from a passing car would lift him off the ground and he could fly.

All these hours he'd been fighting nightmares of rape and torture: of a fragile little body buried alive to feed the alligators in Hell Hole Swamp; of Scotty hidden in a freezer, chopped into convenient parts to fit into the various storage bins.

Now, just like that, he was tunneling out of a place where evil men in masks committed despicable acts of horror and spinning towards nothing more threatening than the topsy-turvy playground of Alice and her friends, a world where accidental mishaps didn't guarantee a fatal ending, where the prospect of happier ever after wasn't one of God's cruelty jokes.

Of course, she could have been poisoned by an undercooked turkey drumstick, or gotten lost in a knickknack mountain of old Broadway memorabilia, or broken a leg tripping over a piece of furniture telekinetically transported from Bela Lugosi's attic. She could have wandered into the dining room, fallen into a pot expecting a raw turkey, and been stewed for bones.

But the dynamic had changed. Because although the guardian of these bones had a zest for terrorizing, it was just part of the show. Cooper had seen Garland Cayce interact with children. She wouldn't intentionally hurt a child. Garland Cayce was a child herself.

He'd agonized over the column. What to say, whether to even write it. But she'd been eager to tell her story, hungry for whatever glimmer of limelight she could get. To her, the Tribe of the Lost Turkeys was a brilliant work of art—her take on the universal themes of life. How many fairy tales and sci-fi classics had been produced in equally imaginative forms?

He would be exposing the sad, bizarre existence of an eccentric woman with enormous pride. Is it exploitation if you don't believe you're being exploited, or if you want to be? His deadline could have been a year away and he still wouldn't have been able to figure it out.

He told the story straight, as though her life were as ordinary as the next person's. And in some ways it probably was, if you could know all the secrets the so-called ordinary people were hiding. Just look at him: He had a daughter he'd never seen, a daughter whose own brain didn't connect up in the typical way. A daughter determined to find her father even though he'd killed his own brother. And against all odds she seemed about to succeed.

Garland bought the turkeys after the sell-by dates had expired. At midnight, when the Piggy Wiggly manager could save himself a trip to the dumpster by filling up her shopping bags and she could pay the bill with nickels and dimes. Then she went home and preserved the perishables with salt and vinegar brine that accounted for the formaldehyde smell.

She tossed the wilted vegetables and overripe fruit to the side, to put in the turkey stew when she made it for the food bank at Blessed Sacrament Church. The volunteers had no choice but to throw it away. But Garland ate hers for dinner, sitting at a card table across from a huge portrait of Simon Cayce propped against a Queen Anne chair.

"If weren't for the Tribe of the Lost Turkeys and for her husband," Cooper had written, "she might be lonely."

Why had it taken him this long to make the connection? The white turban. The old black Cadillac. She'd stopped driving it to New York after a breakdown on the New Jersey Turnpike.

But she continued to spend weeks and sometimes months in the apartment on Central Park South, taking the Greyhound to Midtown Manhattan, suffering through eighteen tedious hours and another fifty minutes before she could parade through the Port Authority, dragging whatever treasures she'd managed to stuff into the suitcases and plastic bags that exceeded the required limit.

From there, it was no more than a twenty-minute cab ride to the building of once modest apartments that a billionaire real estate tycoon had transformed into a condo palace. Simon had leased the apartment decades ago at a frozen rate of $209 a month. The new landlord raised the rent to twenty-five times what the couple was paying, then tried to evict Garland after she refused to shell out. Who was he kidding? She took him to court and won lifetime rights, which she loved to rub in his nose.

◆

Cooper squealed into the driveway on two wheels. What about the medication? Hannah had told him she might be all right for . . . what had she said . . . a few hours? a few days? . . . but in Vegas, a bet on the reliability of a pharmaceutical promise wouldn't draw more than a laugh. What would happen if her heart lost its rhythm? Could she have a heart attack? Pass out and die? Imagining her with Garland in a medical emergency made him crazy.

He beat at the door with the gong, then with his fists. He couldn't get to the windows. The boxwood shoved him away. So he ran toward the side of the house, screaming her name. Not his daughter's name. The name that came naturally. The name of the person he knew.

Where was the car? There, parked in its spot in front of the garage, burning up in the shade. Parked with the windows shut tight. He ran towards it, but his legs didn't want him to get there. Didn't want him to find her. Suffocated. Dead.

All he could see in the car were clothes. Clothes everywhere. Loose on the cracked leather seats and on the floor. Hanging from the jaws of suitcases. Clothes, and a yellow knapsack with. . . .

And then he heard the voice.

" . . . and mister, you might be looking for the lady of the house. . . . "

He wasn't sure how long it had taken him to hear it or where it was. It wasn't in the car.

". . . and if you are she's inside and I can. . . ."

Over in a grove of pears behind the porch. Coming towards him. Pears in her hands. *Light brown hair cut short. Topped with soft bangs. Pale blue eyes. She was frail. If someone tried to hurt her she'd have trouble. . . .* A frail little girl walking, talking, carrying too many pears. She was having a time dragging her dress through the high grass. The dress had spangles on it. Red and white and black. It wasn't a dress for a little girl. Parts of the bottom were missing. There was a pointed scallop and then a slit, another scallop and another slit. The slits were too short and the scallops were too long. They caught in the grass and in her sandals. *Red sandals fastened with Velcro on the. . . .*

". . . go get her if you'd like because sometimes her ears don't pay attention and. . . ." Stopping now, stopping to put down the pears. Pears tumbling out of delicate little hands onto the red sandals. ". . . and I guess you might be lost because you look like you might need some nice ice-cold water like we have in the refrigerator at our house at 2406 Pinetop Road in Charlotte, North Carolina, in a. . . ."

But where was the other dress? The white sundress sprinkled with flowers. This dress was obscene. This must be another child, parading around in a costume that belonged to a tired old stripper in a seedy burlesque show. She must belong to someone else.

And then he was sitting on the ground, leaning against the car, the metal warm on his back. The setting sun was dancing off the spangles, dancing off the spangles and into his eyes, and all he could see were floaters and spangles and light, and a frail little girl standing beside him, asking if he needed help. This frail little child in a spangled dress, asking him if his eyes were hurting or if he had a fever, asking him if he was about to die.

17

The kidnapper was busy in the kitchen, confronting an ugly mess. Soupy brown gravy with chunks of poultry and English peas flooded over the sides of a mason jar filled with turkey stew onto a soiled cloth napkin stuffed into a picnic basket.

"Where's a phone?" Cooper asked.

"Mister Blue Eyes," Garland said, glancing up. "Just in the knick of time. You can help us load."

She'd just turned years into minutes. How many had it been since he'd seen her last? Seven? Ten? Was the last time when he'd taken her to the Dairy Queen for a BLT and butterscotch sundae? Or when she'd called him to pick her up after the Cadillac had died at a strawberry farm in Irmo, which just happened to be three miles around the bend from the home of Maxine and Pierre Springs.

The kitchen looked the same, a galley after the train derailed, but the smell was worse. Although the air conditioning was miraculously blasting through ceiling vents barricaded with rust, mildew and dust, Garland had apparently shut it off the month she was away.

Roaches lay dead on the floor, piled in twos and threes. Turkey entrails were bleeding in the sink.

". . . and they have no appreciation for the sacrifices I make for them. Who do they think they are? Days and weeks, weeks and months go by, and not a single one of my charities bothers to grace the premises with so much as a thank-you-ma'am."

"Garland, I have to call her mother. Garland, listen up. The police should be here any minute. I need a phone."

"The police? No one here is expecting the police."

Cooper crossed the dining room, stepping around enormous pots of brine. The little girl was following, telling him it was very dark in there and that he might fall and hurt his hand on something sharp.

"Did you fall?" he asked her. "Did you cut yourself?"

"Yes, mister, and if you're bleeding that nice lady back there will fix you a bandage out of her hat and you only have to keep it on until the blood dries up and makes a scab."

Garland dug around in a drawer, fishing out complimentary packets of saltines. She had on silk pajamas, the top black and the bottoms periwinkle blue. A contingent of fruit flies swarmed around the guts in the sink. She waved the saltines toward the dining room like an infomercial maven signaling the last chance for a miracle cracker crusher, the deal of a lifetime.

"And just look what they have at their doorstep. None other than Simon Cayce. And what about his bride, highly accomplished in her own right? She could have gone anywhere in the world and they would have rolled out the royal red carpet. But here in this two-bit burg, they turn up their noses, treat her with disdain."

It was hard to see in the drawing room, even though a panel of drapery had been propped open with the marble base of a shadeless lamp. Scotty took him to a black rotary phone submerged in a pile of costumes. He dialed the "0" and got an empty hiss.

"Listen to me, Garland," Cooper shouted. "Does the telephone work?"

"No, mister," the child answered. "That lady in there cooking the turkey she took out of that pot with the smelly colored water in it tried to use the phone, but she had to hang it up because there was no noise on the other end."

"You know more about the operation of the household than she does," Cooper said. He picked his way to the front door and yanked it open. At least the officers wouldn't have to ring the gong. Then he grabbed Scotty's hand and led her back to the kitchen.

"Ah, Little Miss Sunshine," Garland said. "The gatherer of the pears. She returns empty-handed."

She reeled toward Cooper, pointing a finger.

"Shame on you. A child as old as that with no idea how to shimmy up a tree. I had to instruct her to do the best she could on the ground. There's nothing to pick through after the worms and squirrels finish making pigs of themselves. The squirrels are lazy bums. They'd rather eat dreck off the dirt than do a decent day's work on a ladder. No one wants to put himself out any more, even the animals. Succumb, refuse to strive, settle for second rate. No wonder we're in such pathetic decline.

"What were you thinking, rearing a child with no basic skills? Athletic prowess is essential. Makes a girl independent. Self-assured. Women get pushed around even when we're strong. I told her when I was her age, I was competing in. . . ."

Cooper needed to sit but all the chairs were covered in rodent droppings. Garland's flimsy sense of reality had deteriorated in the years since he'd been here. Or maybe it hadn't. His perceptions weren't always on target.

Alice in Wonderland? What had he been thinking? A deranged woman had rescued this child. Anything could have happened. For two days and nights, an innocent nurtured in a haven of reason and order had been incarcerated in a toxic asylum of madness.

Garland wasn't wearing her disguise. The bald patches in her short hair had been dredged by nature rather than the slash of a blade. She was all gray now, and old.

Cooper looked around the kitchen, finally spotting the turban where she'd tossed it, on a small red stool near an open cabinet with more dead roaches inside. He walked over and kicked it to the floor. The gauzy white cotton was ripped where she'd cut it to make a bandage. Suddenly, he lunged towards the counter and leaned across it, inches from Garland's face.

"What . . . what in the hell . . . did . . . did you think you were doing?" He was shaking and couldn't stop. Garland flinched, as though he'd hit her.

"Save me," she pleaded to Scotty. "Help. Please. Help."

Scotty hurried over and grabbed his arm.

"You behave yourself, mister," she said. "No bullies allowed. No bullies allowed in the house or on the playground."

The bully was on the red stool now, a miniature dunce stool for an oversized dunce. Where were the police?

"Tell me, Garland, what gives you the right to . . . to ignore the rules . . . the . . . the most basic laws of society? Do you realize you could be charged with first-degree kidnapping? Do you realize she takes medication for her heart? Look at her. Can't you see she's starving to death?"

But he was the egregious party, attacking a person governed by her own private society, a society where there were no laws; a world he'd accepted until she'd expanded it to include a missing child.

"I intended to bring her over," Garland said, cowed and speaking softly. "Just as soon as we completed the projects. Of course, I'd considered calling, but I couldn't remember where I put your number. I couldn't get it from directory assistance because I've been having a little trouble with my telephone."

"Then why didn't you take her to the police station?" he demanded.

"The keystone cops? Frighten her out of her wits when she was in perfectly good hands with me?"

"But what about her mother? Didn't you know the child was lost? Don't you realize you can't just take a child off a bus and not let anyone know you have her for days? That you. . . ."

She snapped at him then, her black eyes blazing with the old indignant fire. She assumed that her mother had put her on the bus. Why else would a child be riding on a Greyhound all alone? She assumed that he would be there to meet her. The child had produced his name, properly spelled, with only one "t." It was written in magic marker on a piece of paper she had in her knapsack, written in a legible adult hand. According to the child, it was written by the mother. It mentioned he lived in Columbia, and his position, columnist for Odds & Ends. It offered a personal description of his humorous bent and considerate manner. It was even accompanied by a drawing that showed his black hair and blue eyes.

"'What a coincidence,' I told her. 'Your father is one of my oldest friends.' That was before I'd discovered the kind of person you really are." She glared at him before going on. "When I didn't find you waiting outside, I brought her home. What did you expect me to do, leave her wandering around the bus station to be molested by another perverted hooligan?"

◆

"You want it on or off?" Sgt. Mindy Allen asked him for the second time. She was chesty, with tinted glasses, and wore an auburn wig styled in a bouffant flip. Being short, she had to navigate the headrest to look over her shoulder. "Obviously we'll get there faster with it on, except I don't know but what it might upset your little girl."

Cooper stared out the window. The sun was a dull red bruise the color of his bloodshot eyes. It was eight o'clock. He'd been beating up the roads all day in a clunker with no air conditioning, him with no sleep, and only a bagful of undigested Krispy Kremes. But that wasn't what had done him in.

"I don't know, either," he said.

"It's your call."

He ran a hand through his stringy hair. He wanted to ask if he could make the decision lying down. His arms and face were the burnished red of a cooked olive skin. A beard of Clarendon County topsoil grew from his cheekbones down the creases of his neck into the collar of his potholed t-shirt.

"I guess off," he said, but the words didn't make it to the front. "Off," he said again.

"Yessir."

"She takes medicine for her heart."

"We're aware of that."

Scotty was buckled in beside the sergeant, still wearing the spangled costume, a get-up from one of the early Rockettes' Christmas shows at Radio City Music Hall. It had been designed for a number called "Jing-a-Ling the Reindeer Dance." The girls had bells on their antlers and boots, tinkling in synchronized perfection with every kick. Garland had been teaching Scotty the steps.

"I couldn't resist," she'd crowed to Cooper after he'd settled down enough to ask her where the outfit had come from. "That child is gaga over Christmas, isn't she? 'Miss, I sure would like to dance just like you do,' she told me. She has such flair, such joie de vivre, and her manners are flawless. I'm surprised you haven't enrolled her in classes for the performing arts by now. The younger the better, they always say. That certainly proved true in my case. I'd teach her myself except my time is presently taken up with other projects."

Already, the brown Crown Victoria smelled like Garland's house. The costume's glittery fabric was covered in mold. The stained white sequined bodice, fitted for Rockette-sized breasts, gapped open in the front. To hold the top up, Garland had to cut the thin black straps off the back of the dress and tie them around Scotty's neck.

Cooper moved close to the sergeant's ear.

"She'll need to see a doctor," he whispered.

"We're on it," Allen said.

At 6:23 p.m., the Richland County Sheriff's Department had received the 911 report that Scotty had been found. Sgt. Allen, the highest ranking female officer on duty, got the call to check it out. After verifying that the missing child was safe and alert, Lt. Lewis had taken over at the Columbia PD, hurrying to notify Frances, put the ER on standby, and issue a bulletin suspending the search. Then he'd headed to the hospital to wait with Hannah.

"All set, little lady?" Allen asked.

Scotty nodded.

"Then let's give 'em a holler."

Allen's uniform cap was hooked on the radio mike. She passed it over to Scotty.

"Try it on if you want to, honey."

"Thank you, miss." Scotty put the hat in her lap.

The sergeant began speaking in a foreign language of numbers and codes.

The child in the front seat, a 10-57 in transport, was "with the father and appears to be stable." But how could she tell? Cooper wondered. What was the baseline, the criteria? Compared to other children her age, the child in transport appeared fragile, pale.

You couldn't read her eyes. They weren't like her mother's, an intense variegated green that gave her emotions away like a free coupon at the mall. Scotty's eyes were blue, but not head-turners like her father's. The blue was pale, filtered with a touch of gray.

She hadn't been shy when they were in the house. "A regular talking machine," Garland had called her. "Reminds me of this adorable comedienne I once palled around with in the thirties, a real chatterbox, as skinny as a Virginia Slim. Does that description ring a bell with you? My memory for names has deserted me of late. I was chummy with so many of them back then. . . ."

Sgt. Allen patted Scotty on the knee.

"Ready to see your mom?" she asked.

Scotty nodded, but there was no joy in it.

"Wonder if she slept," Cooper mumbled. "And where?"

"I didn't catch that," Allen replied.

"That's okay," he said.

He closed his eyes and saw her plodding through the tall grass, stopping, redistributing the pears, losing a few. Trying to run, tripping on the spangles, dropping the rest of the pears to grab his hand. Tugging, struggling to help him off the ground, toppling onto his chest instead.

He was pulling her away from the old black car, pulling her towards the house, or maybe she was pulling him. Then he changed direction, heading next door toward the bank, squeezing the tiny little fingers tight enough to break one, ducking under the empty clothesline and leading her to a dark blue sedan.

A woman was leaning out the window, using the ATM. She yanked her money from the slot while she locked the door with her elbow. Cooper introduced himself, told her he needed help. She'd recognized him then, and since the bank was closed, sped off to find a phone.

Now, with Sgt. Allen confidently weaving the unmarked patrol car through traffic on the Lexington Highway and the child safe in the front seat, Garland's explanation began to make sense.

What mother would put a child on the Greyhound without expecting the father to meet her on the other end? And when the father wasn't there like he should have been, what person would leave a child in the terminal all alone?

Garland had fed Scotty. She'd given her a dancing lesson and recognized she wasn't able to climb a tree. And what if she hadn't taken her off the bus? What would have happened to her then?

The child had called it right. He was a bully. Garland, difficult and impossible, tiring and self-absorbed, was no more malicious than a nagging sinus headache. He should have been covering her with kisses instead of frightening her to death. Of course she'd intended to take action. To Garland, time was merely numbers on a clock that didn't run. In that they had plenty in common.

Scotty was riding quietly, a tiny porcelain figurine swallowed up by a spangled dress. Sgt. Allen had fastened the seatbelt beneath her arms. Besides being pale and thin, she struck Cooper as plain more than anything else. Until she began to speak. Then she was appealing. Warm, and cute. But it went beyond that. Her animation, the enthusiastic sincerity behind it, the purity of her observations, brought you out of yourself. She gave you a lift.

Most children, adults even, would've been traumatized by a stay with Garland Cayce, but Scotty had been at home. Not good, he thought. But on the other hand, there was the way she'd taken over. Different drummer or not, she had a mind of her own.

"That's right, mister. That big grown bully on the bus was not supposed to put his hands on a strange child because a child cannot let a man she doesn't know touch her on her arm or on her leg or on any of her private places because it's not nice and he should know that he will get in real big trouble because it's her job to turn him in.

"But I did eat, mister. I ate turkey out of that big yellow bowl in the kitchen and a banana that this very nice lady over here had packed in a Ziploc plastic bag with some raisins and some cookies with chocolate chips in them like Miss Mac allows me to have at home for a treat, and the banana was good for me even if it had those brown spots in it that my mom told me to learn to pick out by myself because I'm too old to expect her and Miss Mac to do everything for me, and this morning I had a peanut butter and jelly sandwich from another plastic bag and a drink of water because we were out of juice and milk but that was okay because the doctor said to drink plenty of water to clean out the rusty pipes and for lunch I had another peanut butter and jelly sandwich because I didn't care for any more of that turkey and. . . .

"That's a very nice lady over there, mister. After we finish feeding the people at the church who don't have any money to eat a healthy meal with meat and vegetables in a restaurant, she's taking me to see my daddy, and you can come with us if you can behave. My daddy has a nice big Christmas tree on his porch and a fat brown dog with a red bow around his neck and he can't wait to see me because he loves me very much."

Cooper sat forward, bumping into the wig, recoiling from the watermelon scent of the hairspray. My God, he thought. She doesn't know who I am.

He'd been too rattled to catch it during the inquisition at Garland's, weak and reeling from the wash of so many emotions, the child's rush of words flying at him and over him and around him with the speed of the Concorde while he was fighting to keep from being blown out of the kitchen window by the force of the supersonic tailwinds.

But now he knew why she had turned so solemn. They were taking her to see her mother but she'd come to find her daddy. The daddy who was not an ACOUNTINT who rode to work every day on the bus and on her mommy's AREPLANE and in a big blue car. The daddy with a humorous bent and considerate manner. She'd come to find her daddy and all she'd found was a bully, a coward by the name of Mister.

Sgt. Allen was reaching for the mike again. Another block and they would be at the entrance. Cooper leaned back and put his face in his hands. His whiskers were grimy and rough. In the morning, he'd be sure and ask Sam if K-Mart sold bowties to bullies.

◆

Scotty didn't want to sit in the wheelchair. She didn't want her aunt to lift her up in her arms like a baby, either. She pressed the elevator button when Lt. Lewis asked her to. She was quiet, holding Frances' hand as they rushed through the halls, ignoring the waves and con-gratulations and stares.

"Wait one short second," Frances told her at the door of Hannah's room.

"Okay, Aunt Frances," she said, and darted in behind her, a streak of streaming spangles, a burst of red, white and black fireworks on the Fourth of July, the little red sandals racing toward the recliner Cooper had sat in early that morning, the one where her mother was sitting now, sobbing and holding out her arms.

He sat down on the bed. How could anybody describe it?

The mother standing, buckling, colliding with the child. Both of them falling together in the chair. The thin, white arms wrapped around a tiny set of spangled ribs. The IV pole teetering, eager to crash the party, then Frances, piling into the chair.

Talking, laughing, crying. Hannah, Scotty, Frances. A nurse, the two officers, an attractive female doctor who'd come in to examine Scotty, or Hannah, or both.

"Be quiet," he wanted to shout. "Be still."

But he was transfixed. The child, a hummingbird caught in a net, fluttering one way and then another, looking for a hole to escape from the web of arms. Her mother, too weak to hold on.

And words. About a bus, a very nice lady, her costumes, some very healthy stew for the poor. Words tumbling out, tumbling faster, flooding toward the mother—disoriented and ecstatic as she tried to absorb them, sobbing, giggling, clutching the wisp of a child in a tangle of arms and tubes.

Were you hurt? What are you doing in that ghastly dress? How in the world did you figure out how to ride a bus? Have you had anything to eat? Haven't I told you over and over again not to associate with strangers? Don't you realize you've worried us half to death? Do you promise me on the life of Noodle that you will never, ever, ever, run away from home again as long as you live?

Cooper wanted to address Hannah's questions. He wanted to snatch the answers from his brain, to explain things, to let her know that everything was fine. Her daughter was back. She could come alive now, perk up, look pretty again the way she had when they were young.

Frances had helped her try. She'd combed her oily hair and pulled what she could into a stumpy ponytail, but the starkness sharpened the angle of her cheekbones and accented the hollows beneath her eyes. She'd helped her paint a frosty mauve color on her lips and cheeks, but the color looked ludicrous against the pale. She could have been a prop in a haunted house. Except for the eyes. The Ava Gardner eyes on fire with drugs and joy and love, the most dazzling love Cooper was sure he'd ever seen.

And her daughter, this strangely resilient little girl. From her casual manner, she could've just returned from a stroll in Maxcy Gregg Park down the street. What did she know? How could he know? How could anyone know?

"I'll be outside," he whispered.

He could hear her talking down the hall.

"And Mama, it will be all right for you to stay in the hospital and get your rest because as soon as I can find my daddy he will tell you that I can live with him in that house with the Christmas tree on the porch until you get well and then we can all go to our real house in Charlotte, North Carolina, and. . . ."

The stairwell door was slow to close. Cooper pulled it shut behind him. Hannah would know the right thing to say.

18

Cooper leaned against the door to the bar, holding a mug of beer. Eddie's Lounge was the neighborhood watering hole for weekend bikers. A few authentic bad boys sometimes dropped by, but the regular customers plagiarized their hell-raising feats from Charles Bronson movies and their own embellished dreams.

Jay was one of the regulars. He'd begun auditioning for a gig in Odds & Ends two hours ago, when he'd picked the empty stool on the author's left. He made it through the preliminaries by shooting a balmy breeze and chasing Miller's on tap with BI-LO's cut-rate cashews. Now he was just another swig away from being selected.

Using his pinky, Jay reunited a loose strand of hair with the few left in the center of his crown. "Let me tell you a little secret, son," he said. "Lovin' might grow hair on your chest but it sure dudn' put any on your head." He laughed, an explosion that thundered to an end with "I'm not lyin' to you, hell."

The pencil skidded to a stop in Cooper's subliminal notebook. His Professional Reporter's Notebook, the one with NEWS blocked across the top. *The color. What was the color of his hair?*

He straightened up and cocked his head. Okay, let's see. Definitely in the cordovan family. Think of the rusty old Kiwi tin, the one covered with dust and dings in the corner of the bathroom closet. Think of the color on the rag beside it. But there's a greenish tinge. Could have been a crummy home basin job or it could've been the overhead bug light. That gold distorted things. You'd have to see it in the daylight. Cooper left the line blank.

"Say what?" Jay asked.

"Just talking to myself. Hey, Jay, mind if I ask you something personal?"

"No," he said. "I'll either tell you or clobber you, one."

"Just remember it wouldn't take much to tip me over."

Jay nodded, lifting his mug. "Go ahead. Shoot."

"Okay. If you were quoted in the newspaper, say, in a human interest column, for instance, would you rather talk like you actually do, or like . . . well, more like a commentator for PBS?"

Jay looked baffled. "Like myself, I suppose. Why?"

"No reason. Just something work related."

Cooper set his mug on the window ledge and wondered what Percy was doing. Dancing under the stars in her studio, that's what, the *South Pacific* album scratching away . . . *"Once you have found her never let her. . . ."* No, they wouldn't be practicing this time of night. *"Once you have found her,"* just walk right out the door and into a bar you didn't mean to enter until you found yourself inside getting drunk.

Jay backed up and glanced towards the door. "Um, looks like your man's got lost," he said. "Why don't we go have a seat and chill down, have us one more to grow on?"

Cooper hesitated. "I don't know. I said I'd be out front." Out front practically meant on the street, since none of the structures on the short block had much of a setback.

"Phew. It feels like we been standing here all night," Jay said. He swiped at some sweat under his chin. "What's he rolling, his kid's trike?"

"No way. He's rolling none other than a black Lincoln Continental convertible, circa 1961. Push a button on the dash and the top folds in on itself and gets swallowed up whole by the trunk."

"I'll be dog. He a collector?"

"Yeah, trouble. The car's not his. The woman it belongs to can't see to drive at night. He'll show up in a minute. He had to come from the other side of town."

"Hell, if he's that far away he won't show by the weekend. One of those old granny buggies wouldn't make thirty if you put it on skis and shot it off the top of Caesar's Head. Why don't he just use his own ride and get it over with?"

"He can't. It's in a ditch somewhere in Rock Hill."

"You shittin' me. These people sound like nuts. You couldn't get nobody else?"

Cooper shook his head.

"Damn heat's a killer," Jay said. "Guess I can take it another minute or two. Then I better get on home to Mama. Eddie's about to shut down anyhow."

Business was slow for a Thursday night. A half hour ago, Eddie Limehouse, the owner of the bar, had told the five or six customers left that he couldn't see running up his electric bill so they could blow another point on the breathalyzer.

Cooper had done a column on Eddie once. He was a good-hearted man with wavy gray hair who was famous for making hotdogs. That's all Eddie sold, hotdogs and domestic beer. After he lost his right hand in a bad skid on his Low Rider, Eddie had a friend at the Claussen's Bread plant work up the measurements on a standard-sized bun. Then he'd commissioned a prosthetics outfit to design a customized leather glove to scale. A month later he was back in business.

"Hey." Cooper nudged the air with an elbow meant for Jay. "I think he's coming now."

He swayed toward the curb and waved an arm back and forth. It was dark, except for a dim street light three doors down in front of Kinko's Copy Shop. Eddie's was on a side street in a mixed zoning residential neighborhood around the corner from a small Baptist church.

"Comin' is right," Jay said. "He'd better slow up or he'll. . . . Yo. It's not him, it's grammaw. Move it, dude. Fast."

Brakes screeched. The Lincoln jumped the curb.

"Hold your horses, lady," Jay screamed. "This ain't a friggin' drive-thru."

Margaret didn't hold anything. She managed to swerve past Cooper and Jay, but hooked up with the muffler pipes of a platinum black Harley parked on the sidewalk six feet from where they'd been standing. The bike was a customized Softtail FXST with what seconds before had been freshly polished silver chrome. The rider, a lapsed Hell's Angel named Stray, was inside, finishing a draft before he set out to return the bike to his cousin.

"Get back, everybody," Jay cried.

Tony, a retired Merchant Marine, was standing next to his Road King, talking to an upholsterer's apprentice named Charlie. They ran.

The car lurched forward, carrying the Softtail on its nose.

"She's out of control," yelled Jay.

She was, until she met a stronger force—the cinderblock face of the bar.

The door opened, followed by three customers looking belligerent and bewildered, as if they weren't sure what they might have to fight. Eddie hurried behind them. The last man out was Stray, a dark figure in black dungarees and a black denim vest missing half its fringe. He confronted the scene with his legs spread apart, hands primed near his sides, like he was about to draw.

"God-a-mighty," he said. "God-a-mighty damn."

"She better have insurance," said Eddie, whose glove was stuffed with dirty napkins.

"Don't worry," Cooper said. "She's rich."

The convertible was dancing in place. The Harley's right fender had been decimated by the window ledge. Cooper's beer swam for its life in a sea of crushed glass.

Margaret fastened onto the gear stick again, put it someplace between neutral and reverse, and gunned it. The car skittered in place and then jerked backwards, dragging the bike along with it. The muffler pipes were locked on the bumper.

"Brake, Margaret. Hit the brake."

That came from Malachi, huddled behind her. He'd sat in back when Margaret insisted on driving. When she'd hopped the curb, he made a dive toward a nest of hair on the floor—the spot where her old Springer spaniel crouched when she took him for a Sunday ride.

"Margaret," Cooper screamed. "Cut the engine."

The motor continued racing. The Continental pitched and heaved again, then stopped. Margaret revved it a few more times before it stalled in a gag of black fumes spewing from the exhaust. The stink of hotdogs, cigarettes, and beer the guys had worked all night to earn didn't have a chance against the burnt rubber smoking off the whitewalls.

Cooper crept over and tapped on the glass.

"It's flooded, Margaret," Malachi yelled. "Leave the key alone."

Margaret turned the key. The sound was ugly. Cooper rapped on the window again. "Open the door," he mouthed.

"How?" Margaret asked.

"Lord help the little children," muttered Malachi.

"The handle," Cooper said. "There, by your side."

Tony and Charlie were moving out to the street to get a better look, but Jay barged in front, roping them off with his hefty arms.

"Stand clear," he ordered. "This thing's not over yet."

"Margaret, listen," yelled Cooper. "The door's locked."

Malachi fought the starch in Cooper's white shirt to reach up and feel for the electric panel embedded in the arm rest. Dancing his fingers across the buttons, testing keys on a trick piano, he opened two windows before hitting the right note.

Margaret came out of her funk and hissed an order. "Play it down."

Cooper struggled with the door, dreading the mangled body parts he was about to face, lowering his lids to half mast to cut the view.

"Is anybody hurt?" He bent over to look inside, kneeling to keep his balance. It was hard to see. The Lincoln's interior light wasn't working, the low wattage street light was too far away, and the bug bulb above the bar put out as much glow as a dried-up lemon.

"Talk to me, Margaret. Are you okay?" Cooper reached across her lap to cut the ignition. She looked grim but didn't seem to be bleeding.

"I'll let you know in the morning," she said. "If I can crawl out of bed that's a good indication I'm alive."

"See if you can wiggle your fingers."

Margaret wiggled.

"What about your arms and hands?"

"They're attached."

"Dammit, Malachi. What possessed you, letting her do something like this? She could've killed herself. She's not supposed to drive after dark."

"Her car. Her keys." Malachi was easing up from the floor. Tufts of white hair clung to the back of his light blue Bermuda shorts. He'd shucked the khakis after his trip to the hospital. A man had to stand for something.

"Anything wrong with you?" Cooper asked.

"Nothing a good shot of leg won't cure. But Margaret banged her head. We better take her to the emergency room."

"Go ahead," Cooper said. "I'll wait here."

"Not on your life," Malachi said.

"You're not taking her anywhere, bubba," Stray said. "Not 'til she deals with me first."

"Car's not drivable," Malachi said to Cooper. "We'll have to call an ambulance."

"You let me be the judge of that," Margaret said.

"This is your second crash in less than ten hours," Malachi said. "A subdural hematoma is nothing to fool around with."

"My skull is too thick for any of that," said Margaret. "Now come along. We're wasting time."

"Wait a minute, buddy." Stray moved Cooper aside to lean into the car. The bristles on his Fu Manchu weren't thick enough to shield his breath. Stray had been swimming in Blatz for two days and nights without taking a break to brush his teeth. "That was my cousin's bike," he said to Margaret. "He don't know I took it. You screwed me all to hell."

"Highly unlikely," said Margaret.

Her thin lips were set. Some damp strands of white hair had escaped the clasp of a tarnished turquoise barrette that sat cockeyed at the back of her neck. One sleeve of her silk paisley dress was unbuttoned at the wrist, already purple from a collision with the dash.

She took Cooper's arm, permitting him to pull her out of the car. After looking him up and down, she squinted over at Stray. You would've thought she'd just drawn the short straw for riding pillion on Sonny Barger's bike, bareback. Cooper put a hand over the tear that exposed his nipple.

"I wish I'd known," Margaret said. "I wouldn't have bothered to dress."

She provided insurance information to Stray, and offered to speak to his cousin on his behalf. He told her not to worry about it, that he'd be thumbing to Mexico before his cousin got up to go to work.

Jay, Tony, and Charlie separated the Softtail from the Lincoln, then went inside to look for something they could use to shore up the bumper and keep it from dragging the street.

Eddie inspected the building. The damage wasn't bad—shattered glass and missing chunks of concrete around the window, and a horizontal trail of heavy black scrape marks.

"I'm thinking about immortalizing the spot," he said. "You could take a can of red paint; spray some arrows here and there. Write something like, 'This is where Margaret Motte Burns laid it down.'"

"That would be grand," Margaret said. "But I didn't realize we were acquainted."

"Everybody knows who you are."

"Is that so? Then I suppose I should've been more careful."

"Don't worry, ma'am. Accidents happen to the best of us."

"No, Eddie, she was just being facetious. . . ." Margaret quickly sliced a finger across her neck, the signal for Cooper to terminate.

"Thank you," she said to Eddie. "Well, if I'm being considered for such an enviable distinction, perhaps you can tell me what it was that I laid down."

Eddie explained.

"How disappointing," she said. "I was under the impression it related to my feminine wiles."

•

They were back in the Lincoln, nobody dead, including the motor. Margaret had asked Eddie to try it before he called a wrecker. It caught on the second turn.

"The karma of the privileged class," Malachi said. He'd just come back from the bar. He took a long draw from the plastic cup before swapping places with Eddie. There was no way that Margaret's ten-ton Birkenstock was getting near the gas again, even with a Seeing Eye dog in her lap. Earlier, she'd pointed out that between the two of them, she carried the lesser liability, which was true. But the woman hadn't mentioned the fine print on her own license, a minor omission that almost delivered them to Edisto Gardens.

The problems associated with Margaret's driving were generic to the bourgeoisie—no regard for the chain of command. Calm entitlement. If a lane took longer to clear than she believed it should, she'd pile in anyway and let the other drivers work things out. She was cavalier about it, too. No telling how many insurance claims she left in her wake.

Malachi put the car in gear, thinking the DMV ought to pass a law, update Margaret's whereabouts like a hurricane advisory. Put in routes for emergency evacuation. The steering was better now; less pull. Funny how a wreck could right a car temporarily, like a knock on the head.

Cooper leaned forward in the seat, ready to confess. They'd all been busy with the reunion, he told them, so he slipped out the door and took off. "Left her clasped in her mother's arms," he said. After wandering for about an hour, he'd found himself at Eddie's, three miles north of where he'd started out. The guys cheered when he walked in. They'd already heard. Eddie kept a fourteen-inch black-and-white TV on the end of the bar. Cooper told them he'd parked it on the curb for the night. They understood.

"Quite a self-indulgent little itch you scratched," said Margaret. "Although I suppose you may have earned it."

"No supposing to it," said Malachi. "He can do anything he damn well pleases. Sherlock Holmes wouldn't have solved that case, even in his salad days."

Malachi leaned toward Margaret, lowering his voice. "When his guilt kicks in we'll have to chain him in the attic with old lady Rochester and stuff lead in our ears."

"Has it ever kicked out?" Margaret asked.

Malachi smiled, but all it did was shine some light on the misery. "Guilt," he said. "The bane of civilized man."

"I suppose so," said Margaret. "Although it depends on how one chooses to apply it."

"Hey." Cooper poked Malachi on the shoulder. "I believe I just heard you admit I have some sense."

"Slow on the uptake, aren't you, baby?" he said. "Don't get cocky. It's a temporary condition. Be lucky if it lasts until morning."

"It is morning," said Margaret. "My bedtime passed long since the while."

"Who's old lady Rochester?"

"Look it up. Used to be your favorite novel when you were twelve."

"You kept telling me I was supposed to cry."

"Trying to take up some time. I was being paid by the hour."

"How much did you get?"

"Not enough. After that it was *Catcher in the Rye*. Now that tore you to pieces. I shouldn't have let you read it." A dead brother can kick you in the ass, Malachi thought, but at least Salinger got a classic out of his.

"Caulfield asked all the questions then copped out," Cooper said. "I'm still waiting for the answers."

"The answers were there. Still are, if you know how to read."

"Bullshit," Cooper said.

"Chill. We have a lady in the house."

"She's deaf," Margaret said. "What about the child, dear? We'd like to hear about her if you feel up to it."

"In a minute. Soon as I can figure out where to start."

"Takes a while to do the figuring," Malachi said to Margaret.

"It's nice to be understood," said Cooper.

"Say that like you mean it," Margaret said.

"I do. I love you both so much I can hardly stand it."

"If you didn't it would be one-sided," Margaret said. She patted his arm right-handed to keep from moving her neck.

"Wanna know something?" Cooper said. "I've never seen you two together. It means a lot, having a . . . having you. . . . You're my family, you know?"

"We may be," Malachi said. "Along with half the population of greater Columbia."

"And then some," Margaret said.

Cooper smiled. In a way it was true. His extended family included people he didn't always recognize when they hailed him on the street. But the pair up front, along with Percy, and to a lesser extent Sam and Duke, they were the people he came home to, the ones he allowed to tend to him like he tended to everyone else. He'd never thought about it before, about how the five of them belonged to his life.

"Where's Percy?" he asked.

"She wanted to come," Malachi lied, "but I didn't know what you'd gotten yourself into. Wouldn't be wise, her prancing around a biker bar in one of those foxy little leotards. Don't believe either one of us could stand up long enough to throw a punch in her behalf. She said she'd let Sam know you were back on the radar beam."

"Maybe we should stop by and check on her," Cooper said. "She falls asleep on the couch without locking the door. She's too hard-headed for her own good. A serial killer could be busting in right this minute and no one would even know it."

"You moonlighting for Wackenhut or what?" Malachi asked. "You can't control everything, baby. Percy's a mature woman with a mind of her own."

"Yeah, with a few divots missing in the fairway when it comes to common sense."

"What are you talking about? She's got more common sense in one of her dainty little baby toes than you got in both sides of your skinny...." Malachi glanced at Margaret.

"Hey," Cooper said. "I forgot about the doggies."

Margaret rolled her eyes. "Don't worry, dear. Percy is fine. The doggies are fine. We're all managing more sufficiently than we have a right to be. Now sit back and rest."

"I didn't mean it like that," Cooper said. "I forgot to include the dogs in the family tree."

"Drounk," Margaret said to Malachi.

Cooper lunged forward and kissed her on the cheek. She winced.

"Next time make it dry, with less pizzazz. What did I do to deserve it?"

"You said, 'If I'd known I wouldn't have bothered to dress.'"

"Thank God," she said. "I've been forewarned."

Lying down, Cooper stretched a leg over the top of Malachi's seat. Malachi knocked it off. Cooper put his feet in the windshield. Besides a pair of worn-out loafers, his view was a streetlight now and then, and a black sky.

He used to ride like this coming back into town late Sunday nights after a weekend trip with his parents. Lying in the back seat, attaching his feet wherever he pleased—including on his brother's blond head—watching his father chew a Muriel as he confidently guided the Oldsmobile toward home. His father's best friend was the dealer, so he traded often, sometimes before his kid learned to spot the old one in the elementary school pick-up line. He traded for a new burgundy Ninety-Eight, complete with power windows and power locks, the week his second son was born.

"Have to bring your baby brother home in style," he said.

"Can I come, too?" Cooper asked.

"Can you come? What kind of question is that? The oldest always gets to go first, but he also gets stuck watching out for the poor dickens who has to wait his turn."

Sometimes, when Cooper saw his father's eye move to the rearview mirror, checking for the cop who might catch him speeding, then checking on his boys, he wanted to live his whole life in that very moment. His father had been born to drive a car. You felt like you were sailing on the ocean.

On vacations they were cowboys. Cooper was Black Bart. His baby brother was The Kid. Their mother was Moll.

"Who're you, Daddy?" Cooper would ask him.

"Let's see. Who did you say you were?"

"I'm Bart. Black Bart the stagecoach robber."

"And your brother is The Kid?"

"Yep. And Mama's Moll."

"Well, I guess I'll be Bert," he'd say.

The first time he said it, Cooper and his mother laughed until they couldn't breathe, which made Scooter laugh the same way. How did he come up with Bert? Bert wasn't a cowboy name. Yet in the private playhouses families furnish with pieces only they can understand, they knew Bert was exactly who he should be. Bert didn't use cowboy lingo. They'd ask him a question in cowboy talk and he'd answer like a regular person. Like Bert.

It was the same with the CB. He bought one because they'd begged him to. Scooter because he was coached by his brother, and Cooper because he couldn't wait to use the code.

"Breaker, got your ears on?" a voice would ask.

"Sure do," their daddy would answer.

"What's your handle there, good buddy?"

"This is Barnet, Truluck Motors, out of Charleston? Hope you're doing all right today. Uh . . . by the way, we just passed a patrolman sitting at the underpass at 52, facing east. Best regards."

"You didn't use your handle, Daddy," Cooper would yell. "You're supposed to say 'smoky' and use your handle."

"Use your handle, Daddy. Use your handle," Scooter would repeat.

They'd be frustrated and laughing, too, laughing so hard they could barely choke it out. Their father would look around at his boys and grin that big wide innocent grin he used when he was about to make a joke. Then he'd click on the mike once more.

"Uh . . . this is Barnet again, from Truluck down in Charleston? Calling about the highway patrolman back at 52? Uh . . . make that a smoky. The handle is . . . uh. . . . The Silver Cigar. My boys thought it up."

People were crazy about his father. You couldn't really say what it was beyond the goodness. He was a handsome man. Wavy brown hair, light brown eyes framed by brows that were strong without being bushy, a fine Greek nose, and big white teeth often on display because he smiled a lot.

But it was this look he had more than anything else. Cooper called it his musical chair look, after an expression on his father's face one time in the Smithsonian. He was sitting in a huge chair attached to earphones, listening to *Don Quixote* in Italian. He looked like he wanted to laugh and cry at the same time, like he couldn't grasp what it was all about but couldn't believe his good luck that God had allowed him to be there, allowed him to try and figure it out. Not the language or the plot. The beauty. The beauty and the meaning of the world.

He saw things, their father. They'd be driving down the road, all of them looking for nothing but the next stop, and he'd show them the blue bird.

Sometimes, without saying a word, he'd pull over. Get out and walk over to a spot in the grass beside a sidewalk or maybe on the edge of a field. All you could see were some weeds and trash, but he'd seen something else. He'd come back with it in his hand, a twenty-dollar bill, folded into sections no bigger than a ten-cent stamp, or a stupid miniature wooden treasure chest that said "Made in Florida," or a tacky clip-on tie, gold and fat, out of style even when it was in.

He'd found the clip-on turning around in the parking lot of the Blockade Runner at Wrightsville Beach. They'd been riding around with the windows open, listening to the waves and looking at the stars, and there it was, tangled in a scruffy lantana.

He had plenty of good ties, old Bert, ties other people bought him. But this tie made sense. No pretense to it and ready for action. He wore it every chance he got, even to his boy's funeral, the only time his wife didn't object.

It didn't matter what his father brought back, a nickel, the pop top off a can of Coke. The present was on his face. Cooper intended to be exactly like his daddy when he grew up and had kids.

There was no feeling more secure than floating through the night in his father's burgundy Oldsmobile, the car his brother would die in, knowing in a "hop, skip, and a jump," that they would soon wait sleepily at the door until he pulled out the key and walked in first, to make sure everything was all right.

Back then, his boys loved to tell him he was the best Daddy in the world, and back then he was. Back then, Cooper didn't know he'd have a kid he didn't know he had, and he didn't know that his future Daddy would be the beautiful ragged one-legged drunk looking in the rearview now, mindful of speed and the jury-rigged car and his lack of a license to drive it, careful to stop at every yellow light. Malachi, despite the risks, taking the longest route home, giving him a chance to recover.

"Ya'll okay up there?"

"We're all right," Malachi said.

Cooper raised his arms and stretched.

"Jesus," Margaret said. "What's that?"

"Uh-oh. I may have let the cat out of the box."

"Then embalm him and send him back to Denmark."

"Malachi?"

"Uh-huh?"

"I don't think I feel like talking about it right now."

"Don't worry about it, baby. It'll come in time."

◆

He'd done okay at the hospital. Made it through the emergency room door. Stood firm as the two pieces of glass separated and began to inch apart, then taken Scotty by the arm, and led her in. Lt. Lewis was on the other side, striding across the tiles.

At last, Cooper Barnet, seasoned newspaper columnist for the Columbia *Herald-Journal*, a grown man in his forties, had crossed the threshold of a hospital trauma center, a facility that filled him with such dread that he'd avoided entering one until that night.

His mother died from stomach cancer. Not in a hospital but in her sister's house, aided by her sister, with drugs acquired from her brother-in-law the doctor, who might or might not have known.

His father died in a Catholic-sponsored private clinic. Alcohol-related complications, they called it. They'd saved him the night he was drinking himself to death in his den. It had taken two more months in a coma for the organs to fail. Cooper had been in the newsroom when it happened, writing a column about his inability to kill a wounded bat. He'd taken it to the animal hospital in a cast-iron skillet so the vet could put it to sleep.

Cooper completed the column. His first obligation was to the living. A coward being true to his stripes. He got the gene from the sweetest man the world had ever known. His father wasn't a Catholic. His second wife was.

Two volunteers from the Folly Beach Rescue Squad had taken his little brother to the hospital. Taken Scooter off in a red truck with a red light on top and left him behind—left him with a man he didn't know. He'd run after the truck until he tripped and the man caught him.

"I need to be with my brother," he cried.

"Your parents are taking care of your brother," the man said. "You can't go. You're too young."

Cooper fought and screamed and kicked and hit until the man pinned his arms against his chest. "Don't worry, son," the man said. "They've gone to the emergency room to get help."

But his brother didn't die in the emergency room. He died in the car. Scooter was already dead.

The best Cooper could tell, he killed them all—his brother, his mother, his father. Killed them all, yet he was walking free.

•

Margaret's second Lincoln, a green '77 Town Car with silver trim, was parked in front of the house. Flip Barnes, her driver, was stretched out across the steps, wearing a straw boater and a seersucker sports coat unbuttoned over a white cotton golf shirt. He jumped up and pumped Cooper's hand.

"Say," he said. "What terrific news. How are ya? How's the kid? Joan and I, we were pulling for ya all the way. She sends her best."

Joan, lovely, scholarly, and Boston refined, was Margaret's home secretary and the love of Flip's life, as well as his junior by twenty years. They'd moved to Charleston two decades ago from The Doral Hotel in Miami Beach, where Barnes had been an institution at the front desk.

At eighty-seven, Flip could do a soft shoe as nimbly as a man half his age, and although he wouldn't admit it, he was once a contestant on the Gong Show, singing an old vaudeville ditty with corny asides like "Fish don't perspire" and "You can't swim in a pool hall. . . ." The hotel clientele appreciated his ever-sunny view of life. He received more mail than the entire operation combined, much of it addressed simply to Flip, in care of The Doral.

After Cooper had called from Eddie's, Margaret had sent word for Flip to head for Columbia, conceding it would be too late for her to drive back to Charleston alone. Now, she waited until Cooper and Malachi were inside to tell him that the Dart was in Cayce, and suggest they take the convertible with them and leave the Town Car behind.

"Mr. Barnet is averse to practicality," she said, "but if you're amenable, I suspect he should have air-conditioned transportation that's dependable, for the sake of the child. He insists the contraption he drives is an automobile, but I haven't been able to identify it as anything of the like."

"I should say," Flip said. "Well, we're all set then, are we? Fine, fine. Shall we dance?"

He took Margaret's arm and walked her back to the same car he'd helped her out of a few minutes before.

"Hey, lookit," he said, leaning down to peer at the bumper. "That's a beaut."

"Indeed," Margaret said.

"Boy," said Flip. "She's a mess. Have any idear what might have happened?"

"Is there a reason you expect me to?" Margaret asked.

Flip didn't answer.

"I'm afraid I became engaged with a motorbike."

"Geez. A motorbike." Flip shook his head. "What a shame. Those things shouldn't be allowed on the highway. Gee, I hope . . . er . . . I hope you didn't. . . ."

"Fortunately, with the exception of the building, everyone survived."

"The building? Oh, fine, what luck. What a blessing. Didya say a building was involved?"

"Yes. It's known as Eddie's Lounge. The proprietor has lovely manners. He informed me he has a grandbaby on James Island. He's planning to pay us a visit."

"Fine," Flip said. "That's fine. Hey, must've been some night, huh?"

He helped Margaret into the car and walked over to inspect the frayed yellow extension chord tied around the bumper. "Just look at that," he said. "It's barely hanging on by a string."

"Is that a fact," Margaret said. "Any chance of arriving home by sunrise?"

"Sunrise? Why, that's four hours away. You'll be in bed long before that. You can bet your life on it. Yessiree."

19

What was going on in the building this early in the morning? It wasn't nine thirty yet, and both the staff parking and visitors' lots were full. Cooper shut his eyes and backed into the only spot left, a twelve-minute meter. The rusty rack of a banged-up silver Volvo was nosed over the dividing line. Damn. Margaret's cars were programmed to thwart inconvenience by bashing it in. He didn't feel like leaving a note, and decided to confess in his column instead, which would give him one for tomorrow. Not his best moral moment, but he wasn't thinking that clearly. He'd had three hours' sleep, and Gene Krupa was beating on his head with every drum on the platform, threatening to bust down the stage. Besides, the car looked like it had been chewed up by a junkyard dog before he hit it.

He crossed Lady Street, heading for a less conspicuous entrance. Nobody was in the alcove checking out a staff car, so he slipped inside and walked past the swinging doors that opened into a hallway of neutral offices, the largest belonging to the circulation department. His percussion headache throbbed in time with every step. At the door that led to the elevator, he stopped to check for traffic.

There was plenty. The lobby was packed. Evidently some kind of promotion or charity drive since they were pressing towards the far side of the room, forming lines at two long tables to drop off boxes and bags. A crowd hovered around Jo, who was attacking the switchboard like she was plugging voodoo pins in the head of Robert Mugabe.

Cooper couldn't see the elevator, just the arrow above it. Four ... three ... two. . . .

"Hey. There he is."

"Where?"

"Over there."

"Stop him. Quick."

"Hold that elevator, Cooper."

"Cooper, wait."

That was always the dilemma, how to proceed without giving offense. Margaret's views on his privacy rights were extreme. You write a column, they pay you the courtesy of reading it, you allow the elevator doors to play accordion with your bones and shoot the pain to your pounding head. And you shake hands. One then another then another. Where were they all coming from, this multitude of hands? The lines were breaking up at the tables and metastasizing into a circle around him.

"Wow. What're we giving away?" he asked.

No one had an answer. They watched him, eager, anxious.

"Is there a contest?"

Some of them laughed politely. Others looked blank. Cooper had no idea how to move on, other than morphing into a weasel and snaking up the elevator shaft.

"I give. What am I missing? Somebody clue me in."

"You beat all, Cooper," one of them said; a woman holding a teddy bear.

"That's just like him." A man, standing behind her. His eyes were as bright as the plaids in his shirt. "He's just pulling our leg."

That wasn't Jeff, was it, from the Goodyear tire place? "Hey, buddy," Cooper said. "Running any specials today?"

"Always. Come on by and we'll cook you up a deal."

"Sold, if you throw in a haircut."

They liked that one. But now they were shoving things at him, the things they'd been carrying to the tables.

"Congratulations, Cooper. Way to go."

"We knew you could do it."

"Absolutely. Who needs the cops when you're around?"

They were offering him packages wrapped in paper printed with balloons and dinosaurs and fairy tales characters. Packages with curly ribbons and enormous bows.

"Cooper, I cried from pure joy. . . ."

"Cooper, I was so relieved. . . ."

"Cooper, we prayed and prayed. . . ."

"We could hardly believe it was happening."

And cards, all sorts of cards.

"What did you say when you first saw her?"

"Yeah. What was actually said?"

"Did she know you right off?"

"Did you know her?"

Cakes, brownies, pies, deviled eggs, a ham.

"What's she like, Cooper?"

"Does she look like you?"

Three pounds of Melvin's Brunswick stew.

"Are you gonna write about her for tomorrow?"

"Hey, Cooper, did you bring her with you?"

"Where is she? Bet you're not about to let her out of your sight after this."

"Congratulations, champ." It was George Rogers, heisting a life-sized stuffed animal in the air, a huge Saint Bernard, like it was his Heisman trophy.

Maxine waved from behind the plastic Schefflera, and Tiny Tuttle was next to her, but Cooper couldn't speak because a stooped lady with a three-pronged cane was being helped forward to hand him a bouquet of roses. He took them, just as the elevator doors were closing again. Bang-bang. Shudder-shudder. Krupa drum boogie. His hero, Number 38, threw a body block and reached behind him to press "Stop."

A little girl tapped him on the stomach. A barrette, an apple, was perched in a storm of blond ringlets. She wanted him to take a piece of paper, folded in two.

"Thank you," he said. "Let's swap."

He gave her the roses. His hand was shaking.

"Be careful," he said. "They can prick you."

"Those are the thorns," she said.

He unfolded the paper. It was a drawing from a coloring book, a cozy brick house with a big yellow door and green shuttered windows.

"See?" she said. "I made the windows green and the brick red, and that's the sun." Something purple and fluffy was scribbled over the brick.

"Is that a pansy?" Cooper asked.

"No, silly, it's a flower."

An inscription ringed with more flowers had been printed with a lighter green crayon, traced in black. "To Miss Scotty Barnet," it said. "Welcome Home." Most of the words were misspelled.

Cooper was crying now. "I'm sorry," he said. George wrapped an arm around him. "It's all right, brother. We love you, man."

Then there was Hitch, pulling him forward, leading him through the crowd.

His friends had begun calling early that morning. Maxine first, then Duke and Sam, then Boom-Boom on behalf of the copy desk, and Myrtle and Ginna and Jazz. Percy brought coffee and Danish. Margaret had phoned to check on him—why hadn't he checked on her first?—and told him to inform Mr. Limehouse she had no plans to board a motorbike for a while. All that was in the sphere of expectation, but this. . . .

Cooper tripped over some puffy toes in a blood orange flip-flop. The woman who wore it shut her eyes and made a face. "I didn't mean to step on you," he said, although that was no reason for him to cry.

"I drove all the way from Charlotte," she said, "just to give you a great big hug."

Hitch held up a hand.

"I'm sure my columnist would like to stay and visit, but I'm gonna have to borrow him a few minutes. You can drop off your packages and so on over at the tables. Make sure you leave your names and addresses and phone numbers. We'll see that Scotty gets them all."

◆

Hitch led him past the circulation department to a storeroom, unlocked the door, and slid a hand behind a metal cabinet.

"Aha," he said, and flipped on a florescent bath.

"Mind turning it down?"

"I can't. It only has one speed."

"Then cut it off. It hurts my eyes."

"Those ain't eyes," Hitch said. "They're a couple of smashed Muscadines. Who stomped 'em, Night Train Lane?"

"Skip the editorial. You're supposed to be a newsman."

What was behind him? Cooper turned to see. The best he could tell, nothing. A narrow aisle with shelves along the wall to the right. The only light came from the white shirt Malachi had worn last night, the sleeves still rolled up when Cooper put it on this morning.

His farmer's tan stung beneath the starch. How did he get so much sun? He was still holding the little girl's drawing. He folded it in fourths and put it in his pocket.

What was going on, another surprise party? He hadn't recovered from the first one. Where were they hiding, in the rafters? Okay. You got me. Come on down.

No one showed except Hitch, a fuzzy ghost creeping from shelf to shelf, rummaging through the supplies. "Give me just a minute," he said.

There. A yellow beam, coming from a Coca-Cola bottle. A miniature rubber flashlight, with a keychain swinging from the stopper.

"Payola for that hundredth anniversary crap," Hitch said. "Sent over enough of these gewgaws to light up the Family Dollar store. Wasn't worth the trouble to send 'em back. I meant to give 'em to last year's toy drive."

He lit the way to some cardboard boxes full of copy paper. The light was stronger now, regulated by the amount of pressure Hitch exerted when he squeezed.

"Take a chair."

"You can't be serious," Cooper said, but he sat, facing the long row of floor-to-ceiling shelves. "What are we doing, taking inventory?"

"Thank God we don't have to. That's the newsroom secretary's job. This is her secret stash."

"She goes by 'Ginna,'" Cooper said. The same name her mother gave her when she was born. The same one she's used since she's been working here the last fifteen years.

"I had to take you someplace. The newsroom wouldn't work."

Cooper was fed up with the Hitchcock Wall. There had been no reason to snatch him from the lobby, to disappoint the people who'd come to celebrate a happy ending just to drag him to "the newsroom secretary's" private warehouse. To do what, punish him for his transgressions by making him stare at a bunch of metal shelves?

I might be a master of avoidance, Cooper thought, but Benjamin J. Hitchcock is a master of depersonalization. Negate their validity, keep 'em on the defensive. Ice is the great intimidator. Makes you feel like more is never enough.

Okay, he'd paid his dues with the perfunctory editor bashing. If Sam hadn't been standing on his shoulders in a pair of cleats, Cooper would've thanked Hitch for bailing him out. He'd been on the verge of losing it in a way that would've embarrassed everybody.

He rolled his sleeves another turn. He was sweating like crazy. There was no ventilation in here. Why didn't Hitch get on with it?

The shelves were in flawless order. Well-stocked, nothing out of place, the most utilized products down low, like Ginna. **No. 100 NEWS Professional Reporter's Notebooks** dead center, a bull's-eye for her sweet little arms. Amazing, the amount of light in a Coke the size of an **Alvin Art Gum Eraser, 12/BX**.

"That was wild out there," Hitch said. "They were lined up when Jo got here this morning."

"I didn't handle it well."

Cooper wanted one of those flashlights for Percy. The output was phenomenal. Hitch had it dancing on a shelf three yards from where they were sitting, and even a pair of middle-aged Muscadine eyes could make out the print on a box of **Bates No. 56 Stapler Bun. Gray. Lg**.

Percy had a thing for gewgaws. She might carry this one in the flimsy patchwork sack she used as a purse. Her magic bag, she called it.

Was a person middle-aged at forty-two? Who was Cooper kidding? Any more, twelve was middle-aged. Well, his daughter still had a few months to go. Maybe a miracle would happen.

He wouldn't mind picking up a stapler while they were here. But all he saw were staples. He didn't see a gun. What he needed was a pack of pens.

Hitch hit Cooper with a shot of Coke.

"What'd you think about the Liebman piece?"

"Great," he said. He hadn't read it.

Was that carbon paper over there? Sure was. **Blueblk. 500 Sheets. 15 1/2 x 9.** It was comforting, finding a long forgotten symbol of the good old days.

"You got a lot of booty back there," Hitch said. "Any idea how you wanna deal with it?"

Cooper shook his head.

"What about the night shelter for the food?" Hitch blinked the light off and on, on and off, toward the shelves.

"Sounds good."

"Or we can pass it around up here."

"Either way."

"Take whatever you can use for yourself. They brought it to you."

So they were here to discuss catering plans. This had gone from crazy to absurd. Let's see. **Standard Size Eagle Pencils, No. 2 Lead.** Where were the pens? In the newsroom, they used a lot more pens than pencils. Come on, Ginna, give me a hint. If I had a pen that wrote, maybe life would be worth living.

More blinks, now against a leg of the Sansabelt slacks. Gray today.

"I wouldn't mind having one of those flashlights. If it's not out of bounds. Not for my personal use, for someone else. I don't plan to be doing anything on Coca-Cola."

Hitch rose and walked to the shelf.

"How many?" he asked.

"Just one."

He tossed it over.

"Sure that's enough?"

Cooper nodded. He'd said "for someone else." Not "for Percy." Not even for "my girlfriend." A scene in the life of a stockroom, where what's good for the goose wasn't so hot for the gander. Why did he think in clichés when he hated them so much?

"I need to tell you something," Hitch said. His voice was grave and flat. The light was on his moccasin now. The side was slick where the suede had worn off. Hitch turned his feet out when he walked.

Thank God, here it comes, Cooper thought. Scumbag house, scumbag writer, scumbag dad. You can always judge a man by the clothes he wears if the smell doesn't do you in before you get close enough to check him out. He sniffed his pit. Not bad, for a sitting duck a Coke shot away from being fired. Disappointing, in a way. He'd kind of gotten used to the funk.

"Let's have it, chief," Cooper said. "It's okay."

Hitch took a breath. "They say confession is good for the soul, but I'm not sure I believe it. We'll see after you hear what I have to say."

Confession? Hitch wasn't a confessor. What did Hitch have to confess?

"You remember meeting my sister a few years ago at the Christmas party?"

Vaguely. A good-natured lady with a lisp. Light brown hair. Nothing like Hitch. He'd made small talk with her on a sofa beside the fire.

"She supervises the car rental concessions at Douglas Airport. You know, where Hannah works."

Cooper sucked in air and rediscovered his hangover. Hitch had said "Hannah." He'd used a name. But this was something private. It had nothing to do with his employment here, his job.

He could see Hannah sitting in the Toddle House. The Piedmont bag. The wings on her blouse. She'd told him she worked for Piedmont. A director of scheduling something. Maybe flight attendants. He hadn't been paying attention. But it made sense. She lived in Charlotte. The Piedmont headquarters were in Charlotte. She was wearing the wings.

"They moved to Charlotte," Hitch said.

Did he miss something? Who were "they?" The light was off now. The two of them were crouched on cardboard boxes in the dark, confined in a creepy gunmetal tomb, bracing for the tense atmospheric conditions to explode into a storm of unknown destruction. Cooper had been lured into a séance to wait for a spirit he hadn't summoned, a spirit he didn't want to meet.

"My sister and her husband and the kids, a good many years ago. IBM transferred him to the central division."

So what? Cooper thought. So they were in a storage room and Hitch had lost his mind. Join the crowd.

Douglas Airport. He'd driven there a couple of times before Columbia had gone international. Gone over to pick up Sam and Laura from trips abroad. Piedmont flights, connections from New York or Pittsburgh or Cincinnati. They'd begged him to go with them. They'd been on him since he'd confessed that a girl in false eyelashes had read his palm at a fraternity party. He wasn't in the fraternity, just a guest. She told him he'd meet his demise in Europe. She wasn't an authentic fortune teller, just a party girl high on Purple Jesus, with teased red hair, but he'd spent his life on U.S. soil.

Hitch worked a Tampa Nugget from the inside pocket of his jacket. A blazer, missing a pewter button. One out of three wasn't bad.

Douglas Airport. Hannah was right there in Douglas Airport. They could have occupied other spaces together, too, separated only by a wall or a flight of stairs. Hannah and her baby. Hannah and her child. Charlotte was an hour and a half away. Cooper went to Charlotte for sporting events and concerts. He'd eaten in restaurants there.

"She knew your wife. Your ex-wife." Hitch was confiding to a box of typewriter ribbons. **IBM Selectric. Nylon. Blk**. His voice was gentle, low. "She knew her before she knew who she was, if that makes sense."

It didn't make sense. They were holed up in a storage room. There were too many "she's."

"Of course, she'd already gone back to her maiden name. But one thing led to another and she made the connection. She used to be married to a newspaper reporter in Columbia, she told her once. She didn't usually talk about it, she said. Didn't like to think about that part of her life. Over a cup of coffee I believe it was, or in a cafeteria line. Your wife, your ex, didn't realize that she was my sister, though, wouldn't have had any way of knowing, and my sister didn't say. But when she came back to Columbia . . . you know how everyone always gets around to telling the Cooper Barnet story. She told me about this woman who worked in the airport, told me she'd figured out who she was."

Cooper stared at the side of Hitch's face, yellow in the burning ash. There was no cynicism, no challenge. He was hesitant, apologetic. But he was hard to follow. He had a thing against names.

"This must be going somewhere," Cooper said.

"I knew about your daughter."

There it was, the storm, the spirit summoned in the séance, but it had appeared in a normal human voice, a voice soft and level and subdued. Pained. Heavy with remorse.

"I've known about her for years. I didn't think you were aware of her but I wasn't sure. I thought about asking you, worried over it for months. I decided not to mention it. Maybe you knew and preferred to keep it to yourself. Maybe you didn't know. If she hadn't told you, she must have had her reasons. It wasn't my place to interfere in your personal life. Hell, you never talked about it. After a while it didn't cross my mind again."

Hitch pulled at the waist of his slacks. The ash dropped on his sleeve, near the cuff. It burned a hole in the navy polyester.

It was hard to catch a breath, trapped in an airless cabinet. Hitch's cigar stank. Cooper's father smoked the only cigars that didn't stink; he didn't light them up.

"When I heard she'd run off to find you," Hitch said, "all I could do was blame myself."

"You knew?"

"I've paid royally these past few days. Suffered the tortures of the damned. Had to put the shoe on the other foot, ask myself the tough questions. It's a lot easier making the other fella squirm, I can tell you that."

Clutching the corners of his box seat, Cooper helped himself up. He felt his way along the shelves, walking slowly, towards a dead end. Where had Ginna put the pens? Hitch was following him with the Coke. Hitch, defender of the public's right to know.

"I have to do a column," Cooper mumbled, but didn't turn around.

"I didn't catch what you said."

"I said I have to go."

"Once I knew about a friend whose wife was having an affair."

Hitch was behind him now. Cooper wanted to turn around, but there wouldn't be room to pass.

"One of my best friends. I didn't want to tell him. My wife thought we should. We went round and round. Spent days and weeks on it. Talked it over with other people without letting on who it was. That was more than twenty years ago. They're still together. We never got involved."

What was the point? This was different. This was about a child. Someone's daughter. She didn't know about her father. Her father didn't know about her.

"All right. Was I afraid you might pack up, move yourself and your talent to *The Observer?* I'm sure it must've crossed my mind, although I don't like to believe I could've been conscious of it. A child trumps all that other bullshit, don't you think?"

The light was on the floor. Hitch was patting him on the shoulder, patting him with the cigar hand. Cooper was grateful for the awkward touch. Somehow, it grounded the sadness. It was hot in here. He'd been about to lie down, to curl up on the cement floor.

"I don't want to press too hard," Hitch said. "But after the demonstration this morning. . . . I think you need to come back with one soon. Don't worry about tomorrow. Liebman's filling your spot, doing a piece on the hero's welcome. Might inspire another riot. Damned if he hasn't blossomed into some frigging Elizabeth Barrett Browning or something. If Eyes remembered to load up we'll have some damned good shots."

This shirt was murder. How had Malachi kept it on? "Thanks, but I don't want the sympathy vote. I came in to write a column. I've already got the lede."

Some stupid confession about putting a scratch on the bumper of a car that made the Dart look like the star of a showroom brochure. He could go back to it, but where would he take it? Logically, to the reason he was driving Margaret's car. But that wouldn't work. It would mean calling on the keys that spelled "daughter."

"Hold off a few days," Hitch said. "Get some perspective. If you decide by then you don't want to touch it, leave it alone. Liebman can do an update about mid-week. Maybe you can use some of the letters. Hell, we'll have to rent a couple of boxcars to store 'em in. Then we'll let it die."

Cooper ran a sleeve across his face. He had another column. Something about a man he met last night in Eddie's. But he couldn't remember his name right off. Maybe Percy would give in and cut his hair. It was heavy, too heavy for him to hold up anymore; weighing down his feeble brain.

Hitch knew and didn't tell him. Hitch, a hard-nosed newsman, in the business of reporting the news.

"As far as the other stuff, the cards and toys and such," Hitch said. "We'll get them together; get a circulation truck to drop them by your house. It'll be like Christmas. She'll have a ball."

20

As soon as he managed to convince Margaret's irascible bulldozer to merge into eastbound traffic, Cooper checked the seat beside him. His passenger, a merry little animated run-on sentence since he'd picked her up five minutes ago, had suddenly become somber and silent, digging into her canary-yellow satchel, papers flying, pencils flying—and after opening every zipper and flipping it on its end, a metallic hailstorm—nickels, pennies, dimes, quarters, nickels, more quarters. . . .

"Noodle must have a real strong back to carry all that change," he said. Make that past tense. Noodle had sacrificed his life for a Greyhound ride.

"Let's see. You have a piggybank named Noodle, a dog named Noodle, and I bet you eat spaghetti noodles, too. Lots of noodles floating around, huh?"

No wonder she didn't answer. She'd probably never heard a more inane statement in her life. He slowed for a group of students crossing the street on a green light. They waved their thanks and ran towards a large wrought-iron gate leading to the campus of Benedict College, recipient of Margaret's most recent drizzle of holy water.

Probably late for class, he thought, and glanced toward the child again. Please don't let her miss what she can't have, he prayed. But it was too late for that. She'd missed having a father so much she'd attempted something absurdly beyond her realm to find him. Was that a good or a bad sign?

"Guess you're getting hungry," he said. She was still pre-occupied with the knapsack, turning it inside out and shaking it over her lap. Two more pennies tumbled out, followed by a bracelet crudely woven together with heavy colored threads.

He couldn't figure it out. She'd been as bouncy as a sprite in a bubble bath, and now she was carrying more weight on her shoulders than the chrome draped around the Lincoln. She looked over at him, and then whispered to herself, "It's gone."

What if she started to cry? Stay calm, he told himself. She'll come around, be all right. During the nightmare at Garland's she'd been stoic, as well as during the ride with a uniformed deputy sheriff, buckled into an official patrol car. She hadn't even broken down when she saw her mother in a hospital room, drugged and hysterical, with an IV in her arm. Yet this was his watch, and she was distressed, and he didn't know how to fix it.

At the next stoplight, he turned to face her. It shouldn't take much to divert her attention. An innocuous comment, a compliment, a joke. She was a child. Why couldn't he think of something to say?

He couldn't stop staring at her eyes—the guileless simplicity behind the pale-blue confusion, the trust. He could see everything Hannah had been protecting in that one look. Could see how easy it had been for Garland to escort her from the bus, pack her into her ghoulish black car, and stash her in a house lifted off the set of

Psycho. Scotty grew her world in a secret garden, where goodness bloomed like flowers, true and pure.

Take him, for instance. As anonymous as any person she might pass in the street, yet to her he'd become the actual father she'd created on a piece of construction paper. Just as if he'd removed his bowtie and daubed a few strands of gray into his hair and stepped off the bright green grass she'd drawn with such wide, broad strokes, stepped right off the lawn and right into her life, to remind her to say her prayers and brush her teeth and warn her that whatever she did, to never, ever associate with strangers.

"Daddy, you might be very sad to hear that I lost that small gray shell that I was bringing to give to you for a present, because it looks very pretty and shines like a silver star when you hold it up to the sun."

"That's okay."

"No, Daddy, that is not okay because you have to be very careful with your possessions and put them in the place that you're supposed to keep them in when you finish playing with them and if you don't remember to be responsible you might lose them like I lost the nice little present I was bringing to Columbia, South Carolina, especially for you and. . . ."

Maybe he should return her to the hospital. Frances would know what to do. But she would be gone by now. Hannah had convinced her sister to drive back to Charlotte, to her own children and husband and job, while she spent the next three or four days getting healthy enough to be released.

Scotty had refused to go with her. She intended to see her father, even after they'd told her that he was the same man who'd delivered her to her mother yesterday, a man of such high honor and integrity that he didn't identify himself as the VRAY person she'd risked her life to find. How could they prevent her from seeing him now? How could he keep it from happening?

Ginna had shown up just as he was leaving the stockroom to give him the message. From a phone in the empty pressroom, he'd used every excuse except his hangover: The house was a disaster. His houseguest was a drunk. He had a column to write. Her mother had hidden her existence to keep them apart.

And then, protected by the sleeping presses, he'd headed out the back exit to the loading dock, where Hitch had delivered the Lincoln. The five-dollar parking ticket was still attached to the driver's side wiper when Scotty climbed in thirty minutes later.

Frances had brought her to the car, given him the pills, and apologized for the lack of personal essentials. She'd told him bedtime was at eight, and that keeping her routine was important. But why hadn't she gone over the critical stuff, like what to do when a child in her condition experiences meltdown?

He had no idea what her condition was. He'd allowed Hannah's clichéd description to pass without a single question. He would have never done that in an interview. In an interview, he would have pressed for an explanation.

"A different drummer." What exactly did that mean? The kid in school who didn't fit in, Hannah had told him, like he had been as a child himself. Yet there was something engaging about her. Was he making this judgment as a person attracted to misfits? Comparing her to his menagerie in Odds & Ends? Still, it wasn't like the child should be excluded from the band, just allowed to beat her own time. And when she smiled. . . .

She wasn't smiling now, or talking, either—just staring at the dashboard. The Bowtie Father would reach across the gulf of tan leather, touch her bare little shoulder, catch her nose. But was it proper for him to touch her, him a stranger, a stranger she called "Daddy"?

"I hope you won't fuss at me for losing that nice little shell, Daddy, because I tried to take real good care of it and. . . ."

"Don't worry. It'll turn up, and if it doesn't we'll find you another one just like it."

"But we can't find another one just like it, Daddy, because you have to go see Aunt Julia at that nice beach where they have the very old houses and that fort that the soldiers had to live in when they put bombs in the cannons and started the war."

"Sullivan's Island? You've been to see Julia at Sullivan's Island? The Julia who was your mother's best friend? Jesus Christ."

"No, Daddy, we only saw Aunt Julia at Sullivan's Island, not Jesus. You must know that you have to be good and go up to heaven if you want to see Jesus Christ."

"Of course. You're right."

Why didn't he call her Scotty? That was her name. The name her mother had given her when she was born. The name she'd been going by for practically twelve years. That thing with Hitch and names, they'd all simplified it. Nothing was simple, nothing. Everyone knew that. Jackie, Hitch, Jesus Christ. Everyone but this little girl sitting next to the block of granite posing as her daddy.

You had to pass through Columbia to go to Sullivan's Island from Charlotte, unless you flew. There was no direct flight. If you flew you wouldn't change planes in Columbia. You'd change in Atlanta.

"And Daddy, that fat brown dog with the red bow around his neck might not like it when we have to feed him a small bowl of diet food like that other fat dog eats with the long white fur that Mister Curry brought to our school so he could show all the students in the sixth-grade class his nice little tricks. But Noodle doesn't have to go on a diet, Daddy, because he only weighs thirteen whole pounds and another half of one soaking wet. . . ."

Cooper glanced at the solemn little gamin beside him. Was Audrey Hepburn as delicate when she was a child? The spangles were gone, and she was back in the sundress she'd picked out for her escape. Frances had cleaned up the red sandals and washed her hair. It was shining. Light brown, almost gold. Not auburn like Hannah's had been, or black like his.

The genetics of dominants and recessives . . . how did it go? Cooper's father had been a pure dominant and his mother had black hair and blue eyes. He'd come out like her and his brother had turned out blond, with skin lighter than his mother's, and freckled. Yet Scooter turned brown in the summer, as brown as Cooper and his father did. Of course, you couldn't say how he would've ended up.

Maybe I should have a paternity test, Cooper thought. Maybe she belongs to someone else.

The Velcro fastener on her sandal was coming apart. Hannah said she was clumsy. Accident prone, she'd called it. She'd need a new pair of shoes.

"You feeling better?"

She shrugged, shaking her head like a pair of high-speed windshield wipers. What did that mean? Yes? No? Maybe?

She had a few freckles between her nose and cheeks, like Scooter's. Cooper hadn't noticed the freckles yesterday, or her nose. It was small—a perfect shape. Her eyes fascinated him. At certain moments, the gray behind the blue became more pronounced, like the inside of the lost seashell she'd described, translucent and serene. And suddenly she smiled and the blue lights came on, just like that.

"Daddy, you'll be very happy to know that it will be all right for me to stay at your house with the Christmas tree on that broken front porch because in school Mrs. Wiley read a story about the twin girls with the very nice parents who lived in two different houses and the parents had to learn how to share the twins, and Daddy, would you like to share me and Noodle in your house?"

"Um, well, your mother wouldn't like. . . . You say Noodle is a male dog, isn't that right? And I have male dogs, boy dogs, too. Two boys and a girl. You see, sometimes male dogs are settled in their ways and it's hard for them to take on new friends . . . new people, I mean, new dogs in their lives. Sort of hard for them to learn how to get along."

She turned on the radio, working the dial up and down . . . static, song, static, news, static, static, static . . . her eyes gray again.

"And Daddy, you might be worried that I miss my mama and Miss Mac and our nice brick house with the green shutters that the man without a real voice came over to paint that day. . . ."

Put an arm around her. Tell her the dogs will be glad for Noodle to visit.

"See that big white house over there? That's the Governor's mansion. The man in charge of the state of South Carolina lives inside."

More fiddling with the radio. . . .

She knew all the words, this child bouncing around on the seat singing about exes in Texas; this child nodding her head, even carrying the tune as she clapped her hands against the beat, smiling a big bright happy smile, her eyes bluer now, like a skyful of suns sparkling through a translucent gray shell, this child who was his. . . .

•

And then a remarkably self-possessed Samaritan in white short shorts and bare feet was ushering them up the chipped pink concrete steps, past the pink sign, through the screen door to the studio/den. Cooper wandered over to the sofa and sat on a pile of sequins.

"I'm lost," he whispered.

But Percy had gone off with Scotty, introducing her to Bob, answering questions about cage droppings and ferret odor, taking her to the kitchen for Oreos and milk.

"She's not supposed to have sugar," Cooper called after her. "Unless it comes from fruit."

"Chocolate's a fruit," Percy said, "Isn't it, princess?"

Scotty was knocking back cookies like Nabisco had announced they were baking the last batch tomorrow. She was sitting on a high aluminum stool, nothing to catch her if she lost her balance.

Percy had lifted her there. Tiny strong Percy, her perfect little biceps bulging from the short capped sleeves of a black scoop-neck blouse, her perfect black braid swinging to the side, placing Scotty in the center of the scratched red seat, pouring some milk in a Dixie Cup and setting it on the table.

They were both eating the cookies now, taking happy bites, chattering and chewing with their mouths open the way their mothers had taught them not to. Percy pulled another cup from the stack on the counter. "Hey, doodlebug. How would you like some nice new gloves, like a dancing girl wears?"

Cooper blew a forlorn kiss toward the kitchen, although Percy was too busy to see it. Watching her with Scotty made him sad. She'd confided once that in a life of bad choices, the only one she couldn't live with was the shoddy abortion that prevented her from having other children. She'd made another bad choice after that, attempted to abort her own life. She wouldn't tell him how, only that her brother had found her. She was almost sixteen when it happened.

"I know I'm asking a lot with the recital and all," he'd told her when he called from a gas station phone. "But she needs a woman. We need a woman."

He walked in and sat on the captain's chair. It had belonged to one of the captains, he'd forgotten which one. The base coat was black enamel. Two summers ago, Percy had sanded off a couple of spots on the legs and experimented with other colors—lime green, cobalt blue, shamrock green—before moving on to another project.

She decorated her kitchen with the same amorphous energy, turning it into a haphazard haven of cheer. In her latest brainstorm, to warm up a dreary February, she'd painted the linoleum a shiny turquoise and free-handed glittery yellow quarter moons in each of the four corners and a full moon in the center. The ceiling was bluish-green, a shade lighter than the floor, with lumpy, cracked plaster adding to the comfort level. Built high on bright white walls were red cabinets with fat round turquoise knobs and doors that didn't close all the way. Percy had to launch herself from the counter to grab a box of Chef Boyardee pizza, her favorite home-cooked meal.

"Here," Cooper said. The medicine was in the pocket of his chinos. He put it on the stove next to a pair of salt and pepper shakers wearing tutus. No. Too close to the burners. He moved the bottle to the center of a plastic cutting board next to the sink. "2 X DAY w. MEALS," he printed on a paper towel in black magic marker, large enough for Percy to see from the house next door, and tossed a wad of twenties beside it that he'd withdrawn from the bank on the way to pick up Scotty from the hospital.

"She doesn't have a toothbrush or pajamas." Cooper spoke softly. Krupa and the drums were raising hell again. "Or any underwear, either." He massaged the top of his head. His hair was like a field of weeds after days of rain—wild, with patchy spots of sweat. He could apply for a government farm grant, raise hair for wigs instead of selling shoes. "Or any extra clothes."

"Light traveler," Percy said. "Smart girl."

"She takes these for her heart. Twice a day, after breakfast and supper—and for breakfast she eats wholesome cereal and drinks orange juice and milk. All those cookies. . . . I don't think she was supposed to have that many cookies."

Percy jammed one in his mouth and told him to take his time chewing. "Tell your father he's late for his yoga class," she said.

Cooper grinned. "I just realized something. You can be hung over and hungry at the same time."

"Duke will feed you much better than I can," Percy said. Then, to Scotty, "Like he didn't know."

She took the empty cup from Scotty's hand and threw it in the trash.

"That's called washing dishes," she said, grabbing a paper towel and wetting it. "Here you are, little chickadee. Clean yourself up and come with me. I bet you'd like to check out your room while your daddy takes a little nap with Bob."

The room was a cubby-hole, with a twin blow-up mattress on the floor. Percy made it up with purple polka-dot sheets, pressed dry-cleaner perfect. When Cooper teased her about eating on paper plates and then killing herself ironing all her sheets, Percy would point out that he never complained when he was between them.

"Wouldn't she be better off in a bedroom, with an actual bed?" he was asking her now.

"What are you doing here? We sent you off to take a nap."

"Couldn't sleep." He leaned against the door jamb.

"Children like to camp out in snug corners, don't you, princess? They like to be as snug as a bug in a rug."

Scotty was pointing to a life-size ballerina behind the bed, a figure with short dark hair, one dark eye, and an arm on a barre, performing a plié in a pink leotard. Percy had sketched her directly on the wall, since a canvas that big would've cost her an arm and a leg. One of these days she intended to add a tutu.

"Miss," said Scotty. "I sure do like that picture over there of that pretty little dancer because when I grow up I'm going to be a dancer, too, and I don't have a costume or shoes because my mother says that I might have to wait a while before I can get started and that she'll let me know when the time is right."

"You already have part of a costume," Percy said. "You're wearing it on your wrists. Just wait until we spray on the red paint and add some shiny red sequins. Then you'll really be something."

"Hey, Pops," Percy said, tossing her head behind her, where a military foot locker had been shoved next to the closet. "How about opening that thing up and digging out a pillow."

All Cooper could find in the trunk were some moth-eaten Army blankets, a pair of steel-toed dingo boots, and goldfish paraphernalia. A goldfish bowl filled with colored rocks, two boxes of goldfish food, a book on how to identify different types of goldfish, and a stack of plastic bags with ties, like goldfish come in when you buy one in a pet store.

"What were you, a breeder?" he asked.

"Huh?"

"Look, Miss," said Scotty. "My daddy has a costume, too."

"He sure does," Percy said. "How did he manage that?"

"Sequins," she told Cooper. "Come here." She made a one-handed swipe at his trousers. "I just remembered. Pillows are in the closet. Top shelf. Pick out a skinny one so it won't be too high for her head, and be sure it passes the sniff test. If we have to we'll give it a sunbath."

"Now then, ladybug," she said. "You're going with me."

She took Scotty's hand and led her off down the hall. Cooper heard the familiar thud, bare foot against stuck screen. He selected a soft feather pillow that smelled fine to him, then he sat on the trunk and put the pillow against the wall, resting his head on it while he waited for them to come back. When they did, Scotty was carrying a tangle of Black-eyed Susans.

"Look, Daddy, we found these pretty yellow flowers outside in front of the house and your very sweet friend here said that we could pick them for free because they grow beside a public sidewalk and that I'm allowed to keep them in this same room where I'm going to spend the night so they can make me happy when it's time to go to sleep all by myself."

"Good," he said.

Percy arranged the flowers in a ceramic ballet slipper and put the vase on the orange crate next to the mattress.

"Now. Your daddy's going home to rest, and we're going shopping."

Shopping? In this heat? "Her medicine's. . . ."

"On the cutting board, along with a pharmaceutical handbook."

"Be sure and lock up as soon as you get back," Cooper said at the door, kissing Percy on the bridge of her nose. "It's getting late. Don't you think she should have some lunch?"

"Don't worry, we'll grab a Big Mac."

"But she can't. . . ."

A paper cup tapped him on the elbow.

"Excuse me, Daddy." Her voice was timid and polite. "I'm sure that if you want to spend the night with me in this real old house, it would be all right with your nice lady friend here, because it's not a very good idea to be driving a car when you need your rest, and. . . ."

"Maybe another time," he said, and kicked open the screen.

Scotty watched with calm gray eyes. "It's okay if you're too shy to kiss me goodbye, Daddy, because it might make you feel better to know that sometimes I'm shy, too, and. . . ."

Stiffly, Cooper bent over and pecked her on the head. Before she could thank him VRAY MUSH he was on the porch, the sequins retreating like dull little stars as he limped down the steps to the car.

21

Cooper's friend Remi Raines met him at the staff entrance to the emergency room carrying a set of scrubs she'd just clipped off of a storage caddy in the underground laundry.

Remi was a beautiful Jamaican woman with sparkling black eyes and a head full of long micro-braids. She helped elderly patients about to be discharged from the hospital find places in rehab centers and nursing homes. One of her clients had been Short Stroke Driggers. When she'd scored the nine-time national Putt-Putt champion an apartment in the Leticia Florence high rise for seniors with enough shelves to handle his trophies, Remi became his number one pin-up girl, and Short Stroke had ordered Cooper to write a column about her.

That had been long ago, before the new regulations, and they'd had fun doing the interview—Cooper slowing her down so he could record her Kingstonian dialect in his Professional Reporter's Notebook the way she spoke it; Remi helping him figure out how to spell the words. She loved the column, told Cooper it made her famous, and after that, on the first Tuesday of every month, the two of them met Short Stroke in the Leticia Florence dining room, where they ate the triple-salad cold plate and celebrated Short Stroke's outrageous life.

"Hol' up a quickie, bwoy." Remi hijacked a surgeon's mask from the mattress of a passing gurney and hung it around his neck. "Dat wicked, ee? Okay. Mek haste," she ordered, shooing Cooper into the service elevator.

They were heading to a privileged spot next to the fifth-floor nurse's station, the throne room, reserved for doctors to write up instructions after making rounds. Cooper would be an imposter, which Remi cheerfully reminded him was a federal crime.

"I don't know," he balked. "The plan seemed better at a distance."

Remi stood by the panel that listed the floors, the tip of her long orange nail hovering above the "5."

"You radda play," she asked him, "or stand roun' signin' bedpans 'til your renk ol' booty runs out of juice and dey haul it dung to da bloody morgue?"

"Cold storage might be the better option," Cooper said, sliding the mask up on his forehead.

Remi pressed the button. "Don' be so squirmy. No patient in der right min' is gaan ask a Doc to save 'em when he looks worse off dan dey do. Bee-lieve me."

Now, all alone behind the throne room door, Cooper's renk ol' booty was feeling more and more squirmy. At last he gave in to a hard folding chair—a new father in his faded green scrubs, waiting to ask the particulars of the birth of his child almost twelve years after she was born.

An overhead air duct sprayed him with chilly fumes of micro-waved tuna casserole and dirty mop water. He burped up Brunswick stew. He'd eaten it cold from the carton just before he left. The dogs had cleaned out the pizza.

Hitch had sent over some of the food from the surprise party. A spontaneous reunion, Odds & Ends' Greatest Hits. The essence of the person is there, watching you fidget as you turn the pages of the yearbook. They know you'll get it, as close as you were and all, and you don't want to let them down, but there have been hundreds of them and only one of you, tone deaf from alcohol abuse, no sleep, and no desire to sing.

The bright-eyed old woman with the carton of Brunswick stew . . . something about the way she smacked her lips while she waited for you to . . . to what? To order. Sure. The spectacular Beatrice Brown, an institution at Melvin's Barbecue, the first server they'd hired when they opened up back in 1947. Loaded with alacrity for the work, she buzzed around the tables, earning the nickname stitched in cursive on her uniform—"Miss Bee."

Cooper had written about Miss Bee when she retired on her eightieth birthday. Her husband had been an infantry soldier killed in the Normandy invasion, forcing her to share the skills she'd perfected by waiting on two spoiled little boys hand and foot. The lunchtime mob showed their gratitude by leaving her a fortune in fifty-cent tips. One son became a NASA engineer, the other an associate dean at the South Carolina School of Law.

The tears soothed Cooper's grainy eyes. His daughter's saga had attracted more attention than he'd been prepared for. Newspapers, television, and radio wanted interviews.

"I booked you on Carson," Sam announced. "Told 'em you do an imitation of the Godfather of Soul, and have a pack of trick dogs whose specialty is pissing on sofas."

As soon as he got home from Percy's, Cooper had called Sam at the paper to dictate a statement.

The nightmare of the last 24 hours became an impossible dream come true when a plucky little girl by the name of Scott Norris Smith was found unharmed. For a man whose livelihood depends on making words, I have only two:

Thank you:

To the members of law enforcement who professionally and diligently worked to cover every potential base and check every tip and lead.

To the people who sent so many prayers and positive vibes our way. We felt them, heard them, and needed them all.

To my friends and coworkers for organizing a first-rate coordination of information between the public and the police while continuing to put out a newspaper, and to the editors I've temporarily called a truce with for standing behind us in every conceivable and inconceivable way.

And to the person I most want to thank, an old friend, the heroine who rescued Scotty from the prospect of serious harm by an unidentified predator on the Greyhound bus, then graciously gave her shelter in her own home, where she cared for her and entertained her until I arrived. As always, Garland, you are the star of the show, and there are no honors or accolades large enough for your role in saving the life of an innocent and trusting child.

As you might imagine, Scotty, her mother, and I need some time to adjust, reflect, and heal, so I'm checking out for a few days to do just that. Until then, all I can say for now are the same words I started out with: Thank you, from the bottom of my heart.

Cooper had thanked Duke personally. He'd appeared with a big platter filled with appetizers when Cooper was getting in the car to drive to the hospital. "My girls are up since the crack of dawn selecting toys for Scotty," Duke moaned. "They built Junior Mount Kilimanjaro. Need good pair of hiking boots to reach the top."

It had felt good to laugh. "Tell them one toy each is a generous gift," Cooper said. "She has enough toys at the paper to supply an orphanage."

"No need to bother," Duke answered. "They never listen to me unless they want money. Be warned. A daughter is very expensive proposition. You will be placing collect call to everybody from now on. You like kitchen so much, you can relieve Tiny of dishwashing job; make him very happy. He can hang out in dining room twenty-four-seven. Earn lots more dough."

◆

Cooper stretched his legs and looked around. Throne room? This space was barely twice the size of his bathroom. A skimpy sheetrock wall separated him from the nurse's station. He could hear every beep and blip of the cardiac monitors, every jangle of the phone, every wisecrack and complaint. His heart was riding a pogo stick, jumping from his bowel to his throat each time another buzzer bleated.

He stood up, knocking over a Styrofoam cup of stagnant coffee next to a prescription pad. "10 a.m. Spring Valley" was the cure. Saturday's tee time, less than twenty hours away.

A narrow window treated him to the roof of the physical plant. He paced beside it. He longed for a nap. For three days, his senses had been as random as the sounds beyond the pasty walls. He had two heads, one a feather, the other a cinder block, neither holding a coherent thought.

He started to sit down again. Decided against it. The throne in his bathroom had a cushioned seat, and he didn't have to do time in the federal pen to squat on it.

Everything had been arranged, Remi had assured him. Hannah was having her hair done and would be here shortly. Remi was programmed on hospital time.

A shampoo and set wasn't what Cooper had pictured that morning when Frances told him Hannah was better. Comatose one minute, running off to the beauty shop the next. Women were made from the rebound gene.

Somebody was knocking.

"Remi?"

A woman wheeled Hannah through the door.

"Hello, Mr. Barnet."

"Oh. Hi. I thought you were. . . ."

"Bunny Carpenter. Congratulations. Great detective work. I wanted to meet you yesterday but you snuck off before I had a chance. We have a much-improved patient here, thanks to you."

The doctor, the one who'd examined Scotty while she was locked in her mother's arms. She was even better-looking today. Wild strawberry blond curls, honey brown eyes, and rosy skin free of makeup. No scrubs. Just a shiny black miniskirt over a set of skyscraper legs.

Cooper folded his arms across his chest. Dr. Carpenter gazed at his get-up, ending with the mask on his forehead. Why wasn't she in her office? Remi had told him that's where the doctors spent the afternoons, in their private offices, keeping appointments with patients.

"Just out of surgery?" she asked, and grinned.

"Open heart," he said. Should he remove the smock or leave it on? "Actually, I, um, I assumed Remi would be the one who . . . Remi Raines sort of thought up this crazy scheme to help me escape the. . . ." That's right, throw Remi under the bus.

"Whatever steams your ship," Carpenter said.

"Ordinarily I wouldn't do anything to misrepresent, I mean, anything that compromises the hospital or violates any . . . it's just that the well-wishers, for lack of a better word, they can keep you pretty busy, and I called Remi to see if she could . . . you may know Remi, she's. . . ."

"I get it."

Of course she got it. She was a medical doctor, for Chrissake, programmed to call the next play and move along. "Let them know outside when you're finished," she said. "And make it short if you can. She's been up too long already."

"What's he wearing?" Hannah was eyeing him like he'd just exploded from the trap door of a haunted house.

"I was just trying to save time," Cooper said.

"You did," said Hannah, "on a haircut and shave."

She took a big swallow from the large plastic water bottle she was holding. Evian. Hospitals were amazing institutions. Jailhouse toilet paper, with beauty parlors and designer water.

"You look like the last man standing," she said. Water was rolling down her chin. "Why are you growing that beard, anyway? It looks funny, like it landed on the wrong face. Except for your eyes I wouldn't have recognized you. They show up great against that silly mask. The blue against the white, like sky against snow. God, Bunny, I'm blathering like a fool. I thought you said you were bringing me down. What if this is permanent?"

"Remember, Hannah. Patience and faith. Look how far it's taken you. Now where would you like to park?"

"Park? Oh. Near the cliffs on Capri, I guess. Sorry. Right where I am is fine."

No it's not, Cooper thought. You're too close. Just ask Garland Cayce.

Rage was a new experience for him. It came at you like an avalanche. No chance for bystanders to find shelter. It was like a free trip to Vegas. Made you feel powerful and powerless at the same time.

"You got your hair all fixed up," he told her.

Meet the father, Bunny. The fake doc in the dumb-looking mask. All substance.

"They have a woman, Ruby, who travels around the rooms cleaning up major oil slicks like mine for almost nothing. I bet her a nickel she wouldn't have the stomach to touch the filthy stuff and she won. Prell's miraculous. That's what it was, of all things, Prell concentrate in an unbreakable tube, in case you drop it in the shower. Remember Prell? I used it when we were married."

Cooper nodded, squirming out of the jacket as his colleague slipped out the door.

"Ruby offered to curl it but I wasn't sure how it would turn out. Her hair was teased really high. It was cute on her, though. She looked kind of like Loretta Lynn. Scotty's mad for Loretta Lynn. I have no idea how she heard of her. I had to buy one of her CDs. She's crazy about country music."

"She was singing some of it in the car."

"She sang to you? She felt at home."

"I'm not sure who she was singing to. It could've been the radio."

"I understand she's over at your girlfriend's. Oh, for Pete's sakes, stop the presses, why don't you? Frances left me your number. I phoned and got Malachi. He told me where she was."

"She teaches dancing. She deals with little girls all the time. I called to check on them right before I left to come here." And no one had answered the phone. "She's very reliable. I hope you don't mind."

Hannah was talking over him. She'd turned into an adult model of that doll with the wind-up lips. She was worse than her daughter.

"She wouldn't take no for an answer," Hannah was saying. "And after everything the poor child went through . . . oh God, I swore I'd never allow myself to go there and I'm already going."

"I didn't know what else to do. I mean, if she'd been a boy it might've been easier as far as. . . ."

Hannah wasn't paying attention. He'd have to speak up. He cleared his throat.

"I wasn't sure if I'd say the right things, you know? Or what to give her to eat, and Frances was talking about baths, and shit, Hannah, the house is. . . ."

"Oh, shut up, Cooper. Why do you insist on apologizing for the imaginary shortcomings you impose on everybody else? Surely you didn't think I expected to find you chaste and womanless after all this time, did you? I'll be damned. I believe you did."

"It's not that. I didn't know how you'd feel about me leaving her with someone else. Someone you didn't know."

"Yeah. Like I actually pictured you taking up with a female werewolf, a serial executioner of helpless little girls, a sexual pervert posing as a children's dancing instructor. How about giving a person some credit for a change, will you? What kind of reporter are you, anyway, assigning motives to someone without bothering to let them speak for themselves? Not a good one, as far as I'm concerned. It makes me wonder about the accuracy of your stories."

Hannah stopped, put a finger in each ear, like a child.

"Dear God," she said. "Where is all this coming from?"

Cooper had no idea and wasn't about to assume, not after that lecture. She was right, though, about everything but the accuracy of his stories. She could be right about that, too. Anymore, the only certainty in his life was confusion.

"Well? Cat got your tongue? Don't look like that. I didn't mean to hurt your feelings, okay? My head feels all mixed up. They claim they're sending Timothy Leary packing but he's sure leaving behind a lot of residual madness. I shouldn't have to be held accountable for that. Well, should I?"

Hannah drank more water. Little sips this time, slowing herself down. She was as jumpy as a hot-wired Porsche in Manhattan grid-lock. The black fog lamps were still on, but Cooper was glad to see the green fighting through, flickers of natural light enhanced by the healthy pewter shine in her hair, revived by the miraculous Prell. The scent of home. She had a robe on over the hospital gown. Silky and light blue, tossed across her shoulders.

Looking beyond the physical effects of the medication, Cooper suddenly realized that Hannah's beauty had returned with the reappearance of her daughter. The dazzling youthful allure that had sent him reeling that chilly October night at the State Fair had been subdued by a road-weary vulnerability and deeply embedded determination, but the lovely features were now enriched with the seduction of well-earned substance, which in some ways made her seem more attractive.

He decided he'd better use Sam's technique, his Golden Rule for Female Appeasement—just tell her she's right and you're sorry, then run like hell because the next thing you say will get you killed.

"You're right, Hannah. You're right," Cooper said, and was going for "I'm sorry," but "You're barefooted," came out instead.

"What? Oh."

Hannah raised her feet off the wheelchair supports to look. Her toenails were pink. Gaudy.

"Pretty sloppy, huh? Scotty did it. We paint each other's. It's a Saturday ritual. We go to Woolworth's, eat grilled cheese and drink vanilla milkshakes at the counter. She picks the color. She gets to spend her allowance while we're there. You wouldn't think it would take long to blow a dollar, but she's a careful shopper. We go back home and take off our old polish and get a new lease on life. That daughter of mine goes for splash."

Hot pink in the little red sandals? Such kitschy toes for a kid. How could he have missed them on that daughter of hers? He automatically processed details. It was part of the job.

"They can't find my shoes," Hannah said.

She leaned over to scratch a wheal on her ankle. The blotches didn't look as bad today. Cooper held his breath until she sat up again. People tumbled out of wheelchairs all the time. One of Driggers' lady friends had reached down to pick up a Kleenex and broken her neck. Or maybe it was one of his buddies from the putt-putt circuit.

"Remember how you used to tease me about the way I packed my carry-on for a flight? Like I was a Marine heading off to Parris Island, you said. You made me go over each little tip they taught us, where to put the toothbrush, where to put the underwear, how to fold the extra uniform. One time you held that vase Nana gave us up to your eye. Do you still have it, the one made from carnival glass? I hope you didn't give it away. You pretended to be making a training video. You loved to do those character sketches. He was a real goofball, that instructor. I couldn't believe how you had him pegged. You'd never seen him in your whole life and . . . it was amazing. Right on the money."

Cooper shifted in the throne. Gene Krupa was tuning up again. Matinee performance.

"Why didn't you go gray?" Hannah demanded.

"I did."

"Only a little. You don't have nearly as much as I do. I dyed it for awhile. Now I don't even care. Did you see Frances? Five years older than me and yet to have a one."

"Your hair looks fine. But you're too thin."

"I know."

Cooper stood, stepped out of the scrubs, and went over to the window to check on the physical plant. When he came back to sit again, he saw he'd scraped a black mark on the linoleum. He rubbed at it roughly with the toe of his loafer, yanked the mask off his forehead, and wriggled his chair backwards.

This was it. No more bullshit. No more playing cocktail party. No more playing doctor. He could only play himself, a man at sea with not enough gray in his hair, a mutinous beard, and a castoff white shirt with too much starch. A man looking for shore.

"Listen, Hannah. I heard something from Hitch a while ago."

"Hitch? He's still at the paper?"

"He was as of this morning, when he told me he knew about you and Scotty. From his sister, he said. His sister who works at the car rental place at Douglas. She knew you. She knew about Scotty. She knew we'd been married. He's known about it for years."

Hannah listened, detached, like she was analyzing a movie she'd just seen.

She gulped some water. "It's this stuff they have me on. It makes your throat so dry you can barely talk." She wiped her mouth on the sleeve of her robe.

"Naturally I wondered," she said. "We knew a lot of people together and we were living less than two hours away. I assumed it wouldn't be a problem as far as the people I hadn't known before.

I was divorced, her father had remarried, moved far off to another life . . . but I worried about what I'd do when I ran into someone from back then, what they would think. And of course it started happening. Only on occasion. No one particularly close. Fringe, mainly. Sometimes, when Scotty was with me.

"The first few times I panicked. What in the world should I say? But it never came to that. Oh, once in a while they mentioned you, asked if I'd heard about your latest escapade, your latest prize. But as time passed . . . people take on new lives, new identities. I suppose people forgot our connection, or lost interest, or maybe thought it was no longer appropriate to bring up the past."

A call bell went off. Hannah waited until someone answered, then nodded and went on.

"Funny though," she said. "I didn't have anything to worry about as far as Scotty was concerned. They hardly asked anything about her. Oh, they'd say hello, make a little bit of nervous small talk here or there, what a cute dress, what a big smile, but they hardly ever asked who she was or anything like that. And the way I introduced her, if it was somebody we both knew, I'd just say, 'This is Scotty.'"

She checked to see how much water she had left, then put the bottle to her mouth and wet her lips.

"I'd never realized before how uneasy adults are around children when they detect something's not exactly right. It's fascinating. They try to be polite and act as though they haven't noticed but they overdo it, you know? And the whole situation becomes strained. I guess in a way you could call it artificially pleasant. How do I ease out of this scene?

"It's odd, how they don't ask her any of the questions you usually ask a kid. Where do you go to school, what are your hobbies, do you have any brothers or sisters, things like that. I'm not sure why they don't. Maybe they feel like it's out of bounds, like she might not know the answers or something. And with Scotty rambling on about everything under the sun, everyone sort of gratefully loses their train of thought and the encounter ends in an awkward rush."

Hannah bent over to scratch the wheal on her ankle, wincing as she trailed a finger across the angry reaction. She examined the wet spot on her sleeve, where she'd wiped her mouth.

Cooper watched her struggle. He wasn't going anywhere.

"At first I worried that someone might run into you and mention that they saw me, that I was with a little girl named Scotty, and ask you who she was, but then I realized the connection would never dawn on them, or you, either. It just wouldn't have occurred to them that the two of us could have, would have produced. . . . Besides, when I left, I was only a few weeks pregnant. No one knew, not even Julia. Not even me, for sure. And then the whole time I was pregnant I was living like a hermit with my parents. Only a few people knew that we'd split, knew that I was home, only the ones I told Frances she could call and tell. And I made her promise not to let them know I was pregnant. She told them I was having a hard time, that I didn't want to talk to anybody, that I wanted to figure things out by myself. And after Scotty was born . . . well, because of the way it turned out, I sort of never stopped living that way. I didn't have time for a social life. It all seemed silly. Trivial. I couldn't relate."

Hannah was stranded on the other side of a prison fence. Part of Cooper wanted to help her over, and part of him wanted to pound her fingers with a shovel, impaling them in the barbed wire.

"Of course, there came a point . . . I eventually had to start confiding in my closest friends. If they didn't agree with my decision, they at least seemed to respect my right to make it. Like if your friend decides to get fake boobs, even if you don't think she needs them, you realize it's her choice, you know? I made them swear not to tell you or anyone else who might, and since you didn't find out, I guess they honored my request. My friends are very loyal. I was in a bad place. They felt sorry for me.

"I imagine they thought if they came to you they would be holding down the head of a drowning woman, consorting with the enemy, even if you weren't enemy material. I guess they blamed you for not doing your job when it came to appreciating what you had. I was really hurt. I loved you so much, and it seemed like the more I loved you, the more. . . . It does seem hard to believe, though, when you think about it, doesn't it?"

"Not hard to believe. Impossible."

"I suppose the word could've gotten around through a sort of underground grapevine," Hannah said. "It's nice to believe that confidences are for keeps, but nothing ever is. It's funny, though. When secrets are told they never get told right. Even if you tell them yourself."

"But it doesn't make sense. In all this time . . . almost twelve years . . . I happen to run into someone who'd happened to run into you and they never say. . . ."

"And they never say what? Your ex might have a daughter but I'm not sure. She's not quite right. Is she yours?"

It hit him like a fist in the throat. What did she mean, "They honored my request"? She was commending her friends for hiding his child from him, equating it to keeping a confidence about breast implants, or an illicit affair. How could she be so obtuse, so smug, so matter-of-fact? Like she was the all-mighty queen of England—a scheming, malevolent queen—who on a whim ordered her subjects to withhold information about a plan to drop a nuclear bomb on the entire free world. Like it was an honorable thing when they did it, like they deserved to be knighted and deified with psalms of praise and glory for the rest of their lives.

"Your friends. . . ." he said, but his voice belonged to someone else. It was threatening, contemptuous, visceral. ". . . your devoted co-conspirators, should be ashamed to look themselves in the mirror. They're mindless shallow assholes, every last one of them. Your wonderful sister, too. Especially your sister. And your father, a law-yer. They have no principles, no sense of right and wrong. She was my child, too, Hannah, whether you liked it or not. It wasn't your call to make. Half of her was mine."

Cooper reached forward, grabbing the wheelchair, wrestling it closer. It lurched, then skidded towards him. The brake was on.

"What're you doing?" Hannah said. "You're spilling my water. Let go."

He knelt in front of her, the lazy blue of his eyes dark now, fierce. He locked his hands on the arms of her chair. His face was close to hers. He wanted to hurt her, the same way he'd wanted to when she'd walked into the Toddle House, except then the inclination had passed before it was a threat.

Until that night, the compulsion to commit violence was nothing Cooper could relate to. His outburst towards Garland was a release of unresolved emotions that had been locked in since the morning Hannah had called him in the newsroom—perhaps since he was ten years old—and even before Scotty had corrected him, he'd begun to step back from the edge of the hole.

But this, this rage was the remorseless craving of a sociopath, the unleashed demons of a madman, the inbred trigger of a wild animal pulled by its instinct to lunge.

Heretofore, Cooper had thought of a male who physically abused a woman as a monster who belonged in a cage, a sicko, a coward of the vilest form, and resented having to share a link with him on the human chain.

Yet at this instant, he could see, could actually understand, that there were circumstances that could drive a reasonable, normally compassionate person beyond all sense of himself and his control, because all he wanted to do was stand up, storm behind this woman he despised, grab the handles of her wheelchair, and jerk her back and forth, as rough and hard as he could.

He wanted to scare her, make her scream, make her cry; make her beg him to stop. He wanted to raise her chair as high as he could lift it and sling it toward the wall. He wanted to. . . . Hold on, he told himself. Hold on. But he'd already lost it and it felt so good he could hardly stand it.

"Dammit, Hannah, do you realize you stole a child? You can't do that. You can't just take someone's child away and never let them know they had it. That's criminal, as low as it gets. Do you realize the blatant arrogance, the narcissistic callousness. . .? I thought I knew you. I thought I loved you. I thought you were the most solid, trustworthy woman I'd ever known. How did you fool me like that? For seven whole years, almost eight, I thought. . . .

"It takes one cold, heartless son of a bitch to do what you did, Hannah. I could have you arrested, do you know that? Arrested for kidnapping. For . . . hell, you were the thief all along, not Garland Cayce. Poor, deranged woman, she thought she was doing a good deed, but you, you. . . . Why did you do it, Hannah? Why? Can you just tell me that? Or am I too far out of the privileged loop to have that information?"

"Sssh," she said. "Quiet now. Settle down."

She was crying, trembling. She hiccupped when she spoke, but her voice was soft and firm. She was speaking to him as if she were speaking to her daughter.

"It's all right," she said. "It's okay."

"Talk to me, Hannah. Tell me. Why, Hannah. Why?"

She waited until she'd stopped crying. She was calmer now, more controlled. She covered her face with her hands before she answered.

"Sometimes I don't remember," she said. "Sometimes I don't even know."

"You must think I'm despicable. The worst bastard that ever took a breath of air. What did I do to you? What did I do that would make you pull such a heartless, devious, cheap. . . . She could have died, Hannah. The probabilities were enormous. Do you realize that? She could've died, and it would've been your fault. You would've had to live with it the rest of your life, the fact that your reprehensible behavior was what killed your precious daughter."

Someone was opening the door. A nurse.

"What's happening in here?"

"Go away," said Hannah. "This is a private conversation sanctioned by my physician."

"But you've become very elevated. We can hear you outside."

"Of course we're elevated. You know the story. Everybody and his brother knows the story. We had a baby together and she's eleven going on twelve and this man, my ex-husband, didn't find out until a few days ago. Wouldn't you be elevated if you were him? Wouldn't you be?"

"This is a hospital, Miss Smith. I'm a nurse. My concern is your health."

"My health won't get better until we have this thing out. If he murders me I probably deserve it, and if I get hysterical you can just shoot me up with another round of dope. That's all you've been doing for my health since I've been here. Holding me against my will. Shooting me up with dope."

"I'm going to call Dr. Carpenter," the nurse said, and hurried out the door.

"Sanctioned by my physician?" Cooper said.

They both laughed, and then they cried, and then she started to talk. Some things she told him, some she continued to save for herself, without reservation, because this was the only way it could be.

◆

She'd assumed he wanted children when they married. Didn't every-one back in those days? Go to college, get engaged, have the wedding the summer after graduation. Work two years, have your first kid?

Only he wasn't ready. She was happy to wait. She was crazy about flying. They were madly in love, having fun. But he kept stalling and the distance grew. According to the therapist it happens slowly. The avoidance of topics, the layers of separation, the imitation of feelings that had been real.

Then she'd pulled the sleazy trick. Men are too easy to fool, even the ones who aren't supposed to be. After she'd quit the pill, she kept the empty cardboard dispenser on the dresser for awhile, but got sick of looking at it and threw it away. She hadn't even told her sister.

She was pretty sure she was pregnant when she'd planned the weekend at Sullivan's Island. Yet there wasn't the joy she'd expected. Just panic and shame. Their baby was made from her deceit. She wasn't leaving him, Hannah told herself. Just going away.

She planned to call him as soon as she arrived in Charlotte, tell him what she'd done. She loved him. He loved her. She'd confess, he'd want her back. But it was complicated. She waited. Just another day or two, to sort things out. But each day brought new guilt. More depression and confusion.

Besides, he'd never told her about his brother. This was the part she left out of the narrative, although Malachi may have been right, it may have influenced her more than anything else.

What kind of relationship was that, when a man neglected to tell his wife about the tragedy that had shaped his life? The week before she'd left, the therapist she consulted advised her to confront him about it, but she'd been as determined then as she was now never to betray the man who understood Cooper better than anyone else. Certainly more than she did. Cooper trusted Malachi like a child trusts people, like Scotty does. She wasn't about to destroy that. Who else would he ever have, a man too damaged to let go?

The therapist told her it would be hard, perhaps impossible, for him to change, a person who had experienced something like that, especially when he had repressed it all those years, but at first she'd convinced herself she was strong enough to alter her expectations. Not lower them. Just make adjustments. Mature. Adapt. She would have a baby, their baby. She would make a home for them, fill it with love.

But what if he shut the baby out? Of course it would be unintentional, but would that matter, if he couldn't open himself to the risks of helpless abandon?

The problems started toward the end of the second month. The spotting, the ordered bed rest, the fears. She left Frances' condo and moved in with her parents. She told them she'd scammed Cooper, that he didn't want children. They worried about the toll of additional conflict, worried she might lose the baby. They agreed with Frances that Cooper would have to be informed, but it would be better to resolve everything when the crisis had passed. Then, three months later, after the amniocentesis. . . . Hannah's father took care of the divorce.

That's what she told people closest to her, in different variations, later on. That a man who hadn't wanted a child in the first place certainly wouldn't want one who was compromised. She didn't say anything to the others. By then, it didn't matter anymore.

"When I found out about Scotty's problem I needed strength," Hannah said. "The kind of strength I didn't think you'd have. And the emotional energy it takes, no one understands. There's not much left for reflection or remorse. Or regret. Everything is right this minute, until you tuck her in at night and hear her prayers. And then you're lying in bed praying yourself, dreading the future, dreading the inevitable. What's going to happen when I'm not there to make her life, to make it. . . . No one else knows, Cooper. I'm the only one who knows how, who cares as much as you have to care. . . ."

"I'm sorry, Hannah," he said. "You don't have a life."

"I have the only life I want. I have Scotty and Miss Mac, and I have the other mothers, and my sister and my parents and Julia and a few other friends, if I feel like making the connection. And as far as men go I meet my needs. An occasional dinner, a roll in the hay. The airport's a good place. Plenty of people like me coming and going, between marriages or finished with them altogether. Don't worry, it's all right. It's a win-win process. Instant vetting, everything up front, no strings attached. We pass each other around."

Cooper was no longer kneeling. He was sitting on the floor, grasping her hand. Probably hurting her. He let go and stood. Sat in his chair. The throne. It was a bad day in the palace. The kind of emotions that started wars. Everything and nothing understood.

"You should've told me," he said.

"Yes."

"You were doing the same thing I did to you a little while ago, when I was telling you about Percy. Making assumptions without giving me a chance."

"I guess I was."

"I deserve to know the reason."

"Beyond what I've already told you, I'm not sure I can. . . ."

She was worn out. Head lowered, shoulders sagging, eyes almost closed. He should leave; let them take her to bed. Go check on her daughter.

"I could have just been being. . . ."

Cooper had to lean towards her to hear.

". . . what would I have been? Stubborn? Irrational? Proud? I remember telling myself I was mainly protecting Scotty from your reaction. Or from no reaction at all. But how could I be sure you'd behave that way, with your very own child and all.

"I guess some of it could've been the hostility I felt toward you for shutting me out when I'd done nothing to deserve it. I'd held it in for so long, and the hormones were raging, and, maybe it was the ultimate payback, I just don't know. I just knew that I'd deceived you, and then I had a child who was. . . who wasn't. . . ."

She spoke the last few words slowly, and then they were both quiet.

"You can't imagine how much I agonized. . . . God, the indecision, the guilt . . . and then this miracle happens. You reach the point where you can put it out of your mind. Like a psychotic or a person with a split personality. Without actually realizing it, you manipulate the situation until you've convinced yourself that you're right. You lose all perspective. You lose a sense of reality. Not total reality, with Scotty that would have been impossible. But you can lose reality in one facet of your life. It's amazing really, how easy it is to do."

Cooper listened. For more than thirty years he'd done the same thing, or at least learned to trick himself into thinking he could.

"Malachi told me yesterday, or was it the day before, that I wasn't protecting Scotty," Hannah said. "He told me I was protecting you."

"Malachi came to the hospital?"

"I'm pretty sure he did. I was all alone and then he was there. The whole thing was strange. His appearance, our conversation. I have this picture of him sort of floating above my bed. Then all of a sudden he's gone. He was wonderful, Cooper. Even in my drugged-up stupor he made a lot of sense."

"Malachi's in bad shape. He's just. . . ."

"He's what?"

"Never mind."

"Just what?"

"Just nothing."

"I hate it when you do that," she said. "You start to say something that matters and then you clam up. You're like the President carrying around that little black bag or box or whatever it is, with your fingers right next to the button. Almost ready to press it, almost ready to drop the bomb, but you can't screw up the courage. Maybe the box is just a ruse. Maybe it's only filled with confetti. Nobody ever finds out. Is that the trick, Cooper? Is that how you keep them hanging on? By keeping your finger right on the edge of the button?"

Hannah was getting wound up again. Cooper stood and glanced at the door. The doctors would be coming around before long.

"Wonder what's going on in the halls of *General Hospital*?" he said.

"You'll never change, will you, Cooper? All this time and you really haven't changed at all."

Hannah raised her head to look at him. He could see the scar on her forehead. When she was agitated it used to turn red, or was it white? He leaned towards her to check, but somehow went too low and found her mouth.

It was a gentle kiss, first one side of her lip and then the other. Then both together.

"I'm sorry," he said. "I meant to see about your scar."

"My scar?" She laughed. "Remember when you grew that mustache?"

He ran his tongue over the straw on his upper lip. He seemed to be growing another one.

"It was godawful," she said.

They looked at each other's mouths.

"What color was it?" he asked her.

"Black. Well, almost, anyway. And full, if you didn't count that tiny bare patch. If it had been on someone else it might have been kind of nice. But you weren't the mustache type. You looked like you were trying to hide something. Besides, it never stayed smooth. Some part of it was always jutting out one way or another, like your hair. And when you smiled, the way your mouth does, yeah, just like that, your mouth would go one way and the mustache would go the other. I could hardly look at you without getting tickled."

"Why did I shave it?"

"Just got tired of me kidding you, I guess."

It had happened after Lizzie got sick. She was part boxer, part shepherd, part mystery. They found her on a rafting trip, mangy and abused. When they called her over, she slunk, almost crawling, to the spot where they'd beached the canoe. They brought her home in the Volkswagen. She stank so bad Cooper had to stop the car while Hannah got sick.

"We can't let her in the house," they said. When she was too skittish to cross the threshold, Cooper carried her.

Six months later, they discovered she had leukemia. They fixed up a pallet for two on the living room floor. Each night after deadline, Cooper came home and spent the rest of the night lying next to her.

"She's starting to suffer," Hannah would tell him. "We've got to put her down."

"Not yet," he'd say.

One day after he left for the office, Hannah took Lizzie to the vet and held her while she went to sleep. That night, Cooper sobbed so hard she was afraid.

"Can't I do anything?" she pleaded.

"No. Just stay away."

Early the next morning, she found him lying on Lizzie's pallet, soaking wet.

"Let's be grateful she wasn't a person," she told him. "A little child," she said. "That would be unfixable. Let's try to be thankful for that."

"Yes," he answered softly. "That would be unfixable."

He turned to her and touched her scar. He was tender, yet she could feel the distance. And when she leaned close to kiss him, the mustache was gone.

22

Five other girls were prancing on the dead front lawn but she was the one you noticed, the skinny little squirt dropping a skinny silver baton, the pale kid swallowed up by the long red basketball jersey, LSU's Number 23. What did she do, win it off Pistol Pete in a game of horse?

She was flitting around the stingy shade of a dogwood. Her hair was gold one second; brown the next, after nearly twelve years still trying to make up its mind. It was cut short, a golden brown cap framing the delicate bones of her forehead and cheeks. She could blister, a child that fair, if the sun could ever catch her.

But she was moving, moving all the time, pacing back and forth in herky-jerky motions, a wind-up toy, a Jack-in-the-box. It was some scene. Five of them strutting and flailing their batons and in one case what looked like a cut-off mopstick, none of them in lockstep. And this cheerful little rebel neither strutting nor flailing, just flitting around and talking with all of her might, talking without being heard.

Why didn't Percy take them in, out of the heat? She didn't look his way. In the Lincoln he was just some old codger on the way for a wax job at Elmwood Shell. Besides, he was never early.

All these years he'd driven past this house, everything and nothing changed. The yard thin on grass but thick with patches of petunias, Black-eyed Susans, and the tiny violet blossoms of stinkweeds. The amateurish hand-painted sign, highlighted in pink to match the pink steps. Percy standing on the bottom step in a basic black leotard, her petite body as taut as a nautical knot and sexy with unaffected confidence, her black hair shining in a thick braid all the way to her butt, even the same navy-blue Boston Red Sox baseball cap she had on today—leading a parade of bedraggled children clutching batons; her smallest class, she'd assured him the night they met.

No. 23 hadn't been in the original picture. How old would she have been back then, two maybe, or three? She dropped the baton again, watched it roll, chased it; a red-white blur of helter-skelter improvisation, cluelessly out of sync. Good thing Percy had her on the end, this funny little girl, this little girl who was dancing to the beat of a different drummer, a drummer in a wacky alternative band. Watching her was heartbreaking. Heartbreaking, yet heartening, too.

Cooper puttered around the block—that's what codgers did, they puttered—and then he made the loop again. He would've pulled in the driveway, waited inside where it was cool, if the champion of cartwheel karate hadn't been patrolling the grounds with a weapon.

"A man doesn't belong in a little girl's dancing school affiliating with her teacher unless he's a Daddy coming after his daughter."

But he did have a daughter. The one in the long red shirt. The one dancing to a different beat, cursed by the part of him that made her, the part of him that also danced to the wrong tune. That was what they told him, said to him in various degrees of exasperation or amusement or ire, the people he hung around with, the people who put up with his off-the-wall notions and enigmatic ways. What would he do next?

He stopped at the hill for a funeral procession. Goble Brothers, the mortuary downtown. They had four. He'd be taking their dictation soon. Thank God they were one body short this week.

Touch a button, he remembered, and found one still attached to his collar. He could pass for human today. Sam's wife Laura had rescued his cleaning from the auction block and dropped it at the house early this morning. Nothing unconventional about his wardrobe; khaki britches or chinos, white or blue oxford shirts, all the same.

If you don't touch a button when you pass a hearse, someone you know might die. If you don't have a button on your clothing, your belly button will do. Irene Miller, the lady Hannah had nicknamed "The Hairnet Woman," had picked up this tip from one of the girls at the bingo parlor.

They'd been sitting in his car, Cooper and Irene Miller, waiting on a funeral caravan on the way to Longview Cemetery. "Touch a button," Irene had demanded. He'd told her it was silly and refused, and two days later The Hairnet Woman was dead. Just to be on the safe side, he kept his finger on base as he puttered around the block again.

◆

Percy was pleading. "This is our last practice before the big night and all but two of you are doing everything except what you're supposed to." She nodded towards Lacey Jo, peering shyly beneath thick black bangs heavy with sweat, and then at Myrtle Bailey's daughter Stacey, her silky brown skin glistening beauty and health. "And Li isn't even here." Leyla Chang had called to say she had a conflict with tennis.

"Careful with that stick, Patricia," Percy said, pointing to an Annie Oakley blonde. "You're about to poke out a couple of eyes."

"But it's too long. It keeps getting in the way."

"Only if you let it," Percy said. She held out the yellow dime-store ruler she'd been using to lead the parade. "See, mine's too short, but it's not stopping me. The trick is imagination. You're the star of the show. You're twirling the fire baton. It's blazing like mad. Everybody's on the edge of their seats. It's your finest hour, your chance to shine. Now let's go."

"Why does *she* get to be the star of the show?" demanded Little Linda Lister. "She didn't even remember to bring her equipment."

"Linda, your job is to do your best, hon, and stop worrying about everybody else. Patricia is using that mopstick because her brother turned her baton into a pretzel."

"If my brother did that to me I'd kill him," Little Linda said.

"To put it mildly," Percy muttered.

Scotty left her place in line to go over and pat Linda on the arm.

"Don't worry about Patricia being the star of the show," she told her. "You're a nice large size so everybody will look at you, too."

"Scotty, go back to your assigned spot," said Percy, and turned to face the group again.

"Hello, girls. Do you realize this is your last chance to pull it together? Maybe we should just skip the recital this year."

"Nooooo," yelled the girls. "No, no, no, no, no."

Percy slid the ruler down the inside of her arm, cupping the end in her hand. "Okay, one more time. Get ready, and START two three, and STRUT, strut, strut-strut-strut, and KICK-one, KICK-two, together, AND. . . . What's the problem now, Patricia?"

"She keeps trying to give me her baton, Miss Percy. She wants to trade for the stick."

Percy jammed the ruler down the front of her leotard. "Come here a second, doodlebug." Scotty hurried forward, the baton banging against her knees. Percy crouched to a squat and lowered her voice.

"Listen, honeybunch. Your offer to Patricia is very generous, but I bought that baton especially for you to use. It's a present, and I paid good money for it, and I don't want you to give it away. Understand?"

Scotty nodded.

"Good. Besides, I'm trying to teach Patricia a lesson. She forgets to bring a baton every time she comes. She borrowed mine way back in March and I haven't seen it since. You don't want her to lose your baton, do you?"

Scotty jerked her head from side to side.

"I didn't think so. If you're going to be a famous dancer, you have to go over there and stand in a straight line and watch me real close so you can learn these steps. We have about ten minutes to finish the lesson, so please try not to interrupt again. Okey-dokey?"

"Okey-dokey, miss, I will try not to interrupt your lesson again because my mama says that I need to concentrate on one thing at a time and not do too many things at once, because I have a. . . ."

"Your mother is a very smart lady," Percy said. "Now scoot. Hey, what happened to my straight line?"

Stacey was using Patricia's stick to block the holes in a fire ant bed, and Lacey Jo was trying to grab it and return it to Patricia. Little Linda Lister was bending over, crushing the fleeing troops with the rubber tip of her baton, one hand clutching the back of her blue-jean skirt.

"Little Linda, what's that you've got behind you?" Percy asked.

"Nothing."

"I want to see it. Pronto."

"My zipper just busted," Little Linda said, "and if it doesn't get fixed, my mother will have a hissy fit."

"A hissy fit, huh?" Percy raised her eyebrows and pressed the ruler against her lips, attempting to hide her grin. "That sounds serious. You better leave those ants alone, before you get stung."

"Get some Raid," Stacey said. "Quick."

"Live and let live," Percy told her. "Now, all of you, away from there.

"Linda?" Percy said.

"Ma'am?"

"Have you tried your costume on lately?"

"No."

"Make sure your mother sees me before you leave today."

"Miss Percy?"

"Yes, Trudy."

"Is that new girl gonna have a costume just like ours?"

"She certainly is."

"But her mother's in the hospital. Who's gonna make it for her?"

"That's not your worry, Trudy. Your worry is to memorize these steps before Sunday night. Now, let's get going. The next one of you who goofs off is. . . ."

"I just need to interrupt one more time, miss, because I would like to tell that girl with the braces on her top teeth that she doesn't have to worry about who is going to make my costume for me, because my daddy told me that he will make a very pretty costume for me, and he also said that he will be happy to see me dance with all these nice girls in your real big show."

"Exactly when did he tell you that, cutie?"

"I don't know exactly when he told me that, Miss Percy, because he probably told me a very long time ago."

"Her picture was in the paper yesterday."

"What now, Linda?"

"Her picture. My mother showed it to me. That man that hangs around your house all the time is her father, but he didn't even know he had her until a few days ago. Why doesn't he want her? Why is she over here?"

Percy looked over at Scotty, who'd gone to sit beside the ant bed and was fiddling with the Velcro fasteners on her new tennis shoe.

"Watch the ants, dollbaby," she called out. "I give. Class dismissed."

◆

Cooper pulled in as soon as all the girls had been collected. Scotty was sitting in the grass under the dogwood, surrounded by Black-eyed Susans, holding her baton and watching Percy drag a large green garbage can up the driveway, dodging broken chunks of concrete and bulging roots to park it at the side of the house.

"It's my daddy," Scotty whispered, dropping the baton. "Daddy," she cried out. "I'm staying put over here by this tree where Miss Percy told me to take it easy while she does a few little jobs, and in a minute we can go inside and eat a nice healthy lunch."

"Oh, hi," Percy said, glancing over her shoulder. "I thought you were somebody turning around."

Cooper leaned out the window. "I almost was," he said. He grinned, but his tentative blue eyes gave him away.

His relief that Scotty was alive and unharmed went beyond any feelings he could describe. Still, he couldn't shake the apprehension, the foreboding, even in his sleep. Five hours last night. He'd had a bad dream. He was searching for Reba. He finally found him in an empty department store, scrambling up a rickety escalator, being pursued by a snake that was actually a female Dr. Fue. Cooper was riding on another escalator, unable to save him. He was going in the wrong direction, going down, and he couldn't get off. "Reba. Reba," he kept calling, screaming so loud he could feel his heart about to burst, yet he wasn't making any sounds. He'd kept trying anyway, until Reba disappeared. This morning, he'd given him a side bowl of cabbage to go with his regular breakfast. Reba was a fool for cabbage.

"Your daughter and I have been spending your money," Percy said.

"Yes, Daddy, we've been spending that big pile of money you gave us."

They were both standing beside the car now, waiting. Cooper lowered the other three windows but didn't get out. "Good," he said. "What on?"

"Clothes, what else?" Percy said. "We went shopping again this morning, early. Scotty likes riding with the top down, don't you, sweetie?"

"Shouldn't she be wearing sunscreen?"

"She is. We slathered it on. She had on sunglasses, too, and a straw hat, at least until we drove across the Broad River Bridge."

"Yes, Daddy, and Miss Percy told me not to worry about it because some real lucky fish would soon be decked out in that nice straw hat, and she said that we should be very happy for him."

"I bet it's a perfect fit." Cooper's smile was full of tenderness and sorrow. Percy turned away for an instant, sucked in a breath. "Hey there," she said softly, reaching inside to run a finger along his wrist, which was hooked above the steering wheel.

"Thank you," he said. He glanced at Scotty and quickly moved his hand to the seat. "Her face looks a little pink to me."

"Oh, she's just excited about her stuff, aren't you, Scotty? She got these shorts and three tops that were all on sale, and those Nikes she's wearing, plus a new pair of white sandals. Not the most practical color, but try finding Velcro straps. Your daughter informed me her shoes have to fasten with Velcro. If she's still around on Monday, we'll be learning to tie a knot."

"Yes, Daddy, I have this very nice pair of red Nikes I'm wearing, Daddy." Scotty lifted her foot to show him and lost her balance. Percy caught her, giving her a quick squeeze before she let her go.

"And you can take them off without having to untie the strings, because you may not realize this, Daddy, but it saves a lot of time, and. . . ."

"What about the shirt?" Cooper asked. Scotty turned around to show him what was printed on the back.

"For God's sakes, Percy. *My Daddy's Pistol?*"

"She went for the color first. Said it matches her toenails. Not hardly. No way to duplicate that shade. Then, when we read the message, nothing else would do. Come on, let's go in. It's hot out here."

Cooper sat on the captain's chair. Scotty dragged the red stool beside him and climbed up on it, then climbed down again.

"Daddy, you might like to know that I always wanted a nice new baton like the majorettes use in the Christmas parade but my mama would always forget to buy it for me and your sweet little girlfriend here bought this one before our lesson today and I'm going to take it to my mama and tell her that I'm going to use it in a nice big show and that she can. . . ."

"Nice big show?" Cooper looked from Scotty to Percy. She flipped the Red Sox cap on the counter, a souvenir of husband number two, and snatched a jar of Duke's mayonaise from the refrigerator.

"What show?"

"That nice big show at that church where her oldest brother is not the first boss but another boss who gives the prayers, Daddy, and it will have all those pretty decorations in it that I can take you to see right now, in the room where the squirrel with the very bad smell is living under that old red couch, and. . . ."

"Show me later, okay? I'm talking to Miss Percy right now. Why don't you go play us a concert on the piano?"

"It's simple," Percy said through gritted teeth. The pop top on the Spam had broken off and she was working the lid open with a knife.

"Here," Cooper said. "You'll cut yourself."

"Hannah's not going home tomorrow, which means there's no reason Scotty can't dance."

"Come on, baby, I just witnessed her performance out there." Cooper frowned toward the noise in the den. "There's no way in hell she can. . . ."

"She'll do fine," Percy said. She dumped the Spam in a warped plastic bowl and felt around in a drawer until she came up with a fork missing part of a prong.

"But she doesn't know how to dance."

"Yes, Daddy," said Scotty, already running back into the kitchen after a few random bangs on the keys. Bob crept behind her, keeping a safe distance. "I sure do know how to dance just like those beauty queens in those snug tight bathing suits that dance on that real late television show that my mama lets me stay up to see, and Daddy, you might be surprised to know that they wear a crown just like a real Cinderella princess, and if I could have a crown I sure would take care of it and always keep it in the place where it belongs and. . . ."

"Percy, can she dance or not?"

"Didn't you just hear her say she could?" Percy dumped enough mayonnaise in the bowl to cover Williams-Brice Stadium end to end and added some sweet pickle relish. "She told the girls that you couldn't wait to make her costume."

"That I couldn't wait to . . . don't they make those things in smaller sizes?"

"Sure. You can make one any size you want. You just fit her to the pattern. You should know that, being an accomplished seamstress and all."

"No, I'm talking about those wands, batons, whatever they are. Maybe if she had a shorter length. . . ."

"We got the shortest one they had."

Percy opened a rusty bread box, took out a half loaf of thin-sliced Claussen's and slapped four pieces on the counter.

"Don't look so distressed, old man," she said. She plopped on the deviled ham, then cut one of the sandwiches in fourths and put it on a paper plate with a pile of Fritos and a cluster of green grapes. "We've got it in the bag."

"You might want to eat the grapes first and save the Fritos for last," Cooper told Scotty. "Your aunt Frances said you shouldn't. . . ."

Percy caught his hand and pulled him toward the door. "I thought you had to go by the paper. Don't you want to run over and check on Hannah, too, since Frances isn't here?"

"But she can't just. . . ."

"You better shake a tail feather. You have some sewing to do, and your daughter's expecting you back by six thirty."

Percy settled Scotty at the table and peeked out the window to make sure the car was gone.

"Eat. I'll be back in a skinny minute."

The telephone was in the pink beach chair, on the sands of Happy Isle. She scooped it up, sat in the chair, and dialed.

23

Cooper settled Scotty on the street side of the swing, then sat next to her on a cafeteria tray. Early in the afternoon, Sam and Duke had come by to clear the junk off the porch. They'd shored up the swing by replacing the deteriorated hardware and cleaned up the mildewed seat, but didn't have time to do anything about the missing slats. Cooper reached up to tug on the new chains, making sure the hooks in the ceiling were holding firm.

He could hear his mother's voice. "You have to be on your toes every second." Their father would agree, humoring her in his corny, playful way. "One false move and they're goners." People assumed if you didn't have children it meant you didn't like them, but who wouldn't love a kid?

"Daddy?"

"Yes?"

"I would like to see that nice brown dog with the pretty red ribbon around his neck that you put in your TV show."

His TV show? In another four days, he wouldn't even have a column. He'd overstepped Hitch's golden oldies' bounds yesterday and asked Maxine if she minded writing one for Tuesday. Sam agreed to give it a read, promised he'd tweak the grammar. Maxine was a marvel. She always had new things to say.

Cooper took Scotty's hand and led her into the bedroom where he'd confined Reba along with his promiscuous running buddy. In Scotty's chronicles of Life with Daddy, when he'd dressed up in his jaunty red bowtie and piled her into his big blue car and drove her over to his house to play as long as she wanted, there had been no wild dogs throwing body blocks at the windows, scaring her half to death. Besides, she had laid down the law at Garland's. "No bullies allowed," she'd commanded. "No bullies allowed in the house or on the playground."

The dogs were lying on a pile of dirty clothes, Mount Maxwell using the overhang of Reba's belly for a pillow. Reba was plotting a raid on the Brunswick stew, and Max knew he'd have to be close and quick to have any chance of batting cleanup. Scotty asked to take Reba out to swing, but Cooper explained that he had an exercise complex.

"Anyway, you can't trust him in open spaces. He might decide to hop a Greyhound like you did."

Scotty reached over Max to touch the red bandana, told Reba she had a poodle named Noodle, and wanted to know why they stayed in the bedroom when it wasn't time for bed. "Would it make you happy if I let them run around the house?" Cooper asked. She nodded, but didn't smile. On the way back through the kitchen, he heard Sophie scrambling around in the pantry and offered her as a substitute.

Now Pistol Pete was back on the porch swing, holding the old dog in her lap, patting her with brisk, awkward strokes, as solemn as the smoky twilight. She'd come dressed for the game and warmed up on the ride over with her trademark chatter and smile, but she'd stopped speaking after he'd helped her up the steps, except to ask about Reba.

Cooper turned to her with what he hoped was a look of fatherly enthusiasm. "Remember the toys I told you about?" he asked. "We can go by the paper if you want. You can pick out the ones you'd like to take with you to Charlotte."

"No thank you, Daddy."

"God's not runnin' a beauty pageant, he ain't. Just as long as you got the Lord in your heart, one's just as pretty as the next. . . ." Cooper heard Maxine say, as the brand-new chain creaked in rhythm. He'd published it in a column several months or several years ago–her take on a report about women who have cosmetic surgery before they're out of their teens. Many of the adjustments had to do with noses and breasts.

"God's not runnin' a beauty pageant. . . ." this cheerless evening with daughter and dog. Daughter not talking. That's how bad it was.

•

He'd tried to tell Percy it wouldn't work. "She won't be comfortable," he'd protested when he'd come by to pick Scotty up. "I won't know what to do. I don't have any idea what to even talk about. We better call it off."

"Over my sweet little patootie," was what he got back. "When she asked you about it, you told her you'd see, and a Daddy doesn't tell his daughter he'll see without meaning yes."

As sweet as Percy's little patootie was, it could be a pain in the ass. She lived by a code of laws that Cooper had never heard of until she laid them down, each a rare surprise to him.

Severe depression had rendered Percy's mother useless when it came to passing along tips on leading a life, and Percy had been only eight when her father had been run over by his appliance store delivery truck while prying out a dead limb tangled in the exhaust. How wise could a man be if he parked on an incline with the motor running and relied on the emergency brake in a heap that had been bumping along on the edge for fifteen years?

"That child's her daddy's pistol if I've ever seen one," Percy had announced in the kitchen, where they were finishing off the ginger ale. "She practiced and practiced, and took a nap and practiced some more. She said she wanted to learn all the steps so her daddy would be proud of her tomorrow night and clap louder than anybody else. She said you told her you'd be sitting right on the very first row."

"I'll bring my sewing machine and work on her costume between acts. You're letting her overdo. She said her mother wouldn't allow her to dance until the time was right, which probably means never. She takes medicine for her heart."

"Yes, Dr. Spock, and she remembered to take it herself, after breakfast and supper, like she's supposed to. As far as the timing, it couldn't be more right. God delivered her to a dancing teacher a few days before the recital. Embrace the moment. She's an energetic young girl with a passion for life. If you don't allow her to have one, what's the use of her living? By the way, I wish you wouldn't call them acts. Balanchine's *Nutcracker* has acts. We're not talking Lincoln Center here. We're talking kids running around on a platform at a church in front of their parents and the few other relatives they can dredge up. That's called charming chaos."

It was then that Cooper had given up. In the wake of all the turmoil in her family, Percy had taken over as boss since no one else had wanted the job, and she was good at it. "I guess you have a point," he said. "I'm just a babysitter by default."

"However you want to describe it," she said.

They'd gone to round up Scotty, who'd been lying on the sofa with Bob, watching a rerun of *The Match Game*. Was this the kid who'd never spent a night away from her mother or Miss Mac except for a stint at summer camp?

She was wearing the top half of her costume, a red satin elastic halter with silver stars glittering over each flat breast. The right star was bigger than the one on the left.

"You sure that outfit's appropriate for a children's program in a church?" Cooper asked.

Percy took a few steps back and frowned. The left star was missing one of its points. She stepped over and fiddled with it a little bit, then found the scissors under a heap of crepe paper streamers and cut off a point on the opposite star.

"That's more like it," she said. "Now you're even-Stephen."

Gene Rayburn grinned. Cooper shot him the bird.

"Your father needs to grow up," Percy said to Scotty. "Playing the prude one minute, flashing his digit the next."

"Ssssh," Cooper said.

Percy tugged on the halter, centering the stars above each breast.

"Princess, how about explaining to your old fogy of a daddy that the only time pasties can appropriately be worn any place is by God's children in God's house, and then run to your bedroom and change. I have some work to do on the scenery."

Pistol Pete was back in two minutes, her smile as wide as a backboard, her words careening off it like a gymful of balls pumped giddy with helium, barely able to wait for the next big shot. And then she'd deflated.

"Why are you stopping at this house, Daddy?" she'd asked him.

"This is where I live."

"This isn't where you live, Daddy, because on your TV show you live in that very old house with that very nice Christmas tree on the front porch, and this house is very old but it doesn't have a Christmas tree, and. . . ."

The boob tube, muse for her odyssey. He'd been a fool not to figure it out. Scotty had expected to find the scene in the camera lens, an everlasting Christmas tree and a dog at the window wearing a shiny red bow, all wrapped up in the yuletide spirit of promise and love and joy. On television, a bandana would look like a bow, especially to a little girl who, for the rest of her life, would believe the world belonged to Santa Claus.

From the beginning of January until the end of May, Cooper Alan Barnet, acclaimed columnist for the Columbia *Herald-Journal*, had lived with a Christmas tree on his front porch. A blue spruce with sagging limbs shrouded in funky ornaments and globs of icicles as lifeless as the tired old strippers at the Pickens County fair. For practically six months, he'd walked past it without moving it to the street—until yesterday morning.

"Hold up a second, please," he'd yelled to the man hanging off the end of the garbage truck. "I have something for you. It's gotta go today."

He'd grabbed it up, the delinquent tree, scratching his hands and face on the brittle limbs, leaving a trail of brown needles and busted glass on the porch and sidewalk, running after the truck to heave it in; homemade stand, bastard decorations, sheenless icicles, and all. Ridiculous, becoming attached to a washed-up Christmas tree. It wasn't even alive.

He pictured the well-wishers in the newspaper lobby. So generous, so full of praise: *Congratulations, Cooper. How in the world did you ever find her? It's a miracle, Cooper. A real blessing. You'll be a wonderful father, Cooper. The very best. She's a lucky little soul to have you.*

An instant father? What did they expect? You become a father in the delivery room, holding your wife's hand and telling her to breathe, breathe, breathe, push-push-push, until the baby pops out. That's when you became an instant father. You don't become a father the instant your ex telephones you and announces it was a girl and lets you know she's going on twelve years old. Percy had told him that.

◆

The screen door squeaked. Nothing, then the tip of a crutch. Cooper smelled the whiskey he'd seen on the kitchen table, a quart of Jim Beam. Good old Sam.

"Just a minute. I'll be right there."

"Keep your seat, my man. I'm on the way out."

Malachi was wearing the frankfurter shirt and a pair of khaki pants. The left leg was rolled up and held by two large paper clips. Like Cooper, he was weeks beyond a haircut, on the verge of a legitimate Afro. He'd never worn one in the day. No problem with the style, only trends in general.

"This isn't a good time," Cooper said.

"For you or for me?"

"You were supposed to be asleep."

"You ship a mother to the guest room, you supposed to treat him like a guest."

"A guest is supposed to watch his language around other visitors."

"Too many supposed-tos floating round. What kind of discount they give you for a mattress stuffed with marbles?"

Malachi thudded over to the swing, grabbed the chain above Cooper's head in his free hand. They all lurched backward. Cooper reached for Malachi's shoulder to keep him from busting his nose on the lumber and used his other arm to lock Scotty in. Sophie hit the floor. After catching his balance, Malachi straightened, transferring his weight to the crutch.

"You'll have to forgive your old man, Scotty," he said. "There are times when grown people behave as if they are angry but they really aren't angry at all. They are simply attempting to maintain a distance. In your father's case, the reason he's trying to maintain a distance is because he's afraid."

"Christ, Malachi, you're wasted. You don't know what you're doing."

"Beg to differ, my friend. You're the one for whom confusion reigns."

Cooper reached down and put Sophie back in Scotty's lap. She stroked the dog faster and faster, looking from Malachi's face to his stump.

She wasn't frightened, though. More like excited, happy to see him, as if she'd known him from someplace before. Just showed how accepting she was. Cooper thought about the slicked-down pervert sitting next to her as the Greyhound sped to Columbia, disguising himself as a refreshing lime sherbet in his sleazy lounge-lizard shirt. Draping an arm around her back, moving it lower, exploring his sick predatory cravings at will. A sharp pain shot up his left arm. Nothing but indigestion or a heart attack.

"Mind if I join you?" Malachi asked.

"Yes," said Cooper, although the question hadn't been put to him.

"No, mister, I don't mind if you join me, and if you want I can hold that big high cane while you sit down beside me on this nice swing here, and mister, you don't even have to worry about this little dog trying to bite you because all she wants to do is lie down and take a nap, because she's not allowed to run out in the street in case she jumps on a bus like I did."

"I see," Malachi said, turning around to sit.

Cooper slid over, pressing his ribs into the arm of the swing, and raised up to adjust the tray beneath the block of wood that once had been his butt. Scotty moved forward, pumping to start the swing. Cooper helped her get it going. He could put on the brakes, fling

Malachi off the seat, but Scotty and Sophie would sail along with him. And she was talking again.

"Those pants just came from the cleaner's," Cooper said. "They charge extra for alcohol removal."

"Alcohol removal. Uppity all of a sudden, aren't you? Hell, I can still remember the day you were like the rest of us. Called it liquor, booze, hooch, firewater, sauce. Alcohol removal. Give me a break. Alcohol's what they clean the shit with."

"Spoken with Angeline lately?" Cooper asked. "Next time you do, maybe you better ask her for a refresher commandment on little pitchers and their untainted. . . ."

"And sir," Scotty interrupted, "I meant to tell you that I'm very sorry about that missing piece of leg you have there and ask you if you were born that way like I was . . ." She reached over as if to touch the nub and quickly withdrew her hand ". . . except I have two legs exactly the same size but I have to go to a different school because. . . ."

"Excuse me a minute, Scotty." Cooper cut his eyes toward Malachi as he pointedly pronounced her name. "Drink much in your sleep?"

"In my dreams, baby."

"You've been dreaming way too long. She shouldn't be exposed to. . . ."

"At the moment, that's a peripheral concern," Malachi interrupted, and turned to Scotty. "Now then," he said, "our young lady, Miss Scott Norris Smith here, has been very patient. She wants to finish saying her piece about my piece of leg."

"Yes, mister, I would like to finish saying my piece about your leg. And what did you say your whole name was?"

"My whole name is Malachi T. Patterson. The 'T' stands for Thurgood, after a man named Thurgood Marshall. His given name was originally Thoroughgood, but he had the sense to shorten it when he was a young kid. He was a prominent lawyer who came to be a famous judge on the United States Supreme Court. He's a great man, old as the hills, but still around. Attempted to uncomplicate something that should have been simple in the first place. Have they taught you about him in school?"

"No, Mr. Pat, and you better not try to dance in that very big show with that nice lady with the pretty black tail behind her back like I'm going to do because you might hurt yourself, and as soon as my daddy finishes making that costume with the silver stars on the front. . . ."

"You say your daddy is making a costume?"

"I don't know where she got that idea," Cooper said. Malachi was barefooted. His heel was thick and calloused, the price of working overtime.

". . . although you might know how to dance with that real short leg, Pat, because my mother took me to see those men in wheelchairs that ride around the basketball court in that big Coliseum where the circus is, and they have very short legs, too, and Pat, I just remembered that I wanted to ask you if you were born with that short leg there or if you found out about that special little leg when you got a few years older like I was when my mother told me that I couldn't. . . ."

Sophie interrupted Scotty this time, struggling to stand in her lap. Malachi reached over and picked her up, then handed her to Cooper.

"Dog's in need of a bush," he said, and stopped the swing.

Cooper stood up with Sophie under his arm. He was careful going down the steps. In another hour or so it would be dark. In two hours, the moon would be full. They were all already mad.

"Scotty," Malachi said. "This short little piece of leg that for obvious reasons has captured your interest was not a curse delivered at birth. I had two legs of similar length, just as you do now."

From behind the boxwood, Cooper cleared his throat, the second time louder and more threatening than the first. Malachi had a repertoire of manufactured tales, none of which Hannah would approve of as a bedtime story.

"I lost this leg when I was a grown man, Scotty. At least I thought I was a grown man, but actually I was a baby. A baby of almost twenty-four years. Have you ever heard of a baby that old?"

Scotty shook her head back and forth.

"No, you wouldn't have," Malachi said. "I lost this leg because I was driving too fast. I was angry, see. I wanted to lose more than my leg."

Scotty worked her legs to speed up the swing, but Malachi's foot was stronger, sliding back and forth against the floor, slowing the pace. She gave up. Cooper hooked Sophie by the collar, ready to run back up the steps, grab the kid, and take her inside. But he didn't move.

"The incident had nothing to do with the whiskey that is disturbing your father now. I hadn't tasted the first drop in those days. Didn't need to then. Didn't believe I ever would. In those days, I was solid and cocky, with both legs attached to my body and a mind convinced of where it wanted to go. I'd fooled myself, you see, into thinking the world was my oyster—I'll bet you've encountered an oyster somewhere by now, haven't you, sweet child? I thought I had just as much right to the pearl as. . . ."

Malachi stopped the swing, leaned his head against the crutch. The oak was cracked and streaked with rubber marks. The arm pad was wrapped in duct tape. It was coming unglued.

"Hey," Cooper said. "Malachi? You with us?"

Welcome to an evening in Santa Land, he thought. A nice, wholesome indoctrination to Daddy's wonderful world.

Malachi sat up and rested the crutch against the window sill. "Dr. Clifford Drake, graduate level theory of composition at Yale University School of Music, reserved for a select group of prodigies lucky enough to get in the class, including a few token prodigies like myself. He liked my music, all right, the esteemed Dr. Drake, and he liked my brain, but he didn't like the color of my skin when he found it lying on the sofa next to his daughter. Especially after she informed him that we planned to be married. In the family garden, if it suited, sometime in the early spring. I was the bronze trophy, don't you see. The prize behind the glass case. And the instant I broke it open and stepped outside, I lost the freedom I never had in the first place."

"Malachi." Cooper's voice was low as he edged between two large boxwoods. Stubbly green leaves covered the chest and sleeves of his white shirt. "Maybe you shouldn't. . . ."

"Maybe I shouldn't, but no one told me that back then, see. All they told me was I should; so I did, and all it got me was a hard bed in a basement ward full of miserable people mostly the same color as myself. Except they were the ones with the brains, because they had known they shouldn't long before I did, and I was the only one with a leg ground to mulch in some foul-smelling incinerator for body parts, wondering why the hell I wanted to do it, go to the other side. I'd never had a desire like that before and never have since. Untested waters, the downfall of man. There are sharks in there, little girl, and let me tell you, the waves aren't worth it. Your father over there came to call on me then, Scotty. In fact, he brought your mother with him. It was the first time I laid eyes on her lovely face."

Scotty's eyes were shining blue, riveted on Malachi as he spoke, listening to him tell her things she'd never heard in her life, things she'd never been prepared to hear, as if she had the capacity to grasp everything he was saying.

"Pardon me, child. Your father thinks my description untenable for the ears of such a pure young maiden, and he happens to be right. But this isn't the first time I've failed your father, Scotty. I failed him because I couldn't allow myself to end up just another one-legged black man playing ragtime in a half-empty cellar dive on off nights. Some whiskey-dulled cripple struggling out in the morning to play the fool for two-bit tourists eating powdered sugar and fried dough at the Café du Monde on Jackson Square, jumping around on one leg playing 'Sunny Side of the Street' like there was one. Playing like Meadowlark Lemon with a keyboard, a keyboard racing in high gear because that was the only way the tourists dunking sugared dough in milk coffee would think it counted enough to spare a little change. All the while eyeing the Panama hat on top of the piano, watching it to make sure none of that marvelous short change got lifted by sticky little white-powdered paws. . . ."

Malachi coughed, toed the swing toward the railing and spat the mucous over his shoulder. "In brief, Scotty, I was determined not to become a cliché. Now tell me, little Miss Scott Norris Smith, how well do you think I succeeded? How well do you think I've done at that?"

"That's enough, Malachi. You're drunk. She's a child."

"Your father is uneasy, Scotty. He thinks I'm making a short story far too long, and I suppose I am. Just leave it this way. This skimpy piece of leg you see here is my comeuppance. It taught me everything I needed to know about life, the knowledge I was so certain I would find in books."

He turned toward Scotty. "Would you like to take a look?" he asked her. "There's nothing to be afraid of. It's merely a missing piece of a puzzle. Once you see it, you won't have to be concerned about it anymore."

"Yes, Pat," she said. "I would like to see that place where your leg came off when you drove too fast and got a speeding ticket from a very nice police officer who told you to behave and obey the law."

"Good," Malachi said. "I'm going to roll up these trousers, and you'll see a scar where they had to stitch my skin together after they finished the operation. You've seen a scar before, have you?"

She nodded. "My mother has a crooked white scar on her forehead because a very mean boy hit her with a rock and his mother put a clean white towel over the blood but she didn't have to pay the bill because my mother started the fight."

"My goodness. Here we are, then, Scotty. My missing piece of leg. Would you like to touch it? I don't mind. It doesn't hurt."

Cooper sucked in a breath. Slowly, Scotty reached out and put her hand on the leg. She touched the end where the ridges were recessed from the scar, and then the thigh just above the absent knee. She was curious, engaged. After he'd answered her questions, Malachi took her hand and put it down on the edge of the swing.

"Mr. Pat, I will say a prayer that your leg will get well one day and grow all the way to the ground so my daddy won't be mad at you for rolling up his good pants after he paid to get them out of the cleaners."

"Thank you," he said. "And now, Scotty, I want you to listen hard to what I'm about to say. Can you do that?"

"Yes, Mr. Pat."

"I encouraged you to make a discovery just now because your father is in our presence," Malachi said. "But I want you to promise me that you will never allow a man you don't know to touch you if your mother or father isn't with you. Okay? Such as the man who was sitting next to you on the bus. Remember him? Good. He knew it was wrong when he put his hands on you. He thought he could get away with it because your parents weren't there to tell him no. You're a big girl now, and you must learn to take care of yourself in the face of adversity. Am I making sense?"

She was nodding again, solemn. "Yes, Mr. Pat," she said. "It makes sense that if a strange bully asks me to see his private part again I'll tell him that he has to ask my daddy first, and if he doesn't ask my daddy I'll tell him that a policeman will have to give him a ticket and put him in jail until he learns how to behave."

Malachi smiled. "That's good enough," he assured her. "That's fine."

Cooper stared at Malachi. It had been haunting him, too. Hannah could talk to Scotty in the abstract, but Malachi, still the tutor, had understood that he could make a tangible impression. Even as a drunk, he made the better father. It wasn't even close.

"And now, Scotty," Malachi was saying, "do you want to know a secret? All right, then I'll tell you one. I don't miss this piece of leg right here as much as I miss the pearl. Oh, not that specific pearl. I can't remember her face. The quest is what I miss. Yes, indeed. I do miss that quest for the pearl."

Cooper moved back toward the swing, toward the odor of the man he'd known since boyhood. There was something besides the smell of booze. A fresh, clean, reassuring scent. Zest soap. It was Malachi's soap. Angeline always bought it. Cooper had to have it, too. He begged his mother. If he smelled like Malachi, he'd be like him. Cooper still used Zest after all these years. Scotty must have liked it too, the blend of whiskey and Zest. She had her head on Malachi's shoulder. She was falling asleep. Cooper got up and put Sophie in the house, then came back and sat next to a memory.

"Hey, Malachi?"

"Sssh."

"You were right, what you told her a while ago."

"About what?"

"I'm afraid."

"I know you are, baby. We all afraid."

"Remember when we were kids, those nights on the swing?"

"All those questions." Malachi was whispering now. "Drove my ass crazy. What's this, Malachi? Why are they doing that, Malachi? Look over there, Malachi. Shit. Angeline should have paid me double."

"Too bad you don't get paid for swearing," Cooper said. "You could buy enough whiskey to tide you over to the nursing home phase, maybe have a few dollars left over to buy yourself a pair of pants." But the sad truth was, Malachi wouldn't make it that far.

Scotty was sleeping away. Cooper took a breath, smiled. She hadn't been contaminated after all. She didn't know the meaning of the x-rated language she'd been hearing. Otherwise, she'd have told her friend Mr. Pat to stand in a corner with duct tape over his mouth.

He looked over at Malachi, at the eyes, brooding and resigned, and the circles underneath, ashen remnants of charcoal against his whiskered brown skin. The anger would come back. It always did. It broke Cooper's heart, Malachi and his missing leg advertising the virtues of a hotdog with fried green tomatoes and Velveeta cheese.

"Here we are," Cooper said. "Two grown men, still swinging together on a broken-down porch."

"Ya'll reporters are opportunistic sons of bitches, aren't you, always inventing prose to suit your needs. Only time you're actually creative is figuring out how to squirm out of something when you get caught."

Cooper's grin hung out on its usual corner while he waited for Malachi to finish. Not much traffic going by. North Park was a short street on the back side of Shandon Oaks. No reason to drive down it unless you lived here or had specific business. He listened to the neighborhood sounds. They held a lot of power on a spring evening. They could lull you into feeling connected or make you want to be. Different types of aches, those.

"You know good and well," Malachi finally said, "that Angeline Cordelia Patterson would never allow any porch of hers to be broken down."

Cooper didn't answer. He was writing the head.

"Two friends rust to death in broken-down swing
While celebrating marvelous beauty pageant, life."

"Hey, Malachi."

"Yeah."

"You know all those hours you spent teaching me about music?"

"I was experimenting. Trying to infuse some ignorant white boy with a soul. It didn't take."

"I'm trying to be serious."

"Go on, be serious then."

"Remember what you said about Booker? About how he could speak for you when you couldn't talk for yourself?"

"I do."

"You'd give me another tape or album and tell me to take it home and listen to it over and over again until I heard it in my sleep. You'd tell me, 'Unlock the door with this.'"

"That was inspired by the fear of Angeline. She said you needed to be educated and I should do whatever I could. It wasn't a suggestion, it was an order. And an attempt. Doubt it succeeded, your head is so hard."

At the curb, a streetlight came on.

"Malachi?"

"Hush, now. Whisper. She needs her sleep."

"Don't you miss it?"

"The music, you mean?"

Cooper nodded.

"You jivin' me?"

"No, just asking."

"You got better sense than that. You just asked me if I miss my life."

"The night you played at Township Auditorium? It was the only time I felt that kind of pride. Actually, the first time I had someone to be proud of back then, besides my old man, I mean, when I was a kid. It was the same way you told me you felt the first time you heard Little Booker, like everything you didn't know you had was about to bust right out of your gut and be exposed to the world, and you didn't give a damn who saw it. You remember telling me that? That's exactly how I felt that night when you were sitting up there all alone on that big empty stage and I heard you play."

Malachi smiled. Two children sitting on this swing, one as naïve as the other. The one too big for his lap shifted on the cafeteria tray and ran a hand through his hair, sending it to all the wrong places. Pretty soon, that spunky little woman of his could put it in a braid. Then they could walk around the Columbia Mall advertising themselves as a couple the way people do. Maybe wear matching sweats.

"You looked out at us and asked, 'Ever heard James Booker play '"Over the Rainbow?"'' And we yelled back, 'No.'

"'Well if you haven't,' you said, 'you've never heard the song before.' You had that little mike above the keyboard, bent low toward your mouth, but you were talking so quiet everybody had to strain to hear you. And then you played it, "Somewhere Over the Rainbow." Played it like all get-out. And I remember thinking, That song was written for him to play. Then you sent us home with "Sunny Side of the Street." And you said the same thing, that if we'd never heard James Booker play "Sunny Side of the Street," we'd never heard the song before. And I knew everybody in the audience felt the same way I did. That nobody could've made that song sound any better than you did that night. Not even Booker. You were my hero, man. My idol."

"Then your idol was nothing but a screw-up, baby, just like mine. How much of it he could help, I don't know. Homosexuals weren't accepted all that well back then, especially when they were black and schizophrenic. He was delusional half the time. Thought the CIA had bugs planted up his ass, and he was on every kind of dope you can name to boot. Still, he could bang the hell out of that piano. Nobody could ever take that away from him. Nobody could match him on that."

Malachi didn't have to tell him. Cooper had seen it, too, that night at the Maple Leaf Bar in New Orleans—a wounded eagle soaring toward the sky.

"There's a pretty good story about Booker," Malachi said. "They were recording the *The Lost Paramount Tapes*. He was on methadone then. He could function. The guys could stand to play with him. In fact, they were elated to be playing with him because he was straight. Where they were recording the CD, somewhere on the Paramount lot, they had a roomful of pianos and sent him over to choose one.

"All these fancy pianos, he could pick any one he wanted, and you know what the mother picked? He picked a funky little spinet. Thing played just like somebody had set it in an empty can. But the brother came back excited as a school kid, talking about this hot little music box. Couldn't wait to get rolling and when he did he was cooking, honey, loose as a human can get. Like his fingers had just detached themselves from his hands and were dancing all by themselves. Some of the best music he ever played."

Malachi lowered his chin, rested it a second on Scotty's head.

"As messed up as he was, he knew that crazy little clinker would understand him, make him some fine music if he talked to it right. Man was a genius. Too smart to be sane."

Cooper felt like he was in the back seat of his father's car again. He didn't want the ride to end.

"And now I'm getting ready to turn the tables on you, baby," Malachi said. "I have a question for you."

"Okay, ask."

"I want to know about your brother."

Cooper jammed the swing to a stop, the way he had all those years ago, the last time Malachi had trespassed on the subject. Malachi should've known it was out of bounds then. He had to know it was now. They were sitting here having one of their conversations, he was basking in the comfort of Malachi's presence, the security of his protection, and he'd clobbered him with a sucker punch.

It reminded him of a trick his mother had pulled when he was nine years old. She'd invited him to take a ride to the hospital—"Your daddy just needs to tend to a little business." One minute Cooper was in the car making happy talk with his mother, waiting for his father to come back, and the next a nun was shoving a mask over his face, forcing ether in his mouth and nose so they could pull his teeth.

It was a Catholic hospital, the same place they'd taken his brother. You couldn't act up with a nun.

It wasn't so bad after it happened, though. Cooper dreamed of Goofy and Mickey in a rowboat fishing in a mountain stream. Brightest colors he ever saw. The sky, the lake, the clouds, the mountains, the colors of their clothing. He hadn't seen such vivid colors since.

"What was his name?"

"We called him Scooter."

Cooper was shaky, but it came out easy. It was time.

"Scooter, huh? Little Scooter. How does it feel, saying it out loud?"

"It feels strange."

"It's hard, carrying around something all those years, isn't it, baby? I've had to do it myself, and now I'm getting ready to dump it on you. If I weren't such a sorry coward, I would've done it a long time ago. But first go get me that bottle of Kikkoman in the cabinet, next to where you stashed the gin. Right hand side, behind the Premium Saltine Crackers. Those crackers got to be stale as Bessie Carter's breath. You been hiding liquor there since Jesus was a baby, and that box of crackers hadn't moved yet."

Cooper slipped off the swing. He was careful not to wake Scotty as he lifted her from Malachi's chest and carried her to the futon. It was just where Malachi had dragged it the other night, right inside the front door, where he could hear the phone and be close in case a small child happened to knock.

He found the wine without turning on the kitchen light, or noticing the Brunswick stew container missing from the counter. Malachi had to be desperate. Plum wine was beneath cough syrup with codeine. The vintage was Bangkok Garden, no corkscrew required. Glass, either. Malachi didn't speak until he'd drunk half way down the label.

"How's Hannah?" he asked.

"Better. She was asleep when I went by a while ago, but Percy said she and Scotty talked to her on the phone."

"Percy? Women are glorious, aren't they?"

"That's what they all claim."

"Did you know I went to see her?"

"She told me. It meant a lot."

"She mention anything we talked about?"

"I don't remember. It was a pretty emotional time. I haven't sorted it out yet. I'm scared to."

"Look, sweetheart. There's no way to tell you this but to tell you."

Malachi leaned over to set the bottle down. It tipped over, rolling down the slope of the porch until a column saved it from jumping overboard. Malachi checked the damage. Still half full. His lucky night.

"I disappointed you, shutting off the music. But I betrayed you, too. I told Hannah about your brother, about Scooter, back while the two of you were married. She was making herself crazy, putting your hard times on herself. She didn't deserve it but that didn't give me the right. I was drunk and I broke a confidence. I'm sorry. I'm deeply ashamed."

Cooper started to say something. Malachi touched his arm.

"That's why I went over to the hospital. I figured she'd be beating herself up. It was the reason she hid it from you, in my opinion. Scooter. He didn't have a name back then. I could be wrong, but that's what I believe, and I wanted her to know it."

Cooper raised himself from the tray and stood. He didn't go anywhere, just unbuttoned his shirt and pulled it off. His undershirt was stuck to his chest. Malachi parked the swing, leaned over and righted the bottle.

"She never told me she knew," Cooper said.

"No."

"She shouldn't have made assumptions. It was wrong. She should've given me a chance."

"She should have. But shit, man, we've both been in the car with you when you passed a dead squirrel in the road. Shut your eyes so you wouldn't have to see it, groping for your navel or your button or whatever the hell it was, to what . . . make it all go away? Meantime, you liked to have killed us, acting the fool over something already dead."

"She never understood our relationship. Mine and yours."

"People wouldn't. I doubt we do."

Cooper walked over to the door and squinted through the screen. Scotty was sleeping on her side, wearing the new red tennis shoes, with Mount Maxwell snuggled in the crook of her legs.

"All safe and sound," he reported. "Max is babysitting."

"Yum-Yum? Don't you think the poor child has encountered enough unsavory characters for one night?"

"What do you mean? He's harmless."

"Tell that to my lower extremities. That's where I found his pointed little snout awhile ago. Hell of a wake-up call."

Cooper peered through the screen again. Max's eyes were closed.

"I let you down," Malachi said. There was pain in his voice, and resolve. "Not in the way Booker let me down, but in. . . ."

"No, you didn't," Cooper said, but Malachi shook his head.

"Oh, at one time in some idealistic fantasy, I may have believed in him too much, possibly similar to the way you believed in me, but the only words Booker ever spoke to me came out of his keyboard. I gave you my word and I didn't keep it. It's not just Hannah, baby. That's too easy. Your trusted confidante, he's the one you need to blame. And while you're at it you can save a little for yourself."

Cooper didn't answer. Everything pent up for years, exploding, like a monster from a bottomless grave.

"And now I have another question about your brother. About little Scooter."

Cooper sat down. He was sick to his stomach, but eager to hear what it was. Malachi started up the swing again. The new chain squeaked.

"Your mother told my aunt he suffocated in a car on Folly Beach. That's all she told her. But then your maid, remember? The lady who told your mother about Angeline? She told us later that he'd gotten hurt some way and you were the one who put him in there. That's about all we ever knew. I want to know how it happened, baby. I want to hear you tell me about it. Tonight. While you can."

And so Cooper filled in the blank pages of his Professional Reporter's Notebook. The words had always been available, hovering close and far away, straddling the arbitrary line between conscious and unconscious; the details held firmly in place with a passionate detachment; the story ready to be released like the good writers teach you to do it—by picturing one person you want to tell it to and writing it just like you were talking only to them.

And that person, the only person he felt like he could tell, was the brilliant alcoholic train wreck sitting next to him on the swing, the man who had first asked him about it when they were boys sitting together on another swing more than thirty years ago. Malachi might not understand this, but it didn't matter that he had told Hannah about his little brother. Cooper still trusted him. He always would, with whatever was left of his heart and of his life; and he had kept him waiting far too long.

•

The obit was published in the Charleston News and Courier the morning after it happened—Monday, August 12, 1955. It led the city police round-up. Since the news hole was small that day, it gave only the essentials. The name of the deceased and his age, three years old. The cause of death, suffocation in the family automobile. The fact that funeral arrangements were incomplete. It listed the survivors, and stated that the parents requested donations be made in place of flowers. "In lieu of" is the way they say it in the paper. It also mentioned the location, down at the west end of Folly Beach, across the street from the haunted house.

Everyone around knows Folly. It's your beach if you want to claim it, and if you do, it's a good place to spend your last day. If you prefer fancier beaches, Charleston has them, too, and they're nice in their own ways. But in the midfifties, Folly was just Folly; a punky little six-mile den of delight on the Edge of America; a carnival with waves; a sanddust strip of smoky pool halls with smoking juke boxes, short-order holes with shirtless cooks and swivel stools, and beachwear shops pushing one basic style, bohemian funk with a salty twist, anywhere there was a nail, with a solid or two thrown in for democracy's sake. Still the same feel today, with a few concessions to current trends.

They charge you a dollar an hour now to park by the ocean, and at Lil' Mama's you can order gourmet pizza legitimately made from scratch. Also, a new stucco Holiday Inn faces the new boardwalk where the old pier and rides used to be.

But for regulars the real Holliday Inn—that's two l's and no relation—is a well-seasoned fourteen-room cottage just one block and a few less bucks away; the only Holliday around on the day he died. Sometimes the family stayed there for a week in the summer, though they lived less than seven miles inland after you cross the Folly River Bridge. Maybe if they'd been staying at the Holliday Inn when it happened, his brother would have taken him up to the room instead.

Occasionally they rented a house. That was his mother's job and she was a procrastinator. She'd tried to find something just the afternoon before, but the bungalow they showed her reeked of bug spray, and when she tested the kitchen tap it spewed out rusty water. Back then, the locals didn't build houses with renting in mind. They built conversation pieces with attitude, places that talked a little trash with the hurricanes and with outsiders who wanted to make something of it; structures put together with cement blocks and Coca-Cola crates and Bud bottles liquidated during construction, maybe sometimes with a busted muffler or a blown engine or a lump of Silly Putty stuffed in just because it was handy and cheap.

Later on, the character of some of the houses was compromised for the sake of profit, but not the perspective on surf-

ing. Surfing is synonymous with Folly. The natives consider it their quality time with God, who hangs out over by the rocks at the Wash Out. On high surf days and weekends you're swimming elbow-to-elbow with a congregation riding fiberglass pews, so if you're timid and like to keep to yourself, you'd probably be more comfortable on another quarter mile of sand. The little guy and his family were ocean-savvy and friendly, and often spread their blanket by the rocks. Maybe if they had done this on the day he died it would have been a different story. You can park beside the beach at the Wash Out. More people around to notice trouble.

It was hot that day. Ninety-eight degrees at two o'clock. A hazy heat, no breeze. The jellyfish were bad and he got stung. You could say his parents shouldn't have left their children to take a walk, but that was the customary pattern. Swim in the morning. Sit in the shade under the gray haunted house to have lunch. Eat tuna fish sandwiches and barbecue chips. Rest half an hour. The kids knew the rules. They were both good swimmers. They could go in but not above their knees. That wasn't far, especially for the three-year-old. Even though he would have been four in October, he was small for his age.

He was wearing his Mighty Mouse cape. His mother had made it. By August, the pale freckles across his cheeks and nose had baked to a walnut brown and his hair, a brand new barbershop crew cut, was as light as spun sugar. When he ran for the ocean with his arms extended, singing, "Heerrre I come to save the daaaayyy," his cape stuck to the salt and sand on his back. His nylon bathing suit was still damp from riding the noontime waves in his daddy's arms and was riding up his crotch. The suit was red, to match the cape. His brother started to tell him how dumb he looked but he didn't. Instead he followed him out to the water to make sure he stayed away from the barnacles clinging to the legs of the timber jetty.

The ocean was dull and gray. The slough beside the jetty looked refreshing but it was tepid and slimy. The boys decided to lie around in the shallow waves. They hardly had any time to play before the little one was clutching his foot in his hand, crying hard. The wheal was red and swelling fast. "I want my mama," he said. "I wanna go home." People were watching. He was ashamed. Mighty Mouse isn't supposed to cry.

The car was parked across the street, a burgundy Oldsmobile Ninety-Eight with power windows and locks. His brother carried him piggyback. The boy was heavy and the sand was deep and hot. The pavement was even hotter. His brother almost dropped him as he put him in the car. "Sit right there while I go get Mama and Daddy," he said. Then he shut the door.

Three-year-old kids accidentally trapped in cars can't get out, even if they are Mighty Mouse. Parents can seem far away when you're ten years old and anxious and can't remember the direction they went off in. In the time it takes to find them and bring them back, your little brother can suffocate in the heat.

·

After the funeral, they drove to the Great Smokey Mountains; Scooter's parents and their only son. They walked across a mile-high swinging bridge and rented a canoe. They ate steak suppers and stayed in decent budget motels. At Cherokee Indian Village, Cooper stood beside Big Chief Running Water and had his picture made.

"Why did Scooter have to die?" he'd asked him. His mother had said Indian chiefs were among the wisest men in the world.

Chief Running Water patted his head.

"Good job, good show," he said, and moved on to the next child in line.

"Malachi?" Cooper finally said.

"I'm with you, baby."

"You remember the afternoon my mother dragged me over to Angeline's?"

Malachi nodded.

"It was the second worst day of my life. I'd killed my brother. My mother didn't want me anymore. She'd dumped me on a black family I'd never laid eyes on. I was scared to tell anybody about it, especially my friends at school. They'd beat me half dead."

"Shit. It was worse for me. Ya'll lynched us for much less than that."

"And then you became the only thing in my world that made sense."

Malachi drank until the bottle was empty. He didn't have to worry about dregs.

"Guess that proves we're both crazy," he said.

"Guess it does."

Malachi set the bottle on the floor, laying it on its side, watching it roll back to the column that had caught it before. Cooper leaned over and picked it up.

"Cleaning house?" Malachi asked, and watched Cooper smile.

Malachi smiled back and reached for the crutch. "We better see about the child," he said.

"I guess we better," Cooper agreed, and went in to call Percy to come wake her up and take her home.

24

"Well?" Percy asked him.

Cooper wasn't sure. Everything was in place, but the Fellowship Hall hadn't been transformed into the South Pacific. It still looked like the Fellowship Hall. He started off by easing a toe in the crepe paper waters, testing them out. "Maybe the waves should have been closer together or farther apart," he said. "A deeper green or a brighter blue." A different combination of colors. Something.

Percy bored in. Raised up en pointe to do it, which put her head just past his chin. Those burnished umbers of hers could be scary when they expected a certain answer.

"It looks nice, though," he said. "The kids will love it."

But the scenery was primitive, even for limited expectations. None of the coconuts were shaped that much like coconuts. The palm fronds were stubby, dense clumps, with about as much definition as Garland Cayce's pre-Victorian boxwoods, and the crumpled blue tissue paper ran out before it talked you into believing it was a sky.

Even viewing the designs charitably, as whimsical Kiddie Art meant to represent the students' interpretation of the setting, there was no way you could claim that they turned the drab prison gray of the auditorium into a sunny island paradise.

The stage was elevated by the height of two low brick steps and surrounded by concrete block walls. After they had taped the unassembled pieces of storage closets together with the pieces Percy had joined at home and patched everything loose into place, the whole backdrop was barely more than half the size of a standard backyard swimming pool.

"Some of the girls will be doing the hula in the South Pacific," Cooper told her, "while others are swishing around in front of the State Pen." He should have realized this wasn't a time for humor, but had been thrown off his game for a second, noticing how much a perky dancer's ass can improve a ragged pair of cut-off jeans.

"What did you expect," she demanded, "the entire island chain?"

On top of that, the air conditioning was broken. He made another mistake, asking what would happen if it couldn't be fixed in time.

"Don't sweat it, Barnet," she snapped. "This is the tropics."

She huffed off to pick up Scotty, leaving him to deal with the chairs.

Sixty was optimistic, she'd told him; eighty wishful thinking. He decided to go for fourteen rows of eight, a hundred and twelve. Give them a choice of facing the music head-on or laying low in the back. With only a spotlight, the dancers wouldn't be able to see past the first couple of rows. For all they knew they'd be playing to a packed house. He sat down in the fourth row to take another look at the stage.

"It might be better if there were no lights at all," he muttered.

"Sorry, babe. If you were speaking to me I didn't catch a word you said."

A woman was standing beside him. "Oh, hi," he said. "I wasn't. Just to myself."

"Join the club," she answered. "I do it all the time. I'm Rachel Sills."

Rachel was wearing a pair of lavender Bermudas. A polka-dotted scarf a shade lighter than the shorts was tied over the curlers in her hair, and she was carrying a hard-cover book of Broadway show tunes. She informed Cooper that she'd been tapped for emergency piano duty, but as she'd given her piano to the grandchildren, she had come in to work off some rust.

"I sure didn't expect to find anybody here this early," she said. "You'll have to excuse me, looking like something the cat scratched up. I'm a sight."

"You look fine."

"Good for you. I see your mother brought you up to be a gentleman. Gentlemen are splendid liars. But this is the way it always happens, doesn't it? I finally have a chance to meet my hero and the girl who does my hair is down in her back. My regular appointment is Saturdays at ten. I would've been all fixed up, the living end. Instead . . . well, gracious goodness, just listen to me, froufrouing you to death. A man hates being held hostage to a bunch of silly malarkey, now, doesn't he?"

Cooper winked at her. "A gentleman would have to take the fifth."

She laughed. "Just look at that scenery," she said, digging underneath the scarf to rearrange a roller.

He began doodling in his mental notebook: *Baffling little gizmos. Mini silver mesh sausages. Sausage links, with appendages made of porcupine quills . . . Her scalp . . . ow . . . more indentations than a Titleist after seventy-two holes . . . probably throbs like a tee cracked with a three-wood.*

Rachel winced—could she have been reading over his shoulder?—and reached back under the scarf again. This time, she yanked.

"Got ya," she said.

. . . pulls out broken plastic tee. PINK!!!!!!

"Forgive me if I'm speaking out of school, but I do want you to know how disappointed we were in Dan for calling you out like he did. Your fans, I mean."

Rutledge Manor, his notorious abode. The drubbing in town square. McDonald was taking more heat over it than he was. Depressing that those were the good old days, less than a week ago.

"Don't go too hard on him, Rachel. He was more or less doing his job."

A gentleman indeed, criticizing Percy's harmless make-believe island while his real Shangri-La violated enough codes to earn a condemned notice from the city inspections department, tacked to one of the rotten columns with an ax. "Your fans," the lady had said. They always picked the wrong people.

"Now where did you come from?" A horsefly was dive-bombing Rachel's curlers. They both swiped at it. "Yet and still," she went on, "I imagine you're planning to see to a few things here and there, with your only daughter in your life now and whatnot. I'm sure she'll be coming over a lot, making up for lost time."

Was a couple of hours 'making up for lost time'? When Percy—not her biological mother, not even her official stepmother—had picked Scotty up last night and carried her out to the MG, Cooper had followed, said goodbye, and gone back inside, announcing to Malachi, "I've performed my obligatory custodial visitation for the last eleven years, and for the next eleven, too." Hannah probably wouldn't even have allowed that, if she'd been in her right mind.

Had he missed something? Rachel was thrusting out her chubby right hand. He reached out to shake it, but drew back when he saw the index finger swaddled in a heavy gauze wrap.

"My daughter-in-law banged it with the hammer last night," she told him. "We were trying to hang drapery before the kids got back from the beach. Of course, she didn't mean to. We get along famously well. Sailor could've searched the Seven Seas and never found a more perfect wife. Sailor's what we call our son. He's a submarine captain in the Navy. Been wearing a sailor's cap since he was five years old. Thought he was Popeye. Carried around a can of spinach, too. Cutest thing you ever saw."

My brother Scooter used to wear a Mighty Mouse cape, Cooper almost told her. Almost rolled it off his tongue like a comment about the heat. He'd even slept with it over his pajamas. Their mother loosened the ties so he wouldn't strangle.

After all this time, Cooper could still see his hair, fine and straight and blond—in summer, buzzed short and practically white—could see the sweet hazel eyes full of light, rounded with endless awe, the mouth with its mustache of orange popsicle, the freckles on his sun-browned cheeks. Scooter the Pooter, his baby brother a very long time ago.

"I tell her the only thing I'd change about her, that's my daughter-in-law . . . well . . . she does have a heavy foot."

The finger was still extended.

"Does it seem swollen to you?"

Cooper leaned in to look. He couldn't tell with the bandage around it. To him, all her fingers seemed swollen. "I believe it does," he said.

On the way out, he checked on the palm tree. Percy had taped it to the door leading into the Fellowship Hall. The trunk was made of brown crepe paper. She'd painted in some green fronds, and then colored in her vision of coconuts with a purple magic marker. She'd also printed a purple sign on white construction paper, thumbtacked to the top of the tree.

"The Columbia Academy of Dance Invites You to Enjoy a Journey to Fantasyland."

25

Pleasant Orchards, a large subdivision six miles northeast of the Capitol building, couldn't be more of an architechtural hodgepodge. Although designed in the mid-forties as a neighborhood of traditional ranch houses, builders later expanded the choices to split-levels, condos, townhouses, and apartments, resulting in an ecclectic tangle of winding streets with names rich in vitamin C but no predictable pattern. For Cooper, the upshot was a bad case of acid reflux. The curtain went up in thirty minutes and he had no idea where he was.

He'd gone down Applewood Drive, swerved onto Apple Way, dead-ended at Crabapple Court, turned around to backtrack, and wound up on Bartlett Terrace heading into Anjou Lane.

None of these streets seemed familiar, but he hadn't been in the mood for sightseeing at daybreak when he'd followed Percy to the church to decorate. The 7-Eleven hadn't made any coffee yet and the Town Car, loaded with scenery, every inch of it, inside and out, was barely able to creep along, which Percy seemed to forget each time she'd lost him in an arboreal curve up ahead.

He was in the peach orchard now, distracted by another phantom head. **"Surprise Entry Wreaks Havoc at Local Recital, Chaos Abounds,"** chasing his consciousness from Elberta Avenue to Melba Park Road to Nectar Trail, then into the roundabout on Peachtree Circle.

The last time Cooper saw a sign with Peachtree on it was when a drummer named Sticks Street had phoned from Atlanta to tell him to come get World Book before he woke up and found out they'd hidden his keys. That's what Malachi's musician friends called him, "World Book"—"World," for short.

Five years ago it was, although it could've been ten. Malachi's blowups were an ongoing series of poorly conceived intentions. To Cooper, the dates blurred together the way they did with his newspaper columns, but the scenes were always set with booze and reefer, and the plot involved one or more of the assembled group pushing Malachi's play button with the same explosive results.

That had been a bad night, getting out of bed to drive more than four hundred miles to Atlanta to haul World Book back to Columbia, and Cooper intended to make sure that Sticks got the message before they left.

"Why don't you just give it up, Sticks?" he told him. "Leave the hard-headed fool alone."

"Can't do that," Sticks said. "Cat got the stuff, he's obligated to lay it down."

"But it doesn't belong to you, and you know all it ever does is start something."

Sticks took a while to situate a bottle of club soda inside the heel of a vacant tennis shoe. He'd had the sense to switch over, but still hadn't lost the buzz. Finally, he raised his head and answered softly.

"Don't matter," he'd said. "Gator has to pay for it, regardless."

World Book never told them that denying himself his one true love was his form of self-abuse. But if he had, they would've just told him he was full of shit, something World considered old news.

Cooper pulled over beside a mini park, leaving the car running to keep cool. He'd cleaned up for the show in a lightly starched white shirt, tan dress pants and a pair of dark brown matching socks that turned out to be wool and hot, and he didn't want to swim into the *South Pacific* smelling like a dead conch.

He was in Bonita Park, according to the small wooden sign on a post planted near the jungle gym. The first pleasant spot he'd seen. Black-eyed Susans, a sliding board, swings, a sandbox with more sand on the outside than in it. A tiny concrete building said "Facilities," which might have room for a toilet for one of the gnomes.

Cooper had called Maxine last night. He'd started to ask her something, didn't, and with his usual dedication forgot to check on her progress with the column before telling her he had to go.

Bonita. Bonita senorita. In Pleasant Orchards just another peach. His Bonita senorita hadn't led him into the peaches this morning, or any other morning since a child had been added to his résumé. Not that it had occurred to him until just now.

Sex with children in the house? No way, not until they leave for college. You could tuck them in and they could get up to go to the bathroom, trip on a rug in the dark and fracture their skulls against the tub. They could sneak in the kitchen for a cookie and choke on a chocolate chip. They could wander outside and decide to play in the car. For awhile you'd be listening for their little footsteps and then you wouldn't, and that's when it would happen, two simultaneous climaxes, one delivering temporary ecstasy, the other permanent despair.

A burning pain spread through Cooper's chest into his throat. He leaned toward the floor, reaching for the aspirin bottle. But aspirin caused acid reflux—it didn't cure it—and he was in Margaret's car. He had been wrong, what he'd assumed before. Hannah *had* known. Malachi had told her. She'd acted logically and responsibly, like any mother who loved her child. She was protecting her daughter. Not from a father's ambivalence, but from an unfit guardian in a land of no second chances.

Concentrate. He had to concentrate, to retrace the morning route in his head, picture the entrance to Pleasant Orchards . . . a faded red MG, an outrageous green float limping behind it, crepe paper flying out the windows . . . but his focus dissolved into a storm that was brewing in the South Pacific, with the latest character in his Professional Reporter's Notebook, the **Surprise Entry**, bobbing up and down, lost at sea. A strange little sun-starved child with pale blue eyes and wisps of golden brown hair and a pair of silver pasties glued to a red strip of satin around her chest . . . the little waif washing up on the sand and performing a roving commentary, while the other ill-fated girls marooned on the island with her ducked out of the way and twirled.

His stomach turned a flip. Why had he allowed such a vulnerable little child to be exposed this way? It was killing him. Her one and only aptitude was in the field of talking. How was he supposed to quote her under the new regulations, he wondered? It didn't matter; he wasn't planning on writing anything anyway, not about what was bound to be a full-blown fiasco. Maybe the audience would think she was the narrator.

Only sixteen minutes until eight, according to the dashboard clock, which Cooper was sure Margaret kept calibrated to the millisecond, and he was still idling in Bonita Park. He thought about his own car out in Cayce. He kept a necktie in the glove box, and would cram it in his pocket when he wasn't sure about the dress code. Garland had probably incorporated it into a turban by now. Talk about a trip to Fantasyland. He felt bad for not inviting her, but had been afraid to take the risk.

Thirteen minutes. What if he just camped here until the show was over and slipped in just in time to give her the flowers? "Good job, good show," he would say, invoking the wisdom of Big Chief Running Water. But Margaret's spirit, resident of her car, was ordering him to terminate, get along. Across the road, he saw a young couple walking a lab, and called out to ask directions.

The flowers were in the seat beside him, wrapped in a cellophane vase. So far, they hadn't wilted. Percy had said it was a tradition, presenting them to your child after a performance. He'd bought a mixed bouquet of daisies on the order of the sundress she'd been wearing when she'd run away. The florist had suggested roses but they have thorns.

"Where's that sweet little girl this morning?" Rachel Sills had asked as he was leaving.

"With a friend." It had sounded natural, normal, when he'd said it. Like that's where you'd expect an eleven-year-old to be on a Sunday morning if she wasn't with her parents. But Cooper knew nothing about her friends. Didn't know if she had any. The only mention of anything related to a friend was her poodle named Noodle.

"That's nice," Rachel had replied.

Scotty had gone out with Belinda Lister for breakfast, then to buy a pair of tap shoes. The shop that sold them was closed on Sundays but the owner knew Percy and agreed to meet them there at nine. Little Linda was out of striking range, spending the morning with the seamstress letting her costumes out.

"Bet you can't wait to see her up here on the stage," Rachel had said.

"She hasn't had much time to practice."

"Don't worry, babe. Neither have I."

At first he'd been surprised that Rachel had known about Scotty being in the show, but then he'd realized that Reverend Ray had probably been spreading the word all over the place. That was part of his job.

•

Cooper passed it twice. The first time he didn't see it. The second time he spotted the building but there were too many cars. The paved lot was jammed and people were parking along the edge of the grass.

Had he screwed up again? The labyrinth of neighborhoods and streets, one subdivision after another. Mainline churches built in the suburbs during the Eisenhower years were as predictable as the houses. Red brick, white steeple, white columns, stained glass windows, green grass and shrubs, and a parking lot or two on the side. He slowed to let some children cross and squinted at the marquee. "Ebenezer United Methodist Church. Visitors Welcome."

Nothing unusual for a church in the South to have two events going on, especially on Sunday night. Like a revival in the sanctuary and a function in the Fellowship Hall. Cooper had five minutes to park and get inside. The only place he could find was on an incline that dropped down into a drainage ditch. He stood in the dried muck, about to shut the door, when he remembered the windows. He had to get back in and turn on the ignition to let them down. It took him two tries to connect with the keyhole. Now he had three minutes.

He dodged a van and ran across the street. It wasn't dark yet but soon would be. Daylight Savings could be tricky in spring, depending on the weather. Tonight was muggy, with a gray mask on the moon. The highs were back to normal for late May, in the upper eighties and low to mid nineties, turning slightly cooler by the evening.

Cooper trotted past the sanctuary. No way to see through the painted glass. He hustled toward the colored arrows taped to the sidewalk, each with a word printed with the purple magic marker.

"Follow" ... "Your" ... "Dream" ... "To" ... "The" ... "South" ... Christ, when had she managed this?

He'd promised to sit on the front row. No, just told her he'd see. According to Percy's law, telling your daughter "you'll see" meant yes, but that was crazy.

Besides, it was too late for the front row now. The first number would've begun. He'd slip into a chair in back; move up as soon as the routine was over.

He checked his shirttail, wiped some sweat off his face and tamped down his hair. If it got much longer he'd have to wrap it up in one of those Baha'i towers. Hannah didn't think it was gray enough. That had been two days ago. It was probably white by now. Forget the bowl cut. He was ready to have it shaved.

Maybe he'd do it himself with the chain saw. He'd bought it the week after they'd moved in. Every man needs one to go with his wife and house, right? Evidently not, since he'd never opened the box.

Another series of arrows and he was at the door. Or would've been, if the arrows hadn't stopped after "**South**." What had happened to the "**Pacific**?" Probably an omen. Three steps led down to the auditorium. He stood outside and listened a second. No music yet, just people talking and the scraping of metal that always preceded a performance.

The scraping was excessive, though. Shouldn't they be settled by now? What if the record player had conked out along with the air conditioning? What if they were getting up to leave? Cooper pulled on the handle just as someone was doing the same thing on the other side.

"Sorry," he whispered after he'd stumbled into the room.

"Well, lookie here. The father of the featured attraction."

Samuel A. Reaves, Jr., vaunted, insurgent investigative reporter for the Columbia *Herald-Journal*, renowned for accepting press association awards from the Governor's manicured hand in one of his short-sleeved Blue Light Special polyester knits. Sam was standing before him now in a summer-weight navy blazer, a conservative red-striped tie commandeering the collar of his beige golf shirt.

"Percy roped you into this, huh?"

"Nope. Voluntary attendance. I owe you a few. All Sarah's swim meets and. . . . She's here with me but Laura sends her regrets. Brett's down with some dumb stomach bug."

"That's too bad." Cooper kept his voice down, although with all the commotion it didn't matter. He was in one of those sick panics now, where you feel like you're about to pass out and go to the bathroom at the same time. What were all these people doing here?

Since the call from Hannah, he'd been like a blind frog on hallucinogens, hopping from one absurdity to another. A mere fifteen minutes after the serenity of an unplanned respite in Bonita Park, he'd leapt inside the door of Rod Serling's inner sanctum, where nothing but the unexpected could be expected and the exit sign was a mirage.

"Go on in and sit down," said Sam. "We were just heading out for more chairs, if Stuart can come up with any. He thinks they've just about run out."

"Run out? I put up a hundred and twelve."

Percy's brother, Reverend Ray, came up and shook his hand.

"Pretty good crowd tonight," he said.

"Margaret's saving you a place," said Sam.

"Margaret who?"

"See her? Front row, midway down. Standing over there by Sarah. There's an extra seat for me. Don't let anybody take it."

"Excuse me," Cooper said. "Excuse me, please."

There were too many people. Where would they all sit? Sixty chairs would be optimistic, Percy had assured him. Eighty wishful thinking. It was electric in here, like the vibe before a concert in Carnegie Hall. Or *The Nutcracker* in Lincoln Center.

"Excuse me. Oh, hello. Good to see you. Did I step on your foot? I'm sorry. Someone is saving my. . . . Yeah, sure I do. Eddie? Hey, man. Glad you could come. Who's minding the hotdogs? Oh yeah, that's right, it is Sunday, isn't it? She's fine. Over there somewhere saving me a seat. This is your daughter? Hi. Nice to see you, too. It's kind of chilly, isn't it? It was burning up this morning when we. . . . Boom-Boom? Damn. Are you here for the recital?"

There had to be two hundred people. Maybe three, more than that. Cooper had never been good at estimating crowds. Rod Serling was pulling a masterful trick, trying to finish him off. Serling had put him in a time warp. It was the surprise party all over again, with familiar faces looking unfamiliar in an unfamiliar place, mixed in with strangers. He was supposed to be back in the newspaper lobby, but he'd walked through the wrong wall and ended up on another set.

This couldn't be happening twice in a week, unless he'd died and been sent to columnist hell. Meeting and greeting. Greeting and meeting. Forgetting faces that went with names and names that went with faces. At least no one had asked him for an autograph.

Percy only had thirty-four students. He'd asked her this morning. "Last count, thirty-four going on twenty-nine and a half." It was funny. They'd laughed.

There was Margaret. His buoy. His channel marker. Erect and immobile, dressed in aqua silk, her white hair up in an antique silver comb. She was frowning, guiding him through the maze with firm green eyes that scolded him for being late.

His legs were too long. He stumbled over people as they stood to let him by, had to climb over a chair to reach the first row.

Hello. Hello. Sure I do. How could I forget?

He'd left plenty of room between the aisles this morning but there were no aisles now. The seats were jammed together like they'd been welded that way. The tables had been removed from the back and people were bunched up along the walls, hunching their shoulders and standing sideways to make more space. They had to be breaking the fire ordinance. What if someone fainted or had a heart attack?

Cooper saw his friend Myrtle. That was expected, her daughter Stacey was dancing. But surely she hadn't dragged Ernie and Jazz with her. And Janice Dean, the entertainment editor, who judged every performance she attended as though it were a candidate for a Tony award. Thank God Janice didn't review children's recitals in churches.

And who was that other woman with them? Wow, was she all dolled up. Silver-sequined dress, silver hair to match, earrings down to her chin. She was ready for some nightclub action. Cooper was glad to see her even if he'd gone blank on her name. He was losing his mind. She was someone he was close to. Saw her all the time. Liked her a lot.

According to the word on the street, he liked them all a lot. Even the grandmother on death row for poisoning her fiancé. Spiked his iced tea before a tent meeting. Poor man was too sick to go in and waited for her in the hot car. Also poisoned her father and a few other old folks while she was at it. Lois Stevens was her name.

She couldn't have been nicer, though. Offered him a Lifesaver as soon as he'd gone in the visitor's room to interview her. He told her he didn't eat candy. Okay, he liked her. Was that a crime? Didn't mean he liked what she'd done. They exchanged letters for a couple of years. She said the doctors shouldn't have prescribed all that Valium.

There was Duke, giving him a thumbs-up, he and Layla animated and eager, waiting to see their girls perform. They were talking to Maxine and Pierre. But Pierre hated crowds. Noisy places made his ears ring as well as tick. Cooper hadn't told Maxine about the recital last night. He hadn't told anybody.

Certainly not Short Stroke Driggers, but there he was, some type of miniature oxygen contraption strapped to his back, and Remi Raines manipulating his elbow, smiling brightly, practically airlifting him into a seat.

A pudgy woman patted his arm. "Can you believe the turnout?" she said. That bandage, those fingers. *"Does it look swollen?"* The piano player, Rachel. Why hadn't she mentioned she was coming?

Margaret hadn't said anything about coming, either. She was wearing a neck brace. She didn't tell him about it yesterday when he'd phoned. Told him she was never better.

"Is it broken?"

She ignored the question. He kissed her on the cheek.

"I saw you talking to Mr. Limehouse," she said.

"He asked about you."

"Did he say anything about the memorial?"

"What memorial?"

"The spot where Burns laid it down. My name happens to be Burns, the designated honoree."

Entwined in the veins on her arms and wrists were some ugly bruises, and a layer of goose bumps.

"Those look bad," Cooper said.

"A watch might be in order, dear. If you believe your newspaper, you can buy one at K-Mart. A battery-operated Timex for twelve dollars and ninety-seven cents, if I recall. That wouldn't include the tax. Of course, you would be required to change the batteries from time to time."

Her neck couldn't be broken. Someone her age would be in the hospital with a broken neck. Even Margaret.

"What are you doing out of bed?" Cooper said. "Where did all these people come from? Why haven't they started yet? Have you seen Percy?"

"Your guess is as good as mine on all counts except the last. Miss Sims was just out making a repair to the scenery. The middle section had a gap there, toward the bottom. You seem a little shaky, dear. Wouldn't you be better sitting down?"

"I guess," he said. The metal was hard and cold. It was freezing in here. Margaret sat down beside him, folded her hands and faced the platform. It was past time to start. No one was on stage but voices were carrying from behind the partition. Someone complaining about the temperature. Little Linda Lister.

Half the paper was here. God bless Boom-Boom. The copy desk chief didn't turn out for anything unless it involved a bat with a ball and some beer. That was T-Bone beside him, with a lady and a couple of kids. T-Bone all dressed up, with his family. All these years, and before tonight Cooper had never seen him any place but in the Toddle House wearing an undershirt and apron.

"Speak up, dear," Margaret told him. "I can't make out anything you're saying in this racket."

It wasn't her hearing. His teeth were chattering. He leaned closer to her ear.

"I said, what in the world possessed you to come?"

"I wanted to stake a claim on my car before you got used to it. This happy occasion struck me as a convenient time."

"But how did you know about it?"

"No thanks to you. Your sidekick, Mr. Patterson, was kind enough to pass the word. Malachi is beginning to grow on me. Since we're on the subject of collecting vehicles, I've offered to drive him to Rock Hill tomorrow. It seems one of his acquaintances agreed to have his automobile removed from a ditch, but as far as I can determine it hasn't been located."

"For God's sake, Margaret, stay out of Malachi's affairs. He's an alcoholic. You can't do anything to save him. And tell me you didn't drive all the way from Charleston at night with that contraption around your neck."

"Stop fretting, dear. Mr. and Mrs. Barnes came along. They were pleased to be included."

Joan and Flip Barnes? Cooper glanced over his shoulder, but didn't see them. Who else had she dragged with her, the cook? The woman who showed up on Mondays to do the laundry?

All these people here to see her. She'd be all right. She'd be fine. Percy would be there, prompting from behind the portable basketball goal her brother had plundered from the MYF meeting room down the hall. She'd wrapped gold crepe paper around the pole, and attached balloons and streamers to the backboard and rim. Then she'd joined three of the cardboard partitions with duct tape to make a screen, painted it blue, added some clouds, and propped it against the back of the goal. Cooper had anchored the partition from behind, with cinderblocks he'd found on the side of the church.

"That's supposed to be a palm tree," he yelled in Margaret's ear.

"How clever." Margaret examined her watch.

"They call it Outsider Art."

"I see. Perhaps that's where it was intended to be displayed."

Cover it with a fishing net, dangle a ceramic bass through the middle of the rim, and anybody at Scarborough's would be proud to have it, Cooper thought. He was planning to call Tad Potts in a day or two and thank him. And Yolanda, with her magnificent dimple . . . and Jack Riles. Cooper wondered if the Santee minister was as engaging standing in the pulpit over a Bible as he was sitting in the DINING AREA over a cheeseburger. He missed him with all his heart right then, a man he'd only met once in his life.

"How you like that, Barnet, standing room only," Sam said. The metal squeaked as he squeezed into his chair.

"I thought I left more space than this," Cooper said.

"We had to do some rearranging."

"Well, you better not stretch your legs unless you put on a costume. Is it cold in here to you?"

"Cold as almighty hell. The South Pacific caught a wave to Nome. Damned air conditioning was turned down to fifty. It should be warming up before long."

"Hey, Reaves? What's the switchboard lady's name?"

"You mean Jo? You've only been flirtin' with her for twenty years."

"She's here, and Maxine and Pierre, over there by Layla and Duke."

"Your pal Hitch, too."

"Hitch? You're kidding. You think Percy asked him to come?"

"Come on, Barnet. Get real."

Margaret nudged him discreetly.

"It's almost half past eight," she said.

"How can you be so tuned in to every...." Sam paused to grab Sarah, who was scuttling over a chair. She'd spotted a friend from school. "Try to get something through your thick, empty skull, all right? You saw the lobby Thursday. They love you, okay? They came to support you. You and your daughter. I imagine Hitch did, too."

A daughter. He had a daughter, about to appear on the platform before him and do no telling what. Cooper shuddered, and rolled down the sleeves of his shirt. Why hadn't he brought a sport coat? Something to put over Margaret's shoulders. He glanced at her arms. The chill bumps were gone. Maybe it was warming up.

26

The room went black. A light was looking for the South Pacific . . . in the chairs, across the ceiling, along the wall. The crowd murmured. Finally, a direct hit . . . a tiny island with waves that defied the pull of gravity and a Chicken Little tissue-paper sky and two fat palms bulging with malformed purple growths begging for a visit from a tree surgeon. The audience went nuts. Cooper leaned towards Sam.

"This might be the best part of the show."

Or the only part. Nothing was happening. Just an extemporaneous solo by the spotlight, dancing a jig on limited expectations.

"Is she first?" Sam asked. They'd run short on programs.

"I don't know," Cooper said.

"Here we go."

Scratchy music was blaring now, from large speakers on both sides of the stage. *"Bloody Mary Is the Girl I Love"* . . . screeched off the vinyl after *"Now ain't that too damn bad!"* Sarah clamped her hand over her mouth and giggled, peeking at Sam to see if she was in trouble.

Cooper eyed the cardboard partition. No one was coming out. The audience strained toward the set. Maybe the cheap stereo had exploded from volume shock. Percy wouldn't let Cooper buy a new one. She could be hard-headed. Hard-headed and obtuse, too.

"Bloody Mary?" *South Pacific* was PG, but picking a song with "damn" in the lyrics for a children's recital in a church, little girls prancing around in pasties. . . . Cooper glanced at Margaret. She was smiling.

Come on Barnet, he told himself. Lighten up. You've had a daughter less than a week and you've turned into Jerry Falwell. Sam jabbed him. Little Linda Lister was standing on the edge of Bali Hai, swathed in glistening red. Her arm was raised in serious business, wielding a baton like a billy stick.

Cooper sat forward, ready to dive in front of Margaret if he had to. From behind the partition, a hand snatched the back of Linda's halter.

"Get off the stage." Percy's hiss was rock band decibel level. "The little ones are going on first."

A grating noise. Someone was bumping into the chairs Cooper had put behind the set to brace it up. The crepe paper ocean rippled.

"Ike. Quit it. I didn't, Miss Percy. She shoved first. . . ."

Clanging and banging. The ripples were turning into a tidal wave. Cooper sucked in his breath and forgot to let it go again.

"Shush. Attention, girls, let's count off. One, two, three, four, five, six. Good. Hands extended, right heel out, and . . . What's the matter, Sonja? No you don't. Not now."

If Cooper slunk any lower in his chair, his legs would be on the beach, tripping them up if they ever made it to the sand.

"Well try and hold it in."

Why was Percy talking so loud, airing the family linen in an echo chamber?

"They're all out there, cheering you on. Come on, you can do it. Get in line and throw those shoulders back. Show your stuff in that snazzy new costume. That's right, knock 'em dead. Ready, set. . . ."

Show your stuff? Meantime, the stereo needle was riding a vinyl groove like a bucking bronco, and the speakers were bragging about it, over and over and over.

The instructor of the Columbia Academy of Dance appeared at the edge of the cardboard divider. She had on the cut-off jeans she'd been wearing that morning over a black leotard and tights, and her old pink ballet shoes. Her braid hung out the back of a white sailor's cap, and a red ribbon was bouncing at her butt.

Polite applause started in the rear and filtered toward the front. Meanwhile, the stereo cowboy was still straddling the wild horse, grunting and groaning. Cooper grimaced. Somebody had to be back there holding the needle in the grove.

Percy nodded pertly, peering behind the cardboard, then leaping onto the shores of Bali Hai. She landed with a thud at the base of the basketball goal—swimming through the streamers, breaking off three or four—before settling in her hiding place.

Music blasted. Margaret almost dove into the ocean.

"Bloody Mary is the girl I love, bum-bum-bum-bum, Bloody Mary is the girl I love, bum-bum-bum-bum, Bloody Mary is the girl I love, Now ain't that too damn bad."

The cheers startled Cooper. Marie Chang, her black hair glistening in a high ponytail, strutted out with four other girls right behind her and a sixth, the lagger, holding her hand between her legs. They had on cut-off jeans like Percy's, with fringe around the legs, and white t-shirts with big red anchors stenciled on front, and bright red bandanas knotted around their necks.

They were stepping out on their heels, right first, then the left, and raising opposite arms in the air. Right heel, left arm, left heel, right arm, stomp, stomp, stomp. Kicking one another in the ankles, bumping together, each with her own technique independent of the music and of Percy—dancing the routine behind the coconut goal post—hidden as long as you didn't look.

But the Smallest Fries hadn't found her. They were gaping at everything besides Percy's tree.

Sam pounded Cooper's ribs like Rocky Balboa beating on a slab of sirloin.

"Where is she? Is she the one next to Marie?"

"No. These girls are five and six. She's with Little Linda Lister's group."

"Who's Little Linda Lister?"

Margaret poked Cooper and nodded toward the front. The girls were facing them now.

Kick kick kick stomp. Kick kick kick stomp. Heavy, heavy stomps, hands on hips. Nothing in syncopation. White middy caps salvaged from attics or the sale bin at the Army-Navy Store flopped below brows and rode the crests of noses. Didn't matter that they couldn't see. All they were doing was stomping.

Sonja joined in with both hands, choosing stardom over a pit stop. The audience was clapping madly. Marie Chang gathered up the marauding band of sailors, led them off, and ran back out to curtsey. She waved at her parents. The crowd waved to Marie. Marie waved back. Percy left her post, escorted Marie to the exit, curtseyed, and returned to the tree.

◆

Reverend Ray slipped behind the set and lowered the volume before the seven and eights came out to perform a ballet to "Bali Hai."

Barefooted, in white bathing suits with white carnations pinned in their hair, the girls were too intent on keeping up with Percy and the flowers to be intimidated by the whistles and whoops in the crowd. A curly-headed little blonde Cooper hadn't seen before appointed herself liaison between Percy and the audience.

"Arabesque," Percy mouthed, demonstrating.

"Arabesque," the little girl shouted into the auditorium, extending a leg behind her arched back.

The Smallest Fries minus Sonja came back to make "Happy Talk" in crepe paper hula skirts and more bare feet.

"Adorable," Margaret said.

"You think she's overdone the crepe paper?" Cooper asked her.

"They're dancing to beat the band," Margaret said.

Another group was lining up at island's edge.

Sarah pointed at Linda Lister. "See that big girl over there? She's in my art class. She's really good."

"Get ready," Cooper said, and squeezed Margaret's hand. "This is her group. This is it."

Little Linda blinked at the spotlight, waiting for the music to start. The opening bars of "I'm Gonna Wash that Man Right Outta My Hair" began to play.

"Wrong record," somebody shouted.

The needle made a pass at something unintelligible before it scraped off again. Cooper cringed. Mary Martin would need a new larynx when this was over. Who was operating the stereo?

"I'm as corny as Kansas in August," Mary was programmed to sing, but the "Kan" had been wiped out by a hiccup ending in a lisp. Linda had one hand on her hip and the baton in the other, thrust to the ceiling.

"Stop fidgeting, dear," Margaret said under her breath.

"I'm as normal as blueberry pie. . . ."

Little Linda marched onstage and hurried to the other end, followed by Patricia, carrying a sawed-off mopstick garnished with red ribbons. *"No more a smart little girl with no heart. . . ."*

Here came tall, elegant Stacey striding behind her, stopping downstage of Linda, peering through the spotlight to locate Myrtle and send her a movie star smile. *"I'm in love with a wonderful guy. . . ."*

There was the little black-headed girl Cooper had watched from the car yesterday, legs prancing as high as a prize filly, shiny bangs bouncing across her forehead. He didn't know her family, but they'd brought along a rooting section that would rupture an applause meter.

"That's her," they were yelling. "There she is."

She was a doll, all right. They'd better tone it down, though. The children wouldn't be able to hear the music.

But another one had raced onto the island right behind her. *"I am in a conventional dither. . . ."* It was this last child they were cheering for, this awkward slip of a girl, the **Late Entry**. She was bringing down the house.

Percy gestured behind the streamers, waving her hand toward the center of the stage. Stacey quickly moved over to make room. She collided with Patricia, knocking her off balance with a sparkling red hip.

Then Percy signaled to another child, motioning her to join the others in line. Motioning not to the one with the shiny black bangs but to the one behind her, the **Late Entry**.

She had shiny bangs too but they were fine, not thick, fine and golden brown, and she was wearing a red elastic halter with stars on both sides, stars with only four points, and a red pair of Pete Maravich's basketball trunks.

Had to be Pistol Pete's because the legs were so baggy, so much longer than the other children's. Red glitter gloves stuck out from her slight little wrists, round little Dixie cup gloves that left her hands naked and pale. Was that more glitter on her forehead?

And the lipstick and rouge, applied unevenly to her cheeks, making her seem off balance when she moved, as though one leg were shorter than the other. So much red paint against so much white skin.

Margaret was leaning into Cooper on one side, Sam on the other, sending him their excitement, their support, and something else. Was it concern . . . pity?

But he'd forgotten about his friends, forgotten about everything except the kicking and shuffling and sliding and turning, the tangle of bumbling silver tap shoes and clumsy silver batons and one cut-off mopstick.

Scotty in the middle, in a daze, in a haze, Scotty down on the floor, baton bouncing toward the edge of the stage. Should he jump up and catch it, hand it to her? She ran over and got it herself, then ran back again, going in every direction but the right one, her new silver tap shoes tied with bright red ribbons, ribbons so jaunty, shoes so big, they accented every mistake.

The right star came off her halter and floated to the floor. Scotty stepped on it with her brand new shoe. It stuck to the bottom. She sat down to pull if off but Linda helped her up and told her to keep on dancing. Longest song in the history of the world . . . *"and you will note there's a lump in my throat. . . ."* Longer than the suicide scene in *Madame Butterfly*.

Scotty walked over to the basketball goal and asked Percy a very long question. Percy parted the streamers to answer, straightened the glitter on her forehead. Cooper could see now that it was a sequined headband, that she was one of the Bali Hai Flappers.

Percy sent her back. She tripped on one of the streamers. Little Linda reached out and caught her. Everyone cheered. She dropped her baton and ran off. Stacey picked it up and ran behind her. A standing ovation.

Cindy and Missy Langston, fifteen-year-old twins, sailed through their toe duet to "Some Enchanted Evening" without missing a step. Then Little Linda returned with her troops to *wash that man right outta my hair*. This time, Mary Martin had to compete with a commotion in the back. Chairs clanging and scraping. People arriving late.

Cooper pressed his arms against his pounding chest and waited, but Scotty didn't join the others. Maybe Percy had held her back. Maybe she was ashamed of her performance, crying behind the palms. What if she'd wandered off?

He should check. Just stride behind the set like Stuart Ray had when he'd gone to adjust the volume. But the song was over. The girls deserted Bali Hai. The audience whooped and hollered some more.

"I had a happy time," Margaret said. "Scotty was grand."

Percy popped out from the streamers and strode to the center of the stage. Everyone hushed and waited, jammed together in the narrow aisles or by their chairs.

"I'd like to thank each and every one of you for making this recital by the Columbia Academy of Dance the best yet," she said. A piece of gold crepe paper was looped around her neck.

"I realize it's getting late but if you can bear with us just a few extra minutes, we have one more presentation for you, and I think you'll like it. It's a special solo, a surprise from a special student who's been with us for only a brief while. She's worked very hard, and I know you'll show her your appreciation."

Percy stared into the spotlight and blinked.

"Hey, Stu, cut that thing off, will you, so I can see. Thanks. How about flipping on the lights. Rachel? Rachel Sills, are you out there?"

Cooper looked behind him. There she was, struggling to make her way out of a row midway toward the back, holding her finger in the air. Some people had decided to sit again, but now they were rising to let her pass.

The audience was edgy with impatience. Their anticipation had been spent, their emotions over-played. The show had ended. The children had school in the morning. They were ready to go home.

"For those of you who don't know, Rachel is substitute organist here at Ebenezer," Percy said. "She was kind enough to agree to accompany one of our students on very short notice."

Hesitant, polite applause.

"Now for all of you out there in the audience, this will require some imagination."

Percy folded her hands behind her back, like she was preparing to deliver a dramatic reading, a former Miss America contestant returning twenty years later for a second try.

"This evening, we've been visiting an island in the South Pacific. But we're leaving that spot now—transporting ourselves to Thailand, or Bangkok, or wherever it was that Yul Brynner lived in *The King and I*."

"Bangkok," several people yelled out.

"Thank you," Percy said. "Bangkok. That's what we're doing, stealing a little scene from Bangkok, from old Yul. I've heard he can be a little puffy, but I'm sure he won't mind, and if he does, we'll take up a collection and pay him the appropriate royalties."

The audience tittered. What in the world was going on?

Percy fanned her arms in a wide circle. "This area behind you has been a sad and lonely little kingdom. But a special little princess is about to come in and make it a very happy place. This special little princess is someone you've already met. Her name is Scotty."

Murmurs, then cheers. Cooper got ready to bolt. Margaret had been working on the wrong person. Percy was the one who lacked terminal facilities. His stomach hurt again. He held his breath as Percy turned to the entrance of Bangkok. It was empty.

"Scotty has asked to dedicate this number to another special person, a person she loves very much. He's someone you all know, someone seated right here in the first row. Her daddy. Sweetie, will you please come join us?"

And right away she darted out, the misplaced little princess of Bangkok, her head bent low, looking for something on the ground. Cooper saw it before she did, a gold arrow like those leading to the Fellowship Hall, the missing "**Pacific**"—now scuffed and torn by a tirade of diligent feet.

Scotty spotted it too, and planted both oversized tap shoes on either side, looking at Percy, saying something Cooper couldn't make out. Percy whispered in her ear and adjusted the glimmering red halter, the side that had slid down below her breast. One four-pointed star shone somewhere under her armpit. The other star had disappeared from the bottom of her shoe. Lipstick was smeared on her chin.

After helping Rachel roll the piano closer to Bangkok, Percy sat cross-legged on the floor behind Scotty. Stuart dimmed the lights.

"Don't mind me," Percy told the audience. "I'm just an overgrown mushroom that sprouted up in the courtyard. I don't think I could pass for a flower."

The audience tittered.

"You could pass for a flower in my garden," one man called out.

The audience hooted and cheered. They were getting into it now. Percy eased up to flip her braid out of the way, then positioned her forehead in the middle of Scotty's back, holding her hands to keep her still. Scotty was still wearing the Dixie Cups.

"Ready, princess?"

Scotty bobbed her head. Stuart centered the spotlight on the tiny figure standing on the yellow star. The Fellowship Hall was silent. No one had left.

Percy nodded toward the piano. "Okay, maestro," she said. "Hit it."

Rachel squared her shoulders and played some chords. Cooper noticed she was wearing a smaller bandage. She pounded the chords again and waited. Percy bumped Scotty's back with her forehead. But the princess wasn't ready. She had something to say.

"Excuse me, miss, because I know I'm supposed to follow instructions and not talk except to sing the words to that very pretty song, but I don't see my daddy in this very dark room, and I would like to find him so I can show him my nice new costume with all the pretty red stardust on it, and Daddy, I would like very much to find you in this big dark place because. . . ."

Percy pointed to Cooper.

"There's your daddy, honey. Right there, see? Right in front of your nose. Exactly where he promised he'd be."

Percy raised her voice.

"Stu, how about flashing Cooper for just a second so she can see where he is."

A light skipped from Percy to the basketball goal, walked the ceiling, and attached itself to the back of Sam's head. Sam stood and gestured down at Cooper, low enough in his chair to be mistaken for a contemporary of Sarah's. Stu flashed the light green, then purple, then white.

"Wave to her, Cooper," Percy ordered.

Cooper waved. Scotty shielded her eyes and waved back.

"Okay. Ready?"

Scotty had more to say, but Percy reached up and put a finger over her lips. She nodded to Rachel, who pounded out the introduction for the third time, then beat three counts on the shelf with her good hand.

It was a catchy tune. Sentimental. Cooper recognized it. It was from *The King and I*. He and Hannah had seen the movie. The play on Broadway, too.

But things weren't going right. Scotty was singing too softly, mixing up the words. Percy's prompting confused her. Scotty turned around to consult with Percy, then turned back to try again. The second time was no better. The apprehension of the audience mounted with Scotty's agitation. She stopped singing. Rachel pounded the chords again, but Percy quickly stood, holding on to Scotty's hand.

"Thank you, princess. And thank you again, ladies and gentlemen, for sharing this little visit with us tonight. We appreciate it very much, don't we, honey?"

Scotty stared into the audience where her father was sitting. They both looked lost.

"It's all right."

He was in the back. Cooper couldn't say why, but he had expected him.

"It's all right now, little miss."

It was quiet. Everyone could hear him. It was as if no one else was between him and the stage.

"You just sit tight, and we'll do it the way we practiced. Sit tight for me, baby, and I'll be right there."

Scrambling and the squeaking of chairs. People making room. He made his way through the bodies. Too many bodies, but as it always is for someone with limited mobility, people quickly moved aside and helped him pass.

"Let's have a nice hand for Rachel," Percy said. "Rachel Sills."

Rachel sat a minute, and then hopped up from the bench.

Sam helped him up the steps. He was wearing the blue linen Bermudas with his cream Italian loafer and no sock, and the frankfurter shirt. He smelled of hard whiskey and sweet wine, sweat and Zest soap. He went over and whispered something in Scotty's ear, then limped over to the piano. Rachel offered to help him but he shook his head, used the crutch for balance, and slid beneath the keyboard.

The audience was stunned.

"Now then, little miss," he said over his shoulder. "Let's take it from the top, shall we? Let's show your old Daddy over there how much a tiny little pearl can shine."

Stuart refocused the light. Percy resumed the mushroom position. The introduction was light and breezy. Scotty smiled. No, she beamed. Then she began to sing.

"Getting to know you, getting to know all about you. . . ."

She was on stage, singing a song with Malachi. Malachi leading her without saying a word, prompting her with the keys, showing her where to go. If she got lost or left out a line, it didn't matter. World was a genius at rifts and fills. World Book was laying it down.

"Getting to like you, getting to hope you'll like me. . . ."

It seems I have a daughter.

Margaret reached over and gave Cooper her hand. He clutched it like a life preserver.

"Getting to know you, putting it my way but nicely. You are precisely. . . ."

She left home on a mission.

". . . my cup of tea."

If she isn't found. . . .

But she wasn't lost any more. She was no longer in danger. She was on the stage singing a song. A song she'd dedicated to someone special. She was looking at him now, looking at her daddy. Anchored to the gold arrow, holding her hands in front of her, the sparkly red Dixie Cups pointing together in a perfect plastic V, singing about feeling free and easy. Well, that certainly wasn't a stretch.

Funny, she had a pleasant singing voice. Not jerky and rushed like when she talked. Clear. Clear and sweet and pure. In fact, her voice was more than pleasant. It was a beautiful singing voice. She could be the lead in a Broadway musical. Anna in *The King and I*. A prima donna at the Met. Okay, with a little work.

Margaret needed a handkerchief but Cooper didn't reach in his pocket. He couldn't move.

"If you find her, please tell her that her daddy is looking for her. Please say that. . . ."

"Haven't you noticed, suddenly I'm bright and breezzzzy?

"Because of all the beautiful and new,

"Things I'm learning about you,

"Daayyyy . . . by . . . daaayyy. . . ."

She took it from the top again. This time, she didn't need to worry about the words. The audience helped her. People who had been seated stood alongside people already standing.

Myrtle stood beside Jo, Maxine beside Layla, Pierre beside Duke. Joan Barnes stood near the back, holding tight to the thin arm of a woman in paper bedroom slippers and baggy red knee-length shorts—Cinderella's sobbing mother, whisked to the ball in a '61 pumpkin convertible with a prince she claimed as a first cousin riding at her side.

Margaret stood beside Cooper's chair, singing in an off-key tenor, reaching down to clutch his hand. Sam stood on the other side, his left hand grasping Cooper's shoulder, singing in a fervent baritone.

Malachi jazzed up the encore. The Fellowship Hall at Ebenezer United Methodist Church resounded in song. Everyone was standing but Cooper. Everyone was singing but him. They were all singing with Scotty. They were all singing for Scotty. For Cooper's only daughter. His little girl.

◆

The ride to Irmo took twenty minutes. They were silent much of the way, the golden kind, like the cliché. Scotty was worn out and he was drained. He worried about keeping her up past her bedtime but he had to admit it was a kick, driving a big fancy air-conditioned Lincoln through the country in his undershirt, free of starch and the hot wool socks. He thought of his father, the way it used to feel when they were riding in the car at night. Old Bert.

The bouquet of daisies was in her lap. He had forgotten to remove the cellophane. She still had on the costume, even the Dixie Cups on her wrists. When they'd stopped for the gasoline he'd asked her if she wanted to take them off and she said no.

She did let him take off the tap shoes when they got there. They were rubbing blisters on her heels. It was dark over dark, no stars and a cloudy moon, risky to go barefooted so he carried her. Tricky with the chain saw in his other hand but when he tossed her over his shoulder they did fine.

The tree she selected was small. All right with him. Less to decorate, easier to drag, especially after she told him it would be okay if he wanted to leave the saw at the edge of the woods, "because it has that nice black case over it, Daddy, and no careless little child could step on it and get cut on that very dangerous blade." A real thinker, his daughter.

Before they got back in the car she wanted to visit Snow White and the Seven Gnomes, but the porch light wasn't on, and it was too dark to tell Dopey from Sneezy. She asked him if they could do it another time, and after he made sure she was sitting straight in the deep leather seat and buckled her in, he whispered, "We'll see."

Maxine and Pierre were still at the church. No one wanted to leave. They were all pumped up, World sitting up there on Bali Hai in a wienie shirt playing the hell out of the piano, Eddie Limehouse ribbing him about wearing the competition.

Just your standard upright, the Yamaha missing a few of its letters. Wouldn't have mattered if it was missing half the keys.

They all felt like dancing but no one did. You can dance anytime. Besides, it's hard to keep a rhythm with New Orleans-style boogie stride Latin jazz funk flying all over the place unless you're a professional like Percy, and she was occupied with Hannah, holding her arm to keep her steady as they grooved to Malachi's beat.

His fingers did the dancing for everyone, as if they had detached themselves from his wrists and were freefalling all over the keys, just happening to land on the best notes. Sounded like two pianos playing at once, sometimes three. He stuck with Little Booker. Nothing raucous or raunchy like "Junco Partner." Nothing get-down bluesy or melancholy, either. Not for a children's recital in a church.

He kept it lively and light. Tunes you heard before, tunes you wished you had. Played "Pixie" in honor of the star attraction, even though she wasn't there to hear it. You could see her, though, skipping and tripping and dancing all over the place, talking up a storm. Could've sworn Booker wrote the piece just for her.

This is how Maxine described it for Tuesday's column: "Be nice if you could hear him play sometime. He has this way of summoning up everything you've got in your soul while he's making it right in your heart. Like just for that very moment, you know what you're supposed to know and feel what you're supposed to feel. Something about that makes you happy, even when it hurts."

He sent them home with "I'll Be Seeing You." Maybe he would. Even with a restraint around her neck, Margaret Motte Burns was a formidable force, which has to be taken into account.

One more thing, and Little Booker would tell you this: If you've never heard Malachi Patterson play "Sunny Side of the Street"—well, baby, you've never heard the song before.

###

Greta Medlin grew up on James Island in Charleston, South Carolina and graduated from the University of South Carolina. While a reporter for the *Greensboro News & Record*, she was a two-time winner of the American Society of Newspapers Editors Award and also won the Ernie Pyle and National Headliner's Awards. This is her first attempt at fiction.

www.ingramcontent.com/pod-product-compliance
Lightning Source LLC
Chambersburg PA
CBHW031923060726
47496CB00002BB/264